BY JALEIGH JOHNSON

ORIGINAL FICTION
The Mark of the Dragonfly
The Secrets of Solace
The Quest to the Uncharted Lands
The Door to the Lost

DUNGEONS & DRAGONS
The Howling Delve
Mistshore
Unbroken Chain
Unbroken Chain: The Darker Road
Spider and Stone

MARVEL
Triptych: A Marvel: Xavier's Institute Novel
School of X: A Marvel: Xavier's Institute Anthology

THE
ROAD
TO
NEVERWINTER

DUNGEONS
&DRAGONS
HONOR AMONG THIEVES

THE
ROAD
TO
NEVERWINTER

JALEIGH JOHNSON

RANDOM HOUSE WORLDS

NEW YORK

2023 Random House Worlds Trade Paperback Edition

© 2023 Wizards of the Coast LLC
© 2023 Paramount Pictures Corporation

Excerpt from *Dungeons & Dragons: Honor Among Thieves: The Druid's Call* by E. K. Johnston copyright © 2023 by Wizards of the Coast LLC and © 2023 by Paramount Pictures Corporation.

Published in the United States by Random House Worlds, an imprint of Random House, a division of Penguin Random House LLC, New York.

Wizards of the Coast, Dungeons & Dragons, D&D, their respective logos, and the dragon ampersand are registered trademarks of Wizards of the Coast LLC in the U.S.A. and other countries.

Random House is a registered trademark, and Random House Worlds and colophon are trademarks of Penguin Random House LLC.

Originally published in hardcover in the United States by Random House Worlds, an imprint of Random House, a division of Penguin Random House LLC, in 2023.

ISBN 978-0-593-59815-3
Ebook ISBN 978-0-593-59814-6

Printed in the United States of America on acid-free paper

randomhousebooks.com

2 4 6 8 9 7 5 3 1

First Edition

Book design by Alexis Capitini
Additional editorial by Allison Avalon Irons

To Tim, because ours is a DM and PC love story for the ages.
Also, I'm sorry I almost disintegrated your character that one time.
And I'm sorry I killed him later.
In my defense, I never expected to roll that high.
Anyway, love you tons!

THE
ROAD
TO
NEVERWINTER

PROLOGUE

"Avert your gaze, foul beast!" Edgin shielded his face with his hands. "You have no power over me!"

But no power in Faerûn could protect him from the eruption of giggles that followed his pronouncement. Edgin peeked between his fingers. Also a mistake.

His daughter, Kira, lay on her bed, a cloud of dark brown curls spread over her pillow, grinning up at him with a light in her eyes that was one part adoration and two parts mischief. The cutest basilisk— no man alive could be expected to resist the power of that look.

"Please, Dad?" Kira sat up, tugging on his hand to bring him closer to the rickety wooden chair sitting beside the bed. "Just one story."

Edgin let out a dramatic sigh and sank down onto the chair. "All right. One story, and then you'll go to sleep within ten seconds, right?"

"Right!"

It was never ten seconds.

But Kira was already flopping back down, pulling her checkered quilt up to her chin. A fire burned in the small hearth on the other side of the room, casting everything in warm golden light. Flickering shadows danced on the walls. It was, Edgin had to admit, the perfect atmosphere and the perfect night for a story. Rain clicked softly on the windowpanes of the small cottage, and a faint rumble of thunder promised a storm sometime in the night, but it was still far off, a distant dragon growling in its sleep.

The perfect atmosphere and a rapt audience—truth was, he lived for nights like this. It hadn't always been this way, and he tried never to take what he had now for granted.

"All right, then, which story is it going to be?" He listed them off on his fingers. "The Harrowing Heist of Harkendon? Longsaddle's Bungled Burglary? The Case of the Missing Cabochons?"

"Missing because we stole them," Kira said helpfully.

"Hush, you." Edgin put a finger to his lips. "Dealer's choice, then—what's it going to be?"

Kira stared up at the beamed ceiling, pretending to think it over, but Edgin knew his daughter. She'd already picked her tale.

"I want *our* story," she said. "The story of our crew."

Because of course she did. It was the longest, most tangled story of them all. But it was also Kira's favorite, and those eyes had him pinned to his chair with their hopeful delight.

He was doomed.

"An origin story it is." He leaned forward in his chair, elbows propped on his knees, and cleared his throat. Then he hesitated, glancing at his daughter, the way her cheek pressed into the pillow as she turned toward him. "You know this one starts off sad," he warned her. "Are you all right with that?"

Kira looked thoughtful, and her gaze flicked to the wall above her bed, where a small domino mask with a hairline crack on one side hung in pride of place. A smile spread across her face as she turned back to Edgin.

"It's all right," she said. "There are sad parts, but there are amazing parts too."

Just like any good story.

Edgin nodded, reaching out to squeeze his daughter's hand.

"In the land of Faerûn, there is a wild, dangerous, and beautiful place called the Sword Coast," he began, letting his gaze go unfocused as he pictured the lands he'd walked, skulked, and bled through for most of his career as a Harper agent. Another time, another life—a version of himself that no longer existed—but the memories were as vivid in his mind's eye as staring into a clear pool of water. "Throughout this stretch of the world there are glittering cities, where the wealthy, powerful, and magical hold sway. But there are also vast forests, jagged cliffs carved by time and tide, and humble villages nestled in between. In one of these remote villages, there lived a brave, handsome, capable man named—"

Edgin thought he heard a snort from the next room. Ah, so his audience was bigger than he'd thought. Well, he didn't mind performing for a crowd of two. He could handle it.

CHAPTER 1

TEN YEARS AGO

Edgin tried to remember the last time he'd slept. Sleep, that capricious, lovely siren—he knew he'd been acquainted with her once. He'd even had a bed, a comfortable bed if he remembered correctly. Lately, though, his world had shrunk to the small, scarred kitchen table by the fire, and everything, from the dried herb bundles hanging from the ceiling, to the pot of something cooking—or burning—in a pot on the stove, was just a little hazy around the edges, and it was all because of—

A screech shattered the air in the small cottage, traveling right down Edgin's ear canal and rattling his heart inside his chest. He jumped, jostling the small bundle in his arms and causing it to let out another ear-piercing shriek that he swore was worse than a banshee's wail. And he should know—he'd been up close and personal with one, a long time ago.

This was no banshee. He looked down at his baby daughter. Kira's small face was scrunched up in an expression of misery that Edgin felt, if he was being honest, had no place on a newborn baby whose only concerns in life were eating, sleeping, and defecating in alarmingly large quantities.

Whereas Edgin's concerns were many and varied.

He no longer had a job, for one. He'd left the Harpers, the do-gooder group to which he'd sworn an oath and dedicated his life, because that blind devotion had resulted in his wife's death at the hands of the Harpers' enemies. The grief and guilt of that had opened up a hole inside of Edgin, a hole that probably would have swallowed him—or he would have jumped in willingly—were it not for the squirming child in his arms.

Kira. The only family he had left. He would die for her. He would walk through fire, face down a horde of kobolds, kill anyone who tried to harm her.

He also occasionally wished he could toss her out a window to get some peace and quiet and sleep, which was a strange thought to have alongside the fierce love and protectiveness swirling in his chest.

Was this what being a parent was supposed to be like?

There was no one around to ask, so Edgin had just been muddling through these last few months.

He poured himself his fifteenth or sixteenth cup of tea from the dented kettle in the center of the table, trying to keep himself alert while Kira continued to wail in infant misery.

"I'm sorry, sweetie," he crooned, rocking her in his arms. "I don't know what you want."

Getting his daughter to stop crying was just one of the things he'd been failing at. Another was the fact that they were out of firewood, and their pantry, already meagerly stocked to begin with, was now almost completely empty. Whatever he'd been cooking over the fire was giving off a distinctive burnt stench that filled the cottage and made his eyes water, but he didn't want to put Kira down long enough to deal with that, and when was he supposed to go out and get supplies while she was crying and with what money would he buy them since he no longer had a place among the Harpers . . .

Edgin shook himself out of that downward spiral and took a big swig of tea with his free hand. He grimaced. It was hot and bitter and doing nothing to ease the fog that swamped his brain. He needed a hot meal, some fresh air, and a change of scenery. If he stayed in this cottage for another minute, he thought he might start howling right alongside Kira, and then where would they be?

He reached into the pouch tied onto his belt and felt around inside for some coins. He came up with a couple of silver from his emergency funds. It would be enough for a small meal at the local tavern and some milk for Kira, and maybe the trip outside would be enough to distract Kira from her misery.

Too much to hope that it would distract him from his, but at least it would keep him awake.

THE TRIP AND Shuffle Tavern was an aging single-story building with simple fare and a loyal local crowd, in addition to the travelers that wandered in to shake the road dust off their boots and have a pint or two. A large, white stone fireplace dominated the back corner of the room near the bar, and there was even a small stage on the opposite side of the room for bards and other entertainers to try their luck with the crowd. Once upon a time, Edgin might have been one of those entertainers.

In another life.

Tonight, he bypassed the stage and the bar and headed for a table near the crackling fire. He settled Kira in her bassinet, and whether it was the warm fire, the faces of the people to look at, or just the change in scenery from the dreary cottage, Kira's crying gradually tapered off. She drank half a bottle of milk, then shoved two pudgy fingers into her mouth and stared around the tavern in bleary wonder.

Edgin slumped on his stool and enjoyed the relative quiet.

A few minutes later, someone put a bowl of thick stew with large chunks of potato, carrots, and meat in front of him, along with a tall tankard of ale and a wooden platter of bread. Had he ordered that? Or did someone take one look at his face and think, *New father starving, get that man some meat!* At that moment, Edgin didn't particularly care. He tore into the hot bread and used it to mop up every bit of stew he could from the large bowl. It tasted like bliss. Rich, meaty bliss. And the ale—Edgin let out a moan of pleasure as the cold, sharp drink slid down his throat.

Why had he waited so long to do this?

Kira had fallen asleep, mouth slack, arms above her head, and for the first time in what felt like years, Edgin had a hot meal in his belly and ale ready at hand. The fire was warm, flushing his skin and making his eyelids droop. He was going to sleep so good tonight.

So good.

EDGIN SNAPPED AWAKE to a sharp pain in the side of his face and a puddle of drool around his chin. What in the Nine Hells had hit him?

He was lying on the floor of the tavern. Through his swimming vision, Edgin could see the place was still packed, and people milled about the room, talking and laughing and not paying him any attention whatsoever.

He supposed that was fair. People passed out in taverns all the time, and it certainly wasn't the first time he'd woken up like this—facedown on a flagstone floor with his head throbbing and no idea how he'd gotten there. Most of the time it was after a night of drinking, but sometimes it was because he'd taken a punch that put him on the ground.

Had someone attacked him from behind? Oh Gods. Edgin's groggy senses finally started functioning again.

Kira. Where was Kira?

In one fluid movement, he pushed himself up off the floor. Or, at least, that's what he'd intended to do. In reality, he flopped around like a fish in a net until he got his arms underneath him and levered himself to a sitting position.

He'd fallen next to his table. His tankard and bowl of stew were still at his place waiting for him. But Kira . . .

Again, it took Edgin's rattled senses a moment to process what he was seeing.

Kira, his baby daughter, the center of his existence, the only thing in his life he had left that was worth a damn, was currently dangling from the outstretched arm of a grim, muscled woman with long dark hair and tattoos on both arms, wearing fur-lined, travel-stained clothing, with the biggest axe he'd ever seen strapped across her back. Seriously, he had no idea axes even came in that size.

"Let her go!" The words ripped out of him, and he lunged for the woman, intending to tackle her and grab Kira, shielding her with his own body if necessary.

Again, that was the plan.

Instead, the woman calmly stepped out of the path of his charge, and Edgin skidded across the stained tavern floor on his belly. His body felt like it'd been weighted down with stones. This, after one ale? What was wrong with him?

He sprang to his feet. The room tilted crazily around him, but he shook off the feeling and went for the woman again.

"I said, let her—"

He never got to finish. This time, the woman shot him an exasperated look and grabbed him by the throat with her free hand when he got close enough. And Edgin just sort of . . . stopped, dangling like a doll from her steady grip. She wasn't hurting him—much—but it wasn't at all pleasant to be held by the throat. At least she had a much gentler grip on Kira, holding her by the collar of her nightgown.

In fact, now that he looked, Kira seemed strangely . . . happy? She swatted the air in front of the stranger's face with her tiny hands. Edgin recognized the game she was trying for—it was Got Yer Nose. Everyone in the baby business knew that game.

Except this woman. Eyebrows lifted, she seemed to be trying to figure out what it was Kira wanted. Edgin couldn't tell her either, because of the whole *being held by the throat* situation, so he just stood there and gasped. It was pretty humiliating.

Finally, the woman seemed to translate Kira's squeals and coos, and she leaned forward. Kira's pudgy fingers closed on the woman's nose, and she let out a triumphant baby giggle.

Oh Gods, Edgin thought. The woman was going to get angry now. She was going to hurt Kira. He squirmed in her grip, desperate to free himself.

The woman opened her mouth and said in a low, deep voice, "Honk."

Kira erupted in a fresh stream of giggles.

Edgin stopped struggling. His sleep-deprived mind finally registered what he probably should have realized immediately: The woman wasn't trying to hurt Kira. She looked like she'd maybe never

seen a baby before and certainly had no idea how to hold one properly, but she wasn't about to eat Kira either. The relief of that made
him sag in her grip.

The woman flicked her gaze to him, gave a short nod, as if sens-
ing his surrender, and dropped him to the floor. Then she took Kira
in both of her arms and sat back down at the table—his table—with
her, bouncing her clumsily but gently on her knee. Kira was wearing
her smitten expression, the look that Edgin had thought belonged
only to him. He shook off the little stab of jealousy and climbed to
his feet, taking the stool next to the woman.

"So," he said, his voice a little raspy from having her fingers
around his throat, "do you often come to taverns and randomly grab
people's babies?"

She glanced over at him. "You always leave your kid unminded
while you sleep?" she said gruffly. "You were passed out when I saw
you."

"I was not!" Edgin lowered his voice when a couple of the other
patrons looked their way, but his outrage didn't cool. "I had everything under control before you butted in."

"Whatever you say." The woman had turned her attention back
to Kira, who'd grabbed a fistful of her long hair and shoved it into
her mouth.

How had he lost control of this situation? What was even happening here? "You," he started, pointing at her with his index finger,
as if that lent him some sort of gravitas, "should mind your own
business." Then he hesitated, mouth still open to give a lecture, as
something dawned on him.

Kira wasn't crying. She was giggling. She was *happy*, and being
entertained by someone other than Edgin for the first time in
months.

And his ale and stew were waiting on the table, unfinished.

"But since you're here, why don't you tell me your name and
where you're from and how long you're in town and what's your life
story," he finished in a rush as he grabbed his tankard and took a
swig. It had warmed while he'd been unconscious on the floor, but
warm ale was better than no ale.

The woman sighed loudly, as if he were far more trying than any baby could ever be. Which was fair. "Holga," she said.

Edgin decided to go out on a limb and take that as her name. He waited for the rest, but that was all he was apparently getting, because Kira had grabbed Holga's nose again, and they were both absorbed in the Got Yer Nose game.

Well, he supposed a name was a start. He leaned forward in his chair and dove into the food. When the bartender passed their table, he flagged the man down for two more ales, glancing at Holga for permission. She gave a short nod and added, "Potato, please."

Edgin blinked, but he was sure he'd heard her. He turned back to the bartender. "Two ales and a potato," he said, a little uncertainly. He looked back at Holga. "Roasted, I assume?"

Holga nodded again.

The bartender left.

It was one of the stranger meals Edgin had ever shared with another person, in that it mostly consisted of Kira giggling and grabbing Holga's nose, and Holga eating a roasted potato that she gripped in her bare hand, even though Edgin could see the steam rising off it. He ended up ordering another bowl of stew for himself. Kira had all the milk she could drink, and at the end of the meal she let out an impressive burp against his shoulder. Holga grunted in what sounded like approval.

"Good kid," she said. "Strong. Cute too, like a little bug."

"A *bug*?" Edgin said. At Holga's frown, he said quickly, "Hey, if you like bugs, who am I to argue?"

He glanced out the window. It was fully dark and probably late. He'd lost track of time during dinner. And when he'd been unconscious. All the warm food in his belly was making him sleepy again. His eyeballs felt like they'd been sanded, and his head kept doing that dip-and-jerk dance of fighting sleep. "We'd probably better be getting home," he said, yawning hugely. "Early bedtime for the little bug. You know how it is."

"Oh," Holga said, looking suddenly downcast. "Right."

Edgin paid their bill, wincing only a little bit at how much lighter his coin purse was afterward. Worth it, he told himself firmly.

Holga followed him out the door. Edgin stood in the dark for a moment, the light of the tavern spilling out at his back, breathing in the fresh, cool night air. Kira was asleep in his arms and, exhausted as he was, for the first time in months, he felt a bit human again, like he was no longer a sleepwalker stumbling around in a nightmare.

He was savoring that moment of tranquility when he realized Holga was still standing beside him, looking up at the star-filled sky.

Well, this was awkward. Although he supposed he hadn't said a proper goodbye. "Thanks for looking after Kira while I was . . . you know . . . indisposed," he said.

"Sure," Holga said, but she made no move to walk away.

Edgin felt a tiny bit of his earlier suspicion creeping back. Did Holga intend to murder him and kidnap Kira once they were away from the crowded tavern? He tightened his grip on his daughter instinctively, and she murmured a little protest in her sleep.

Maybe he should go back inside the tavern, wait another hour or so, and then walk home with one of his neighbors. On the other hand, he was so tired, if he didn't get to his bed soon, he would probably fall asleep in one of the neighbors' tomato gardens.

He was still weighing options when Holga spoke up. "Want me to walk you home?" she asked, her voice tentative. "Make sure you're—I mean, the baby—is safe?"

Edgin looked at her, but Holga wouldn't meet his gaze. Her expression was sad, so sad that it pulled at the place in his chest where Edgin's heart used to be. Though, figuratively speaking, he hadn't used the muscle for so long, it was hard to tell what he was feeling. Despite his suspicion, he took a chance and asked, "Do you not have somewhere to stay tonight, Holga?"

"What?" Color rose in the woman's cheeks, and she scuffed a boot in the dirt. "'Course I do. Just looking out for the kid, is all."

During his time among the Harpers, Edgin had learned a thing or two about reading people, about looking for deceit, exaggeration, or sometimes just bald-faced lies in the people he interacted with. And since he'd recently joined the ranks of the lost souls of Faerûn, he knew how to recognize a kindred spirit.

Holga had lost something precious to her too. She didn't have anywhere to go, and she was feeling just as anchorless as he was.

Maybe that was why he found himself saying, a bit to his own shock, "You know what, why don't you escort us home and stay the night, just to be safe? There could always be murderers waiting in dark alleys." In this small village in the middle of nowhere that almost no one knew about.

Holga perked up immediately, although she didn't smile. Her lips didn't even twitch. Edgin doubted her face was capable of contorting in the general direction of a smile, but he could be wrong.

Well, it was no business of his what kind of burdens she carried. He had his own history, and he definitely wasn't keen on sharing it with a stranger.

Besides, it was only for one night, he reminded himself as they started walking back to his cottage. He'd stay up and watch over Kira to make sure Holga didn't try anything, and in the morning, the woman would be gone. End of story.

Or, at least, that's how he'd planned it. In reality, he was half-asleep on his feet by the time they reached the cottage. Somehow, Edgin ended up sleeping on the floor again instead of his bed, but when he woke up, there was a warm fire in the hearth and a full basket of firewood sitting nearby. Holga was outside, chopping more wood, while Kira was propped against a nearby stump, watching her and giving her baby claps of approval.

She hadn't cried at all.

CHAPTER 2

A month later, Holga was still living with them. Edgin was beginning to think she had no intention of leaving.

And that was absolutely fine with him.

He stood in the kitchen, drinking a cup of tea, watching Kira through the window. She was in the yard, in the reinforced cradle Holga had made for her, wrapped up snug in her blankets, cooing and happy. Holga was sitting a few feet away from her, repairing one of the rain barrels that had sprung a leak.

As far as he knew, there was nothing Holga couldn't repair around their cottage. Besides the barrel leak, she'd fixed the roof leak, tightened the shutters on the windows, and sealed some cracks in the cottage walls that Edgin hadn't even realized were letting out precious heat.

She was almost as terrible a cook as he was, but it didn't matter, because she was an extra pair of hands to hold Kira while he muddled his way through preparing a meal. She was another voice to soothe his daughter in the middle of the night so he could finally get enough sleep to become a fully functioning human being again.

She was just . . . *there*, and even though they didn't talk much, Edgin realized how much he'd missed having another adult in the room. He hadn't noticed how alone he'd been until he wasn't anymore.

Not to say that she was the perfect roommate. Far from it. She snored and belched more impressively than Kira. She wore clothes way past the point where they could be considered acceptably clean. And sometimes she was just . . . *there*, hovering like a silent, hulking shadow. It could be unnerving.

But it was a small price to pay, so Edgin had never broached the subject of her leaving, and Holga hadn't brought it up either. They'd settled into an odd, calm coexistence that seemed to suit them both.

"Barrel's fixed," Holga said, interrupting his thoughts as she stomped into the kitchen, setting Kira's cradle down near the table before seizing the kettle to pour her own cup of tea. That was another thing about Holga. She did nothing quietly or gently. Well, she was gentle with Kira. He'd give her that.

"Well done," he said. He leaned around her in the small space and lifted a soup pot from the rack on the wall. "There's a hole in the pot. Think you could fix that?"

Holga eyed the ancient pot skeptically. "It's rusted through. Time for a new one."

Edgin shook his head. "Not a chance. New pots are not in the household budget this month."

Or any month in the foreseeable future.

Holga sighed and opened the empty cabinets one after another, wincing as the unoiled hinges squealed. "You own *one* pot." She threw a pointed look at the kettle and two cups, which were all that was left of a once lovely tea set. At the single dull knife stuck in the cutting board on one end of the table. "How do you cook?"

"Listen, the kitchen used to be full," Edgin said defensively. "I just had to sell a few things to make ends meet, that's all. There's a pawnbroker on the edge of the village who took everything. As soon as I got back on my feet, I was going to buy everything back."

He was still waiting for the day he got back on his feet. Fortunately, he didn't need to explain any further. Though they never talked about it, he sensed that Holga understood what it was like to be at rock bottom and trying to claw your way back up.

She crossed her muscled arms, thinking. "Would he loan a couple things back? If he knew . . . you know . . . you really needed them?" She shifted uncomfortably as she spoke. Edgin hadn't told her about his wife, not in so many words, but Targos was a small village, and gossip got around. She'd probably heard by now that he was a widower.

He shook his head. "Good thought, but as much as I love the idea of pathetically throwing myself at the mercy of my neighbors to help me out of the gutter, Raylin Pendro won't have any pity for me. He's a dirty, coin-hungry snake."

And Edgin was pretty sure Pendro occasionally did side jobs for the Zhentarim.

Also known as the Black Network, the Zhentarim was an organization whose goal was to amass as much power and influence in the world as possible, through any means available. They didn't care much about staying on the right side of the law, and if people got hurt in the service of their ambitions, so be it.

Edgin wasn't a Harper anymore, but he could smell Zhentarim corruption a mile away, and Pendro reeked of it. He'd long ago resigned himself to the fact that he'd probably never get back the rest of the tea set Zia had loved so much, or the pots and pans she'd cooked with. He ignored the knifelike pain twisting in his chest and gave Holga a cavalier shrug.

"He runs a pawn shop?" Holga mused, glancing around the empty kitchen again. "Interesting."

"What are you thinking?" Edgin put down the rusted pot and stared at her. "Are you thinking . . . what, steal the stuff back? Sneak over there tonight and clean him out?" It wasn't like he hadn't considered it, some nights. He was pretty sure his skills hadn't atrophied over the months he'd been away from the Harpers. He could still sneak, skulk, and pick a lock or two when needed. A small-time Zhent agent's shop in a little village like Targos wouldn't be much of a challenge, and Gods knew Pendro deserved to get burgled. He was no saint.

Holga blinked at him. "I was just thinking I could sell some stuff too," she said.

Edgin felt his face get hot. "Right, sure, that's what I thought you meant."

Great, already Holga thought he was a terrible father with no household skills and an empty kitchen. Now she thought he was a criminal too.

He went to Kira and made a show of adjusting her blankets, even though she'd fallen fast asleep in her cradle and didn't need him fussing with her.

When he was finished, he risked a glance at Holga. She hadn't moved, arms still crossed, thinking about . . . well, really, it was hard to tell with Holga. She could have been contemplating deep life questions or fighting a sneeze. The frown and brow furrow were similar for both.

Finally, she looked over at him, meeting his eyes. "Or we could do your thing," she said quietly.

Oh.

"To be completely clear," Edgin said slowly, not wanting to misunderstand and embarrass himself further, "do you mean—"

"Sneak over tonight and clean him out," Holga said flatly. "That one."

Well, they were already at rock bottom. Might as well make themselves comfortable.

AT NIGHTFALL, THEY took Kira over to Edgin's neighbors, Jon and Veri Talvick, who were more than happy to watch Kira for a few hours, and whose nine-year-old daughter, Miriam, was over the moon to get to hold the baby. Edgin was grateful and a bit sheepish that he'd never considered going over to his neighbors to ask for help before. Zia was always better at that sort of thing. The truth was, Edgin had been gone so often on business for the Harpers, he didn't even remember their names until Holga broke the ice by sticking out her hand and introducing herself with a gruff "Holga."

With Kira safely taken care of, the two of them then snuck over to Pendro's pawnshop, which was conveniently located at the edge of the village, with the nearest other businesses several yards away. There they waited until Pendro came out, locked the place up, and headed into the village, probably to the tavern for a long night of drinking. Edgin had casually asked around and discovered Pendro was a regular. He wasn't well liked by the other villagers either, which made what they were about to do all the more satisfying in Edgin's mind.

The pawnshop wasn't in the best shape. The roof thatching was old and picked over by birds and other vermin, and there was an alarming lean to the whole thing that made Edgin wonder how long Pendro intended to stay in business in Targos. Working for the Zhentarim must not have paid as well as he'd thought.

They circled around to the back door, and the lock there was pitifully easy to pick. Edgin almost wished it had been a bigger challenge. As it was, the door swung open quietly, and they crept inside. Well, by "crept," he meant Holga stomped a bit less violently than usual.

Wan moonlight illuminated the dusty shop interior. The back room they entered was full of floor-to-ceiling shelves with all kinds of knickknacks and household items. A thin, moth-eaten curtain separated this back area from the front of the shop.

"Poke around back here if you want," Edgin whispered to Holga. "I'm going to take a look up front."

To find the coin box. He didn't say it, but Holga gave him a knowing look and a small nod.

Glass display cases were arranged in a U shape in the main room of the shop. Some notched weapons and mediocre art hung on the walls, nothing that jumped out at Edgin as being particularly valuable. He paused by one of the cases when a flash of green caught his eye.

It was a tiny emerald ring fitted to a simple gold band, intended to be worn on the smallest finger. He'd given it to Zia as an anniversary present several years ago. It had killed him to pawn it, but Kira needed milk, and he knew Zia would have clapped him upside the head for even hesitating when it came to feeding their kid.

There was a lock on the glass case, but it too was easy to pick, and a moment later, Edgin was slipping the ring safely into his pocket. Back where it belonged.

He would give it to Kira one day.

If he'd had any doubts before, any pricks of conscience about what they were doing, they'd all vanished. It was every person for themselves in this world. He'd had to learn that lesson the hard way, but he'd learned. Anyone who worked for the Zhents deserved every terrible thing that happened to them, as far as Edgin was concerned. From now on, he'd put his family first, no matter what.

He felt around behind the cases, looking for hidden drawers, a locked chest, anything that might lead him to a stash of coin. A slight creak made him pause. The section of floorboards here was loose. Edgin could feel them give under his weight. He crouched down to inspect them carefully, and soon his fingers found the seam of a trapdoor. He wedged his hand underneath and lifted, revealing a hidden space.

A small, brassbound chest was nestled within.

Holga emerged from the back room, carrying an assortment of pots and pans, as Edgin was lifting out the chest. She hadn't found the teacups. Edgin supposed it was too much to hope that Pendro hadn't sold them already.

"Pendro's going to know it was you stealing from him if you just take your own stuff," Holga pointed out as he worked the lock on the chest.

"I thought about that," Edgin admitted as the lock clicked open. He pushed back the lid of the chest and whistled at the amount of gold and silver coin stashed inside. Awful lot of money for a pawn-broker in a village this size. He raked up a fistful of coins. "The thing about our man Pendro is, he's predictable. And I had a feeling, being the slippery coinmonger that he is, he'd be skimming from his Zhen-tarim masters, and I bet this is some of the profits. So, I think we're going to help ourselves to this and anything else in here that we need."

And that wasn't all. He wasn't a Harper anymore, but Edgin was still wily enough to plant a whisper in certain ears, let it get back to the Zhents that Pendro was skimming. Once they came looking for their money and Pendro couldn't pay, he'd have bigger problems than accusing Edgin or anyone else in the village of stealing from him.

He closed the chest and relocked it, hoisting it onto his shoulder.

He pointed to a rack on the wall. "Grab those knives, the bigger serving platter—oh, and that washboard too, we need a new one—and let's get out of here."

Holga scooped up everything he pointed to, plus a few more things, and they slipped out the back door.

It had been so *easy*. Standing in the moonlight outside the pawnshop, Edgin finally acknowledged the tremor of excitement in his limbs, the euphoria of having enough coin in his arms to feed his small family for months. He had not one ounce of regret either. Pendro had had it coming, and his loss was their gain.

They snuck back to the cottage together, and although Holga wasn't smiling, Edgin thought he detected a bit less stomp in her step, a lightness that he hadn't seen before. They worked well together. He wondered if she might ever consider doing something like this again.

Now, there was an idea.

INTERLUDE

"You were already a thief," Kira said, grinning at him. She'd propped herself up on her pillows—probably so there was no danger she'd fall asleep during the story. "You knew you were."

"Lies," Edgin said, grinning back at her, one ankle resting on his opposite knee as he leaned back in his chair. "Who's telling this story?"

"What happened to Raylin Pendro?" Kira asked, ignoring him. "You never said."

"Well, you see, I was right—as usual—in that the Zhents our poor Pendro was working for eventually returned to Targos and gave him notice that they were coming for the money he was holding for them. Tragically, he was unable to give them what they wanted."

"Huh," Kira said. "Imagine that."

"Right?" Edgin scratched the stubble at his chin. He decided he needed a shave. "And since Pendro came up short on the coin, he had to skip town in a great hurry. Shame, really. He left behind all the trinkets people had had to sell him over the years, so gradually, people drifted in and out, reclaiming their property in case the building collapsed from neglect."

"But it didn't," Kira said, pulling her knees up to her chest.

He gave her an exasperated look. "Again, who's telling this story?"

"I just want to make sure you don't leave out the good bits!"

"The good bit is that Pendro's nephew—or something, it's not really clear how they're related—turned up in Targos one day, fixed the place up, and opened a bakery that now serves the best cinnamon rolls on the Sword Coast."

"I *love* those cinnamon rolls," Kira said with a dreamy expression.

"I am at least fifty percent responsible for their existence," Edgin said loftily, "so you're welcome. Now, can I continue the story in my own way, please?" He gestured for her to lie back down.

Kira rolled her eyes, but she did as she was told.

"Now, I'm going to skip ahead a few years," Edgin warned her. "I assume you're all right with that as long as I cover—"

"The Neverwinter Haunting Job!" Kira burst out.

"I wouldn't dare skip the Neverwinter Haunting Job," Edgin said, laying his hand over his heart.

The fire burned low, but the story was just getting started.

CHAPTER 3

NINE YEARS LATER

"We'll all be murdered by the faceless dead!"

It was definitely a challenge to pick a lock while the lord and lady of the house were screaming their heads off downstairs, but Edgin was a professional.

"Set the scene for me, Holga," he said, glancing over his shoulder. "What's Kira doing?"

Standing watch at the door to Lord Bantakent's study, Holga was shaking her head in pure admiration. "Told you that invisibility pendant would pay off, Ed. She's a master."

The lock clicked open. Edgin threw back the lid of the chest and buried his hands in a pile of gold and gems. Sweet victory. He scooped the loot into a bag and tossed it over his shoulder before joining Holga at the door.

Downstairs, the Lord and Lady Bantakent, one of the most unscrupulous merchant power couples in the city of Neverwinter, were huddled together in their nightclothes in the center of their grand foyer, while a pair of what looked like priceless vases floated around their heads. The rest of the room was a shambles. All the paintings had been turned upside down or pulled off the walls, tables and chairs were knocked over, and through it all, a high-pitched, disembodied voice intoned, "Yooooouuuu shall join me in the emptiness of the beyoooooond!"

"She improvised that line," Edgin said, nudging Holga.

The servants had all fled as soon as Kira started throwing plates and dinnerware against the dining room walls and howling in a voice of ghostly despair. Lord and Lady Bantakent had retreated to the foyer, where an invisible Kira had cornered them to continue the haunting while Edgin and Holga cleaned out the upstairs.

"Miffles!" Lady Bantakent wailed. "No, not my baby!"

"Oh, that's a nice touch," Edgin said, "using the dog."

He watched Lord and Lady Bantakent quail before the sight of Miffles the terrier sailing through the air, dipping up and down, his pink tongue lolling out the side of his mouth, to all appearances having the time of his doggy life.

"Time to go," Holga said, pulling Edgin toward the half-open window and the rope they'd left hanging there.

The three of them met up at the rendezvous point in an alley a few streets away, Kira appearing in front of Edgin with a huge grin on her face. "Did you see me, Dad? Did you see?"

"Fantastic job, kid," Edgin said. "That was a one-in-a-million haunting."

"Profitable too," Holga said.

IT WAS WELL after midnight by the time they got back to the cottage.

"It's time to admit the truth," Edgin said with a sigh as he, Holga, and Kira sorted the loot at the kitchen table. "I'm a damn good thief."

Holga snorted. "Ought to be, after nine years of practice."

"Well, I've always known it, of course, but I'm a humble man," Edgin said.

Kira laughed as she sorted the coins from the small pile of gems. Edgin did a double take every time he looked at her these days. She'd grown from a squalling newborn to a nightmare of a toddler and was now all skinned knees, skinny arms, and dark curly hair at nine years old. The change from baby to *person* had seemed to happen in an eyeblink.

Of course, as soon as she was old enough to understand what they did for a living, Kira had insisted on joining him and Holga on their heists. Edgin had been unsure at first, but she'd quickly become invaluable. The rest of the time . . .

Edgin had hoped that when she was able to walk, dress herself, and take care of the basics of being a person, to speak and tell him exactly what she needed, things would get easier when it came to raising Kira.

Oh, what a sweet, innocent, naïve man he'd been.

Being able to walk meant that she could *run*. With sharp objects. Toward horses or deep bodies of water.

Being able to speak meant that she had *opinions*. Suggestions about when her bedtime should be, or critiques of his cooking.

He still had no idea what he was doing. Without Holga, he'd be lost.

"Bedtime soon, bug," Holga said fondly as Kira threw her arms around Holga's neck and hopped onto her back. She growled in mock anger and stood up, spinning Kira around three times until she shrieked with delight. When Holga put Kira down, the little girl stumbled toward him, dizzy, flushed, and laughing, and wrapped her arms around his waist in a tight hug, causing him to lose track of the coin he was counting.

"Listen to Holga," Edgin said absently, patting her back before disengaging himself. "Time for bed."

Kira's face creased in disappointment as she stepped back, her smile wavering. "Fine," she said, sighing and toying with her invisibility pendant. She was rarely without it ever since Holga had presented her with the magic item, taken from one of their early heists. Edgin had to admit it came in handy on jobs like tonight, but still, giving an invisibility pendant to a kid as a gift—who did things like that?

"Night, bug," Holga said as Kira shuffled off to her bedroom.

Once she'd shut the door behind her, Edgin went back to counting out the coins on the table. It took him a minute to notice that

Holga had stopped helping him. Instead, she sat back in her chair with her arms crossed, glaring at him.

Ah, the intimidation pose. He was familiar with it. Or, as it was more colloquially known, the *Edgin has screwed up again* pose.

"What?" he said, grinning and flipping one of the silver coins across the backs of his fingers. "Spit it out. Or, monosyllable it for me. What did I do this time?"

"You going to tuck her in?" Holga said. "Or tell her good night?"

His grin faded. "I did tell her—" Wait, *had* he told her good night? "Listen, I'm in the middle of important work here," Edgin said, gesturing at the coins. "Then there's the next heist to plan. It's been a long night." Why did he feel so twitchy and defensive? "Besides, you're usually the one who tucks her in, so the real question is why aren't you in there right now?"

"Because she wants her dad," Holga said flatly. "You remember that's your job too, right?"

Well, that was going too far. Edgin could summon an impressive glare of his own when he needed to, and he leveled it at her now. As usual, she didn't seem impressed. "I have done nothing over the past nine years but think of Kira. Everything I've done has been for her. Why are you on me about this all of a sudden?"

Kira was safe, fed, with a roof over her head and money when they needed it, thanks to a carefully cultivated thieving career he'd built over the past nine years. And now that Kira had become part of their little crew, she was rarely out of his sight. That's how responsible of a father he was. What more did Holga want from him?

She was looking at him with her brow furrowed, as if she wanted to take him apart to see how he worked. He hated it when she looked at him like that. "You don't talk to her," Holga said finally. "You don't spend time with her, unless it's on a job." She glanced at the closed bedroom door. "She needs you."

Edgin slapped a hand to his chest. "Thank you for twisting the knife," he muttered. "I can't help it that I don't have a lot of free time. I'm busy, working to feed—" He started to say "our family" but the words got tangled up in his throat. That wasn't what he and Holga had anyway. Theirs was just a convenient roommate arrangement. That had lasted for nine years.

"That's another thing," Holga said. "You make these heist plans, and you don't leave the house for days." She leaned forward and sniffed, wrinkling her nose. "Haven't bathed either."

"Look who's talking."

Holga shook her head. "You need to get out more."

Edgin checked his shirt. It was clean. Sort of. From a distance. And he'd surely gone into the village for supplies just . . . how long ago had it been? Gods, maybe Holga was right. He was going to become one of those scary recluses who grew a beard to his knees and fingernails that turned yellow and curled into claws.

"Well, what about you?" he countered, because deflecting was a skill that could be honed just like thieving.

"What about me?" It was Holga's turn to hunch up, defensive and wary.

"Oh, come on," Edgin said. "You turn up in our lives out of nowhere, and all I've gotten to know about you in the past nine years is your name and that you're an outcast from your tribe. Maybe I'm hiding in my work, but what are you hiding from, Holga?"

The room went silent. Edgin realized, belatedly, that he might have crossed a line. Holga's mouth was set in a grim frown, brows lowered, like she was ready to reach for her axe.

But then, as quickly as her fury had risen, she seemed to deflate. Her expression shuttered, and she walked over to the stove, checking the dampers and making sure the fire was still going inside, as if she needed something to do with her hands.

Edgin swallowed. Well, this was awkward, and he hated awkward. This was why their arrangement had worked so well up until this point—because they never talked about anything personal. Once you got personal, things got messy.

"Look, Holga, I—"

"His name's Marlamin," Holga interrupted, her voice rough.

Edgin was confused. "Marlamin?"

She nodded, refusing to look at him. "My ex-husband. He was an outsider, not a member of the Elk tribe. I married him anyway, and that's why I was exiled."

"You fell in love with an outsider and left everything behind to be with him." Edgin had painted a few imaginary pictures of Holga's past over the years, but nothing he'd conjured up had looked anything like that.

This time Holga did look up, and she glared at him. "Laugh, and I'll put your head in the stove," she warned him.

"No one's laughing." He raised his hands in a placating gesture. "I'm actually impressed. That's really romantic, Holga." He hesitated, wondering how far he should pry, but he was terribly curious now. "You said ex-husband. What happened?"

She shrugged, and it was such a defeated gesture that Edgin kind of wanted to hug her, but he knew if he tried, she really would put his head in the stove. "People change," she said softly. She looked up at him, her eyes imploring. "But he was good, you know? Made me feel safe, protected." She sighed. "Like I didn't have to be the strong one all the time."

"Yeah." Edgin knew exactly what that was like—and how gut-wrenching it was to lose it. "I felt that way once too, with my wife." He glanced away. "We had a great life, and I thought I was doing good work as a Harper. But I didn't realize how dangerous that life would be for the people I loved. After I crossed our enemies one too many times, they found out where I lived and . . ." The breath sawed in and out of Edgin's lungs. The memories were still fresh, even after so long. "I wasn't there to protect my wife, and she died protecting our child," he said. "After that, I left the Harpers, and I swore I would do whatever it took to keep Kira safe. I wouldn't fail my family again."

He'd never spoken about this to anyone. Holga listened in silence, and, thank the Gods, she wasn't looking at him with pity. He couldn't stand that.

"My tribe exiled me, and you exiled yourself from the Harpers," she said at last. "We're a pair, aren't we?"

Edgin gave a half-hearted laugh. "I guess we are."

He cleared his throat. Judging by the anvil in his chest and the sheen in Holga's eyes, they were in dangerous territory here. *Feelings* were getting involved. They needed a new direction for the conversation before one of them said something they'd regret—something that led to a healthy emotional catharsis. It would be horrifying.

"Maybe you're right," Edgin said, running a hand through his hair. "I haven't been getting out enough lately." Or really, doing any sort of living for the last nine years. He'd had a good reason, though. He'd been absorbed in work and providing for his family, but he could change that. It wasn't too late.

Was it?

"What do you suggest?" he asked, surreptitiously checking the length of his fingernails. Hangnails for miles, but still short, thank the Gods, and he could shave today.

Holga shrugged. "I don't know. I'm no expert." She glanced around the room, as if trying to get inspiration from something in the kitchen. At least it wasn't as sparse in there as it used to be. The cupboards were full of pots and pans, fresh herbs were piled on the cutting board, and there was a vase of purple and white wildflowers sitting on the table, courtesy of Kira.

Even his lute was sitting in the corner, waiting to be played. He hadn't thought about the instrument—or performing—for a very long time.

It was as if Holga read his mind. "You could sing," she said tentatively. She toyed with the ends of her hair, looking uncomfortable. "The Trip and Shuffle has performers. I watch them sometimes."

She was right. There was a small stage at the tavern where traveling bards often performed for coin, and some of them had even gained a degree of local fame among the villagers. He nodded slowly, thinking it over.

"I could maybe do that," he said, but he held up a hand when Holga started to speak. "Just me, though. I don't want Kira to know about this."

"Then what's the point?" Holga sighed, disappointment clear on her face. "She hasn't heard you sing since she was a baby, and she wouldn't remember that."

Edgin bristled. "How do you know I've never sung to her?" Maybe not lately, but surely sometime in the past?

"I've got ears," Holga said. "You haven't sung to her in years." She picked at an old stain on the kitchen table, trying to be nonchalant. "She'd love it."

Holga was probably right about that too. She was right about so many things, though Edgin would swallow his own tongue before he'd admit it. But the idea of getting up on a stage and performing in front of people—a part of him felt a thrill of exhilaration at the prospect. Another part wanted to throw up just thinking about approaching a stage.

It would be so much easier not to do it at all. He was busy with his work. Work that kept Kira fed and safe. She was a happy kid, and she had Holga to tuck her in at night. She didn't really need him.

But she was also growing up so fast. He couldn't believe how tall she was already, how sharp. Was he missing out on important things, not spending enough time with her?

He looked up at Holga, firming his resolve. "One solo performance, just to see how it goes," he said, and before she could argue, he added, "If the first time goes well, I'll bring Kira to the next one, and I promise I'll start spending more time with her. Happy?"

Holga appeared to consider this. Finally, she nodded. "I'll take it."

They shook on it across the kitchen table. Edgin hesitated, a thought occurring to him. "I don't suppose I could convince *you* not to come to the first performance either?"

Holga's lips twitched. It wasn't really a smile. Kira was the only one who could make her break one of those out, but it was close enough that it made him squirm. "Not a chance," she said. "I wouldn't miss this for anything."

CHAPTER 4

E dgin had intended to put off arranging his debut performance at the tavern for as long as possible, but Holga dragged him there the very next day, and before he could fully reconcile himself to the idea, he had the first slot of performances that evening.

Holga kept her word and didn't tell Kira what was going on. She was sent to the neighbors to spend the evening with Miriam, who'd been her babysitter and friend for years, so she didn't suspect a thing. This left Edgin plenty of time and space to pace up and down the cottage, trying not to throw up.

"Here," Holga said, pouring him a bit of their strongest whiskey, kept on hand for emergencies. This certainly qualified.

Edgin took it in one gulp, feeling the liquid burn all the way down his throat as stars exploded in front of his eyes. He slammed the glass down on the table and felt a little calmer.

"We'd better get going," Holga said, glancing out the window at the orange glow of the setting sun. The breeze was crisp and cool coming in the open window. Autumn was in full glory in the reds and yellows of the leaves on the trees, and the neighbors' pumpkin crops were ready for harvest. "They'll be starting soon."

It would be a full house too, on a nice night like this, Edgin thought as he followed Holga out the door. He paused in the yard, glancing back at the whiskey bottle left on the table. Maybe one more little drink wouldn't hurt.

"I'll catch up," Edgin called after Holga.

"You better," she said without looking back at him. "Or I'll drag you by the hair."

"Have some faith!" Edgin made a rude gesture to her retreating back, and then he dove for the whiskey bottle.

Just one more drink to steel his nerves . . .

WHEN EDGIN ARRIVED at the Trip and Shuffle, he was drunk. Un-equivocally, weaving on his feet, sloppy drunk.

He felt glorious.

His tuned his lute as he made his way through the crowd toward the stage. When had it gotten so big? The two steps leading up to it looked gigantic. It took him a couple of tries to get his footing and hoist himself up.

Distantly, he heard what sounded like Holga sighing from some-where in the crowd, but he didn't have time to concentrate on any-thing but finding his way to the center of the stage—*oops, almost fell right off there*—and turning to face his audience.

The room was packed. A standing-room-only crowd come to see him perform. Edgin was so touched he almost teared up. Except, it was possible he was seeing double and there were really half as many people as he thought. Still, he vowed he'd give every one of them a performance they wouldn't soon forget.

He wished he'd brought the whiskey bottle with him, though. That stuff was incredibly drinkable once you got used to the burn. Was it a bad thing for singing if he couldn't feel his lips?

"Good evening, folks," he addressed the crowd, putting on his best performer's smile and hoping it didn't look like a sloppy drunk-ard's grin. "I'm s-so happy to sh-*see* you all here tonight. Who's ready for some lively entertainment?"

His voice rose, emphasizing the last word, and maybe a little bit of spittle flew from his mouth, but he was pretty sure nobody would notice in the low light.

There was a smattering of polite applause in response to his enthusiasm, but Edgin was definitely getting an uncertain feeling from the crowd. Not a great start, but he'd get them warmed up. He pasted the smile more firmly on his face, lips pulled back from his teeth, and forged ahead. "Sit back, relax, and enjoy the snow. *Show!*"

The crowd went back to eating, drinking, and talking, while Edgin stood alone on the stage. His hands itched. He didn't know what to do with them. Did he hold them at his sides? Clasp them? They were just two flailing appendages attached to his body. Wait, that's right, he was carrying a lute. He should definitely focus his hands on that if he expected to play it. But now he realized his palms were sweaty, his lips were still numb, and—

Focus!

It was just a simple village tavern crowd, not a king's court. He could handle this. Edgin forced himself to stop fidgeting. He looked out at the sea of blurry faces—and there was Holga, sitting at a table near the center of the room, right in his eyeline. Their gazes locked. Had she sat there on purpose, so he'd be sure to see a friendly face in the crowd?

Oh Gods, this was not the time to get a lump of emotion caught in his throat. He needed to sing! *Right, time to do this.*

He'd start with an old favorite, something he could sing in his sleep.

So Edgin opened his mouth, feeling the music swell within him, the familiar tune that he'd learned years ago. Everything else dropped away, and he might as well have been alone onstage.

"When the battle is over, friends become lovers, sons embrace mothers," he sang, and it was like all those years away from performing had never happened. He heard the clear, ringing tenor of his voice cutting through the noise of the crowd, making the patrons turn curiously in their chairs so he could snare their attention one by one as he continued the song.

"Where once were contenders now are befrienders." His voice rose as he gained confidence, striding across the small stage, making eye contact with the audience, watching their faces light up, and even the patrons who weren't paying attention were tapping their feet in time with his song. He had them, his first audience in years, and it was like he was his old self again, belting out classic tunes in taverns or singing to Zia on the night he'd asked her to marry him . . .

Edgin's voice faltered as pain filled his chest like a black morass. He spun away, putting his back to the audience to recover himself, making it look like he'd intended the move. But dizziness from the whiskey overcame him, and the candlelight shining on either end of the stage blurred in his vision in streaks of gold.

He was losing it. He could feel it. Desperately, he reached for the song, but his fingers felt like sausages on the lute strings. No matter. His voice was his best asset anyway. He'd finish the song with his back to the audience if he had to. Whatever he had to do to get through it.

But he'd lost the words.

He'd been in the second verse. He *knew* how this went. *Where once were contenders now are befrienders* . . . what was the next line?

Sweat broke out on the back of his neck. Slowly, he turned around, hoping he could reconnect with the audience, find the words in the performance, anything. But he found no help there. Murmurs flowed through the crowd, though he tried to block them out.

"Is the man all right, Mama?"

"Was that the whole song?"

"Five coppers he pukes on the front row."

This last prediction, by a dwarf who'd also been sitting near the center of the room, was immediately followed by a grunt from Holga and a yelp from the dwarf as she kicked his chair. Edgin flashed Holga a weak smile of gratitude.

And he put his lute down and walked right off the stage, leaving the instrument behind.

At first there was confused silence. Maybe the crowd thought he had an urgent need for the outhouse, but soon enough, the heckling began. It wasn't too bad, mostly a few jeers and foot stomping from the drunker patrons. The dwarf threw a potato at him, but Edgin had the wherewithal to dodge, and Holga kicked his chair again before getting up to intercept Edgin on his way to the bar.

"Well, that was fantastic," Edgin growled as he signaled the bartender for a drink and turned to see the next performer, a young, red-haired halfling woman, also carrying a lute, trotting up to the stage like nothing had happened. She chatted up the crowd like a natural, and scant moments later, her beautiful voice and her own lute music filled the room—because why not pour a little salt in his wounds?—and the crowd completely forgot about Edgin's disastrous debut.

"Ale," he said, leaning against the bar to put his head in his hands.

Holga perched on the stool next to him. "Ale and potatoes," she added to Edgin's order, and clapped him awkwardly on the shoulder. "What happened?"

"What happened is I listened to a terrible idea and it resulted in this terrible night, which I'm about to flush right out of my memory with multiple tankards of ale," Edgin said, though his words were muffled by his hands over his face, so he wasn't sure how much of it he'd communicated to Holga. She must have gotten most of it, because she shrugged.

"Least you tried," she said.

And at least Kira hadn't been here to see the extent of his humiliation.

Their drinks—and potatoes—arrived, and Edgin reached into his pouch to pay for this first round.

The bartender waved him off. "These are paid for," he said, "by an admirer of your performance." He didn't quite manage to keep a straight face as he said it, but Edgin couldn't bring himself to care. Free drinks were not to be sneered at, even if they came with a steaming side of mockery.

"Who might this patron of the fine arts be?" he asked instead.

"Ah, that would be me," said a voice from behind him.

Edgin turned to see a human man with pale white skin who looked to be in his early forties, his hair starting to go to silver, with a few wrinkles around his eyes that somehow made him look worldly instead of old. He was dressed in simple traveling clothes and a well-worn leather vest. The corner of his mouth was quirked up in a smile.

"Forge Fitzwilliam, but please, just call me Forge," he said, holding out a hand for Edgin to shake.

CHAPTER 5

Edgin clasped Forge's hand in a brief greeting, all the while taking in the man's charming smile and relaxed posture as he slid onto the barstool on Edgin's other side and casually held up a hand to order a glass of wine.

"I enjoyed your song," he said as Edgin took a long drink of his ale. The first drink was the best, while it was still sweetly cold, with that thin layer of foam on top that tickled the nose. Edgin was going to get so much drunker tonight that Holga would have to carry him back to the house.

Or more likely drag him home by his boots, but Edgin could live with that.

He was dimly aware that Forge was saying something, but Edgin was having a hard time focusing while his lips were locked onto his ale tankard like a man who'd found his lost love.

". . . really thought you had something going up there, and that audience—you had them in the palm of your hand," Forge droned on. "Shame about the stage fright, but it gets to even the best performers sometimes."

Edgin's head snapped up so quickly he dribbled a stream of ale down the front of his shirt. Oh well, Holga said it needed washing anyway. "I didn't get stage fright," he said indignantly, but then he stopped, the ale going sour in his stomach.

What was he going to say? That he apparently had untapped wells of grief hidden inside him that he was still discovering, even after nine years? That he'd had an identity crisis, a screeching internal conflict between the Harper he'd once been and the thief he was now, that was somehow represented by the song he couldn't remember the words to?

"No, you're right, it was a nasty case of stage fright," Edgin said, and went in for another long, lingering drink.

"You want a bigger tankard? Or a bucket?" Holga rumbled from his other side.

"Maybe later," Edgin said, wiping his mouth with a satisfied belch. "Tell me about yourself, Forge." He patted the man clumsily on the shoulder. "What brings you to our little village?"

Forge laughed good-naturedly and took a sip of wine. "Oh, I'm just a simple merchant, passing through. Used to operate out of Waterdeep, but I decided I should explore a bit more of the world before settling down and raising a few children, so I decided to expand and see more of the Sword Coast." He glanced around the tavern. "Truth be told, I'd hoped to find a good Three-Dragon Ante game going, but it looks like Tymora isn't smiling on me tonight." He shot a hopeful glance at Edgin. "Unless you and your friend there would care for a game?"

Edgin couldn't remember the last time he'd sat down to cards with anyone. It wasn't a terrible idea, and it might help wash out the memory of his performance onstage. He did a few quick calculations in his head to determine how drunk he was.

One plus one is two. Two plus two is four. Three plus three is yellow. Solid.

"I'm in." He slammed his tankard down on the bar. "What about you, Holga?" he said over his shoulder. He sensed he was speaking just a bit too loudly, even for the crowd noise, and he was still occasionally seeing double, but it was fine. He could play Three-Dragon Ante in his sleep.

"No," Holga said, and went back to munching on her potato.

"I'll get us a table," Forge said, and he left them to weave his way through the crowd toward the back of the room.

"Come on, at least come watch," Edgin said, grinning and tugging on Holga's arm in a way he'd seen Kira do when she wanted something, until Holga sighed heavily and got up.

"I don't like him," she said, grabbing their drinks.

"I know what you mean," Edgin said, nodding with extra emphasis so she would know he was hearing her. "He has those soulful eyes and that face that's a little bit swoony, but at the same time I kind of want to punch him. You ever know anyone like that?"

Holga glanced sidelong at him. "Yes," she said.

She understood him so well. Edgin loved that about her. He reached up to pat her cheek affectionately, but Holga turned her head at the last second and he missed, so he ended up tugging on her shirt collar instead.

"Sure you're sober enough to play cards?" Holga asked, looking him up and down doubtfully.

"I'm m-more than up for this challenge," Edgin said, waggling his eyebrows.

She started to say something else, but Forge was signaling them from an empty table he'd found in the corner. Edgin grabbed Holga's wrist and towed her across the room.

"Last clean table in the place, I think," Forge said as he sat down and pulled out a deck of cards. He paused in the act of shuffling, as if a thought had just occurred to him. He reached in his belt pouch and pulled out a handful of gold coins. "You know, I was going to break these down for some silver, and it completely slipped my mind." He glanced at Edgin. "I don't suppose you want to play for these kinds of stakes, do you?"

Edgin hadn't realized they'd be playing for any stakes at all. He looked down at the not insubstantial pile of gold in Forge's hand and felt a little prickle at his scalp, the hairs on the back of his neck lifting. He liked to think of it as a kind of sixth sense—his *hustling* sense, as it were. It made him sit up straighter in his chair and regard Forge with renewed interest.

"Oh, pfft, I think I have a few gold coins somewhere around here," he said, making a show of patting down his pockets. He removed a pouch from his belt and set it on the table with a loud *clunk*.

Forge lifted his eyebrows, his genial smile widening fractionally. "I'll deal, then, shall I?"

Three-Dragon Ante wasn't a hard game. A round, or "gambit," of betting was followed by him and Forge taking turns laying out cards into flights of dragons and activating their powers based on the cards' competing strengths.

Forge had a lovely deck, with impeccably detailed artwork of the various chromatic and metallic dragons done in expensive, showy inks. Even Holga looked at the cards in appreciation, though it was clear she had never played and wasn't really interested in following the game anyway.

Edgin wasn't following the game that closely either, if he was being honest, until he noticed how much coin he was losing.

Huh. Now that was peculiar. The drunken haze that had set in over his brain had made him feel a bit detached, but he'd still thought he was doing better building his flights than that. That hustling sense went off again, like sharply ringing bells in his ears, but this time it was directed at the man sitting across the table from him.

"Just a round of bad luck to start," Forge said as he swept the latest pot over to his side of the table. His lips curved in that genial smile again, the smile that said, *I'm rooting for you. You can do this.* "But if you'd like to stop, I absolutely understand."

Edgin looked at Forge. He looked at the cards scattered over the table, the gleaming-scaled dragons staring back at him with hungry eyes. He looked over at Holga, who'd finished her potato and had her chin propped on her hand and her eyes half-closed like this was the most boring night she'd ever spent in a tavern.

"No, let's play a few more rounds," Edgin said. "Maybe I can right the ship."

"That's the spirit." Forge scooped up the cards.

Edgin held up his tankard, signaling for more ale, and then he cracked his knuckles and leaned forward in his chair as Forge began to shuffle.

They started a new game, but Edgin stopped paying attention to his own cards, and instead he watched Forge's hands. To the casual observer, it probably looked like Edgin was in a drunken stupor at this point. To be fair, he was. But he was also falling back on years and years of training that had never really left him, no matter how far removed he was from the Harpers.

Forge's hands moved fast, snapping cards and flipping coins, but in Edgin's hyper-focused mind, they might as well have been going in slow motion.

There it is—he dealt from the bottom of the deck. Oh, very smooth. He used the coin flip as a distraction. Nice nail beds too. No hangnails in sight.

Forge's sleeves, now that Edgin really looked, had little embellishments on them that from a distance looked like fancy decorative embroidery, but in reality they were there to conceal slits in the fabric, large enough and positioned in such a way as to hold cards if he needed them while he rested his elbows on the table.

Oh, there he goes, slipping one out to put into his hand, and another goes in.

Forge was very good. Edgin could always admire a sleek, well-orchestrated hustle. It was like standing in front of an oil painting and leaning close to study the brushstrokes, or listening to a piece of music and trying to separate out the role of each instrument that contributed to the whole beauty of the piece. Yes, Edgin was a connoisseur of hustling, even in a drunken stupor.

Actually, he was even better at hustling when he was drunk.

"My turn to deal?" he asked after Forge swept up another handful of coins. Edgin's own pile was getting dangerously low, and Forge glanced at it with a good-natured wince on his behalf.

"Are you sure you don't want to call it a night?" he asked, but he handed the cards over willingly enough when Edgin made a vague gesture for them.

The halfling bard was still onstage and had just launched into a jaunty tune that was perfect to stomp his feet to. Edgin noticed his lute still lay untouched on the stage. He'd almost forgotten about it, but he wasn't worried. He'd get it later.

"I sense a comeback in the making," Edgin said, rolling his shoulders and shuffling the cards.

And Edgin began to cheat. Shamelessly, effortlessly, and all the while he watched Forge's face to see how long it took his fellow hustler to notice.

To his credit, it wasn't very long.

Edgin had just collected his second victory pot when Forge's brow furrowed. He leaned against the table, tapping his cheek with the index and middle fingers of his right hand. He began to watch Edgin's hands. Edgin was tempted to slow his pace down, just a bit, to give Forge a chance, but no, he decided now was a good time to see how skilled the other man really was.

He saw the moment Forge realized Edgin was cheating too. A muscle in his finely sculpted jaw ticked, and he smoothed a hand through his graying hair. His gaze lifted from the table, and their eyes locked for an instant, neither making a move. They were just frozen there, watching each other, one hustler recognizing another, and it was like they were introducing themselves to each other all over again.

Hello, I'm Forge, and you should know that story about being a merchant on the verge of settling down was a load of steaming horse dung.

Hello, I'm Edgin, and I know you wanted to fleece me while I was drunk and vulnerable, but you should understand the drunker I get, the better cheater I am.

Nice to meet you.

At least, that's how Edgin imagined it playing out in his head. In reality, all that happened was a slow smile spread across Forge's face, and it wasn't his *aw shucks,* laid-back smile, or the patronizing grin he'd worn when Edgin was losing so much coin. No, this was the hustler's smile. This smile was tight, and it was all teeth.

"Another round?" Forge asked, picking up the deck and tapping it on the table.

"Absolutely," Edgin said.

After that, neither of them even tried to hide their techniques anymore. Edgin pulled out every trick he knew and presented it to impress Forge, and Forge did the same. Even Holga started to notice, but when she opened her mouth to call out the blatant cheating, Edgin cut her off.

"It's all right," he said, clinking his tankard against hers. "We're just putting on another performance, aren't we, Forge?"

Forge chuckled and slipped another card from the bottom of the deck. "It's been the most educational evening I've spent in some time," he said. "Truly, the way your fingers caress the cards to distract from what you're doing. You must teach me how it's done."

"Gladly," Edgin said, with a little half bow in his seat. "And you simply must tell me who your tailor is. I have to get one of those shirts. It's perfect for this sort of work."

"Oh, this old thing?" Forge lifted his arms carelessly. "I made it myself. I can give you the pattern."

"You're too kind."

Holga rolled her eyes. "I'm going to the bar," she said, and left them to their mutual fawning.

It wasn't the way Edgin had expected the evening to go at all, but he discovered, to his shock, that he was actually enjoying himself immensely. He hadn't been able to perform onstage, but he'd had no trouble slipping into this performance, and he appreciated Forge as a worthy opponent. Maybe that's what it was—to play well against a worthy adversary made him feel like he hadn't lost as much as he'd thought. It made him feel more like himself.

And then the door to the tavern burst open, slamming against the opposite wall so hard the building shook.

Edgin looked over his shoulder and noted that the draft coming in the open door was quite chilly, but before he could yell at someone to shut it, the gnoll raiding party poured into the tavern.

CHAPTER 6

The inn was packed, standing room only around the bar, so the effect of the gnoll incursion was immediate and terrifying. Screams filled the room as people scrambled up from their seats and charged in a frightened mass for the back exit through the kitchen. This immediately created a dangerous bottleneck, with everyone trying to push through the narrow kitchen doorway at once. Glass shattered, tables and chairs were knocked aside, and people fell and were trampled in the chaos.

The barkeep and the few patrons who were armed grabbed their axes, cudgels, and swords and engaged the gnolls, and things got bloody very fast.

Edgin and Forge jumped up at the same time. Their eyes met, and Edgin nodded at their table. Forge said, "Right," and together they tipped the heavy wood table onto its side, putting their bodies between it and the back wall for some cover. Sifting through the broken dishes and cutlery now littering the floor, Edgin came up with a blunt knife.

"Are you serious?" Forge asked when he saw what Edgin was brandishing.

"Best I got," Edgin said tersely. Well, that wasn't actually true. He glanced around, looking for Holga in the chaos, but she'd disappeared.

A gnoll slammed its hairy, muscled body into their table, and he didn't have time to think about her anymore. Teeth gnashed the wood as the creature tried to scramble over the barrier to get to them. Edgin stabbed at the gnoll with his supper knife, aiming for an eye. He missed, only just managing not to lose a finger in the process.

Forge drew an impressively long dagger from his boot, and that gave Edgin an idea.

"I'll pin—you stab," he shouted, and without waiting for agreement, he drove his shoulder into the table, putting all his weight into it. The wood groaned, and the blow knocked the gnoll off-balance just enough for Edgin to shove the table down on top of it, pinning it with his weight.

The gnoll snarled and pushed back, claws scrabbling along the wood, trying to free itself. Edgin pressed down harder, but the creature was clearly stronger than him. It was only a matter of time before the gnoll threw him off.

"Forge!" He winced as the table bucked, banging his chin hard enough to make him see stars. "This is the stab part!" A sharp pain shot through his knee as the table banged against it. "Stabbing would be good now!"

Forge finally maneuvered his way through the frantic crowd so he stood behind where the gnoll's head poked out from beneath the table. Bracing his foot against the edge, Forge drove his dagger into the creature's eye. There was a high-pitched squeal as the gnoll jerked, its body convulsing.

When it had stopped thrashing, Edgin slid off the table and stood up, looking around. Things were grim. At least four of the townspeople had been killed, and several others lay moaning on the floor, clearly injured. He counted eight gnolls in the raiding party. Including theirs, only three of them had been killed.

One of them had had its head split in half by an axe blade.

Following the blood trail, Edgin spied Holga with another gnoll cornered by the fire. Face twisted in a snarl, blood dribbling from a cut on her forehead, Holga reared back and planted her foot in the middle of the thing's chest, sending it flying into the fire. The smell of burning hair and seared gnoll flesh filled the room, making Edgin gag.

"Not that this hasn't been fun, but we should probably be getting out of this death trap," Forge observed. Though winded from the stabbing, he appeared calm enough. "Front door maybe?"

Edgin nodded in agreement. The remaining gnolls were looting the bodies of the patrons they'd killed and grabbing whatever other valuables they could find. At the speed they were moving, it didn't look like they intended to be here long either. Smash and grab, take the loot to their lair. That was what this looked like.

Then Edgin remembered that his and Forge's coin had been scattered all over the table, and he'd left his lute on the stage.

He whirled around and, sure enough, two gnolls were sweeping over the floor like ugly, scraggly brooms, collecting their discarded coin. One of them had Edgin's lute slung over its shoulder.

"Hey!" Edgin scrambled to get to the creature who'd taken his stuff, but another gnoll got in his way and tackled him to the floor. "Drop that lute! We cheated for that coin fair and square!"

The gnoll squealed and rolled, trying to get on top of Edgin. Edgin's knife flew out of his hands, but Edgin held on, and they rolled across the floor, tripping several people along the way, until they slammed into the back wall. Edgin, unfortunately, ended up on the bottom, and had to use both hands to hold back the gnoll's snapping teeth. Its breath was hot and rancid on his face, and Edgin's heart hammered wildly as he looked around frantically for another weapon.

"Holga! Little help here!"

"Busy!" she shouted back.

Wonderful. He was going to get his throat ripped out by a gnoll on the worst night of music and the best night of cards he'd ever had. He started to yell for Forge, but out of the corner of his eye, he saw the man wrestling with another gnoll, who was trying to rip his dagger out of his hands.

Fine, he'd do it himself.

Edgin planted his forearm in the gnoll's throat. The thing choked, tongue lolling grossly from the side of its mouth. With his other hand, Edgin felt around the floor and came up with a mostly intact serving plate. He smashed the gnoll in the face with it as hard as he could. The creature shrieked and recoiled, allowing Edgin to shove it off and scramble to his feet.

A high-pitched, keening cry pierced his eardrums. Edgin cursed and slapped his hands over his ears. A gnoll standing near the door had made the horrible sound, and the rest of its cohorts looked up, dropping everything—and everyone—and charging for the door in a rush.

Edgin ran after them. Holga met him at the door, just in time to see the group of creatures running off into the night toward the edge of town. They'd gotten as much loot as they could and were in full retreat. Smash, grab, and go.

Behind him, Forge cursed like a drunken sailor. "They got every bit of my coin—our coin," he amended when Edgin shot him a look.

And Edgin's lute. It may not have been his best night performing, but that didn't mean he was ready to give up his lute to a bunch of flea-bitten, overgrown hyenas. Edgin looked around at the ruined tavern, the bodies on the floor. Some of them were people he'd drunk with or waved to on the streets, even if he didn't know all their names. At the edge of the stage, the halfling bard was cradling a broken wrist and gathering up the shattered remains of her own beautiful lute, tears streaming down her face.

Edgin gritted his teeth and looked at Holga. She read his expression perfectly, because she nodded once, wiping a streak of blood from her face. "Let's get 'em," she growled.

EDGIN TRIED TO scrape together a plan as he, Holga, and Forge pelted through the forest, following by torchlight the tracks and blood trails and scattered bits of loot left behind by the escaping gnolls.

It was all well and good to shout *Let's get 'em* and run off into the night like a band of avenging idiots, but they needed a strategy here, because it was dark, they were still outnumbered by the gnolls, and if they chased them all the way back to their lair, there might be even *more* of the creatures waiting for them, besides whatever other dangers lurked in this forest. Edgin didn't know if they had the numbers for that kind of fight, even counting Holga as two or three people.

He'd also lost his supper knife, so he didn't even have a ready weapon. At least Holga still had her axe. He hoped Forge had kept hold of his dagger.

"All right, let's slow down," Edgin said as they plunged deeper into the forest, Forge struggling to get his footing among the mossy rocks and underbrush. The torchlight was uneven but still bright enough that it effectively announced their presence to anyone nearby. Edgin leaned against a tree to catch his breath and waited for Holga and Forge to join him.

"Going to lose them if we stop," Holga said.

She was right. They could hear the squeals and shrieks of the gnoll raiding party getting fainter in the distance.

"We're not stopping long," Edgin said, "but we need a plan. We can't just charge right into their lair."

"An ambush, then?" Forge asked. He gestured to himself. "I may not look like it, but I can move stealthily when I want to. It comes in handy in my line of work."

"As a merchant?" Holga said, her eyes narrowed.

Forge looked hurt. "You know, I wasn't lying about that part. I do sell a diverse and valuable product line." He shrugged. "Most of the time the product just isn't mine."

"Ethics aside," Edgin said, "you seemed pretty decent with that dagger of yours earlier."

"Oh, this?" Forge drew the blade out of his boot. He'd wiped the gnoll blood off of it at some point. "It's lovely, isn't it? It isn't mine either, but thank you."

Holga sighed. "Can we go now?"

"We're going," Edgin said, "but back off with the torchlight once we get close to their lair. They might have scouts or sentries. We go in quiet, execute an ambush if it's feasible, take back our loot, and celebrate afterwards."

"Agreed," Forge said, and Holga offered a grunt of acknowledgment.

They moved quickly through the forest, keeping as quiet as possible, with Holga bringing up the rear and doing her best to conceal the torchlight. Luckily the moon was full enough to provide them some additional light. A cold breeze blew across the back of Edgin's neck, ruffling his hair.

Despite the danger, a flood of excitement had him clenching and unclenching his fists as they moved, the blood pumping in his ears. They finally broke into a narrow clearing that slashed through the forest to see a tumble of rocks and a yawning cave entrance marking the gnolls' hideout.

Gnoll squeals and shouts echoed eerily from deep within the cave as Edgin approached. There was no guard at the entrance, but that didn't make him feel any better. It just meant they needed to expect other defenses.

"Watch the ground for any sign of traps," he whispered over his shoulder. Holga and Forge gave a nod, and they ducked inside the dark cave.

The passage sloped downward sharply at first, so much so that Edgin braced himself with his hands on the ground and half crawled into the tunnel. The air quickly became stale, and it reeked of gnoll waste. Edgin's boots squelched in something soft and rank. He didn't look down to see what it was. He knew.

Luckily, the passage leveled out after a few more feet, and they could all stand upright again. Edgin stayed in front, with Forge behind him and Holga in the rear with the light. The cries of the gnolls were growing louder, but the sounds were also more diffuse, as if the main group had split at some point. Sure enough, the passage curved and then forked, and they had a choice to make.

"Harder to ambush two groups," Forge commented, echoing Edgin's thoughts. "Maybe we should have brought some of the more heavily armed villagers with us."

Edgin shook his head. "More people just ruin the element of surprise, which I still think we can use." He gestured to the passage that angled off to the left. "The two of you stay here and watch that tunnel to make sure none of them come out. If they do, douse the torch, back off, and hide."

"What are you going to do?" Holga demanded, scowling at him.

"I'm going down the other tunnel to see if I can get an idea of how many we're dealing with. Most of the noise is coming from there anyway," he said. When Holga's frown only deepened, he added, "I'm not going to try to be a hero, believe me." Those days were far behind him. "If there are too many of them, I'll come right back."

He dearly hoped he wouldn't have to. They'd stolen a lot of coin from him—and a little bit from Forge—that he couldn't afford to spare, and he wanted his lute back. Hopefully, it was still in one piece.

Leaving Forge and a scowling Holga behind, Edgin crept down the right-hand passage. The torchlight illuminated the space a few yards ahead of him, but even that meager light was quickly gone, and soon he was just feeling his way in the dark. He pushed away a jolt of fear and claustrophobia. Surely, there'd be light once he got close enough to where the gnolls were living—torches, or at least fires for warmth and cooking. Until then, he kept one hand on the wall to his left, fingers trailing over cold, slimy stone. He suppressed a shudder.

Finally, after what seemed like an age of creeping through the dark, a faint, flickering light appeared ahead of him, enough to allow Edgin to see that the passage was widening. The sounds of the gnolls were growing louder too. Edgin slowed his steps and crouched low to the ground, sneaking up to the mouth of the tunnel to peer into the room beyond.

His stomach dropped. It appeared he was looking into the gnoll equivalent of a dining hall, and the room was packed. A quick count showed over a dozen gnolls in this room alone. They were gathered around what could loosely be described as a table. Really it was just a pile of flat stones pushed together, and on this they'd dumped the loot from the tavern: piles of coin, jewelry they'd stolen off people's bodies, and some good-quality weapons and tools.

And in the center of it all was his lute, sitting abandoned and unwanted by the gnolls in favor of the other shiny objects they'd picked up.

Edgin's heart sank. He was going to have to leave it. There was no way they could take on a dozen gnolls, especially when they didn't know how many were down the other passage. It had been a foolish impulse to come here. He needed to get out before the gnolls saw or heard him.

Moving carefully, his heart in his throat, Edgin began backing down the tunnel in the direction he'd come. He tried to stick to the same path he'd taken to get to this point, but the darkness enveloped him again like a suffocating cloak, and he was on edge enough that he didn't pay attention to where he was putting his feet. His toe caught painfully on the edge of a large rock, and he stumbled, hands flailing. He regained his balance, but when he braced his feet, his right foot sank a few inches into the cave floor, and he heard a soft click, like some sort of mechanism activating.

Oh Hells . . .

He tried to run, but as soon as he put his weight on his right foot, a section of the cave floor gave way beneath him, and he was suddenly falling into the dark.

CHAPTER 7

The shaft of the pit trap was narrow. It was the only thing that saved him.

Edgin thrust out both hands, forearms and elbows scraping over loose dirt to slow his fall. He flailed, reaching for something, anything, to grab on to.

Don't scream. Don't scream. Don't scream.

His hands found the roots of some ancient tree thrust deep into the soil, and he grabbed on with both hands, jerking himself to a stop. Loose dirt and stones rained down on his head from above, but that was the only sound in the narrow tunnel. He hung there by the ragged root and listened for any sign that the gnolls had heard their trap trigger and were coming to investigate.

To his immense relief, there was nothing. The creatures must have been too absorbed in shrieking and cackling over their treasure hoard to notice that their pit trap had swallowed him.

Except that also meant that Holga and Forge had no idea where he was either, and Edgin's arms were already burning like they'd been wrenched out of their sockets. He wasn't going to be able to hold himself here for long.

Breathing heavily, he braced his feet on either side of the shaft to relieve some of the pain in his arms. It was then that he felt something, the faintest draft of air blowing against his face. It seemed to be coming from somewhere right beside him, but it was pitch-black in the shaft and he couldn't see anything. But a draft might mean there was another tunnel jutting off the shaft right next to him, and if there was another tunnel, there might be a way out.

Oh Gods, he was about to do something that could turn out to be monumentally stupid. He let go of the root with one hand and thrust it out in front of him, feeling around in the direction of the draft.

His hand slapped onto a flat, horizontal surface. He was right. There was another tunnel that connected to this shaft.

With a heave, he swung his body toward the tunnel mouth and grabbed on to its ledge, bracing himself on his elbows. He started to crawl forward, hoisting himself up, when his head hit the dirt ceiling and his shoulder scraped the wall.

Edgin groaned. Not really a tunnel then, but more like a burrow for some creature that just emptied out into the pit. Still, anything was better than hanging above a dark abyss with nothing but a tree root between him and a fall that might break both his legs or impale him on some sharpened spikes. There were *always* sharpened spikes at the bottom of pits like these. They probably sold them in pit-trap mail-order kits.

Groaning softly, he wedged himself as far as he could into the tiny tunnel. He was still braced on his elbows, but only his feet were dangling off the edge now, so at least he could rest and figure out how to call out to Holga and Forge without drawing the attention of the gnolls.

He'd come up with a plan. He always did.

As he pondered, a soft squeak echoed through the narrow tunnel.

Edgin froze. His breath quickened, sounding loud in the darkness. Maybe he'd imagined the sound. Maybe—

Nope, there it was again, a chittering squeak followed by the flap of what sounded like tiny wings.

Bats.

Great. He had his head sticking down a tunnel into absolute darkness, and there was a nonzero number of bats resting somewhere in the darkness ahead of him. Edgin forced himself to remain calm. He took a deep breath in and let it out slowly.

Bats weren't aggressive, at least not that he knew of. He wasn't a bat expert. They were probably more afraid of him, and *he* was the one who'd come poking into their territory. As long as he stayed quiet and still on his side of the tunnel, there was no reason to think they and their potentially hundreds of friends wouldn't stay on their side.

Because he could hear more movement now. Scuttling, flapping, squeaking, and chittering, from just a few feet away—and were the sounds coming closer? It was getting a lot harder not to panic. Edgin licked dry lips and took a few more deep breaths.

It wasn't that he was afraid of bats. He'd just never envisioned getting close enough to kiss them in a pitch-dark tunnel with a dozen gnolls above his head.

A small, flapping missile buzzed down the tunnel and smacked Edgin in the chest.

At first, he was too surprised to be scared. He thought bats were supposed to be good about navigating in the dark. They shouldn't be running into him like this. Of course, not all bats were equally intelligent, and maybe this one was just a really dumb bat. Edgin supposed those existed, and—wait, why was it still attached to his chest?

Before Edgin could gather his scattered thoughts, the small thing that had smacked into him stirred and suddenly plunged what Edgin could only surmise by the intense pain was a needle the size of his index finger deep into his chest.

Edgin threw back his head, poised to release the scream that was rushing up the back of his throat and definitely would have brought the gnolls roaring down on top of him, when he smacked his head on the tunnel ceiling again. Stars exploded in front of his eyes, and, in a haze of pain, he slid backward out of the tunnel and off the ledge, his weight dragging him toward the pit again. The bat—some part of Edgin's pain-fogged brain acknowledged it might not actually be a bat after all—stayed attached to his chest the entire time.

Edgin retained the presence of mind to catch himself at the lip of the tunnel before he plunged into the pit. It occurred to him that he was essentially back where he started, dangling above certain doom—except this time he had a tiny bloodsucking demon attached to his chest, so this night was continuing to go downhill fast.

"H-help," Edgin whispered, his voice hoarse and shaky. He knew it was a risk, calling out, but honestly, given a choice between the white-hot pain in his chest and the pack of gnolls, he would have taken on the gnolls at this point. "H-Holga," he tried again. "Forge. Little . . . help . . . here."

"Edgin? Ed, is that you?"

Oh, sweet deliverance. Holga's voice. Edgin tilted his head up and, sure enough, a wavering golden light appeared about ten feet above him, and then Holga and Forge were looking down at him in concern.

"We thought the gnolls got you," Forge said, keeping his voice low. "Are you all right?"

"Absolutely fine," Edgin said in a choked voice. "Holga, do you have any rope with you?"

"What's that on your chest?" Holga asked. She handed Forge the torch as she began untying a length of rope from her belt.

Oh. Right. He could see now. Edgin glanced down at the thing attached to his chest and flinched, almost losing his grip.

Definitely not a bat.

The creature was the size and general shape of a bat, and it had leathery wings like a bat, but there the similarity ended. In fact, it more resembled a gigantic mosquito, but with pinkish, almost translucent skin and sparse hair all over its body. Its face was essentially one big needle, and it had plunged said needle deep into Edgin's chest and was extracting his blood. He knew this because his limbs were starting to go weak, and because he could literally see his blood traveling up the ugly little mosquito bat's translucent snout. It was just chugging along, happily draining him dry.

Edgin dredged up the name for these creatures from his memory. "Stirge . . ." he said, keeping his voice at a whisper, for several reasons: He still didn't want to draw the gnolls' attention, and he had the sneaking suspicion, going by the other squeals and wing-flaps he heard from down the tiny tunnel, that he might have stumbled on an entire nest of stirges, and he didn't want to disturb that nest. If he did, he was pretty sure he was going to become a stirge pincushion, and he had *not* signed up for that tonight.

Forge leaned farther into the pit to get a closer look and winced. "Is that painful?"

"A bit, yes." Edgin was starting to feel light-headed. "How's that rope coming?"

Just as he said it, the end of a length of rope came sailing into the pit and bounced off his head.

"Sorry," Holga said, steadying it. "Grab on."

Edgin lifted a hand and snatched the end of the rope, wrapping it around his wrist twice. He let go of the ledge with his other hand and held on tight as Holga hauled him up the shaft, back toward the main tunnels.

The stirge hung on for the ride, contentedly drinking his blood the entire way.

When he reached the top, Holga hauled him out of the trap by the armpits and let him sprawl on his back, staring up at the cave ceiling, which Edgin was pretty sure was twisting and warping before his eyes. Then Forge leaned over him and impaled the stirge on his dagger, ripping the creature off Edgin's chest.

Edgin sat bolt upright, and this time he would have screamed, stealth be damned, because when someone rips a needle the size of an index finger out of your chest when you aren't ready for it, it's an *experience*. Luckily, Holga clamped her hand over his mouth at the last second and kept his scream to a muffled howl.

When she took her fingers away a moment later, Edgin sucked in several heaving breaths and put his hands to his chest in a feeble attempt to stop the bleeding.

"Here," Forge said, sticking a potion bottle under his nose. "Drink. You'll feel better."

Edgin sniffed the open bottle. A pleasant scent like cold cider on a warm fall day reached his nostrils. He took the bottle and drank. Almost immediately, warmth spread down his throat and out from his stomach to his entire body. The pain in his chest faded, and so did the weakness in his limbs.

"Thanks," he said hoarsely, looking up at the two of them. "I scouted ahead. There's at least a dozen gnolls in the chamber I found."

Holga frowned. "We should probably leave."

"The numbers are definitely against us," Forge agreed, "though I hate to lose all that coin."

The numbers. Yes, that was the real problem. If only they had thought to bring more people, Edgin was confident they could have overcome the gnolls.

His gaze fell on the corpse of the stirge as Forge flicked it off his dagger and wiped the blade on a patch of cave moss. He glanced at the pit.

He'd just had another terrible idea. Except it might also be brilliant. Too soon to tell.

"Hear me out," he said, beckoning them closer. "What if I said I could make up the numbers and even the odds here? Would you both still be in?"

Forge shrugged and nodded, but Holga looked skeptical. "You going back to the village?" she asked.

"Don't need to," Edgin said, pointing to the stirge. "I found a whole nest of those things down in a tunnel off that pit shaft. If we can flush them out, they'll do our work for us. We'll stand by to clean up whatever's left."

Forge's eyebrows lifted, and he gave a low whistle. "It could work," he said. "Or you could bring a nest of angry stirges down on *us* instead, and we could all die."

Holga looked intrigued. "Might be fun," she allowed.

Edgin grinned. "That's the spirit. It'll work, I swear."

He had no idea if it would work, but he thought he had a solid plan. Judging by the behavior of the stirge on his chest, the creatures were only looking for blood. He had a feeling that, given just a little push, they would go where the banquet was biggest.

CHAPTER 8

This time when Edgin entered the pit, he had a rope tied around his waist, a torch in one hand, and Holga above him, lowering him down slowly. Forge had lit another torch and stood ready to funnel the stirges where they wanted them to go.

Still, Edgin's palms were sweating and his heart was beating hard against his breastbone as he descended into the shaft. His plan relied on a bit more hope than he usually liked to factor into a given situation. Hope that the stirge nest was big enough to affect the gnolls and their numbers. Hope that they could get the stirges to attack where they wanted, and hope that he and his friends would get out of this cave alive.

But they'd all agreed, and so here Edgin was, dangling in front of the small tunnel jutting off the pit. Bracing his feet on the wall below the tunnel mouth, he brought the torch in front of the hole.

"Ready?" he called up quietly to Holga and Forge.

"Ready," they answered.

Edgin pushed his worries aside. He hurled the torch down the narrow tunnel as hard as he could, then he grabbed the rope with both hands and scrambled to one side, out of the way of the tunnel mouth.

The effect was instantaneous. A cacophony of tiny shrieks, cries, and flapping wings came closer and closer, and then an explosion of stirges poured out of the tunnel mouth and flew upward, away from the fire that had so rudely invaded their nest.

"Incoming!" Edgin shouted. No longer any point in being quiet, as he'd just released a storm of needle-pointed death.

And what a storm. Any worries Edgin had had about there not being enough of the little nightmare creatures was gone as he pressed his body against the wall of the shaft to try to discourage any of them from taking a stab at him again.

He looked up as the stirge swarm ascended the shaft toward Holga and Forge. Forge frantically waved his torch as they came, funneling the creatures down the tunnel toward the gnoll dining hall. A few of them broke away and went for Holga, but she swatted them aside with her bare hand while still managing to hold on to Edgin's rope with the other.

There was a beat of silence as the swarm disappeared, but Edgin didn't waste any time. He began climbing back out of the pit, Holga hauling him up even faster.

The sound of gnoll screams greeted him when he reached the top. He tossed the rope aside and fell in behind Holga and Forge as they ran back to the forked passage and took the left-hand tunnel. By now every gnoll in the place was alerted to something wrong, but Edgin hoped they could take the gnolls in this other room, as it had sounded like there were a lot fewer to contend with.

The passage opened up into a smaller chamber than the dining hall, one that reeked of rotted food and more gnoll waste. Holga came into the room swinging, right into the middle of a group of three gnolls who'd been on their way to investigate the source of the screams. Holga's axe knocked the lead gnoll completely off its feet with a deep wound in its flank. It shrieked and scrambled away, clutching its side. Forge stabbed at another gnoll, but it slashed him in the arm with its claws, and he dropped his dagger.

Edgin came in low on the third gnoll, driving his shoulder into its torso. It was like hitting a furry brick wall, knocking the breath from his lungs, but he held on and shoved it back across the chamber. It lost its footing and banged its head into an iron wall near the back of the cave. It slid to the floor, looking dazed.

No, that wasn't a wall. Breathing heavily, hands braced on his knees, Edgin tried to make sense of what he was seeing.

The entire back wall of the chamber was taken up by cages of various sizes and strengths. Most were made of thin logs crudely lashed together, but some of the other ones were iron, sized to hold livestock or other large animals.

Or a child, in this case.

Huddled in the back of the cage, his back pressed against the wall, was a boy who couldn't have been more than four years old. He had pale blond hair that stuck up at the back of his head. There was a shallow cut under his left eye that had already stopped bleeding but had left a dark trail down his pudgy cheek. His hands and feet were bare and filthy. Edgin recognized him at once. It was Sief, who'd been at the tavern eating dinner that night with his father, Jon. Sief was Miriam's little brother. Miriam, who was at home babysitting Kira right now, completely unaware that her brother had been captured by gnolls and was being held in a filthy cage awaiting a fate that Edgin couldn't bear to think about.

Or maybe she did know. Maybe her father had gone home and told everyone what had happened, and they were all going out of their minds with worry right now. In their place, Edgin would be feeling the same.

If it were Kira inside that cage . . .

An image of his daughter huddled in the dark flashed through Edgin's mind. His brave, clever, amazing daughter, kidnapped by gnolls and held in this terrible place.

Something inside him snapped.

A tight, hot ball of rage formed behind Edgin's breastbone, and he thought he understood for the first time how Holga felt when she went into battle, her eyes unfocused, a cry of fury ripping from her mouth.

His own yell wasn't nearly as impressive as hers, but it was raw and loud, and it distracted the gnoll who was still slashing at Forge with its claws. It whirled around just in time to take Edgin's fist to its face. Its head snapped back with a satisfying crack, even though Edgin felt like the blow had shattered his knuckles.

Opposite him, Forge staggered back out of reach of the gnoll's claws. He'd taken a deep wound to his shoulder and wasn't looking so steady. Edgin scooped up Forge's dagger and whistled to get the man's attention. He tossed over the weapon. Forge caught it with a hand drenched in blood and grimly stabbed the gnoll in the leg before it could snap at him again. The gnoll gibbered and flinched back, and Holga came in to finish it off with a quick axe swipe. Then she finished off the dazed gnoll that Edgin had tackled near the cages.

"Sief?" Holga gasped, recognizing the boy huddled inside. Her expression turned ferocious, and she began hacking at the lock on the cage door.

"Let me work on that," Edgin said, hurrying over and grabbing her arm. She shot him a dark look, and he raised his hands. "We'll get him out, I promise. I just think the lock will respond better to picking than chopping."

"Hurry," she barked, and went to watch the exit for more gnolls. Forge stood beside her, swaying on his feet. He wasn't looking so good. They needed to get out of here fast.

"Hey, Sief," Edgin said, kneeling in front of the cage to inspect the lock. Holga's axe blade had dented it, but he thought the mechanism was still intact. He met the boy's eyes as he pulled a couple of lockpicks from his pouch. "You remember me, right? Kira's dad? We're going to get you out of here." He cleared his throat to keep his voice steady. "Don't be scared."

But that reassurance only seemed to open the floodgates. Sief's large blue eyes filled with tears, and he started to wail for his mother.

"All right, that's fair," Edgin said, working faster on the lock. Finally, after an agonizing moment, it sprang open. He swung the cage door wide and opened his arms. Whether the kid recognized him or was just thrilled to be saved, he didn't hesitate to launch himself at Edgin, clinging to his chest almost as hard as the stirge had.

"We're out of here!" Edgin hauled the boy into his arms and ran toward his companions. Forge was leaning against the wall, still bleeding, while Holga gleefully cut down gnolls covered in stirges who were fleeing through the tunnels, quickly and efficiently looting their bodies. By the swell in her coin pouch, she'd more than recouped their losses.

And she had his lute slung over her shoulder by its fraying strap. Edgin would have kissed her if he hadn't known she would disembowel him.

"Holga! Come on, you beautiful killing machine!"

She left off fighting when he called to her and turned to help Forge, slinging an arm across his shoulders.

They ran.

At the mouth of the cave, Holga stopped them. "Here, take this," she said, handing Forge over to Edgin. Sweat coated the man's upper lip, and his skin had a grayish cast Edgin didn't like.

"Whatever you're doing, hurry it up," he said, looking back down the tunnel for any more gnolls. "Forge is going to pass out, and I can't carry both these two." Sief had curled up into a tight ball in his arms, hiding his face in Edgin's bloodstained shirt. Leaning heavily against his shoulder, Forge looked as if he wanted to do the same.

"Almost done," Holga grunted.

Edgin hadn't even noticed what she was doing, but now his mouth dropped open as he saw her pushing a particularly large boulder in front of the narrow cave entrance to seal it shut. The sounds of squealing stirges and screaming gnolls faded as she wedged the boulder into place. After tonight, Edgin doubted the gnolls would be mounting another raiding party on the village anytime soon. Or maybe ever.

"Devious, isn't she?" Forge commented.

"It's what I love most about her," Edgin agreed.

CHAPTER 9

Their return to the village caused a huge uproar.

Guards with weapons and torches had been posted at the edge of the forest in case the gnolls returned, and a rescue party had been gathered to find Sief, so Edgin, Holga, and Forge were met by what looked like half the town on their way to the Trip and Shuffle, where they'd been told Sief's father was having a broken ankle tended to. He'd had to be physically restrained from joining the rescue party, even though he couldn't stand up by himself.

They walked into the still-wrecked taproom to tears, cheers, slaps on the back, and tankards raised. Jon took his son from Edgin's arms and hugged him so hard Edgin was afraid he was going to suffocate the boy. Then Jon hugged Edgin so hard that Edgin was afraid of the same thing. Luckily, at that moment, Forge passed out, and everyone got busy sitting them down with drinks and hot food, patching up their wounds, and getting their story out of them.

"Free drinks for a year for our very own village heroes!" the barkeep shouted, to more cheers from the crowd that had stayed to help and hear the tale.

Edgin's skin crawled at the word "hero." He started to speak up, to deny it, but Holga nudged him and muttered, "Free drinks," so he fell silent. And he was glad he did when the barkeep came around later with a pouch of coin, a collection taken up by everyone in the inn as a thank-you for saving Sief. Even Forge rallied at that generosity.

Let them think what they wanted. Edgin would take the coin, but he was no hero.

A few minutes later, the door to the tavern burst open, and Sief's mother, Veri, and sister, Miriam, ran in, Kira right behind them. When Kira saw Edgin and Holga, her face did that thing Edgin dreaded—her eyes got huge and shiny, and then the tears started, and she threw herself into Holga's arms.

"I thought you were both dead!" She reared back and punched Holga in the shoulder as hard as a crying nine-year-old could, which wasn't hard at all, but Holga gave a decent performance of being injured as she rocked Kira in her arms.

"It's all right, bug," she murmured, stroking Kira's hair. "It's over now."

"We were never in any real danger," Edgin said, leaning over to pat Kira's back.

Nearby, Forge moaned in pain as the barkeep cleaned his shoulder wound.

Kira lifted her tear-streaked face from Holga's chest to glare at him. "You left me behind!" she accused. "You didn't tell me where you were going. You could have been killed!"

"In my defense, I didn't know we'd be fighting a bunch of gnolls and stirges when the night started," Edgin said. "I just thought I'd get onstage and sing and then . . ." He trailed off as Kira's eyes widened.

"You sang tonight?" she said in a small voice, her face crumpling with hurt. "You didn't tell me."

"Well, I didn't actually end up singing," Edgin said, trying to explain, but the hurt on Kira's face was making him wish she'd just punch him like she'd punched Holga. "I'm sorry," he said feebly. "I didn't want you to know in case it was a disaster, and it *was* a disaster, but now you know and somehow it's even worse, and—"

But Kira had turned away from him to bury her face in Holga's chest again. He looked up at Holga to find her glaring at him too, which Edgin didn't think was fair at all. Holga should have been in as much trouble as he was.

"Let's go home," he said, sighing. He was tired, his chest still ached from the stirge stabbing, and he'd disappointed his daughter yet again.

"It's been fun, Forge," Edgin said, waving to the hustler, who was still being bandaged and fed while he counted his share of the reward. Now that he had coin in his hands, he was looking much better. "If you pass this way again, come see us."

"Oh, I will," Forge said cheerfully. "I had no idea meeting you would be so . . . fruitful."

It was true they'd worked well together, though Edgin doubted they'd ever see the con man again. People like Forge Fitzwilliam couldn't afford to stay in one place for long or he risked people catching him at his act.

By the time they finally extricated themselves from all the questions and attention of the villagers and headed for home, it was well after midnight. Holga was carrying Kira on her shoulders, and Edgin expected her to be asleep by the time they reached the cottage, but she wasn't. Wide awake, she slid off Holga's back and went straight to her room, slamming the door behind her.

Edgin winced as the vibration knocked a small painting askew on the adjacent wall. "Was that for me?" he asked Holga.

Instead of answering, she just raised an eyebrow.

Edgin sighed. "Fine, I'll go talk to her."

Edgin turned his back on her and went to Kira's door. He knocked softly. "Sweetheart?"

"Go away!"

Right, well, he was the parent, so . . . he knocked again as a warning and then pushed open the door.

A pillow hit him in the face.

"Nice shot," he said as she glared at him from where she sat on the edge of her bed, arms wrapped tightly around herself. Edgin held up his hands. "I'm unarmed. I just want to talk. Can we do that?"

Kira huffed, and the defiant tilt to her chin reminded him so much of Zia it took his breath away. He had to swallow a few times and gather his thoughts. Great. Just what he needed to make things harder.

He pulled up a chair by her bed and sat down. "Look, I realize that you and I haven't been getting along very well lately, and that's my fault," Edgin said, a rough edge to his voice. "I'm sorry. I know it doesn't look like it, but I'm trying to do better."

Kira had been staring fixedly at the quilt on her bed, but at this she looked up at him. "Then why did you leave me behind tonight?"

The plaintive note in her voice twisted his heart. He really was a terrible person. His shoulders slumped. The last thing he wanted was to admit what was really going on, but at this point, he owed her an explanation. He'd already done enough damage by lying—to her and to himself.

"Because I'm tired of you seeing me fail," he said quietly, swallowing against a sudden tightness in his throat.

She looked perplexed. "Fail at what?"

He made a gesture that encompassed the room, their cottage, their whole world, really. "I used to have a plan for everything," he said, "and it wasn't this. You deserve better than a father who can barely make ends meet, one who has to turn to thievery to survive and—"

"I like what we do," Kira cut in. Her hand went to her invisibility pendant. "I like sneaking around with you. It's fun."

"That's the problem!" Edgin raked a hand through his hair. "I shouldn't be dragging you into this life, taking you down into the gutter with me." He bowed his head, the shame pressing on him from all sides. "You deserve more, Kira."

If Zia had lived, everything would have been different. What would she think if she could see them now? Edgin shuddered to think about it.

Kira shifted on the bed, and Edgin felt her small hand come to rest on his knee. "What if all I want is you and Holga?" she asked softly.

He lifted his head, and her eyes were so big and earnest that he was absolutely powerless against them. "Aw, kid, you're killing me," he said and reached over to haul her into his lap. She wrapped her arms around his neck, holding on tight.

When she pulled back, she wore a curious expression. "What songs did you sing tonight?" she asked. "Before the gnoll attack."

"Ah. Well." He'd hoped to avoid this conversation entirely, but he should have known better. Kira had gotten her tenacity from his side of the family, obviously.

"I didn't sing any songs," he said, half standing so he could set her back on the bed. "I tried, but I forgot the words."

Her brow furrowed as she lay back on her pillow. "How could you forget? I hear you singing songs all the time."

"That's not . . . no, I don't," he said, feeling oddly exposed. "When have I ever done that?"

She waved a hand. "Well, maybe not *sing*, but you hum all the time when you're working outside by yourself. I hear you."

She was right, he realized. He wasn't really conscious of doing it, but now that he thought about it, he had been humming his songs, especially lately.

In the old days, he used to sing for his fellow Harpers to lift their spirits after a particularly tough mission or to make them laugh when they needed a distraction. Maybe he'd been doing the same thing for himself without realizing it.

"So, which one was it?" Kira demanded. "Was it the one that went like this?" She hummed the opening lines to the song he'd attempted earlier—sweetly, but incredibly off-key. Maybe she got her singing talents from her mother's side of the family.

"It's more like this," Edgin said, and hummed the opening verse. He added the words, singing soft and low. "When the battle is over, friends become lovers, sons embrace mothers."

The next bit was what he'd forgotten onstage. Yet sitting there next to Kira's bed, with only his daughter's eyes on him, the words came easily to his lips, the song reverberating in his chest. And with it came that familiar excitement of performing, of standing on a stage with the attention of the crowd.

Except there was no crowd here, just his little girl staring up at him adoringly as he rediscovered each verse of the old song, a kind of wonder in his voice as he sang.

A floorboard creaked at the bedroom door, and a prickle at the back of Edgin's neck told him that Holga was still lurking there in the kitchen, listening. Even that didn't bother him. He continued to sing, and when that song was done, he found another, and another, singing Kira the bedtime songs with no instrument except his voice. Finally, she fell asleep, and he leaned forward to cover her with her quilt.

"Night, Kira," he murmured, kissing her lightly on the forehead. "Thank you."

CHAPTER 10

Edgin wasn't sure what he expected to happen in the village after the excitement with the gnolls, but he wasn't used to strangers greeting him by name in the streets or at the tavern. He wasn't used to people asking him if any gnolls had been spotted by patrols on the village outskirts—they hadn't—and he had to tell them each time that he wasn't in charge of those things. He had no authority in the village. But they looked to him anyway, so he did his best to reassure them that he thought the gnolls were gone for good.

Scouts had gone to the cave to find the boulder had been rolled away from the opening, but there were more gnoll corpses near the entrance. As for living gnolls, there was no sign, and tracks leading away from the cave indicated they'd cleared out to find a new hideout. Good riddance.

Most of all, Edgin was not used to, nor was he comfortable with, the people who toasted him and Holga in the tavern whenever they walked in, calling them "heroes."

He was *not* a hero. He had no interest in being a hero.

Thankfully, life moved on, even in a small village. Fear of gnolls turned into fear of crop failures and the size of the harvest, and people eventually stopped talking about the attack, though their affection for Edgin and Holga remained, and no one mentioned Edgin's disastrous performance that night in the tavern ever again.

Edgin and Holga went back to thieving, and though it wasn't a life he was proud of, he never stole from anyone who couldn't afford it, and the money they made kept a roof over their heads and food on their table.

Everything was back to normal, and Edgin had never felt closer to Kira. Things weren't perfect, of course, and they never would be—just like the hole inside him that Zia's death had left behind would never truly be filled—but for the first time in years, Edgin felt like he was actually *living,* rather than just existing from day to day.

It was peaceful. It was wonderful.

Which meant, of course, Forge Fitzwilliam had to trot back into his life with his punch-able face and con man's smile and mess everything up.

It was Kira, of all people, who answered the door when Forge knocked on it, with Edgin a few feet away washing dishes with a bucket and scrubbing brush. Kira and Forge regarded each other politely for a second before Forge sketched a bow that was worthy of a king's court.

"Well met, lady of the house," Forge said in his most charming voice. Edgin barely managed not to roll his eyes. "May I speak to your father, please?"

Kira gathered up some imaginary skirts—she most often wore trousers—and returned a delicate curtsy. "Well met, good sir," she said. "He's washing the dishes. Won't you all come in?"

All?

Edgin grabbed a towel, drying his hands as Forge and another human man and a half-orc woman crowded into the small kitchen. Luckily, Holga was outside chopping firewood. He didn't think they would all fit comfortably in the space. The man's leathery skin was deeply sun-burnished, and he walked with a stoop, as if he spent most of his days hunched behind a plow. The half-orc woman wore a faded kerchief over her short dark curls.

Kira directed the man and the woman to sit at the table.

"Forge," Edgin said, shaking the hand Forge held out. "Didn't expect to see you here again so soon."

"Well, it has been a few months," Forge said, accepting the cup of tea Kira handed him, "and you did mention if I ever came back this way, I should stop in and say hello."

Edgin *had* said that, hadn't he? That was his biggest problem. He was too kind and generous. He didn't know why Forge was here, but if the con man was involved, it meant trouble. The question was, was it the kind of trouble Edgin loved or hated?

Kira was serving tea to the man and woman—she was a much better hostess than either he or Holga—and was offering them a plate of muffins she and Holga had baked this morning. They were only a little blackened on the bottoms. And tops. And a little under-baked in the middle, but the couple gamely took one and shared it.

"So," Edgin said as Forge also made himself at home at the kitchen table, "how's the merchant life treating you?" He gave Forge a pointed look before he sat down in the only other chair and let Kira perch on his knee.

"Oh, you know," Forge said, waving a hand. "Buying, selling, transporting, liquidating—I won't bore you with the tedious details."

"Oh, please, bore us. We don't mind." Edgin smirked, and Forge shot him a dirty look while the couple were chewing their muffin.

"Actually, I'm here on behalf of these fine people," Forge said, indicating the couple. "This is Grace and Del. We shared some drinks at the local tavern when I was visiting their village recently. Word had spread of our heroic rescue and fight with the gnolls, you see, and they asked for my help."

Edgin winced at the word "heroic." "What sort of help?" he asked warily.

"Do you need more gnolls slain?" Kira spoke up. She was bouncing up and down in excitement. "I could help this time!"

"You certainly could," Forge said with that *punch me* smile, though it seemed to have the effect of charming Kira, which irritated Edgin for some reason. "Alas, this time I don't believe it's anything as straightforward as gnolls. We've a bit of a mystery on our hands," he said, gesturing to Grace. "If you'd like to tell your story?"

Edgin started to tell her not to bother, this wasn't the sort of work he did, and he wasn't sure why Forge had shown up here hoping it was, but Kira stopped him by leaning across the table to pour more tea for the woman.

"Go ahead," she encouraged.

The woman cleared her throat, warming her hands on the mug of tea. She worried her lip with her short tusks. "Well, as we were telling Mr. Forge, one of our drinking buddies, Feltin, went missing several days ago," she said. "We'd hoped, hearing what you did—finding that little boy in the gnoll cave—that you might find him and the others too."

"Others?" Edgin's eyebrows lifted. "How many missing people are we talking about here?" This was exactly why he didn't want to get into the hero business. Once word got around about something like the gnoll incident, everyone thought you could work miracles. The Harpers had had that reputation with some people. Hells, even Edgin had felt that way about the group when he'd first joined up. He'd believed in their cause with his whole being.

But the Harpers were just people, flawed like everyone else. They weren't miracle workers. In fact, their work regularly got people killed. Edgin hadn't learned that truth until it was too late.

Grace went on, "I'm not sure how many there are exactly, but I only really care about Feltin. Even if he is a fool, he's good drinking company."

"It's that cursed island that took him!" Del put in, blowing on his tea to cool it.

"I'm sorry, what?" Edgin asked, confused. "An island kidnapped your drinking buddy?"

"Ah, yes, this is where the mystery comes in," Forge said, smoothly taking over the story. "Grace and Del's village is situated very near the coast, you see, and there's a small island less than a mile offshore. Rumor has it that lately people from the village and travelers along the coast have been hearing voices, cries for help coming from the island. Some brave souls have ventured out there to investigate, but again, according to rumor, none of these would-be saviors ever returned."

Edgin leaned back in his chair, crossing his arms. "Let me guess," he said. "Feltin was the latest person to hear these voices and try his luck going out to the island."

Forge nodded. "His boat was found adrift several miles down the coast, but Feltin had disappeared."

Grace shook her head. "Something's not right with that place, I'm telling you, and I just know something terrible's happened to Feltin." She looked at her husband for support. "Our village even hired a sorcerer two days ago to go to the island and see if he could use his magic to find Feltin or the others," she said. "We promised him a big reward, but now he's disappeared too!"

She thumped the table with her fist, as if she'd just definitively proven there was something fishy going on.

Edgin had to admit it did sound odd. He met Forge's eyes across the table. This wasn't a hustle or a con job. Something had obviously happened to these people, and now Forge wanted to put them all in a position to be the next ones to vanish.

No. No way in the Hells was he getting involved in this.

Still holding Forge's gaze, he shook his head minutely. Forge tilted his head, mouth twisting in an expression of incredulity.

Edgin sighed. "Forge, can I have a word with you in private?" If he had to spell it out, so be it.

He led Forge out of the kitchen and into his small bedroom, which was situated on the opposite side of a narrow hall. He left the door slightly ajar so he could keep an eye on Kira and the couple and lowered his voice. "No," he said.

"Now, Edgin," Forge said, laying a hand on Edgin's shoulder. "I know you were reluctant that night at the Trip and Shuffle when everyone was declaring us heroes, but you have to admit, it's paying off. Our reputation has spread, and now we have another offer of paying work."

"By embracing a reputation that I didn't want any part of," Edgin said. "You're walking around acting like we planned to run into that gnoll cave to save Sief, but the truth is we were after the coin and my lute. We didn't even know the kid was there. That doesn't make us heroes. It just means we got lucky being in the right place at the right time."

"Such is life," Forge said, waving a hand. "The important thing is not how our reputation came about, but how we can use it to our advantage now. Think about it, Edgin. This is probably going to turn out to be a simple looting job. We go out to the island, discover those missing people suffered some unfortunate misadventure, collect any valuables they might have left behind, then return to Grace and Del's village to report what we found."

"That's not a compelling argument," Edgin said. "What makes you think I want to go around messing with dead bodies?" He shuddered. "It's icky. Besides, I'm not going to get these people's hopes up by promising them something I may not be able to deliver."

Instead of answering, Forge pulled the bedroom door all the way open and went back into the kitchen, Edgin on his heels. "Grace, did I hear you correctly earlier?" he called. "Did you say you offered that sorcerer a 'big reward' if he found out what happened to those missing people?"

"We took up a collection. Everyone chipped in." Grace elbowed her husband. Del produced a large pouch and dropped it on the table with a loud clinking sound. He worked the strings open and poured out a handful of gold coins that glittered in the sunlight coming through the kitchen window.

Forge blinked and turned back to Edgin. "Don't look now, but I believe Del just spilled a compelling argument all over your table."

"All right, you make some good points," Edgin said, briefly mesmerized by the pile of gold.

The idea of disturbing the dead left a sour taste in Edgin's mouth. On the other hand, they *always* needed coin. Food prices were higher because the harvest hadn't been plentiful. Kira was growing fast and constantly needed new clothes. Now the roof was leaking in three places, and they needed to get it fixed before the next downpour flooded the cottage.

But the hero business was never anything but trouble.

While he was having this inner battle, he forgot to pay attention to what Kira was doing. He tuned back in just in time for his daughter to say, with all the confidence of a nine-year-old who knows nothing about the world, "We can definitely help you. My dad and Holga are the best trackers in the village. They'll find your people."

"Kira!" he said, voice slightly strangled. "Let's not get ahead of ourselves here."

But it was too late. Grace and Del didn't care if the promise came from a child—they smiled and hugged Kira gratefully, and came around the table to pull him and Forge in for a hug too.

In the midst of all the group hugging, Edgin squirmed away long enough to glance up and see Holga leaning against the door to the yard, arms crossed, a not-quite smile on her face as she watched him and the others. He wondered how much she'd heard—probably everything, going by her expression.

He pushed past her and took refuge outside. She followed him, shutting the door so they wouldn't be overheard.

"You think this is a good idea?" she asked.

"Absolutely not!" Edgin raked both hands through his hair. "I was about to say no!" Actually, he'd been about to cave and say yes, but she didn't need to know that. Besides, he was outnumbered in this fight anyway, with Forge all smiles and charm, and Kira jumping in to serve tea with that endless optimism she had. He wasn't sure where she got that from.

"You still could," Holga pointed out. "Say no."

The sound of happy voices and chatter could be heard clearly through the closed door. Edgin glared at her. "Very funny."

Holga grew serious. "Sounds like those people ran into serious trouble," she said. "Maybe they found another gnoll hideout or a monster lair. Wouldn't take much to check the island and see."

She was right, but Edgin couldn't escape the idea that heroism was something associated with his old life, a person who no longer existed. A person he no longer wanted to be. His going out and playing hero was what had gotten Zia killed. The last thing he wanted was to bring that kind of danger back into his life.

And he wasn't bringing it anywhere near Kira.

The cottage door opened, and Forge stuck his head out. "Everything all right out here?" he asked, glancing between Edgin and Holga. "Already having a planning session, are we?" He still wore that charming smile as the breeze tousled his hair, which did nothing but emphasize his handsomeness. Kira came to the door too, and Forge put his hand on her shoulder companionably, as if they were the best of friends.

"Yep, just getting our thoughts together," Edgin said cheerfully.

Someday, he was really going to punch that man.

But he wasn't going to turn down the job. They needed the coin. It all came back to that, and that was the only reason Edgin was willing to take this on.

"We'll check out the island," he said as Grace and Del stepped outside to join them. "No promises beyond that."

CHAPTER 11

Kira wasn't going with them.

Edgin had decided this immediately after agreeing to take the job, and he believed he was fully prepared for the explosion and temper tantrum that Kira was going to throw when she found out.

Wishful thinking on his part. As it turned out, he was completely unprepared for the look of shock, hurt, and betrayal that she gave him instead. All things considered, he would have preferred the tantrum.

"Am I being punished?" she demanded.

They were all gathered in front of the cottage as Edgin, Holga, and Forge saddled the horses they'd rented from the village stables.

"What?" Edgin turned to see that Kira was making a valiant effort to hold back tears, but her chin was quivering and she looked miserable, which made Edgin instantly miserable too. "Kira, no, you're not being punished. I just don't think it's safe for you to go. I'm trying to look out for you."

"But you take me on heists with you all the time," Kira argued.

"I've *helped* you both." She turned a pleading look on Holga. Maybe it was petty, but Edgin was glad Holga was being dragged into the line of fire this time too.

Holga left off tending to the piebald mare she'd been given and walked over to them. "Not the same, bug," she said, crouching in front of Kira and tugging her in for a hug.

"Holga's right," Edgin said. "A heist is different. It's more like a game. I plan everything out, I know the layout of the place, the players involved—there's not a lot left to chance."

But a strange island, voices, missing people, and, most worrying of all, a missing *sorcerer* who might have run afoul of whatever happened to Feltin and the others left too many variables for Edgin to feel good about bringing Kira.

"We don't know what we're walking into here, sweetheart," he said. "It's just too dangerous."

"But *you're* all going anyway," Kira said, pulling away from Holga, her small hands clenched into fists. "You're all taking risks while I'm just supposed to wait here alone." Her voice caught, and she gulped back a sob.

Edgin started to point out that she wasn't alone. She was going to stay with Sief and Miriam and their parents, and even Grace and Del said they'd check in on her while they were staying at the local inn. But he bit back the words. That wasn't what Kira meant, and he knew it.

"I promise we'll be fine, and we'll all come back safely," he said. He opened his arms for a hug, though he half expected her to turn away and retreat into the house. So, when she ran to him and threw her arms around his neck, he had to swallow a few times before he could tell her a proper goodbye.

"Don't worry, Kira," Forge said as they broke apart. He'd mounted his horse and was waiting a few yards away. "I'll make sure these two stay out of trouble."

"I'm really going to punch him someday," Edgin murmured, and heard Kira's soft chuckle.

"He's all right," she said, giving Edgin the side-eye. "He's a lot like you."

That was probably why Edgin wanted to punch him, but he didn't have time to get into the psychological implications of that desire.

They mounted up, waved to Kira, and set off for the coast.

GRACE AND DEL'S village was only a few hours' ride away. They could have done the journey on foot, but Edgin wanted to get this over with and get back to Kira as quickly as possible.

A mile or so outside Targos, they took to the road, passing a small caravan that was headed in the same direction they were, but one of the wagons had a damaged wheel, and so they were stalled until it could be fixed. Edgin waved to the caravan master as they rode past.

After about an hour, Edgin felt himself relaxing into the journey, settling back into the saddle to watch the scenery pass on either side of the road. At first it was just farm fields stretching as far as he could see in the distance, but soon enough they left those behind and began passing through groves of towering oak and ash trees. The sunlight filtering through the leaves dappled the road ahead of them in shifting golden light.

Edgin had forgotten how soothing it could be to be on the move like this, when winter hadn't yet buried Targos in ice and snow and there was no immediate danger to be found. Of course, they had to keep an eye on the denser clusters of trees to make sure there were no bandits lying in wait, but otherwise the way was peaceful.

Forge drew his horse alongside Edgin's. "You have a remarkable daughter," he commented. "Very smart, very sweet. Is it true she accompanies you on your heists?"

"Most of them," Edgin clarified. "You could say it's become a family business."

"That's wonderful," Forge said, and he seemed to genuinely mean it, though of course it was hard to tell with the con man.

"Do you really not have any children, or was that just a line?" Edgin asked.

"Oh, I was being entirely truthful about that," Forge said, "which, I grant you, is a rarity. But no, no children that I know of. I always thought I might have them one day, once I attained proper fame and fortune, but things on that front are taking longer than I expected, and I'm starting to wonder if it might be too late." He gave Edgin a wistful smile and a shrug.

"Well, you never know," Edgin said. "Life can change everything on you when you least expect it." He knew that all too well.

"True, true," Forge said. "But there are things I need to accomplish first before I really think about settling down, and one particular mountain I have yet to climb, so to speak."

"Oh?" Edgin prompted, curious in spite of himself. "What's your mountain?"

"Neverwinter," Forge said, his gaze going dreamy. "That's the prize I've always coveted. The wealth in that city is staggering, and it's all just ripe for the taking." He leaned conspiratorially across his horse. "I've heard there's a dragonborn wizard there who's lived so long and amassed so much coin that he built himself an estate the size of a small city in the countryside. Can you imagine?" He leaned back in his saddle, not waiting for a reply. "Someday, I'm going to have that kind of wealth, and then all the doors of the city will be open to me." He shrugged. "After that, I can make a family of my own and give them whatever they need."

"Well, you don't dream small, I'll give you that," Edgin said.

"We *all* should dream bigger than our place in the world, Ed," Forge said, giving him a meaningful look. Then he glanced over his shoulder to where Holga was trailing behind them, watching the trees carefully. "What about you, Holga? Any family out there in the world?"

Silence fell like a stone. Inwardly, Edgin winced, both for Holga and for Forge. This was not a subject he'd been encouraged to talk about with Holga, even though they'd been living together for years now.

He shot Forge a look and gave a little shake of his head. Forge bobbed his head in acknowledgment and pointed into the trees. "Ah, you see that stream over there? I have a story about that from the last time I passed through here . . ."

And they rode on in the sunshine.

Dusk had fallen by the time the dark ribbon of the coast came into view. They'd left the road behind to follow a lesser-used track through sparse trees to where the soil turned rocky and eventually gave way to a small strip of sand. They skirted Grace and Del's village and tethered their horses to a small stand of trees near where two large boulders were propped against each other like sentinels.

Edgin could see the dark outline of the so-called haunted island in the distance, tree-capped and hilly and larger than he'd been expecting. This wasn't just a small pile of rocks. The island was large enough to get lost on or suffer some other misadventure, as Forge had suggested.

"We going out there tonight?" Holga asked doubtfully as she too surveyed the island.

"Not a chance," Edgin said. "We'll have better luck at first light. Let's camp here tonight and get everything done in the morning."

"I think I'll stroll into the village," Forge said. "We need to make arrangements to get a boat down here anyway. I can take care of that."

Left unspoken was that he'd probably find the local tavern and see if he could squeeze in a card game or two.

Edgin gave him a look. "No trouble tonight, Forge," he said. "I don't want this job to be any more complicated than it already is."

"Fair enough," Forge said. "I will be the picture of discretion."

Holga snorted softly as she gathered wood for a fire.

Once Forge had gone, Edgin got out his pack and sifted through the food they'd brought. Nothing fancy—some jerky, a handful of apples and dried fruit. Just enough for one night.

After a while, Edgin glanced over at Holga, who'd been silent since Forge left. "You all right?" he asked.

She was concentrating on making the fire, but she looked up at him in surprise. "Why wouldn't I be?"

She was good, but Edgin recognized the defensive hunch to her shoulders. "You probably weren't expecting Forge to ask about your family. I'm sorry if he blindsided you."

"It's fine." She adjusted the pile of sticks she'd made, then adjusted it back to where it had been. "I never had any kids either," she said softly. "I wanted to, but . . ." She trailed off, her expression clouding. She worked on the fire some more, until a little stream of smoke rose from the sticks, thin and fragile, but she coaxed it into flame.

"What happened?" Edgin asked, watching the smoke curl and rise and eventually dissipate on the wind.

"Marlamin and I split up before we could start a family." Holga added more sticks to the little fire and shrugged. "Maybe I wasn't enough for him," she said. She sat back on her hands, watching the fire spread on its own. "Never thought much about family or kids before him. Now I just . . . I just want to be enough for someone."

Edgin nodded. "Doesn't seem like so much to ask," he said gently.

"You wouldn't think." Holga shook herself, as if chasing away old memories. She grabbed Edgin's pack and looked inside, wrinkling her nose after a moment of searching. "You didn't bring any potatoes," she said, sounding forlorn.

Edgin got up and went over to his saddlebags. He removed a smaller sack and tossed it to Holga. She caught it, undid the string, and looked inside. A rare smile spread across her face, and Edgin's chest *might* have swelled two sizes with pride.

"Have a little faith," he said, grinning back at her.

CHAPTER 12

They took turns keeping watch and passed a quiet night with a warm fire and the stars shining softly overhead. Edgin had the last watch as dawn broke and mist curled around the trees and rocks where they'd made camp. Only once had he heard a rustle at the edge of the camp during the night, but a quick search hadn't turned up anything, so he chalked it up to the usual forest critters moving in the night.

When the sun was a molten gold line across the horizon, he roused the others. They packed everything away, checked that the horses were secure, then dragged the skiff Forge had rented from the village down to the water's edge. It was about ten feet long, with plenty of room for the three of them. Holga manned the oars, and they slid away from shore. The boat rocked from side to side just as Edgin was sitting down, which caused him to lose his balance, but he caught himself on the side of the boat.

"Steady," Forge said, putting a hand on Edgin's arm. He gave him that affable grin. "Takes a minute to get your sea legs."

"Sure," Edgin said, glancing behind him to see if they'd hit a rock or something. But there was nothing but sunlight glittering on the blue-green surface of the water. He turned back and looked toward the island, shielding his eyes with one hand.

It wasn't very far away, and the waves were relatively calm. There hadn't been any storms recently, and the breeze was soft and salty on his face.

A gray, rocky strip of beach gradually came into view as the island loomed in front of them. Up close like this, the hills on the island were larger than Edgin had realized, steep inclines dotted with fir trees at the top. The forest was denser too. It drew in the sunlight, swallowing it and casting long shadows that reached out and covered their boat.

"Help! Can someone help me?"

It was a woman's cry, faint, panicked, and coming from the island.

Holga lifted the oars from the water and let the boat drift in silence as they all listened. A few seconds later, the voice came again.

"Oh, please help me!"

Edgin shook himself. "All right, that's extremely creepy, and I don't like it, but do we think it's a genuine call for help or a trick?"

Forge said, "Could it be a ghost luring people to their deaths? Are we dealing with a haunted island here?"

If it was a haunted island, they should have asked for more money.

"What if it's like the Neverwinter Haunting job?" Holga pointed out. "That was no ghost."

"True," Edgin said. "We might be dealing with bandits running their own creepy con to lure people in. Either way, let's be on the lookout for anything."

Holga resumed rowing, and a few minutes later, the skiff scraped sand, and Holga jumped out, Forge following, and then Edgin. Edgin dragged the boat the rest of the way onshore by himself, grunting with the effort. The skiff was heavier than it looked, or he really needed to get back in shape.

"We should start searching along the shoreline," Forge said as he and Holga walked up the beach to get out of the wet sand sucking at their boots. "Any tracks will have been washed away, but we might still find something."

Left unspoken was the possibility that if Feltin or any of the other missing people had drowned on their way out to the island, their bodies might have washed up here.

Edgin walked along the shore behind the others. Smooth rocks and shells had collected in piles along the beach, and lines of dried seaweed whipped in the wind. He crouched to sift through a pile of shells, absently thinking of taking some home to Kira, when he noticed something strange about the nearest patch of seaweed. There was an oily sheen to it, and an odor wafting off it that reminded him of . . . decay. He wrinkled his nose and bent closer.

"Hey, you two, come over here," he called down the beach. He poked at the seaweed with his fingers. They came away stained black and dripping with an ichor-like substance. The smell intensified, and Edgin had to swallow to keep from gagging.

"What is that?" Holga demanded, her boots appearing in his peripheral vision.

"No idea, but it's disgusting." Edgin wiped his fingers on the sand, but there was still a faint black stain on the tips like dye. "I thought it was seaweed."

"It's all over the beach," Forge confirmed. He brought over a shell in the shape of a wide, shallow dish, which had a bunch of the black substance collected in the bottom. He swirled it around. It moved begrudgingly, like molasses, and it reeked just as bad as the other patches.

"Another sign something isn't right here," Edgin said. Despite the warmth of the morning sun shining down on them, he felt a chill sink into his bones.

"Here's one more," Forge said, holding up a finger for them to be quiet and listen. "No animal sounds or insects," he supplied when they just looked at him.

"Oh, wonderful," Edgin said. "No animal sounds is pretty much the universal sign proclaiming *something evil lurks in these woods.*"

"Better track it down, then," Holga said, climbing up the sand bank toward the dark line of trees at the edge of the beach.

A howl echoed from deep within the forest, like a wolf or some larger beast. The sound pricked at the edges of Edgin's calm, and Holga paused, listening to its eerie echoes fade away.

Forge called after her. "Not that I don't admire your 'take charge' attitude, because I do," he said. "But shouldn't we take some precautions before we go charging into the unknown?"

Holga drew her axe. "Good enough?"

She turned away before Forge could form a reply.

They found an overgrown footpath leading into the woods, and the light from the sun dropped away as they pressed deeper, heading toward the center of the island. The temperature dropped, and the silence was deeply unsettling compared to the sounds of nature they'd heard on their journey here, or even the crashing of waves on the beach.

Suddenly, Holga went very still. She didn't say anything, just stood there in the middle of the path, looking at something Edgin couldn't see.

Holga hesitating was enough to raise the hairs on the back of Edgin's neck. Holga *never* hesitated to rush headlong into a fight, not in all the years he'd known her.

"What is it?" he asked, stepping past Forge to get to Holga's side.

He stopped short and swallowed hard.

Ahead of them a few feet off the path was a dead tree, a massive thing of gnarled, leafless branches and roots so thick they were practically knee-height to Edgin. On its own the tree would have been impressive, but it wasn't what had drawn Holga's attention or stopped the breath in Edgin's chest.

Surrounding the tree were dozens of dead birds. They were mostly starlings and sparrows, with a few bluebirds scattered among them. None of them had been dead very long, to Edgin's eyes, and a few of them even twitched feebly where they lay, wings splayed, not quite ready to expire.

But there was more. The trunk of the old tree was covered in black, oily vines that glistened and almost seemed to *move* in the shifting light. They twined around the trunk and around the bodies of more birds, and even a pair of squirrels and a vole, sealing them to the tree. The vine-wrapped animals appeared to have been dead for much longer and were rotting away, flesh sloughing off to reveal bleached skulls poking out of the sea of black.

Edgin turned away, trying not to gag at the smell of rot that wafted on the breeze. "All right, this is past my level of tolerance for creepiness."

"I'm not an expert on wildlife," Forge said with a shudder, "but I didn't think that death by tree was something that actually happened." He drew his dagger and approached the nearest dead starling, prodding it with the blade.

"Don't touch it!" Edgin cried as his skin pebbled with gooseflesh. "Whatever they had might be contagious."

Holga snorted. "Can you catch a disease from a tree?"

"Come to think of it, I'm not so sure it's the tree," Forge said, pointing with his dagger at the black vines. "Doesn't that remind you of the stuff we found on the beach?"

"You think the island's being taken over by killer vines?" Edgin asked skeptically. "But if that's the case . . ." He trailed off as a horrible thought occurred. Would they find Feltin and the other missing villagers tied to trees, wrapped in black vines?

He and Holga shared a look. Holga nodded and hefted her axe. "Let's see what happens when they're poked."

Edgin and Forge took a step back as she waded through the bird corpses and brought her axe down on the tree trunk, slicing through brittle bark and vines in a single swipe. She jumped back as the severed vines writhed and twisted, as if seeking a way to rejoin. Holga made a noise of disgust and chopped at the vines over and over until they lay in several small pieces on the ground. Breathing heavily, she stepped back. Her axe blade was stained with the same black, tarry substance they'd seen on the beach.

"I'm not sure what that accomplished, but it was satisfying to watch," Edgin said, and Holga gave a huff of laughter, breaking some of the tension and fear that had overcome the group.

"Shall we go deeper into the woods then?" Forge asked. "If the vines aren't aggressive to larger prey, we should be safe enough."

Edgin would not have called anything related to this island "safe" at this point.

He sighed inwardly. This was why the hero business was bad news.

"Let's go a little farther," Edgin said, as the others were looking to him to make a decision. "But at the first sign of trouble, we're getting out of here."

They went back to the path. Nobody had any desire to get lost in the woods. It was still dark and gloomy. The sun had gone under a cloud, and a distant rumble of thunder promised a storm coming. Edgin didn't want to still be on the island when it broke, so he quickened their pace.

They found more dead trees covered in choking black vines, more animals that had been strangled or poisoned or both. The vines weren't always attached to the trees either. Some of them slunk along the ground in coils and strands, with jagged crimson leaves the size of serving bowls sprouting from them. There was a strange citrus and rot scent coming from the leaves.

Forge stepped to the edge of the path to examine one of them. He sniffed, wrinkling his nose. "Like spoiled fruit or—" He stopped speaking and swayed, his eyes rolling back in his head.

"Whoa!" Holga caught him before he fell and dragged him back to the path. While she held him up, Edgin slapped him once, then twice across the face.

He blinked. "I'm all right. I just—"

Edgin slapped him a third time. "Are you all right?"

Forge scowled at him. "Yes, that's what I was just trying to say. Why did you hit me again?"

"Just a reflex," Edgin said. "To keep you conscious, I mean."

Holga bit her cheek to keep from laughing.

"Right, so I suggest we stay away from those red leaves," Forge said. "Their scent obviously has a sedative effect. Anyone else getting the impression this . . . corruption . . . or whatever it is, is getting worse the closer we get to the center of the island?"

Edgin had noticed it. The land was also sloping upward, getting steeper as they walked. "This path was probably made by people coming to the highest part of the island," he said, gesturing ahead of them. "As a lookout point, it's good to see for miles and—" He broke off, squinting into the trees.

"What is it?" Holga asked. "Did you see something?"

"I thought I did, but now there's nothing there." Edgin waited, eyes straining. "There!" he said. "There's a switchback in the trail up ahead, but look beyond it."

"I see it," Forge said, shading his eyes against what meager sunlight there was. "It's some kind of flashing light."

"It's just the sunlight," Holga said.

"It's not," Edgin said. "It's flashing in a pattern. One, two, three, pause. Then one, two, three again."

"Looks like someone's trying to send a signal," Forge said. "You think it's Feltin or one of the other villagers calling for help? Or maybe our missing sorcerer?"

"Let's hope it's one of those," Edgin said. The other option was that it was a trap, another strange plant meant to draw them in and poison them.

They continued on the path climbing the hill. The way turned steep, slowing their pace, and Edgin could feel the breath burning in his chest. Forge wasn't doing any better. Holga was the only one who didn't look winded.

"Watch your step," she said, catching hold of Forge's arm when he slipped on some loose rocks and began to slide backward down the slope. She grabbed Edgin with her other hand and steadied them. Edgin shot her a grateful smile.

Thunder rumbled, much closer than it had been just a few minutes ago. Edgin looked up at the sky. Dark clouds scudded across the sun, and with the dense forest already stealing the light, it felt like a false night had fallen over the landscape. A chill breeze blew across Edgin's skin, and he shivered involuntarily.

Finally, the trees thinned, revealing a cluster of massive boulders dominating one side of the hill adjacent to the path. Holga scrambled up the huge rocks, finding hand- and footholds faster than Edgin's eyes could follow. She stood at the top and turned in a circle, admiring the view across the sea.

"Not bad," she said. "If you like that kind of thing."

"Any sign of the source of that light?" Forge asked, but Holga shook her head.

"You're going to get struck by lightning standing up there with that huge axe," Edgin called up to her. She shot him a rude gesture in return, but she had the sense to come back down when another crack of thunder, this one louder and much closer, echoed all around them.

When the boom died away, they heard a voice again.

"Help! Help! Is someone there?"

CHAPTER 13

It was a young man's voice this time, not a woman's, and it was coming from just up the path. Edgin tensed. "Careful," he whispered to the others. "Keep an eye out for anything suspicious."

Holga nodded, axe held tight in front of her, while Forge readied his dagger. Edgin took point and moved south on the path in the direction from which the voice had come.

"Hello!" he called out. "Who's there?"

"Oh! Yes, I'm here, please help me! I'm trapped!"

Edgin suppressed a sigh. *I'm trapped* was the oldest trick there was. Still, he kept moving toward the sound.

A twig snapped behind him, and all three of them whirled.

The path stretched dark and empty back down the hill toward the shore. They stood silent a moment, listening, but there was nothing there.

"I've decided I hate this place," Forge declared. "I'm through with haunted islands after this. Make a note in the records."

"Noted," Edgin said. "Holga, drop back and cover our rear," he said. If this was a game or a trap, he was tired of it.

He moved forward, pushing through some stubby trees and underbrush that had overgrown the path. Beyond them was a small clearing and another one of the older, gnarled trees like they'd seen earlier. This one was still alive—or at least part of it was, the palm-sized green leaves slowly being overtaken by black vines. These were bigger too, some as thick as Edgin's arm.

They were wrapped around the body of a young half-elven man in torn, dirty traveling clothes. His eyes were wide with fear as the vines slithered and tightened around him, his brown skin sheened with sweat.

"Oh, thank the Gods," he said when he saw them, and the relief was so obvious in his voice that Edgin gave up on the idea of this being a trap. "I thought I was going to die here. Please, you've got to help me!"

"How did you get like this?" Edgin asked as Forge approached with his dagger. "The vines we saw down by the shore were easy to cut."

"Gross, but easy," Holga said, going to help Forge.

"I don't know what happened," the man said. He tried to squirm, but the tree held him fast against the trunk, covering him from ankles to neck, and when he spoke, he sounded breathless, as if the vines were slowly choking him. "I was . . . examining one of those crimson leaves. I got a little dizzy, and the next thing I knew, I woke up tied to the tree. Please hurry!" He yelped as a small vine split off from the others and slithered across his cheek.

So that's how the plants attacked. They knocked a person out, made them helpless so the vines could do the work of . . . what . . . killing and then digesting a person, the way they'd consumed the flesh of the birds and squirrels? If that was the case, the sooner they freed the man, the better.

Holga looked at her axe and then at the vines dubiously. "You do it," she said to Forge, indicating his dagger. "I might cut him in half."

"Accidentally," Edgin emphasized.

"Please don't." The half-elf looked like he might pass out. "Here, let me help." He flicked his index finger—it was about the only movement he could make under the circumstances—and a trio of spherical lights drifted down from among the trees to illuminate the area.

"Well, that explains the light we saw," Forge said. "Are you our missing sorcerer?" he asked as he began sawing at the sticky vines.

"I *am* a sorcerer," the half-elf said. "My name's Simon. I was hired to come out here to find some people who had gone missing."

"Sounds familiar," Edgin said, keeping one eye on the path behind them. He had the strangest sensation of being watched, though that could just be the general spookiness of the forest and the creepily aggressive plants. "We were hired to find them too."

"You could say we're your replacement," Forge commented lightly.

"Wait, what?" Simon was indignant, which was a hard look to pull off while covered in vines. Edgin was impressed he'd managed it. "No, no, no, I was hired first. If anyone's going to collect the reward for solving the mystery, it's going to be me!"

Forge stopped sawing at the vines, taking a step back. "And yet," he said, making a show of looking around the tree Simon was tied to, "I don't see any of the missing people anywhere, do you, Holga?"

Arms crossed, Holga shook her head.

"What about you, Edgin?"

"Not a trace," Edgin said, with a *what are you going to do?* shrug. "By all means, though, if we're getting in the way of your investigation, we can move on and leave you to it."

"Absolutely," Forge said. He started to sheathe his dagger but stopped when he saw it was covered in the weird black tar.

"Wait!" Simon called frantically when the group started to walk away. "All right, I get it. I'm not in a position to give orders, but listen." He waited until they'd gathered by the tree again. "I think I know where the missing people are. There's a cave not far from here, but the entrance is well hidden. Get me out of these vines, and we can go after them together and share the reward at the end of this."

Edgin leaned against the tree next to Simon, careful to avoid the vines. "How do you know they're actually down in that cave?" he asked. "Did you see anyone go in? Did you hear voices coming from inside?"

Simon gave him a mulish look. "No, but I've already been over every inch of the rest of this Godsforsaken island and found no trace, so they *have* to be down there. It's the only place left."

"Process of elimination—I can accept that," Edgin said, nodding at Forge to go back to cutting the vines. He also didn't want to waste time searching the rest of the island if they could wrap this up with a quick underground expedition. "But if the cave was the last place you had to check, why haven't you been down there yet?"

Simon looked away. "I was about to," he said defensively. "I was just . . . you know . . . working up my courage. Don't know if you've noticed, but there's something not right about this island. And even if everything was normal, you never know what you're going to find in a dark cave."

"Wisdom of the ages," Edgin murmured, absently rubbing his chest where the stirge had stabbed him.

"Look, if we partner up, I promise I can make this worth your while," Simon went on. "This investigation wasn't just about the reward money for me. It was a means to an end. I was going to use the coin to buy a hot tip on a much bigger job with a huge payoff, enough for all of us to get a generous share. Surely, that's got to interest you?" He looked at the group hopefully.

Edgin considered. The promise of another job with a "huge payoff" was tempting—and probably a lie. Still, if they needed to investigate a deep, dark cave, it couldn't hurt to have a sorcerer with them. Strength in numbers.

He exchanged a quick glance with Holga, who gave a nod.

"All right, Simon, you make a strong case," Edgin said. "I think we have a deal. Let's get you out of here, and we'll go rescue the missing villagers together, one big merry troupe of fools. Any day now, Forge," he added.

Forge gave him an irritated look. "You could help, you know. Carry a sword, a dagger, a kitchen knife—basically anything pointy with which to defend yourself and others?"

"I could," Edgin said, "but I don't because—"

He never got a chance to finish. Suddenly, all the uncut vines still wrapped around Simon went rigid. Another vine shot out and coiled around Edgin's throat, cutting off his air supply before he could react.

Get back! Edgin tried to shout, but all that came out was, "Gah ack!" He clawed at the vine, trying to get his fingers under the sticky tar. Another vine snaked around his waist, yanking him against the tree.

All right, this is serious now.

"Holga!" Forge dodged another vine aimed at his throat, chopping off the end in midair. The area around the tree had become a storm of writhing, whipping vines. "I think it's time for some axe work, damn the risk!"

"With pleasure."

Holga hefted the axe over her head, eye gleaming, aiming at the narrow space between Edgin's and Simon's bodies.

Oh Gods, Edgin thought, *she really is going to split me down the middle. Quicker death than being choked, though.* Spots of blackness danced at the corners of his vision, and his chest was starting to heave with the need for air.

The axe blade came down with a soft hiss, passing within inches of his ear, cleaving through the layers of vines holding him and Simon captive.

"It's hard being this good," Holga said with a satisfied smirk.

Edgin lurched away from the tree, but the vine around his neck hadn't been severed. It still tethered him like a sticky leash. He fell to his knees, trying not to pass out, pointing frantically at Holga then at his throat.

"Hol—" he choked. "Hel—"

Forge was suddenly at his side, his dagger neatly severing the vine. Edgin tore the loose ends off his throat and sucked in gulps of air.

"Let's get clear!" Forge flung an arm around Edgin's shoulders and hauled him up. Together they staggered a safe distance away from the tree. Nearby, Holga deposited Simon carefully on the ground.

"That was . . . close," Edgin said, his voice raspy. He glared at Holga. "Didn't you see me making the 'save me' signal? You're supposed to respond to the 'save me' signal."

"I was helping Simon." Holga grinned at him. "And enjoying my hero moment. You're fine."

"Yes, you're welcome, by the way," Forge said, waving his dagger from where he sat on the grass.

Edgin lay down on his back, enjoying the taste of sweet, fresh air. Well, not fresh. The stench of rot was still in the air, and it was getting worse.

"Looks like the vines are more aggressive than we thought," he said, rubbing his throat. The sticky black residue was like a disgusting collar around his neck. The remnants gave off a faint burning sensation like a rash. "Or at least they're more aggressive here, near the heart of the island."

"I noticed that too," Simon said. "I think it's because something is controlling these vines and plants, and whatever it is knows we're here and is reacting to the fact that we're getting closer to it." He had his head between his knees, and he was looking a little green. "Thank you for saving me. I probably would have died up here if you hadn't come."

As he spoke, lightning flashed above their heads, striking the top of a distant tree with a loud crack that made Edgin flinch. The storm that had been threatening was finally here. Instead of a few drops of rain to herald its arrival, though, the clouds let loose all at once, the rain coming in thick sheets of water that soaked them to the skin within seconds.

Edgin stood up as the ground turned to mud at his feet. He almost suggested taking cover in the forest, but then he remembered that would just put them back within reach of the choking vines.

"Terrific," he said, wiping water out of his eyes so he could see the path ahead. "Let's get to this cave!"

CHAPTER 14

Edgin and Simon took the front, with Forge in the middle and Holga jogging at the rear as they moved quickly in the direction Simon indicated. The path was now a muddy hazard. Soon Edgin was slipping and sliding and ruining his clothes trying to reach a cluster of fir trees ahead of them. As he staggered and swore and fought his way forward, the only reason he kept going was that there didn't seem to be any vines around these trees, though he wasn't sure that made him feel better.

In fact, a feeling of creeping dread was slowly wrapping around his heart, and it wasn't the storm or the misery of being soaked or the memory of being nearly choked to death by the vine.

It felt like Simon was right, like something *waited* for them at the heart of the island, and every instinct he had told him to run from that thing. Yet here he was, leading everyone into danger anyway, all because he'd promised to be a hero again, when he'd sworn to leave all that behind him.

Another fearsome howl echoed in the distance, making him flinch. It was on the tip of Edgin's tongue to call it all off and lead the group back to the boat when Simon grabbed his arm. "There it is!"

They'd reached the fir trees, and the fresh scent of them and the rain temporarily chased away the rotting smell that had clung to the vines and was now all over Edgin's skin. He was going to soak in a tub of hot water for days and days after this. He looked where Simon pointed, through sheets of rain and lightning that left dancing spots in front of his eyes.

"It's just some more rocks!" He shouted to be heard over another percussive clap of thunder.

Simon went over to the boulders, dark and slick with rain, and ran his hands over a layer of moss that covered the largest one. Then, to Edgin's surprise, he lifted it aside like a curtain to reveal an opening beneath.

They all gathered around the cave entrance. The tunnel beyond was narrow. They'd have to stoop and walk single file. Edgin was painfully reminded of the stirge nest. "Does it get any wider as you go in?" he asked hopefully.

"I don't know," Simon said. "This is as far as I got."

"How did you manage to find this entrance to begin with?" Forge asked, pointing to the moss curtain. "Seems to me unless you knew where to look, it would be impossible."

Forge had a point. Edgin prided himself on being a good judge of people, and he didn't think Simon was lying about anything he'd told them up until now, but he'd been wrong before.

"I used a spell to detect the presence of evil." Simon reached into a pouch he had tied to his belt and pulled out a small scrap of blue cloth. It looked like part of a sleeve. "The spell led me up here, and I found this." He showed them the torn fabric. "I rooted around for a while, looking for tracks, and I stumbled on the cave entrance."

"Nice work." A sorcerer with brains and some tracking skills. That was a handy thing to have, Edgin mused, especially in the heist business. But that was a thought for another time, after they got off this island.

"We going in or not?" Holga asked, sounding impatient. She raked her soaking hair out of her eyes and wrung it out like a mop.

"No way to light torches out here," Forge said. He waggled his fingers at Simon. "Can you bring those lights back?"

"Oh! Of course." Eagerly, Simon sketched a pattern in the air, drawing what looked like three circles, then held his hands about a foot apart and murmured some words that Edgin couldn't understand.

Nothing happened.

Simon's brow furrowed. "It should have . . . wait, give me just a second." He concentrated and repeated the words.

Oh no, Edgin thought, *please don't let him be an amateur sorcerer. Please don't let him be an amateur sorcerer.*

Simon sighed. "I just need a minute. Sorry, I'm kind of . . . um . . . an amateur sorcerer."

"You don't say?" Edgin suppressed a groan. Forge put his head in his hands.

"Try again," Holga coaxed, frowning at Forge and slapping Edgin smartly on the back of his head. Edgin glared at her.

"All right." Simon took a deep breath and closed his eyes. He spread his fingers and made the delicate hand gestures again, then whispered the arcane words. This time, Edgin felt a surge of something pass through the air, almost like a tiny bit of the energy of a lightning bolt. It manifested as a blue point of light that slowly grew between Simon's hands. A hopeful smile spread across the half-elf's face. He crooked his finger three times, and the light split into three spheres, shining golden now like miniature suns.

All right, Edgin had to admit that was impressive, and it was more than he could do. "Good job," he said, clapping Simon on the shoulder. "Let's keep the light a little way back though. I don't want to announce our presence to whatever is at the end of this tunnel."

Armed now with the dancing lights to guide them, Edgin took point, with Forge just behind him, then Simon and Holga at the rear. As predicted, they had to go single file, crouching to keep from banging their heads on the tunnel ceiling. They hadn't gone more than a few feet down the tunnel before that sickly sweet, rotten stench assaulted them again. Edgin put his hand on the tunnel wall and jerked it away when he encountered a cold, slimy surface. He examined it closer and found more vines slithering along the stone, leaving behind wet, tarry trails that slowly dripped down the walls. Edgin shuddered against a wave of revulsion.

"Watch the vines," he said over his shoulder, "in case they get grabby again."

"Hold up a minute," Forge said from behind him. "I think I see some tracks here."

Edgin looked down and saw that Forge was right. He'd been so focused on the slimy walls that he hadn't noticed the set of footprints leading down the tunnel ahead of them. They hadn't seen any tracks leading up to the cave, but of course they wouldn't have. The torrential rain would have immediately washed them away on the muddy path.

"You think these were made by the people we're looking for?" Holga asked.

Simon flicked a hand to bring the lights down closer so they could examine the tracks. He traced the indentations in the dirt with his fingers. "These seem really small," he said, "like a child's footprints." His voice stuttered as the implications of that hit them all at once.

A child, and another potential victim of whatever corruption lay at the heart of this island.

"These tracks look pretty fresh," Edgin said, trying to reassure them all, but especially himself. "If we hurry, we can find whoever made them before they get into too much trouble."

They picked up the pace. The tunnel wound slowly into the earth, sinking them deeper and deeper into that rotting stench. Edgin felt like they were crawling into the belly of a massive beast, and that was not a place anyone should ever be.

Finally, the passage opened out into a large, high-ceilinged cavern. Stalactites hung down everywhere like jagged teeth, swaddled in more of the dripping black vines. A dark pool of still water divided the room in half, and on the other side of this was a wide patch of smooth, verdant green moss interrupted by clusters of stalagmites and pale gray toadstools growing here and there. In the center of this patch of life there squatted a small hut built from what looked like a hodgepodge of tree branches, pine needles, mud, and moss, with a slightly crooked door sporting a shiny brass knocker and latch.

Tiny pink faerie lights danced around the hut like fireflies, but no light came from within the dwelling itself. The two round windows flanking the door were like dark, unblinking eyes staring at them.

The tracks ended ominously at the pool of dark water. Edgin stopped at the tunnel mouth as the others gathered around him.

"This . . . was not what I was expecting to find at the bottom of this evil rabbit hole," Edgin said, keeping his voice to a whisper, even though to all appearances, the cavern was empty.

"You know, under any other circumstances, this would be kind of cute," Simon observed. The others turned to stare at him incredulously. "What? It's like something out of a storybook, you know? Faeries in the woods?" They continued to stare at him. He shook his head. "Fine, none of you've ever read a bedtime story. I get it."

That tickled something in Edgin's brain. "Simon's right. The creepy-cute house could have something fey living in there."

"Something that can twist the native flora and fauna to its own designs," Forge mused. "It could be."

"So is it at home?" Holga asked, ever the pragmatist. "Should we knock or just bust in?" She gestured to the door with her axe.

The very last thing Edgin wanted to do was approach that door, but he knew they were going to have to check to see if someone was inside.

"I'll go see if anyone's home," he said, unable to believe the words that were coming out of his mouth. But they were all looking to him. Whether he'd earned it or not, he was the leader of this odd little alliance, so he'd better act like it.

Squaring his shoulders, he walked to the edge of the dark pool. At its narrowest point it must have been at least fifteen feet wide, so there was no jumping over it. But there was also no boat tethered anywhere nearby, so he hoped that meant it was shallow enough for him to wade through.

Wading through dark, murky water where he couldn't see the

bottom and where anything might be waiting to take a bite out of him.

Terrific.

He glanced over his shoulder. "You don't happen to have a spell that could get me over this pool, do you?" he asked Simon.

The half-elf shook his head, his expression rueful. "Sorry, maybe another time. I already used some of my best spells just getting to this point."

Edgin bit back the retort that maybe Simon should have mentioned he was short on spell power *before* they crawled down into the death cave. That might have been helpful. Too late now, so he turned back to the pool.

The toes of his boots had just touched the surface when he noticed a shadow in the water. He stumbled back, but whatever the object was, it didn't appear to be alive. It was floating near the surface, weighted down by something unseen.

Suspicion tickled the back of Edgin's mind, though he hoped he was wrong.

Carefully, he went down on his knees, keeping one eye on the hut as he reached into the water and fished the object out.

It was a shirt that had once been light blue, darkened now with mud and silt, with part of one sleeve torn away. It was being worn by a partial skeleton with bits of flesh still clinging to the skull.

Edgin swallowed hard and resisted the urge to throw the thing back into the water where it had come from. "I found one of our missing people," he said quietly.

He heard Simon's breath hitch and Holga mutter a soft curse. Forge said nothing but came to kneel beside Edgin. "Are those . . . um . . . teeth marks?" he asked, pointing to the exposed rib cage.

Edgin nodded slowly, trying to keep his breakfast down. "It looks like something had a snack and then tossed away the bones," he said. He glanced up at the hut again, seeing it with new eyes and a sinking feeling in his gut. "I think I know what's living down here."

"What is it?" Holga asked, in a tone Edgin recognized. It was her *I'm going to carve something up into little pieces* voice, but Edgin didn't want any part of a fight with the thing in that hut.

"Back when I was a Harper," he said, ignoring Simon's and

Forge's looks of surprise at that revelation, "for a few months, I worked undercover on a ship called the *Midnight Fire*. We ran a few smuggling missions up and down the Sword Coast. Occasionally, we'd attract stowaways. Most of the time we caught them as soon as they hit the deck, but one night there was a storm, and our night watchman went missing. We thought he'd been swept overboard, until we found his chewed-up body in the cargo hold. Turns out, we'd attracted the attention of a Sea Hag, and she came aboard to see if she could clean out the ship. Took quite a few of us to put her down."

"There's only four of us here," Simon pointed out unnecessarily.

"So that's what you think we're dealing with here?" Forge asked. "A Sea Hag?"

Edgin considered. "Could be, but it could also be a Green Hag, going by the way the plants on the island are being warped and corrupted, and the mysterious voices and beast sounds we've been hearing. There are several different kinds of hags."

"Doesn't matter what kind it is," Holga said. "All I heard is it can die." She was standing at the water's edge, bouncing on the balls of her feet, her gaze zeroed in on the hut.

Edgin reached up and grabbed her wrist, shaking her until she turned to look at him. "The people that came to this island are obviously all dead," he said. "Their bodies are probably sunk in this pool. There's no bringing them back, and I don't like our chances fighting this thing, let alone in its own lair. Let's just sneak out of here quietly before the hag comes back, and we can warn the villagers to declare the island off-limits to everyone. If they want to do something about the hag, they can gather a hunting party, or, better yet, appeal to the authorities in Neverwinter or Waterdeep for help."

Simon immediately nodded agreement. "He's right. This is too much for us." Hands trembling, he leaned around Edgin and lifted a leather cord fastened around the skeleton's neck. Dangling from it was a small pendant depicting a simple sheaf of grain—the symbol of Chauntea, Goddess of Agriculture. "We can take this with us as proof of what we found," he added.

"That's good enough for me." Forge drew his dagger and severed the cord so Simon could put the pendant in his pouch.

Holga gripped her axe, knuckles white on the handle. She was making a visible effort to calm herself. "Fine," she muttered, "but I don't like it."

"There's nothing here to like," Edgin said tersely. He should have known this was going to happen. The villagers were going to be devastated, and he was going to have to be the one to tell Grace and Del what had happened to their friend.

That was it. Coin or no coin, after this, he was done trying to play at heroism. Let someone else do the job. He'd done enough.

Gently, he let the remains sink into the pool again and stood up. He was about to turn away when a sound from above made him look up.

Vines uncoiled from at least ten of the stalactites surrounding the hut and dropped, hitting the ground on the other side of the pool, writhing and twisting like a forest of tarry ribbons. It looked like they were reacting to something, almost like a trap had been triggered, but there was nothing there.

There came a soft cry, a child's voice, and a *thump*. Then there was silence. The vines went rigid, then resumed their frantic twisting.

"What's happening?" Simon asked, voice tight with fear, but Edgin ignored him. The blood was roaring in his ears. His heart threatened to pound right out of his chest.

That cry—the voice was familiar. He'd have known it anywhere, but it couldn't be her. It couldn't be. It *couldn't* . . .

"Kira!" Holga shouted. The sound reverberated off the cavern walls, breaking the spell of denial that fogged Edgin's mind.

Terrified as he was, several things clicked into place for Edgin all at once. The footprints they'd followed down the tunnel. That sensation he'd felt of being watched as they explored the island. Even how heavy the boat had seemed when they dragged it ashore earlier.

And it wasn't like he hadn't seen it before. He'd just told the others as much.

Occasionally, we'd attract stowaways.

Kira had followed them. She'd probably caught a ride with that caravan they'd passed on their way out of Targos. She'd stowed away on their boat to the island and been following them when they found Simon. As soon as she'd heard Simon describe the hidden cave, she'd gone to investigate, because of course she did, and now she was somewhere near the hag's hut, in that forest of writhing vines.

Invisible.

"Kira!" Edgin shouted with Holga, but there was no response. She must be scared, or hurt, or . . .

No! He refused to think it. Instead Edgin plunged into the dark water, no longer caring how deep it was or what might be lurking just out of sight. He had to get to his daughter.

He was knee-deep in the water when Forge grabbed his arm, hauling him back.

"What are you doing?" Edgin struggled to break free, but Forge was surprisingly strong when he wanted to be. "Holga! We have to get to her!"

"No, he's right, look!" Simon was yelling too, and it was only a matter of time before the hag heard them and returned to her lair and Edgin was going out of his mind, but he looked where Simon was pointing.

On the opposite side of the pool, there was a larger stalagmite rising like a lone snaggletooth amid the moss. More vines uncoiled from its base, but these looked slightly different from the black vines dangling from the ceiling. They were brownish and rubbery and—

"Is that a *mouth*?" Edgin said incredulously, as a split in the sta-lagmite's surface opened, revealing rows of jagged, stony teeth. Above it, a smaller slit opened into a fist-sized amber eye.

"It's alive," Holga growled. "Seen these things in caves before. Ropers." She raised her axe, looking almost gleeful at having a target that wasn't a plant. "I'll take care of it. Rest of you get over there and find Kira."

"Is someone there?"

A woman's melodic voice echoed through the cavern, silencing all of them. Edgin's skin erupted in gooseflesh. He automatically looked toward the hut.

The two windows were no longer dark. They were lit now with a golden glow tinged with sickly green. There was the sound of a latch clicking, and with an ominous creaking sound, the door to the hut swung open.

CHAPTER 15

The figure that stepped out was stooped, leaning on a cane made of dark polished birchwood. She wore a tattered brown cloak over a green velvet gown that looked like it had patches of moss and mushrooms growing from it. The gown's sleeves were pushed back to reveal a tattoo of a blood-red flower on one arm, and a bird with a broken neck on the other. Her nails were long and black. A brown braid hung down to her waist, woven with feathers, gems, and what looked like tiny animal skulls.

When she pushed back the hood of her cloak, Edgin was surprised to see that she looked human—mostly. From the right angle. Her skin was as pale as bleached bone, her cheeks too gaunt, her eyes sunken in her skull but watching them with a malicious intelligence.

"So much noise out here, it's hard for a lady to get her beauty sleep," the hag said, using her cane to close the door behind her.

Every instinct Edgin possessed told him to run to Kira, to put his body between her and that creature only barely wearing a human face. But he didn't dare. Kira could be anywhere on the other side of the pool, and if she was hurt or unconscious, her invisibility was the only thing protecting her from the hag.

And if Edgin couldn't protect her with his body, he was going to be the most obnoxious distraction on the face of Faerûn. Whatever it took to keep the hag away from her.

"I *deeply* apologize, my lady," he said, bowing to the hag. "We are terrible guests making an awful first impression. Please forgive me and my colleagues and allow us to introduce ourselves?"

The hag stood up a little straighter, placing both hands on her cane. Edgin suspected she didn't really need it, that, like the rest of her, it was a cleverly crafted façade. "Well, at least you display some manners," she said. Her voice was beautiful, like a song that would lull you to sleep and ensure you never woke up again. "Tell me your names, then, and why you've come to see Drueena."

Edgin knew that names meant something in fairy tales, that they could be used to hold power over someone. He'd never really believed those stories as he spun them for Kira at bedtime, but right now, talking to a creature who could command plants to attack, he didn't want to risk giving her anything of his.

"I'm called Bartholomew Gibbons," he said confidently, "and these are my . . . family. Hester"—he pointed at Holga, then at Simon—"Tibbsey, and Gus," he ended, gesturing at Forge. "We're the Gibbonses."

"Er, that's right," Forge said, shooting Edgin a look. "Gus Gibbons, at your service."

A faint smile curved the hag's lips as she regarded Edgin. "I see. And why have you come to see me today, storyteller and song maker?"

"How did you—" Edgin stopped himself and stared at her, unsettled by her knowing expression.

"How do I know you're a song maker?" Her smile widened. Her teeth were sharp and white, tinged with green near the gums. Edgin didn't want to look at them. "I can hear the music in your voice, though it wavers from time to time." She turned a piercing look on Simon, who visibly flinched. "I can taste the magic in your blood, though you cower from it."

Holga was next. "I can feel the fire burning you up from the inside." Then it was Forge's turn, and by him she seemed especially intrigued, sketching his outline in the air. "Oh, look how you glow. I can see the envy that claws at your heart, though you try to hide it.

Such lovely flaws and weaknesses and hidden truths to complicate all of you." She paused, assessing them, stroking one long black nail across her chin. Then she tilted her head and sniffed the air. A delighted grin split her face. "Oh, yes. And I can *smell* the one who's trying to hide from me. Well, if you wanted to play hide-and-seek, all you had to do was ask."

The hag vanished.

Edgin descended into full-fledged panic. His vision grayed at the edges. The hag could smell Kira. Which meant the hag could *find* Kira, and he couldn't see either of them.

Not fully conscious of what he was doing, Edgin was suddenly wading into the pool, moving as fast as he could. Holga was right there with him, the water only coming to her thighs. The rational voice in Edgin's mind, what was left of it, knew they'd never get across in time, and that if they did, the roper would stop them, but he screamed the voice silent. The hag was probably already tracking Kira, searching like a child looking for a lost toy.

Suddenly, arms went around him from behind, hands covering his eyes and jerking him to a stop. Edgin had to throw his arms out to keep his balance.

It was Simon. Edgin recognized his voice, muttering more arcane words, and for an instant, Edgin was so stunned, he didn't resist. Then, as quickly as it happened, the hands were gone from his eyes, and Edgin's vision had turned strange.

Everything was the same as it had been before, but he could see *more.* Details he hadn't noticed before, like the dark veins he now saw running through the vines that seeped the black liquid, were suddenly clear to him. The tips of the stalactites seemed sharper, more distinct.

And he saw what had been hidden from him before—Kira, lying on the ground on the other side of the pool, eyes closed, her invisibility pendant shining at her neck—its spell broken as she lay unconscious.

He could see the hag too, moving steadily toward Kira.

"Go get her," Simon said at Edgin's ear in a shaky voice. "If it worked, that is. We'll hold the hag off if we can. Point at where she is."

Edgin didn't hesitate. "There!"

Holga threw her axe right where he pointed. The gigantic blade was not really meant to be used as a throwing weapon, but it caught the hag's attention more effectively than Holga's battle scream, which shattered the air and echoed off the cave walls like something out of a nightmare.

The hag dropped to the ground to dodge the axe, baring her teeth and hissing like a cat. Her cane went spinning away, tangling in the curtain of vines. The axe smashed one of the hut's windows and bounced to the ground by the door.

"Kill them!" the hag screeched, and it looked like she was talking to the roper. The air around her form wavered, and Edgin saw Holga's eyes widen, her gaze fixing on the hag. She must have become visible again.

The next instant, three of the roper's rubbery tendrils shot out, wrapping around Holga and pinning her arms to her sides. Holga screamed again, her eyes wild, but the tendrils were obviously strong. They reeled her in toward the roper's wide maw, dragging her through the water like a fish on a hook.

Another tendril launched toward Edgin. He dove into the shallow water, barely managing to dodge. He looked back long enough to see Forge wading in toward the roper, fending off another tendril with his dagger. Simon was still on the opposite bank, making frantic gestures that Edgin hoped meant he was casting another spell.

Edgin reached the other side of the pool just as the hag was getting back to her feet. Streaks of light flew past his vision—for a second, he thought it was Simon's light spheres, but these were thinner and quicker, like glittering arrows tearing through the cave. They slammed unerringly into the hag, driving her back to her knees.

Simon again. Edgin could have kissed the man. He charged into the jungle of black vines, feet slipping on the slick moss, and then he was finally at Kira's side, gathering her limp body into his arms.

"Kira?" She was breathing, thank the Gods. Frantically, he looked for injuries. No blood, no visible wounds, only a vine wrapped around her ankle, leaving a livid red mark on her skin. It must have tripped her. She probably hit her head and got knocked unconscious.

Rummaging in his pouch, Edgin found a healing potion he'd packed just in case and yanked the cork out with his teeth. Hands trembling, he held the rim of the vial to her lips and, as gently as he could, poured the healing liquid down her throat.

Kira's eyes flew open, focusing on him. "Dad?"

A boulder Edgin hadn't realized had been sitting on his chest was suddenly gone, and he sagged, clutching Kira to him so tight she squeaked in protest and tried to pull free. "It's going to be all right," he said in a choked voice.

She squirmed even harder. "No, it's not—Holga!"

Right. They were still in a battle. *Huh.* Edgin suspected he might be in shock.

He turned to see Holga still struggling against the roper's tendril. It had pulled her to itself and sunk its jagged teeth into her shoulder.

They were losing. They'd gotten Kira back, but they were losing the battle.

"Dad!" Kira was yelling at him, tugging on his arm. A sharp pain stung his cheek. Did she just *slap* him? It worked though, snapping him back to reality. He turned to face her and realized she was pushing something into his hand, or trying to, since he was currently still hugging her to the point of suffocation. He eased his grip.

"Take my knife!" she said frantically. "Help Holga!"

She shoved her small knife into his hands. He'd given it to her a few months ago to put in her boot in case she needed it in a tight spot.

Damn, he was so proud of her.

"Thanks, Kira," he said. They sprang up and ran to Holga's side, Edgin blindly stabbing the roper with the knife. The roper recoiled, its tendrils shivering. Holga used the moment of weakness to flex her arms, veins standing out in her neck, face turning purple with exertion. She let out one more earsplitting battle scream, and the tendrils holding her snapped.

She was free. She grabbed the knife still sticking out of the roper and stabbed it twice more before another tendril knocked the blade out of her hand and into the water, where it sank out of sight.

"Little help here!" Forge gasped. His dagger was gone, and a tendril was wrapped around his neck, choking him and dragging him toward the roper.

Suddenly, the hag let out a loud cackle. She spoke some arcane words like Simon had, though these managed to be far creepier, and she pointed across the cave at the half-elf. A globe of darkness appeared around Simon, swallowing him up and blocking him from view. Now the only light in the cave came from the hag's faerie lights and the golden glow from her windows.

The vines were trying to wrap around Edgin and Kira. Cursing, Edgin peeled them off, but they just came back, sticky and relentless.

"We need to get you out of here," Edgin said, trying to gauge the distance to the exit tunnel, but the hag's darkness spell had covered that entire section of the cavern. "I want you to get across the water while I distract the hag and try to disrupt her spell. If you get the chance to escape, run and don't look back. You hear me, Kira?"

"Dad, no!" Kira pointed to the roper. "She's controlling the monster with magic. I saw her! We just need to free it, and it'll stop attacking us!"

"What? No, that's not how monsters work!" Edgin didn't have time to argue about this. A vine slapped him across the face, leaving a burning, tarry imprint on his cheek. He batted it aside. He was never going to own any houseplants after this. "We're outmatched, Kira! We need to leave!"

He tried to pull her to safety, shielding her with his body, but the vines were everywhere, and the roper's tendrils whipped around like a storm. Forge was turning red and gasping for air, and Holga had gotten caught by the ankle with another tendril and couldn't get to him. Simon had stumbled out of the globe of darkness and was looking around, lost and terrified.

Edgin swore he'd come back for them. Just as soon as he got Kira out of here.

"There!" Kira pointed at the hag, yanking on Edgin's arm to get his attention. "On her finger—Dad, look!"

Edgin looked. Sure enough, on the hag's bony index finger there gleamed a gold ring etched with markings Edgin didn't recognize. The ring glowed faintly with its own inner fire. "You're right, it's probably magical. So what?"

Kira threw up her hands, like she was the parent who'd lost patience with her kid. "She's casting spells out of it, obviously! I saw her earlier, when I sneaked up to her window to peek inside!"

"You . . . sneaked all the way up to her hut?" Edgin was both impressed and seriously going to confiscate that pendant of hers if they lived through this.

"It's called *reconnaissance*. Maybe you've heard of it?" Kira shook her head. "I think she's using the ring to force the monster to attack. We need to end that spell." She put two fingers in her mouth and whistled across the cavern to Simon. "Hey! Aren't you a spellcaster? We need you to get rid of a spell on the roper! Can you do that?"

Simon turned a bewildered look on Kira. "Um . . . maybe? I can try?"

"Do it, then!" Kira pointed to the edge of the pool. "There's Forge's dagger! Holga, get it for him!" She turned back to Edgin. "Dad, I need to go invisible again, and you need to fight. Come on!"

He stared at her, at his daughter just . . . taking charge . . . like he should have been doing, if he wasn't so scared that she was going to get hurt.

She was right, though. The only way they were going to make it out of here was together. And to do that, they needed to take down the hag.

The hag cackled again, interrupting his thoughts. She had turned her sharp-eyed gaze on him. "Are you going to fight me, song maker?" she taunted. "Or will you waver, just like your voice?"

All right, that was one taunt too many. Edgin straightened, pulling Kira behind him. "Do what you have to do," he told her quietly. "Just watch those vines and tendrils, you hear me?"

"Got it." Kira vanished.

Edgin focused on the hag, telling himself she'd be all right. She had to be. He shot a quick glance at Simon, who looked like he was preparing a spell, but going by the expression on his face, he could also just be constipated.

It didn't matter. Right now, he needed to distract the hag, keep her attention on him.

He raised his empty hands. "You want to play," he said. "I'm right here. Come and get me!"

120   JALEIGH JOHNSON

He expected her to cast another spell, or to talk at him some more. He never expected how fast she would move, scuttling across the mossy ground, her nails lengthening into sharp claws, her youthful appearance sliding off her face like paint running down a canvas, revealing dark-green wrinkled skin, black teeth, and eyes that were twin black pits, too big for her face.

Then she was on him, claws raking his skin, leaving burning trails of pain and blood. Edgin cried out and grabbed her wrists, trying to push her back, but she was stronger than she looked. Her breath blew rotten on his face when she laughed.

"The flesh on your bones will taste so sweet, so raw and tender," she sang, shoving him until his back collided with the cavern wall. Immediately, two vines slithered around his neck and waist, tightening and holding him in place. She looked him up and down, running a black tongue over her cracked lips. "Or maybe I'll cook you in a stew or bake you in a crusty pie. Meat and bone, meat and bone, savory and divine."

"Simon, hurry it up!" Edgin shouted before the vines tightened on his windpipe.

Over the hag's shoulder, he saw Forge's discarded dagger lift into the air, seemingly by itself. Kira, of course. She ran it over to Holga, who took it and used it to cut away the tendril holding her ankle. Finally, she could get to Forge, freeing him just in time. He collapsed in the pool, gasping for air. He would have gone under the water, but something held him up, dragging him away from the roper. Kira again.

"Simon!" The vines tightened, and Edgin saw stars. *Note to self: Stop getting into deadly plant choke holds.*

Finally, the sorcerer shook himself, squared his shoulders, and raised his hands, sketching some fast gestures in the air. Sweat beaded his forehead, and Edgin thought he saw sparks of light flick from the half-elf's fingertips, but that could have just been a sign Edgin was about to pass out and be eaten by a hag.

"Dispel!" Simon shouted, pointing at the roper.

For an instant, nothing happened. Edgin's stomach plunged, but then, the roper shivered all over, like a dog shaking off water, and it let out a guttural cry of rage. Edgin had never heard a rock scream.

He decided it was the creepiest thing he'd experienced on this trip so far, and that was saying something.

The vines loosened their grip on Edgin, and for the first time since they'd entered her lair, he saw fear flash across the hag's face.

Seizing the moment, Edgin wrenched the vines free of his neck, put his head down, and full-on tackled the hag. Something else he could add to his list of new experiences: wrestling with a Green Hag. The mossy ground was slippery and wet, and the hag's long, stringy hair was in his face, her claws ripping through the air like razors, tearing gashes in his clothing and skin.

"No fair using fingernails!" Edgin rolled them over and over across the ground, trying to get the hag close to the roper. A claw caught him on the eyebrow, barely missing his left eye, and he decided it was time to forfeit the match.

Planting his foot in her midsection, he shoved her away from him. She rolled, her back colliding with the base of the roper, just below its slavering mouth.

"Eat that!" Edgin yelled.

The roper was only too happy to oblige. It closed its toothy maw over the hag's face and bit down hard. Edgin turned away at that point. No one needed that nightmare fuel.

He ran to the hag's door, where Holga's axe had ended up. He grabbed the weapon—hefting it nearly made him throw out his back—and ran toward his friends, who had regrouped on the opposite side of the pool. Kira was visible again, with Holga standing over her protectively.

"Holga!" Edgin held up the axe once he had her attention. "Catch!"

He threw the weapon as carefully as he could. He got it across the pool, but it fell several feet short of Holga's waiting hand. She gave him an exasperated look.

"You're welcome!" Edgin plunged into the pool, making his way across as fast as he could, careful to avoid the roper's tendrils, some of which were still flailing and snapping like striking snakes, although the creature seemed fixated on eating the hag who'd been controlling it.

Payback was tough.

Kira helped him out of the pool, and together they ran for the tunnel, back toward the light. The vines that had been slithering along the walls were curling in on themselves, withering before their eyes.

Withering because the hag was dying.

They'd done it. And lived.

Edgin kept a tight hold on Kira as they left the lair behind.

INTERLUDE

"You're no fun," Kira said, giggling. "You never describe it right—the roper grabbed that hag *by the face*! Wrapped her up and had its revenge! You have to embellish it!" She put both hands over her face and made loud crunching noises.

"See, it's times like this I worry that I haven't given you a normal childhood," Edgin said, stretching and using the break in the story to take a drink of water. "Normal children don't know the sound a roper makes when it's chewing on a hag."

"Normal children are boring, then," Kira said, dropping her hands from her face with an evil grin.

"Good point." Edgin looked at her, bouncing up and down on the bed, her eyes alight, completely caught up in the story. "I can't help but notice that this bedtime story is still doing nothing at all to make you tired."

"Well, that's because you're such a good storyteller," Kira said, batting her eyelashes in a blatant attempt to butter him up.

He decided he'd allow it. "It's true, I do always underestimate my own strengths." He raised an eyebrow. "I take it there's no way you're going to let me leave this story for tonight and do part two tomorrow?"

She pretended to think it over, but in the end, she shook her head. "All the main characters are here now. You can't just leave it for the night."

What she really meant was that Kira was in the story a lot more from this point on, but Edgin couldn't blame her. Who didn't want to be the hero of their own tale? And she deserved every bit of the time in the story he gave her. No embellishments there.

"All right." He made a show of stretching again and sat back. "One last chase through the dark, and we burst out of that cave to find the storm had ended, and the sun was shining."

He wasn't even making up that part. The sunset that evening after the storm had been particularly spectacular.

Too bad he'd had a few things on his mind and couldn't enjoy it. But that was just another part of the story.

CHAPTER 16

No one spoke on the boat journey back to the mainland. Everyone was exhausted or injured or both, and Edgin was trying to get a handle on the fact that he was at once relieved that Kira was safe, incredibly proud of the part she'd played in getting them out of that cave alive, and angry at her for disobeying him and running off.

Holga, sitting next to him in the boat and nursing the roper's bite wound, seemed to sense his inner turmoil. She put a hand on his shoulder. "Don't be too hard on her," she said in a low voice. Kira was up front with Simon and Forge, showing them her invisibility pendant and regaling them with tales of how she'd used it on past heists. Simon looked shocked, but Forge appeared impressed and was regarding Kira thoughtfully.

"You're going to take that pendant away from her when we get home," Edgin said, ignoring Holga's words. "You should never have given it to her in the first place, and today it almost got her killed."

Holga drew back, frowning at him. "You're blaming *me* for this? She used that pendant to help save us, remember?"

"Did you forget the part where she also used it to sneak into a monster's lair?" Edgin countered. "You're not her mother. You shouldn't have given her a magic item like that, so yes, I blame you, and I blame Forge for talking me into this job in the first place, and I blame myself for agreeing." The only one he didn't blame for anything was Simon, but if he thought hard enough, he was sure he'd come up with something.

"We can hear you, you know."

Edgin looked up to see Kira watching them. The excited light had gone out of her eyes, and she clutched her pendant defiantly. Forge was watching him too, and Simon had shifted away, pretending to study the horizon with great intensity.

"Good," Edgin said, turning on his best dad glare, "because you and I need to have a talk. About how I told you to stay home, and you snuck off on your own. You could have *died* at any point over the last twenty-four hours and no one would have known, Kira!"

Kira lifted her chin. "Yes, I did sneak off. *I* did. So, it's not Holga's fault or anyone else's. You should only be yelling at me."

"I'm not yelling!" Edgin was yelling. A part of his brain whispered that he probably should take a minute to calm down, but all of the fear he'd been suppressing since the fight with the hag was coming out of him now that the danger had passed. "I'm telling you that you did something dangerous and foolish and you're going to give up that pendant and you're not going on any more heists. Ever." He was on a roll now, and not in a good way, but he just kept going. "In fact, you're not leaving the house until you're eighteen. No, twenty-six!"

"Maybe I'll just run away before then!" Now Kira was yelling too, rocking the boat with the force of her own nine-year-old rage. She looked around as if she wanted to stomp off and run away right then, but she'd forgotten she was on a boat. With an audience. Well, Simon still looked like he was trying to curl into a ball to make himself as inconspicuous as possible. Holga had her arms crossed, fuming.

Only Forge seemed to be at ease. He leaned forward. "I hate to interject into what is clearly a . . . delicate family discussion—"

"Then *don't*," Edgin suggested through clenched teeth.

But Forge just seemed to take it as an invitation. "I thought Kira performed admirably in an extremely tense situation. If she hadn't pointed out the hag's ring and the spell she was using to control the roper, we might not have been able to turn the tide in the battle." He hesitated, then went on. "One *might* even say she was the key to our success. The hidden card up our sleeves."

Kira practically glowed under the praise, which for some reason made Edgin even more angry and miserable. That, and the fact that Forge was right. Kira *had* been the key to their survival.

"That's not the point," he growled, giving Forge a glare that he hoped would keep the man quiet.

"Then what *is* the point, Dad?" Kira exploded, throwing up her hands. The boat rocked dangerously this time, and everyone had to grab the sides to steady themselves. "What can I do to prove that I can help? That I can be a part of your crew? That I *belong*?" Her voice and chin wavered on the last word, and her eyes filled with tears.

"You can prove you're trustworthy by not lying and sneaking out and putting yourself in danger!" Edgin retorted.

Kira scoffed. "It won't matter if I do that or not! You still won't let me be a part of this because you're too scared. You didn't even let me come to the tavern the night you were going to perform because you were scared!"

"Yes!" Edgin said, gripping the sides of the boat, his face flushed with shame and anger. "I told you I was terrified you were going to see me fail, and today I was terrified I was going to lose you!" His voice dropped, some of his anger fading, replaced with exhaustion. "You're all I have, Kira," he said in a choked voice. "I've lost too much in my life. I can't lose you too."

"You're talking about Mom." A tear slipped down Kira's cheek. "But don't you understand? *I* lost her too. We both did, and I never even got to know her." She wiped her face, smearing tears and dirt. "But sometimes I feel like . . . like I'm losing you too, Dad. Like you're slipping away, and I don't know why. Was it something I did? Is that why you don't want me in your life?"

"No!" Edgin scooted forward on the small bench, wanting to hug Kira, but she shrank away from him. "Kira, that's not it at all. I want you to have a *better* life than one that involves stealing and risking death. I know how capable you are, how smart and brave, and that's what scares me."

Because she was just like him—or, at least, the person he once was. Strong, brave, confident enough to take on the world. Gods, the Harpers would be lucky to have someone like her on their side.

He pushed that thought away. No, the Harpers didn't deserve her either.

"I don't need a better life," Kira insisted. "I'm happy with the life we have. I just want *you* in that life too. That's all I ever wanted."

"Kira." Edgin wanted to say she was wrong, that she'd always had him and that she always would, but the truth was, she was right. The older she got, the more he'd been pulling away from her. It wasn't because she reminded him of Zia either. He loved the fact that she took after her mother—in looks, in kindness, and in courage. It was a reminder that a part of his wife lived on.

No, if he was being honest with himself, he was pulling away for a completely different reason.

"I feel like I'm just going to keep messing everything up," he said quietly.

The boat had reached the shallow water near the shore. Holga and Forge got out and dragged the boat onto the sand, so Edgin had a moment to collect himself as they disembarked and spread out on the beach.

Kira followed him to where they'd left the horses tethered. They were still there, happily grazing and enjoying the shade, with not a care in the world.

Sometimes it was just better to be a horse, Edgin thought with a sigh.

"What do you think you're messing up?" Kira asked, letting Edgin's horse sniff her fingers. She wasn't looking at him, but she didn't sound angry when she asked the question either. Edgin sensed the answer was important to her.

Well, if he was going to bare his soul to someone, it should be to his daughter, right? So why did Edgin feel so terrified?

"It's my fault your mom isn't here with us, because I couldn't keep her safe," Edgin said. "And if she'd been here, we'd be doing this together—raising you, being a family. Making mistakes together. But we don't have that, and it's because of me."

And he hadn't wanted to make it worse than he already had. To prevent that, he'd left more and more things to Holga, thinking

Kira would be better off in the long run with other people caring for her.

Obviously, that wasn't the case. He was still screwing everything up, and now he was hurting Kira in the process.

Kira had stopped petting the horse. Edgin noticed that Forge, Simon, and Holga had all moved a discreet distance away to give them some space, though not, he noted with exasperation, so far away that they couldn't hear everything that was said.

"It wasn't your fault that Mom died," Kira said, her brow furrowed in confusion. "You told me it was because of your work with the Harpers."

"Exactly." And Edgin had sworn if he ever got his hands on the ones responsible, he was going to take them apart piece by piece. "If I hadn't been a Harper, that kind of trouble would have never come to our doorstep."

"You don't know that," Kira persisted. "Besides, if you and the Harpers didn't fight against bad people, wouldn't we be in even more danger?"

"That's . . . it doesn't matter," Edgin said. He was not about to debate the merits of the Harpers with her. They hadn't been able to protect Zia either. As far as he was concerned, the Harpers could take a flying leap off the nearest cliff.

Edgin sighed and crouched down so he was at eye level with Kira. He didn't have to go as far down as he used to, another reminder of how fast she was growing up. "What I'm trying to say is that I'm tired of messing things up for us. I'm sorry. I should have let you come to the tavern to hear me perform, even if it was a disaster. I should have trusted you to come on this mission. Forge was right. You came through for us right when we needed it. If you hadn't been there, I don't know what would have happened." He reached out, tentatively. "I promise I'm going to try to do better, if you'll give me the chance."

She looked down at his hands. "Does that mean you'll let me be a part of the crew? No more pulling away?"

"No more pulling away. I trust you, but that trust has to go both ways," he said firmly. "No more sneaking off on your own without telling me or Holga. We might be boring killjoys sometimes, but we really do it for your own good. Understand?"

She thought about that, her chin lifted stubbornly, but then she gave in and nodded. "You're right. No more sneaking off on my own. If you trust me, I'll trust you."

"Deal," Edgin said. "Shake on it?" He still had his hand out, hope squeezing his chest into an uncomfortable knot.

She gave him her hand, then at the last second changed her mind and threw her arms around his neck. Edgin felt a wave of relief crash over him, and he hugged her back tightly. "I love you," he whispered.

"I love you too," she said, sniffing.

Edgin thought he heard a sniffle or two coming from Simon's direction, but he was too relieved to say anything.

CHAPTER 17

Edgin's relief and good mood lasted up until they arrived back in Targos to find Miriam and her parents tearing the village apart looking for Kira.

They dismounted, and Edgin nudged Kira toward Miriam, who was running to them with tears of relief streaming down her face, her mother and father close on her heels.

"I'm leaving you to deal with that," Edgin said when Kira started to dig in her heels. "You wanted me to trust you and treat you more like an adult. Well, being an adult means cleaning up your messes too."

Edgin knew this was a bit hypocritical on his part, since he didn't especially like cleaning up his own messes. In fact, he avoided his own messes wherever and whenever possible.

Kira looked up at him, wavering for a moment. Holga and Simon gave her an encouraging look, and Edgin patted her shoulder. Sighing, she nodded, put her shoulders back, and ran to meet Miriam, apologies already spilling from her lips.

Which left Grace and Del, who were emerging from the Trip and Shuffle to see what all the commotion was. Forge went to talk to them, and Edgin half hoped he could slip away and avoid having to share in breaking the bad news about Feltin and the others' fate, but when he took a sneaking step back, he collided with the immovable wall that was Holga.

"Oof," Edgin said, looking at her in irritation. "Do you have bricks in your clothes?"

"They're called muscles," Holga said. "You wouldn't know about them."

"You're making jokes now, huh?"

"No." She eyed him. "Are you trying to sneak away?"

"Absolutely not," he said, feigning outrage. "How dare you make that suggestion."

"Good, because part of being an adult is cleaning up your messes."

"So many jokes now," Edgin said, dragging his feet forward to face the music. "I liked it much better when you ate potatoes and barely said two words."

"I bet you did."

This time, there was an edge to Holga's voice that Edgin hadn't heard before. He looked at her more closely, but she was making a concerted effort to keep her face expressionless, so it was hard to tell what she was thinking.

Was this about what he'd said in the boat? He knew he'd gotten a little hot back there, and he hadn't really stopped to think about what he was saying. But as he dredged up the memory, he realized he owed Holga an apology. A big one. His face flushed with shame. He hadn't meant any of the things he'd said, and he'd been so focused on repairing the damage to his relationship with Kira, he hadn't stopped to think about how the things he said might affect Holga.

Before he could say anything, raised voices drew their attention back to Grace and Del. Forge had obviously broken the news to them about Feltin and the others.

Simon ran up to Edgin and shoved something into his hand. It was the pendant of Chauntea, but before Edgin could say anything about giving it to Grace and Del, Simon had scurried off again. Edgin glanced over at Holga, but she had mysteriously vanished as well.

"Really?" Edgin said to the empty air. "Forge and I have to deal with this by ourselves?"

He walked over to the group. Grace and her husband, his cheeks stained with angry red blotches, were holding hands. Edgin didn't bother sugarcoating it. He handed Grace the pendant. "I'm very sorry," he said. "It was too late when we got there."

"From what we could tell, the victims didn't suffer," Forge said comfortingly.

Edgin thought this was a big stretch of the truth, but he didn't say anything. Forge was good at comforting, giving out the lies effortlessly. It made Edgin wonder how much he could ever really trust what Forge said. The man would probably smile that affable smile while stabbing you in the back with his dagger. Still, Edgin had to admit Forge had fought just as hard as the rest of them in the hag's cave, and he hadn't shirked danger.

"You didn't even bring any of the bodies back as proof," Grace said, hands on her hips. "How do we know you're telling the truth about this hag creature?"

"Well," Edgin said, "now that the hag is dead, your village can get a group together and go back to the island for the remains, and you'll see that we were telling the truth." They'd have to watch out for the roper too, but Edgin suspected it might have moved on to other lairs by then. There were caves up and down the Sword Coast that would be better for a creature like that to hide in, assuming it could make its way off the island.

"In the meantime, we'll just collect our discussed fee and leave you and the other villagers to grieve in peace," Forge said in the gentlest *please pay me and leave* voice Edgin had ever heard. The man really was a master at this.

But in this case, he'd underestimated the couple. Grace shook her head, glaring at him. "Not a chance!" she snapped. "You just offer us a trinket and some wild story and now you expect us to hand over all our hard-earned coin? You were supposed to bring our friend back. We're not paying you anything!"

"That wasn't quite the arrangement," Forge started to say, but he closed his mouth when Del clenched his meaty fists and took a menacing step forward.

"My wife's right," he said. "You didn't do anything, so we're not paying." He shook his head. "You're no heroes."

Well, Edgin could have told them that much. He'd tried to, actually, several times.

He glanced at Forge, who shrugged, looking distinctly unhappy. What were they going to do? Ask Holga to threaten innocent villagers? Edgin was a thief, but he had certain lines he wouldn't cross.

They had no choice but to watch Grace and Del stomp off angrily.

The whole thing left a bad taste in Edgin's mouth. Conveniently, Forge was right there to take it out on, and the rest of his crew—minus Kira, who was still being hugged and lectured by Miriam and her parents for running off—were skulking nearby as well.

"Glad you could make it back," Edgin said, waving his hand at Simon and Holga. "I could barely see you two through the dust trail you left behind when you took off."

Simon had the grace to duck his head. "I'm not good with people."

"Yeah," Holga agreed. "You two are the talkers and the faces."

"I've been called worse things," Forge said. He rubbed a hand over the back of his neck. "Well, that could have gone better."

"Yes, Forge, as a matter of fact, it *could* have gone better," Edgin said with false sweetness. "If we'd stayed out of the hero business and just stuck to ordinary, garden-variety heists that don't have any moral gray area, we'd probably be rolling in coin right now."

"But the coin that Grace and Del were offering was so tempting," Forge said, with a longing look in the direction the couple had disappeared. "You have to admit, the way everyone pulled together and did their part—it was a seamless operation, in my humble opinion."

Had Forge been watching the same "operation" Edgin had been? "From where I was standing, it wasn't that seamless, but thanks for the vote of confidence," he said.

"But you're right," Forge went on as if Edgin hadn't spoken. "We should stick to what we're familiar with in the future. And now that we have a sorcerer in the crew, I think we can diversify. Branch out. Spread our wings."

Simon spluttered. "But I'm not . . . I mean . . . I'm a sorcerer, yes, but are you . . . inviting me to be part of your crime club?" He looked hopeful and scared at the same time.

"That's not what we call it, but in essence, yes," Forge said cheerfully. "And didn't you mention something about a hot tip on an even bigger job that we might be interested in?"

"I did, but I don't have the coin to buy it now," Simon said glumly. Suddenly, he perked up. "Unless we all pool our coin, then maybe—"

"Hang on," Edgin said. This conversation was a runaway wagon, and he needed to slow everything down. "Firstly, Holga and I are—" He got tripped up on exactly what to call them. Not for the first time, the word "family" drifted in and out of his mind, but he didn't say it. It wasn't what they were, and even if it might, sometimes, from a certain angle, feel that way, he certainly wasn't going to speak for Holga. "We're partners," he finished smoothly. "We've had occasion to work with Forge as well." Forge gave a half bow of acknowledgment. "That doesn't mean we're forming a crew."

Not that it hadn't crossed his mind. Back on the island, Simon's magic had definitely come in handy, and, despite some hiccups, the half-elf had been there for them when they needed it most—especially for Kira.

But this was all moving too fast. He needed time to think this over, and he wasn't convinced this "tip" Simon had mentioned was actually real.

"Oh, sure," Simon said, doing his best not to look crestfallen. "I understand. I should really be going anyway." He gestured behind him toward the village. "I need to find a place to stay tonight and get something to eat before I figure out my next move."

Edgin had started to give him directions to the Trip and Shuffle when Kira interrupted them, dashing up like a ball of bouncing energy. She jumped unceremoniously onto Simon's back. He gave a startled squawk, but he kept his balance.

"Simon can stay with us!" Kira said eagerly, turning an imploring look on Edgin. "Can't he, Dad? Please?"

Edgin opened his mouth to say that their cottage was barely big enough for three as it was, but between Simon's hopeful smile and the imploring look in Kira's eyes—she'd somehow learned to weaponize those eyes over the years—he was overcome.

"He can stay with us," Edgin said with a sigh, and turned to Simon. "By the way, what you did in the cave—casting that spell so

I could see Kira and the hag—that was huge. Kira needed help, and you came through." He put his hand on Simon's shoulder. "I won't forget that."

Kira slid off Simon's back and came around to face him. "You did that?" she asked, fixing him with an adoring gaze. "Thank you."

She threw her arms around him for a hug, and Simon absolutely melted. It was endearing to watch, actually, as he patted her back and blushed.

"It was . . . nothing . . . er, you're welcome," he said, and looked up at Edgin, giving him a nod as well. "I'm just glad the spell worked. They don't always, as you saw."

"Well, they did this time," Edgin said, "and I'm grateful." He took Kira's hand and started toward their cottage. "Whoever's coming to stay the night, you're helping with dinner!"

"Forge is staying too, right?" Kira said, tugging on Edgin's hand.

Edgin looked down at her in exasperation. "How many rooms do you think our cottage has?" he asked. "Also, Forge has his own home." He gestured vaguely. "Somewhere."

Actually, he wasn't sure if Forge did have a house. He struck Edgin as the kind of man who just had a place to squat in every village and city the length of the coast.

"Well," Forge said, hesitating and making a show of looking forlorn when Kira was watching. "I don't have a place to stay here, as it happens. I was planning on traveling on to Triboar, but with night falling soon and bandits on the road . . ." He let the thought trail off.

Edgin resisted the urge to roll his eyes. It was nowhere near dusk, and Forge had probably traveled these roads his entire life.

But Kira's eyes got as big as saucers, and she yanked on Edgin's arm again. "He has to stay with us, Dad. He has nowhere else to go!"

And Edgin was once again taking the full brunt of her adorable, weaponized eyes.

"You really are my daughter," he murmured, ruffling her hair. "Fine, Forge, we'll squeeze you in somewhere. Anyone who snores is sleeping outside!"

CHAPTER 18

Space, as it turned out, wasn't an issue, because everyone ended up on the floor in front of the fireplace. Edgin hadn't been planning on joining the impromptu sleepover. His comfortable bed was calling his name. Or it had been until Kira blazed through the house, stripping the blankets and pillows off *all* the beds, starting with his own, and piling them on the floor by the fire, so it turned into a blanket fort without the fort part.

Holga opened a bottle of wine they'd been saving, and everyone started relaxing and telling jokes. The fire was warm, the wine was delicious, and Edgin even found himself bringing out his lute to play softly while the evening carried on, the fiery orange streaks of sunset deepening to rich violet outside the windows.

It felt strange but comfortable, almost like they'd all known one another for years. Even Simon, after a bit of initial shyness, slotted in seamlessly with the group. After a second cup of wine, he opened up about his family and his life before they all met.

"My family has always been absorbed in magic—or, at least, that's their reputation," Simon said glumly. "The name 'Aumar' carries weight, but I didn't realize how much until I decided to study magic myself. You wouldn't believe the pressure to measure up to my ancestor."

"Your . . . wait a minute," Edgin said, sifting through his memories, trying to recall where he'd heard the name Aumar before. "You're not saying your ancestor is *Elminster* Aumar? *The* Elminster, the Sage of Shadowdale? The *archmage*?"

"See," Simon said, pointing at Edgin and then at Forge's slack jaw and Holga's eyebrows, which had climbed toward her hairline. "Everyone reacts that way, and when they find out I'm his descendant, they suddenly expect me to be able to part the seas, kill a dracolich, or blow the top off a mountain."

"That is an intimidating legacy to live up to," Edgin said, pausing in his music to take a sip of wine. "I'm glad it's not mine."

"But you did really well in the cave," Kira said staunchly. She was roasting a potato over the fire for Holga and a marshmallow for herself. It was impressive multitasking. "You were a hero down there."

"I don't know about that." Simon hunched his shoulders, as if the praise from a nine-year-old were a weight in and of itself. "Anyway, it doesn't matter, because no one was around to see. I feel like I'm supposed to do great things and then wait for the bards to show up and sing songs and tell tales about those great deeds. But things never seem to work out that way for me. Whenever someone's watching, the magic doesn't work, or I mess it up."

"If you ask me, you're going about the application of your magical studies the wrong way," Forge put in. He stoked the fire with the poker, sending a stream of orange sparks up the chimney. "The only person you should be out to impress and advance is yourself. If you do that, it won't matter what people think of you, and you'll have the security of knowing you can look after yourself." He put the poker away and slid his arm companionably around Simon's shoulders. "*We* all saw what you did down in that cave, and based on that, I'm convinced you could do great things as a part of this crew."

Edgin always hated to admit when Forge had a point, but Forge had a point. The more he considered what Simon brought to the table—magic was something none of the others had—he realized that even though it could be a wild card, it could also mean the difference between success and failure under the right circumstances.

"You just need to cultivate some confidence," Edgin said, putting aside his lute. "Joining up with us might just be the way to do it. Isn't magic fueled by confidence? Or so I've heard." He hadn't, really.

"I'm not sure that's how it works," Simon said slowly, taking a bracing drink of wine, "but you're right, I do need to be surer of myself. Maybe joining a crime club is the better way to go."

"Again, that's not what we're calling it," Forge said.

Note to self, Edgin thought: *Come up with a good crime club name.*

Simon sighed. "If I could have just gotten that reward money, I'd have been able to buy Alyanna's tip, and maybe then I would have had a way to prove to my family that I can be a real sorcerer."

"Who's Alyanna?" Holga asked. She plucked the wrapped potato off the stick that Kira handed her.

"Yes, maybe you should tell us more about this tip," Edgin encouraged. "What's the payoff, and what does it have to do with you being a sorcerer?"

Simon took another drink of wine. "Alyanna's a servant who works on this big estate out in the countryside near Neverwinter. Maybe you've heard of it—West Carrawey Acres?"

"I know it," Forge said, his voice deceptively casual to Edgin's ears, "but I was under the impression it was just a leisure house for a dragonborn wizard or something, a country sanctuary for the rich and eccentric." He flicked a glance at Edgin as he spoke, and Edgin recalled their conversation on the way to the coast, about a dragonborn wizard from Neverwinter who was unimaginably wealthy.

Edgin sat up a little straighter, turning his wineglass in his hands. "It is," Simon said, "but the wizard doesn't go there to rest. He throws huge parties instead."

"Sounds amazing." Kira took a careful bite of her charred marshmallow. "All that food and dancing, beautiful clothes, and a big mansion. I'd love to dress up and go to a party like that." She blushed and grinned apologetically as Holga reached out to tap the bottom of her chin, gently reminding her not to talk and eat at the same time.

It was one of those small parenting gestures that Edgin never thought of but that Holga seemed to manage without ever making a fuss or overly embarrassing Kira. Edgin took another gulp of wine, reminding himself that he still needed to apologize to Holga for what he'd said on the boat. Except, the longer he waited, the harder it was getting to find a way to bring up the subject.

"Trust me, these are not the good kind of parties," Simon was saying, "or so I've heard."

"All right, what kind of bad parties are we talking about here?" Edgin asked. "Is the wizard a poor host? Do people get food poisoning? What is it?"

"Yes, do tell, Simon," Forge prompted. He wore a lazy smile, but Edgin wasn't fooled. Underneath the façade was Forge's hustler smile, and there was a familiar sparkle in the con man's eyes. "We'd love to hear more about this rich, opulent mansion and these terrible parties."

"It's not that the parties *themselves* are terrible," Simon clarified. "I mean, I've never even been to one, but Alyanna told me stories. The wizard, his name's Torlinn. People say he's been alive for centuries, and he's famous for once fighting a magical duel with a beholder."

Edgin whistled. He'd never seen one himself, but a beholder was the stuff of bedtime nightmares: a monster with no arms or legs, just a floating, bulbous sphere with a massive central eye and ten smaller, creepier eyestalks that each had a different, dangerous magical power. "That's an impressive claim to fame . . . if it's true," he said.

"Why wouldn't it be true?" Simon looked affronted, like Edgin was trying to steal his thunder.

Edgin held up his hands. "I'm just saying, any wizard can claim to have fought a beholder, especially if they also claim they won, but how many people do you know who have ever even seen a beholder up close and personal? Most people would wet themselves and run away screaming."

"That's just it," Simon said. "People say Torlinn won, but that for his victory, he paid a terrible price." Simon's voice took on an ominous note on the last two words. He was a decent storyteller. Edgin had to give him that. "They say the wizard was never the same, that he lost part of his soul in the duel, and now he's just a cruel, hollow shell, throwing parties night after night to impress people with his wealth and his magical collection."

"Magical collection, you say?" Forge leaned forward eagerly. He shot a quick glance at Kira. "I don't suppose you'd toast one of those marshmallows for me? They look divine."

"Coming up!" Kira said.

"Now, then." Forge turned back to Simon. "This friend of yours—"

"Alyanna," Simon supplied. "She's not a friend, she just offered to sell me information about the wizard's mansion and the magical items he has in his collection. I thought if I could steal even one of them, I could use it to increase my reputation as a sorcerer. Alyanna and I were going to split the profits from the job, but now I can't even afford to buy the information."

Edgin could see the wheels turning in Forge's brain. He couldn't help being tempted by it himself if he was being honest. An isolated manor house in the middle of the countryside, with no authorities close by and the promise of a juicy treasure hoard.

But was it too good to be true?

Forge opened his mouth, but Edgin beat him to it. "Forge, I can see where you're going with this line of questioning, but wipe the drool off your chin and let me interject a few problems with this scenario."

"Problems?" Simon's brow furrowed in confusion. He'd failed to note the direction of Forge's leading questions. "I'm telling the truth."

"I'm sure you are," Edgin said. He reached across and snagged the toasted marshmallow from Kira before she could hand it to Forge. She giggled and started another one as Forge put on an exaggeratedly sad face. "It's just a lot of this feels like gossip and rumors blown out of proportion to me. Sure, this wizard might have a magical collection of artifacts, but they could also turn out to be fake trinkets."

"Agreed," Holga murmured. She was holding her half-eaten potato and eyeing the toasted marshmallows as if considering whether the two would taste good together.

"Try a sweet potato," Edgin suggested.

"I'm a purist," Holga said, turning her nose up.

"It's not made-up," Simon insisted. "Alyanna works for the wizard, and she knows. But she hates him, too. She says he mistreats his employees. They work long hours at thankless tasks and sometimes . . ." He hesitated. "She says sometimes people vanish too, and it's not always clear whether they left voluntarily—or alive."

"Dragonborn aren't generally known for their cruelty, but if what Alyanna told you is true, it sounds like she needs to quit and get out of there," Edgin said, taking a bite of marshmallow just as Kira handed Forge one of his own. "A-ow!" he said, voice muffled by his mouthful of molten sugar. "Hawt!"

"I told her the same thing, but it's not that easy," Simon said. He shook his head when Kira offered him a marshmallow. "The wizard pays better than most employers, even if he is terrible. He really is rich, and it's not a joke about the magic he has—or, at least, not about one of the items. He brings it out at every party to demonstrate for his guests. It's something called the Staff of Aorth."

Edgin and Forge both froze in the act of eating their marshmallows. Their eyes met again, and Edgin shook his head. "That can't be right," he said, as if Simon had just told a good but ridiculous joke.

"It *is*," Simon said stubbornly. "Alyanna is there at every demonstration. She'd know better than anyone."

"What is it?" Kira asked. She'd run out of people to toast marshmallows for and had her elbows propped on Holga's knee, looking sleepy as she listened to the conversation. "What's the Staff of Aorth?"

"It's a powerful magical item that was supposed to have been destroyed centuries ago," Edgin told her. "But it's also like a bogeyman story for artifacts."

"Legend has it that the staff has a dual nature," Forge said. "It carries immense radiant and destructive power." When the others looked at him, he elaborated. "I have a rather eccentric . . . well, he's probably a wizard, but let's call him a 'client,' who buys the oddities and stranger things I acquire in my travels. Years ago, he gave me a standing order that if I was ever to acquire the Staff of Aorth, he was to be my first and only buyer, and he'd make me richer than ten kings."

"So let me get this straight," Edgin said. He turned to Simon to back him up. "You're telling me Alyanna watches this dragonborn wizard demonstrate the Staff of Aorth's power by, what, blowing stuff up at his parties?"

"Well, no," Simon admitted. "He doesn't do that, but the staff has secondary powers, like Forge said, and that's what he demonstrates— harmless stuff."

"I'm surprised no one's ever tried to take the staff from him," Holga said, "if he's that flashy with it."

"They may have," Simon pointed out. "They just haven't succeeded."

Edgin's thoughts raced, going in directions that were both tempting and ridiculous. He glanced at Forge and found the man watching him, a ghost of a smile on his face. He knew exactly what Edgin was thinking, because he was thinking the same thing.

Edgin gave a small shake of his head. This wasn't something either of them should be considering. So far, Edgin had been successful at small-time heists because he chose targets that had it coming and that were less capable than his crew.

Taking on a dragonborn wizard in his own estate—a wizard who had been around for long enough to have amassed a sizable collection of magic—was a big risk, even with a sorcerer of their own.

Edgin tried to communicate all this to Forge with just a glance, but, of course, the man chose that moment to be as dense as a post.

"Seems to me," Forge said as Edgin suppressed a groan, "that you need a bigger crew for this job, and we might just be able to help."

"You think so?" Simon asked, looking hopeful.

Forge steepled his fingers as he gathered his thoughts—and everyone's attention. "This wizard has the Staff of Aorth. I have a client who'd love to pay us all handsomely for it. So, it's simple. We go to one of the wizard's parties, steal the staff and any other coin and magical items we can get our hands on with Alyanna's help, sell the staff, and the profits make us all rich enough to do whatever we want for the rest of our lives."

CHAPTER 19

The room fell silent except for the crackle and pop of the fire. Edgin had to give Forge credit. He knew how to drop a juicy bit of bait and wait for everyone to come licking their lips. He let them all imagine everything they could do with the kind of coin an artifact like the Staff of Aorth would bring.

Edgin couldn't help imagining it himself. With the share that he, Kira, and Holga would get, they could build a bigger house, maybe with some land attached to it. Kira's future would be secure, and Edgin wouldn't have to do dishonest work anymore if he didn't want to. The money meant safety, possibility, and—there he went, licking his lips and chasing dreams that were likely to come back and bite him.

A log snapped in the fireplace, bringing the group out of their collective daydreams. Holga reached over to poke the fire, a pensive look on her face. Simon's brow was furrowed. He looked like he was thinking so hard he was about to get a nosebleed.

It was Kira who spoke first. "I want to go to the party," she said, her eyes sparkling. "Would we get all dressed up?"

Forge smiled at her. "I know a pair of tailors in Longsaddle who owe me a favor," he said. "They make the finest suits and gowns you've ever seen. Hats and masks too."

Kira beamed at him.

"I know Alyanna hates Torlinn and hates her job," Simon said slowly, glancing at Forge. "If I pay her for the information, she'll help us, but only if she got a full share of whatever we steal."

"As our spy inside the mansion, she'll be absolutely crucial to the operation," Forge said. "Of course that entitles her to a full share."

Edgin wasn't sure he liked that part of the arrangement. Alyanna was a wild card, and Edgin didn't trust wild cards, but they'd address that problem later. He turned to Holga, nudging her knee. "You've been quiet," he said. "What do you think about all this?"

Holga looked down at Kira, who had crawled into her lap and curled up as if she meant to sleep there. Holga didn't seem to mind. "It'd be nice not to worry about the roof leaking all the time," she murmured.

Forge leaned forward, laying a hand on her arm. "You could hire a full-time carpenter to make sure you never have another roof leak," he said, as if the way to Holga's heart was through carpentry. Maybe it was.

"All right, before everyone takes off for the wizard's mansion tomorrow, let me remind you of a few things," Edgin said pragmatically. "If we believe the rumors, then this wizard has been around for a while, which means he's not stupid. He's survived this long—survived a battle with a beholder—by protecting himself and his household. That means we wouldn't just be contending with his magic. That house is bound to be full of traps, security measures, guards, and staff that we're going to have to disable, bypass, or bribe in order to get anywhere near the loot we're after."

"It's true," Simon said. "Torlinn will probably have all of those things."

Edgin spread his hands. "There you go. You thought the ending of the hag job was bad? This could be much worse if things go badly."

"We wouldn't be doing this on a whim, Edgin," Forge said in that reassuring tone that Edgin knew was dangerous, because it got people to agree to things they'd otherwise never consider agreeing to. "I swear, there'd be careful planning, weeks of it, practice runs, training sessions beforehand so we see how we all work together as a crew." He gestured at all of them, sitting around the blanket fort with their marshmallows and wine. "I'm not about to ask anyone to do anything that makes them uncomfortable, but we have an opportunity here with this group. With all of our talents combined, we can think bigger than small-time robbery and sneaking around in dark caves. We're capable of more, and I just think we should explore that. How often does a group like this come together?"

Once again, Edgin had to admit that Forge had a point. During his time in the Harpers, Edgin would have killed to have such a well-balanced group of people working at his side. Forge with his charm, Holga with her strength and fearlessness, Kira with her sneaking and hiding, and now Simon with his magic. They fit, and that had shone through—eventually—in the fight with the hag.

Maybe Forge was right. Maybe Edgin was the one who was thinking too small, holding them back when they should be using their talents for bigger jobs with greater rewards. This wasn't the kind of life that favored the thief in the long term. Sooner or later, they'd do one too many jobs, and they'd be caught. Better to do fewer jobs with bigger rewards, maybe even retire after this if the score was rich enough.

Just to have the option, the freedom to decide, was tantalizing.

But he wasn't going to just be talked into this job and swept along like last time. "If we do this," Edgin said, ignoring the sudden frisson of excitement that went through everyone in the room, "and I'm saying *if*," he emphasized. "We're going to plan out every last detail. We leave nothing to chance." He turned to Simon. "I need you to get a message to Alyanna and have her come meet with us. If she's not in on this, the whole thing breaks down before it starts, and we also need to know we can trust her."

"I'll do it." Simon nodded emphatically. "I just know she'll help us if we help her."

Forge produced, as if from nowhere, a bit of parchment, a quill, and an inkwell, which he handed to Kira. It was as if he'd just been waiting to break it out. "If you'd be so kind, Kira, we can start getting a list together of everything we need. Let's brainstorm."

Kira adjusted her position on Holga's lap so she could write on the parchment, and they all gathered around.

"Complete layout of the manor would be helpful," Holga said, starting them off. "No surprises when we go in."

"Exactly." Edgin pointed to the list. "Write that down."

Kira wrote it at the top. "Party clothes," she said, then amended, "Disguises would be even better!"

"Yes, they would." Edgin looked at Simon. "Does this wizard ever hold masquerade parties?"

"He holds all kinds of parties," Simon said. "Each time there's a different theme."

"We'll wait for a masquerade ball, then," Forge said. "That's bound to come up at some point—people love them."

Edgin rubbed his chin in thought. "If we're going to be part of the party, we need to find a way to get on the guest list," he said. He looked at Forge expectantly.

"Well, forgery happens to be one of my specialties," he said, grinning. "It's right there in the name."

"Yeah, I always thought that was a little too on the nose," Edgin said. "Kira, add party invitations to the list."

The energy in the room was palpable. The disappointment from the failed mission with the hag had completely evaporated in the face of this newest opportunity.

It could work, Edgin thought. They'd need time and careful planning, and maybe a few minor jobs here and there to refine how they worked together as a crew, but it could work.

On that point, Edgin looked at Simon. The half-elf seemed to be feeling comfortable enough with the group. He was adding suggestions to the list and making good points about magical security, but Edgin still wondered about him. Was he confident enough to take on a job like this? On first glance, he didn't strike Edgin as being the type to be part of a criminal operation, but looks could be deceiving.

"Simon," he said, drawing the young man's attention, "I understand you wanting to prove yourself as a sorcerer, but what is it you'll be getting out of this job? Why do *you* want to do this?"

Simon froze under the attention of everyone, drawing back a little into himself. But then Kira put her hand on top of his where it rested on the floor and gave him an encouraging smile. He smiled back tentatively.

"Ever since I was a kid, my family told me stories of my ancestor." He shook his head in wonder. "I didn't believe half of them. The things he did and saw before he was even my age—it's a lot to live up to, but that's what's expected of me, of my family. Magic is who we are, and I have to do great things, just like my ancestor did."

"But, becoming a thief—is that what your family had in mind?" Forge asked as delicately as possible.

"It's not just about that," Simon insisted, "it's about learning to use my magic when it counts. I have to get stronger, build a reputation, like I was saying." His eyes took on a faraway gleam. "But if I could steal the Staff of Aorth from that wizard, if word got around that I'd been a part of that . . ."

"It would certainly impress people in magical circles," Edgin said. "No one would underestimate you if you'd done something like that."

All right, then. It seemed Simon had just as much motivation as the rest of them to carry out this job. That was reassuring.

"Well, then," Forge said, "I believe we have a start. A good night's sleep, and then shall we get to work?"

It was later than Edgin had realized. Holga fell asleep on the floor almost at once, snoring softly with Kira curled up next to her. One by one, the others drifted off in front of the fire in a tangle of blankets made slightly sticky with marshmallows, but no one seemed to mind.

Edgin lay awake for a while, staring at the dying fire, the glowing embers lulling him into a relaxed haze. He hadn't expected to feel this good after the hag job had gone sour, but here he was, looking forward to the next morning and the plans he had yet to make.

Could it always be like this? Surrounded by friends, with the excitement of a job ahead of them and all the possibilities that came with it? He hadn't thought it was possible, after Zia died, to make any kind of happiness for himself. It had always been about providing for Kira, making sure she was happy and taken care of. Nothing else mattered.

But Edgin had slowly been feeling himself come back to life, feeling things he hadn't felt since Zia died. Was he betraying her, by being happy? Deep down, he knew the answer to that. She'd throw food at him if she heard him saying anything like that. She would want both him and Kira to be happy and not to be mired in grief forever.

But happiness, even if he'd found it again, could be snatched away so quickly. Life was like that. Easy come, easy go. He would have to be careful. He'd promised Kira she could be involved in his life and his work, and he'd keep that promise, but he'd also find a way to protect her and the rest of their crew.

That was his responsibility. He wouldn't fail them.

CHAPTER 20

The next few weeks passed in a blur of meetings and preparations. Forge and Simon stayed in the village, renting a temporary room for themselves over the blacksmith's shop, though most nights they were at Edgin's cottage, poring over the drawings of the wizard's manor house and grounds that Simon had requested from Alyanna.

They were meticulous drawings, incredibly detailed, and it was obvious even to Edgin's untrained eye that Simon's contact had both an artist's touch and a criminal mind. Simon had been deliberately vague when he wrote to her about what he wanted, in case someone saw the letter and suspected something, but Alyanna had known right away what he was asking, and she was completely on board. She'd come to visit a couple of times to meet with everyone, though she hadn't been able to stay away from the estate long in case it aroused Torlinn's suspicion.

Edgin wasn't sure whether he was more relieved that they had an experienced hand on the other end of this, or suspicious of her motives and intentions. Both, if he was being honest.

But that was why they were being so careful, planning every-thing out step by step. He wasn't leaving anything to chance.

He and Holga stood in the kitchen during yet another day of planning, putting together a lunch of roast chicken with potatoes and carrots. Holga was picking apart rosemary sprigs while Edgin minded the stove, wrapping himself in a sky-blue apron that Kira had bought for him from a traveling merchant. He kept shooting glances at the drawings on the kitchen table, specifically the drawing of the main ballroom where the parties took place.

"Something's weird about that room," he said, wiping his hands on the apron. "Doesn't it look weird to you?"

Holga laid aside her herb bundle and went to the table. "It's a ballroom," she said, shrugging. "I don't spend time in ballrooms." She squinted, as if that would make things clearer to her. "What's wrong with it?"

"I guess it's nothing," Edgin said. "It's just shaped weird, is all, like they were going for a hexagon and then the builders got drunk when they did the last side."

Holga shrugged again. "Wizards are eccentric," she said, as if that explained away a host of strange decisions.

With wizards, it usually did, and Edgin didn't spend much time in ballrooms either. He sighed and turned back to his cooking, rub-bing his tired eyes. All this planning meant he hadn't slept much the past few weeks. He was tired, his eyes hurt, and they still had a lot of work ahead of them.

He was having the time of his life.

"Nooo, Father!" came Kira's panicked shout from the front yard.

Edgin nearly dropped the chicken he'd begun trussing. Heart lodged in his throat, he ran outside—apron, chicken, and all—to find Kira on her knees in the grass, wailing over Forge's supine body.

"What in the Nine Hells is going on here?" Edgin demanded, waving the chicken to get Kira's attention.

Forge, who was luckily very much not dead, cracked open one eye. "Wonderful, Kira, really put your soul into it," he encouraged, then closed his eye and went limp, doing a fair imitation of a corpse.

"Someone help me!" Kira cried, laying her head on Forge's chest and sobbing. "My father is dying!"

Edgin's heart slowly returned to its normal rhythm as he realized that no one was actually injured. It was just another of the practice cons Kira and Forge had been devising between themselves for the past few days, ever since Kira had expressed an interest in learning the card tricks Edgin and Forge had been practicing on each other. Forge had been delighted by the idea, and he'd quickly suggested that Kira was capable of much more elaborate cons.

As Edgin watched, Simon came running up, looking like the most awkward extra in their little drama play.

"Oh no, whatever is the matter, child?" he asked in a stilted voice. Edgin winced and just managed not to chuckle.

Kira sprang up and ran to Simon, clinging to him as if he were the only port in a storm. "My father!" she wailed. "Attacked by *bandits*! They came from the woods! Can you help us, please?"

Simon patted Kira's back. "There, there, little one," he said, deepening his voice for no apparent reason other than maybe he was trying to sound heroic. "I'll help you and your father."

"Oh, thank you, good sir." Kira pulled away to beam at him, an adoring smile on her tearstained face. Real tears, Edgin noticed. *Impressive.*

Simon ran offstage, stopping a few feet away, and Kira triumphantly pulled out Simon's coin purse, which she brandished before Edgin. "I got it!" she said. "He never knew I took it. Did you, Simon?" She turned to Simon with a hopeful expression.

"I didn't know," Simon said, "I swear." He grinned at her. "You did good, Kira."

"She did grand!" Forge opened his eyes and propped himself on his elbows. "Well done, Kira. What should we call that one?"

"The Heartbreaker!" Kira said without hesitation, and tackled Forge as he was starting to get up. He fell back with an *oof.*

"Help!" he cried. "Edgin! Holga! She's a beast! She'll eat me alive."

Holga, who'd come out to stand beside Edgin, snorted. "Lunch is going to be late, you howling dogs," she said fondly, and nudged Edgin in the ribs. "It's your fault too. I need that chicken."

"I thought my daughter was in mortal danger," Edgin protested. "I didn't see you running out to help."

"They're the ones in mortal danger." Holga snorted again. "She's got both of them wrapped around her little finger."

Watching Kira wrestle Forge into submission, while at the same time holding Simon's coin pouch just out of reach, Edgin couldn't help but agree.

Over lunch, the conversation turned to what their next steps would be.

"Operation: Party Invitation," Forge insisted, waving a chicken leg for emphasis. "All of this is for nothing if we're stopped at the wizard's door."

"There's always the option to have Alyanna sneak us in," Edgin said. "We could pose as servers at the party."

Simon winced. "It might be too noticeable if she sneaks in all of us," he said. "Maybe me and one other person at most."

"Let's do it," Edgin said. "It'll give us access to the servant's areas, which the party guests won't have. That'll help us in moving around the house." He glanced at Holga. "You up for posing as a servant on this one?"

"It'll be the easiest way to get your axe in," Forge pointed out. "They'll be checking the guests for weapons."

Holga nodded. "Didn't want to get dressed up anyway." She shuddered at the idea.

"Which leaves Kira, Forge, and me to be guests who need invitations," Edgin said. "Forge, you said you knew someone who could help?"

"Well," Forge said, drawing the word out a bit too long. "When I said she could help, I actually just meant I found out she has an invitation to the party herself. All I really need to do is study it so I can forge us invitations of our own."

"And?" Edgin prompted when he didn't elaborate. He suddenly had a bad feeling about this. "Is this woman going to let you take a look at her invitation?"

"It's true she's helped me with delicate matters like these before, but alas, when the esteemed Lady Sofina and I last parted ways, it was under less than cordial circumstances, due to a misunderstanding that I will regret for the rest of my days," Forge said. He lifted his chin. "More than that, I'm not at liberty to say."

Edgin dabbed his lips with a napkin. "Let me guess. She caught you in a compromising position with her diamond necklace."

"How dare you." Forge sniffed. "They were emeralds. Earrings."

"Where does that leave us?" Holga asked, tossing a stripped-bare chicken bone down on her empty plate.

"I was thinking that Edgin, Kira, and I would pay Lady Sofina a visit tomorrow and I could beg her forgiveness and ask to copy her party invitation," Forge said, gathering up some of the empty plates.

"Oh, really," Edgin said, crossing his arms. "And why exactly do Kira and I need to be there for your groveling?"

"Kira will come along to use her natural charm to soften Lady Sofina," Forge explained. "It probably won't work, but it's worth a shot. You, Edgin, will be there in case she needs some extra convincing to help us."

Edgin considered that. "All right," he said. "We'll go along as your backup, though I assume you're going to have a pair of emerald earrings and maybe a diamond necklace or two to help smooth the way?"

Forge bowed his head. "I always do."

Edgin turned to Simon and Holga. "Meanwhile, the two of you should be practicing serving drinks and blending in."

Holga paused with another hunk of chicken halfway to her mouth. "Thought you were kidding about that."

Edgin grinned. "Oh no, I never kid about proper dinner party etiquette. We need you both to be able to carry a full tray of wine-glasses without spilling a drop."

Holga sighed mournfully. Simon looked pained.

CHAPTER 21

Longsaddle was nowhere near the bustling metropolis of a city like Baldur's Gate or Neverwinter, but it still felt worlds away from their tiny village when Edgin, Kira, and Forge rode into town. Kira pointed and gasped at the street performers and the crowded city market with goods on offer from all corners of Faerûn. Sitting behind her on the horse, Edgin could feel her excitement as she bounced in the saddle.

He should travel with her more, Edgin thought, chiding himself for not thinking of this earlier. There were places he'd seen in his time as a Harper that Kira would love. She would be dazzled by the Walking Statues of Waterdeep or the skyline of Baldur's Gate at sunset.

Once they had the profit from this score, he'd take her out of Targos, and they could see more of the world together. They'd take the whole crew, in fact. It would be amazing.

Again, Edgin felt that glow of happiness nudging him in the chest. He tried not to dwell on it too much. They still had work to do, he reminded himself.

That didn't mean they couldn't have fun though. He poked Kira in the shoulder as they passed a merchant's stall with flowing silks and gems. "We need to go fancy clothes shopping while we're here," he said.

Kira's face lit up like a sunrise. Edgin soaked it in.

Fifteen minutes later, the glow of happiness had evaporated. "Seriously?" Edgin said as they stood in front of Lady Sofina's townhouse.

"I swear it's not as bad as it looks," Forge said.

Edgin gave him an incredulous stare. "Prisons are more accessible than this place," he said, pointing to the barred windows and the large, reinforced oak door, not to mention the iron fence that ran the length of the property and the guards standing in front of gates that barred entry to a sculpted strip of lawn and rose beds leading up to the house.

"It wasn't like this the last time I was here," Forge said, with a rueful expression. "It's possible that Lady Sofina, after our last encounter, didn't feel she had adequate security measures in place for the more nefarious characters in Longsaddle."

"Meaning this is your fault," Edgin said flatly. "You're the reason for the guards and the iron bars."

"Regrettably, yes."

Kira looked at Forge with a raised eyebrow that she'd clearly learned from Holga. "What did you do to her?"

"Never mind," Edgin said quickly. He looked at Forge and gestured to the guards. "Go on," he said. "This is your show. Give it your best shot."

"You can do it," Kira said encouragingly. Forge offered her a faint smile.

"I suppose you're right," he said. "Time to face the music."

Edgin clapped him on the shoulder. "We'll be standing right back here in the street a safe distance away if you need us."

"Wonderful backup you are," Forge said, but he gamely approached the guards. After a short conversation and a discreet offering of coin on Forge's part, the taller of the two guards left them and went inside the townhouse. He emerged a few minutes later and gestured for them all to come inside the gate.

They were in.

The guard escorted them to Lady Sofina's parlor, which was a long, rectangular room with a large bank of windows on the back wall that afforded a beautiful view of the rear lawn and formal gardens, with a stone fountain burbling at the center of it all. There were plush sofas and wingback chairs all throughout the room, and a polished grand piano had pride of place in one corner.

The lady herself was sitting at said piano with her back to the group. Or at least, Edgin assumed the figure was Lady Sofina. She wore a day gown of rich velvet brocade with an attached hood that she had pulled up to shield her face. The shadows of the room seemed to collect around her, and as she played a soft, mournful tune on the piano, Edgin felt a small shiver go through him.

She's just rich and eccentric, he told himself. *That's all. It's perfectly natural to wear a hood and sit alone in a room playing funeral music in the middle of the day.*

The music stopped, and Edgin jerked to attention.

"Well met," Lady Sofina said, rising and turning to the group. Her eyes were very dark, and as she surveyed them all, Edgin had the strangest feeling that he was back in the hag's cave. He pushed the unsettling thought away.

"Sofina," Forge said, stepping forward and holding out both hands to her. "It's been too long."

"Forge," Sofina said in a flat voice, ignoring his outstretched hands. "I'm surprised to see you here after our last encounter."

Forge's charming smile dimmed somewhat. "Yes, well, you see, that's why I've come. I wanted to apologize profusely for my behavior. It was unacceptable, and I've been racked with guilt ever since we parted." He began rummaging in his vest pocket, producing a small black velvet bag.

While Forge groveled, Lady Sofina turned her attention to Edgin and Kira. "And what have we here?" she asked, her gaze sweeping over them in open curiosity. The intensity of her eyes made Edgin take a small step forward, subtly putting himself between the woman and Kira.

"My daughter and I are business partners with Forge," he explained. "We understand that you recently received an invitation to the wizard Torlinn's party at his country estate." He was tempted to try a charming smile of his own, but his gut told him the woman was having none of it. Straightforward was the way to play this. "We want to attend the party too, but we need invitations of our own."

"Ahhh," Sofina said, and Edgin had never felt more like a mouse confronting a jungle cat. "So you need my help. Interesting." She turned back to Forge and held out her hand for the bag.

"I am *truly* sorry," Forge said, dropping the velvet bundle into her small, pale hand and bowing his head.

Sofina wedged the bag open and looked inside. She made a hum of approval and tucked the jewels away into the pocket of her dress. "Tell me," she said, "what is it you want with this wizard?"

There was a pause, and then Kira spoke up. "His parties are supposed to be amazing," she said. She faltered and shrank back against Edgin's hip when Sofina turned that dark gaze in her direction. "Or at least . . . um . . . that's what we've heard."

Edgin put a comforting arm around Kira. The last thing he wanted to do here was give out too many details about what they intended. He didn't want Lady Sofina demanding her own share in the heist. "Who says we want anything?" He shrugged casually. "Maybe we just want to see what all the fuss is about at these parties."

That coaxed a small, knowing smile from her lips. "If you wanted to use that line, you shouldn't have come here with Forge Fitzwilliam," she said. She moved from the piano to the sofa and sat down, gesturing for the rest of them to sit as well. "Why should I help you, then? What if you mean my dear friend Torlinn harm?"

At that, Forge scoffed good-naturedly. "Come, now, Sofina, I don't believe for a moment that you have any 'dear' friends."

She cocked her head, but still the hood and the position of her body kept her face mostly in shadow. "It's true," she said. "And I have my own questions about Torlinn and his activities." She glanced at Edgin. "If you're not careful, you may find more than you bargained for there."

"We'll be ready for whatever comes," Edgin said, though he couldn't help but feel as if this conversation were a deep, dark pool he was wading into with no sign of the bottom. There was an aura around Lady Sofina that reminded him of magic, though he hadn't seen any clear evidence that she was a spellcaster. Still, he kept up a false smile and an easy bravado. "The question is, was Forge's 'apology' substantial enough to make you help us?"

Sofina considered them all again as she sat back against the sofa cushions, her hands folded in her lap. "As apologies go, yours was . . . adequate," she said to Forge. "But I'm far more intrigued to see what you'll do at Torlinn's party. For that reason, I'll help you."

"Thank you," Kira started to say, but Lady Sofina had already risen, her gown whispering over the rug as she moved to a small writing desk in the corner. The drawer squeaked in the quiet as she slid it open and removed a rolled sheet of parchment with a broken seal.

Forge stood up from his chair and quickly took the parchment from her when she returned to the sofa, as if afraid she would change her mind. He unrolled it and examined the elegant script of the invitation. He nodded slowly.

"Yes, I can copy this," he said. "It shouldn't take long, and I've brought the necessary supplies."

"Let's get to it, then," Edgin said. "We don't want to take up too much of the Lady Sofina's time."

And he wanted to get out of this house as soon as humanly possible.

WHEN THE INK had dried on the parchment of three forged invitations, Lady Sofina led them downstairs to the door herself. In fact, besides the guards, Edgin hadn't seen a single servant since they walked into the house.

"Thank you again, Sofina, for your grace and understanding," Forge said, adding, "and for your discretion in this matter."

"Of course," Sofina said, and Edgin thought they were going to get away with no more words, but she called after them as they walked down the front steps of the townhouse. "I hope to see you at the party, Edgin."

Edgin didn't know if there was a tone in her voice that promised she would, or if he was just being paranoid. Either way, he threw a quick wave over his shoulder and hustled Kira and Forge away.

CHAPTER 22

"Well, I'd call that a successful operation," Forge said as they moved quickly down the street, putting as much distance between themselves and Lady Sofina's townhouse as possible.

Kira was half jogging to keep pace with them. "Yes, but Lady Sofina was . . ." She trailed off and shuddered. "I didn't like her."

"Neither did I," Edgin said. He shot a suspicious glance at Forge. "Is it possible that Lady Sofina is a sorceress, and you forgot to mention it?"

They passed into the shopping district, weaving through other foot traffic and dodging carts, so it was a few minutes before Forge could answer him.

"Did I?" he said, waving a hand. "Well, I really don't think she's much more than a dabbler in the arcane, no real power to speak of. Why, did you think she was trying to charm you?"

He grinned that affable grin. Edgin laughed and slapped Forge on the back—probably a bit harder than necessary.

"No, but I think it would be a good idea if you shared details like that with us in the future."

And now Lady Sofina was another variable in the upcoming party. She would be there and was bound to be curious about their activities. Lucky for them it was a masquerade ball, so they could stay hidden, but still, they'd have to be careful.

"You worry too much," Forge said, still wearing that relaxed grin. "You had that entire conversation under control, just like I knew you would." He leaned in closer. "You always handle any obstacle that gets thrown your way, Ed. You just need to trust yourself and your abilities more. I can think of no better leader for this crew."

"Agreed," said Kira, taking Edgin's hand as they walked into the tailor's shop, the signboard swaying above the door depicting a silver needle resting beside a spool of green thread.

Forge seemed sincere, and Edgin couldn't help but swell a bit under the praise of both him and Kira. Maybe he was worrying too much. They'd accomplished their mission, and Simon and Holga would help them watch out for Lady Sofina at the party.

Still, he reminded himself that Forge would likely stab his own grandmother in the back if it meant getting what he wanted. Once a con man, always a con man.

Inside the tailor's shop, which was dubbed Bristle and Brettons, was a colorful world of sparkling fabrics and deftly tailored suits arranged on rows of cloth dummies. Hats of all shapes, sizes, and decorative flourishes lined one wall, hung so high that a rolling ladder sat nearby to reach the topmost row.

Kira was entranced. She walked the aisles, touching the fabrics with the tips of her fingers. "This place is amazing," she said in a reverent whisper.

"It is," Edgin said, waving to the man and woman who'd just come out from the back room. "You don't need to whisper here, though. We're not in a shrine."

"The lady respects good clothing," said the man, a short, balding human with a wide smile, wearing a deep blue shirt and trousers embellished with big silver buttons.

"I like her already." The woman, a tawny-furred tabaxi with deep red spots speckling her flanks, held out her hand to Edgin, her claws politely retracted. "I'm Bristle, and my partner is Brettons. What can we do for you folks today?"

Edgin shook her hand. Just then, Forge came out from behind one of the cloth dummies. "Brettons, you're looking well! Haven't seen you in an age."

"Well, damn my eyes, if it isn't Forge Fitzwilliam!" Brettons clasped Forge's hand and gave it a hearty shake, clapping him on the back at the same time. "Welcome! Welcome! Finally took me up on my offer to come see the shop, did you?"

"Absolutely," Forge said, gesturing to Edgin and Kira. "My friends and I are attending a party in the country, and we need proper attire. Masks, formal wear, the whole bit. Can you help us?"

"You're not going to one of those strange parties that wizard throws at his country estate, are you?" Bristle asked, narrowing her golden eyes. "They're in very poor taste, from all I've heard."

"Guilty," Edgin said, putting on his charming smile as he sensed a path to getting a bit of free information. "We got roped into it by a friend who said we simply *had* to see what goes on behind those closed doors. Why, have you heard something unsavory?" He leaned in as if whatever the woman said would be their secret.

"Well," Bristle said, her tail swishing back and forth across the floorboards, "if you believe the local gossip—"

"Which I *always* do," Edgin said, and that earned him a snort of laughter from Brettons.

Bristle chuckled. "It's whispered that every time the wizard Torlinn throws a party, one of his guests disappears." She clenched a fist and then opened it, waving her clawed hand.

"Disappears?" Kira said, frowning. "Like forever?"

"Indeed," Brettons said, running his hands over his shirt buttons. "You know how these things are, though. It's always a friend of a friend, never anyone you know directly. And it almost always turns out the person just left town and didn't tell anyone."

"True," Bristle said. "That Sembian wine merchant skipped town to avoid a debt."

"And that Waterdhavian nobleman left the city to go 'adventuring,' whatever that means." Brettons shuddered, as if he couldn't imagine such a thing.

"Still," Bristle said thoughtfully, "it doesn't stop the rumors that strange things go on in that house. Some people even think it's haunted."

"Haunted?" Forge's eyebrows rose. "Well, now you've just made us that much more curious about the place. We simply must discover the truth. Right, Edgin?"

"I think we'll definitely discover some interesting things," Edgin agreed.

Privately, he was trying to make sense of all this. A dragonborn who mistreats his staff, throws wild parties, and lives in a haunted house where people periodically disappear and are never seen again.

It had to be made up. Otherwise, surely someone would have investigated the place by now. But if all this was simply rumors, did that mean the Staff of Aorth was just a story too? He hoped not. They'd put too much time and planning, too many hopes on this job for it to turn out to be yet another disappointment.

No, he had to believe the wizard was hiding something in that house. Too many stories coming from too many different people. Whatever was going on in there, Edgin was going to find out what it was and find a way to profit from it.

"Well," he said, clapping his hands together, "if we're going to find out for ourselves what these unsavory parties are like, we'd better get proper attire, as Forge says." He looked to Bristle and Brettons in turn. "What do you recommend?"

Bristle circled them, humming in her throat, while Brettons glanced at the fabric samples and displays around the store. Once their survey was done, their eyes met, and they grinned at each other.

"We have just the thing," Bristle said.

FOR THE NEXT two hours, Edgin tried on more clothes, hats, shoes, and masks than he'd ever done in his entire life. He probably would have brought the session to a close after the one-hour mark, but Kira was obviously in heaven, trying on gowns in all different colors and fabrics, and letting Bristle weave ribbons and beads into her hair in increasingly complex styles. Edgin didn't have the heart to hurry her along when she was having so much fun.

And he had to admit, once they moved on to trying on masks, even he was starting to feel like a kid again.

Kira picked out a black-and-white domino mask festooned with glitter and long purple ribbons. It went perfectly with her black gown and its skirt that shone when she twirled. That had been one of her requirements for the dress, apparently. It had to be properly twirl-able.

Edgin and Forge chose tailored suits in black and gray, respectively. Forge's mask was more of a jester's mask, complete with a comical grin and bells on the side tassels.

"You look amazing!" Kira told him when he stepped out of the changing room.

Edgin thought he looked ridiculous, but he kept that one to himself.

For Edgin's mask, Bristle started to present him with something green and shimmery and covered in elaborate feathers, but Kira got to him first, shoving a white cat mask in his hands.

"Try that one, Dad!"

Edgin looked doubtfully at the mask. "Isn't it a bit . . . cute?" he asked.

Kira nodded, her eyes sparkling. "That's why it's so great. It'll be perfect!"

Edgin sighed. There were those weaponized eyes again, and he was helpless to resist. He slid the mask over his face and turned to the nearest mirror. The shop was full of them, so he barely had to move.

He stared at himself in the glass. "You know, you might be onto something," he told Kira. The cat mask paired well with the elegant black suit, and it had a sly look to it that Edgin hadn't noticed at first. It was a mask that said he knew something everyone else didn't. He liked that.

"I think this will do," he said.

"We still have to get masks and outfits for Simon and Holga, don't forget," Kira said.

Edgin hadn't forgotten. They'd decided that, even though Holga and Simon were going to pose as servants, they should have formal wear and masks too, so if they needed to slip between the guest areas and the servant's areas, they could do so freely with a quick costume change.

Even if they hadn't decided on that plan, Kira wasn't going to let them leave the shop without picking out a nice outfit for Holga. She'd been talking about it for days.

Forge helped her select a set of robes embroidered with dragons in flight for Simon, along with a dragon mask that glittered pale bronze.

"To give him the courage of a dragon," Kira said.

But shopping for Holga proved to be more time-consuming than even Edgin had anticipated, and, as a result, their visit stretched into hour three. Forge spent the time haggling over prices with Brettons and then excused himself to go in search of some gear that Edgin knew would include anything they could possibly need to get through locked doors or scale walls if it became necessary.

"Oh, look at this!" Kira held up a thick cloak of deep crimson with a fur-lined hood. "This will go perfect with her hair, and it's got pretty fur just like her other clothes. And she can wear whatever she wants underneath."

Edgin made an approving noise. "It's not too flashy either, which definitely wouldn't be Holga's style. What mask are you picking out for her?"

Kira perused the selections on display, climbing the ladder and pointing to a mask every now and then so Bristle could get it down for her to examine. She kept shaking her head, though, until finally she spied an antlered beast mask on a lower shelf. She pointed to it excitedly.

"Is that an elk?" she asked.

"Hmm . . . maybe?" Bristle brought it over to the counter and handed it to Kira. "Maybe a deer or something?"

"Close enough," Kira said. She held it up for Edgin's inspection. "What do you think, Dad? It's her tribe: the Elk."

Edgin took the mask, turning it over in his hands. "I don't want to burst your bubble, sweetheart," he said gently, "but Holga might not like to be reminded of her past with her tribe. You know it didn't end well."

Kira bit her lip. "I know, but I asked her once about her tattoos, if she ever wished she didn't have them anymore, because they remind her of her tribe. She told me that the tattoos actually made her feel better, like she was still a little bit connected to her family. To her, they were good memories, not bad ones. So maybe the mask could be like that too?"

Edgin wasn't sure what to say for a moment. He'd never known Holga had shared that much information about her past or her feelings with Kira. Though really, he shouldn't have been surprised, as often as Kira imitated Holga, trying to be like her. It reminded him that Holga had a whole other relationship with Kira that he wasn't a part of. He tried not to feel jealous of that. And he wasn't, not really. He knew Holga would never hesitate to step between Kira and danger, and she'd do whatever it took to care for her and make her happy. He was glad Kira had someone in her life who could be a mother figure for her.

That thought brought him up short, his chest tightening. Was that what Holga was to Kira? She'd never known her own mother, so it made sense in some ways. Edgin had never really stopped to think about it before, and for some reason, it made him uncomfortable to think about it now.

No one could replace Zia. That was impossible. But Holga had never tried to do anything like that, he reminded himself. She'd never claimed to be a parent, she'd just helped Edgin raise Kira the best she could, never asking anything in return.

And that day in the boat coming back from the island, Edgin had thrown all that back in her face, telling Holga that she wasn't Kira's mother. His stomach clenched at the memory and the fact that he still hadn't apologized to Holga for that. At first, he'd gotten distracted with all the planning over the past few weeks. Later, it felt like things were back to normal between them, so Edgin had tried to put the incident out of his mind. Surely, she didn't hold it against him?

He shook away those thoughts as he realized Kira was waiting for him to say something. He handed the mask back to her. "You're right," he said, swallowing thickly. "I think she'll love this, especially since it came from you."

CHAPTER 23

The night of the party arrived faster than Edgin had expected, even after several more weeks of planning and preparation and going over the plan until everyone was sick of talking about the plan, bickering over the small details of the plan, and running through the plan in their sleep.

That's when he knew they were ready.

They left for Torlinn's manor on horseback the day before the party, passing the outskirts of Neverwinter and camping in the woods about a mile from the house. This gave them the entire day to scout the outer perimeter of the grounds and to allow Simon to locate any magical security measures and traps they should avoid during their escape.

Alyanna met them at sunset, bringing along the wagon they would use to load and transport the bigger pieces of loot. The half-elf was a little bit older than Simon, her long auburn hair pulled back into a neat braid, her hazel eyes bright and sharp as she assessed the group—Edgin, Forge, and Kira in their formal wear, Simon and Holga in their servant's livery.

"You know, when Simon came to buy my tip and bring me in on

this job, I wasn't sure about you all," Alyanna said, leaning casually against a tree. "But he was very convincing. He really talked every-one up."

"I didn't!" Simon sputtered. "I mean, yes, I did, but it was war-ranted."

"Oh really?" Edgin spread his hands theatrically. "How have we measured up since?"

"Eh," Alyanna said, shrugging.

"I set myself up for that one, didn't I?" Edgin said, glancing at Holga, who nodded in confirmation. His humor faded when he glanced back at Alyanna. "I think we'll all be taking each other's measure tonight. This job is going to require a degree of trust on both our parts. Right?"

"True," Alyanna said neutrally. "I've met a lot of smooth talkers in the past, and very few of them could deliver results." Her expres-sion darkened. "I've got a lot riding on this. When the dust settles and all this is over, Torlinn will be looking for the inside person who betrayed him, so I need to make enough money off this heist to dis-appear to a land far away. Understand?"

"Not to worry," Forge said, in a tone that basically made him the poster boy for smooth talkers. Edgin coughed to cover his laugh. "We're all professionals here, and we've been able to plan well, thanks to your inside information. Everyone's prepared to do their part to make this operation proceed as smoothly as possible and make us all as rich as possible. Life-changingly rich. Does that suf-fice?"

Alyanna nodded, accepting that promise, because, really, what other choice did she have at this point? They'd come too far to turn back now.

Edgin raised his hands to get everyone's attention. When the group had all gathered around, he said, "All right, here's the plan."

Their collective groans drowned out anything he might have said next.

"Daaaaaad, we've gone over this a hundred times!" Kira whined.

"This is different," Edgin insisted. "This time, I want you all to close your eyes and imagine what's going to happen. We're talking full-on theater-of-the-mind stuff. The last dress rehearsal before the big show." He waited, arms crossed, until they all reluctantly shut their eyes, still muttering complaints.

"Picture it," Edgin said, dropping his voice and invoking all his storytelling prowess. "A glittering ballroom full of mysterious masked party guests. Music fills the air, and—"

"Dancing?" Kira cut in.

"Of course," Edgin said. "Dancing, drinking, laughter, and into the middle of the revelry step me, Forge, and Kira. We're the face of the operation. We mingle, we fraternize and familiarize ourselves with the layout of the mansion in person. Meanwhile, our team on the inside—Holga, Simon, and Alyanna—will blend in with the servants and work on getting us access to Torlinn's treasure room upstairs. You three know your parts there?"

"We swipe the key—which is magical and not easily copied— from the butler's set after I spike his drink with something to knock him out for a few hours," Alyanna said. "After Torlinn's demonstration of the staff, he'll take it upstairs himself and return it to the treasure room. Team Party Guests will wait for him to return to the ballroom and then sneak upstairs to meet us."

"Exactly," Edgin said. "Once we're in the treasure room, we clean the place out, grab the staff, and, after making sure there's no magical protections on it, Simon will use an illusion to disguise it as a walking stick and take it out the servant's entrance. The rest of us will split up and leave on our own with a portion of the loot. We rendezvous at the wagon, which Holga will bring around to the back of the mansion. Then we ride off into the sunset together."

There was no complaining about that part, Edgin noticed.

"We know what we have to do," Edgin said, "and I trust each and every one of you to play your parts to perfection." He grinned. "Let's go get rich."

There was a chorus of agreement.

Venturing stealthily out from their camp, the group was able to have a front-row seat when the first of the party guests began to arrive. Ornate carriages with large teams of horses in decorative harnesses rumbled up the long, circular drive of the mansion, past hedges sculpted to look like wyverns, giants, and unicorns. There was even a full-sized beholder sculpture fighting a draconic figure with horns, which must have been meant to represent Torlinn, but the topiary had grown a bit out of control and looked more lumpy than dragonborn.

Eventually, Simon and Holga headed around the back to the servant's entrance with Alyanna, while Edgin, Forge, and Kira mounted their horses and rode up the drive at a slow, stately pace, joining the line of carriages and horseback riders waiting to gain admittance to the party.

Night had fallen by then, and torches lined the way to the house, their fires burning orange, green, blue, and white, periodically shooting sparks into the air that made the horses shift restlessly.

"A little pre-party entertainment for people waiting to get in," Forge commented as he rode up next to Edgin.

"A lot of casual magic to be throwing around," Edgin said with a raised eyebrow.

"I'm glad to see it, actually," Forge said, glancing at the spitting torches. "Makes me more convinced that we're going to find the real Staff of Aorth tonight. And it's going to be ours."

He smiled at Edgin, and Edgin couldn't help but smile back, a wave of excitement building inside him. They were actually doing this. They had a plan in place and they were executing it. Everyone had their angle, and if everyone did their part, the heist would go off perfectly.

He had a good feeling about tonight.

Fifteen minutes later, they finally reached the main doors, which sat at the top of a short flight of stone steps. The doors themselves looked like tall obsidian blocks with gold etchings running along their edges. Not particularly welcoming, but servants were waiting to take their horses, and the doors swung open by themselves when they reached the top of the steps.

As soon as they crossed the threshold, Edgin felt a tingle at the back of his neck, and the sensation of someone watching him was suddenly very strong. He looked around, trying to be casual about it. They were in a small foyer lit by four magical driftglobes. Another set of double doors, smaller and less intimidating than the ones they'd just passed through, led into the main party, which, judging by the muffled sounds coming from within, was already in full swing.

But two guards stood by the doors, wearing plate armor and holding ornate spears, effectively blocking the way.

An elven woman with short black hair stood off to Edgin's left behind a small podium. "Invitations, please," she said. She wore a dagger on a chain belt over her pale blue gown.

"Of course." Forge immediately produced three rolled pieces of parchment sealed with wax—exactly as they'd seen Lady Sofina's invitation presented.

The woman broke the seal and unrolled the parchment, laying each invitation out flat on her podium. She waved a hand, and one of the driftglobes floated closer to give her better light.

Edgin tried not to hold his breath. This was the first big test. If they couldn't get in as guests, Simon and the others could theoretically still sneak them in via the servant's entrance, but it would make what they had to do a lot harder.

The woman examined the invitations for an agonizing minute. Kira was fidgeting next to him. Edgin put a hand on her shoulder and gave her a quick wink, like they had this.

He hoped they had this.

The woman looked up at them. "Everything seems to be in order," she said, and Edgin gave a quiet sigh of relief. "Enjoy the party."

They moved toward the main doors, donning their masks as they went. Kira stepped between Edgin and Forge, taking each of them by the arm. "Let's go," she whispered excitedly.

The guards pulled the doors open to let them enter, and a wall of sound immediately enveloped them as they entered the grand ballroom.

Edgin had been studying the layout of this place for so long, it felt strange to be seeing it in person for the first time. The two-story hexagonal ballroom was tiled in glittering black marble. A balcony circled the entire second level. Golden damask draperies adorned the windows, which were tall and thin and interspersed with stained glass scenes depicting dragons in flight or cityscapes in faraway places such as Rashemen or Amn. Everything was bold, bright, and just a bit garish, but somehow it all worked.

Maybe it was because the room was full of equally bold, garishly costumed party guests. Humans, elves, dwarves, gnomes, tabaxi, halflings, dragonborn, and others Edgin couldn't see—masked and dancing, or standing around in groups drinking, laughing, and soaking up the general atmosphere.

"Where's the music coming from?" Kira asked, looking around for the orchestra as the dancers twirled and pranced across the floor to a waltz.

"Not sure," Edgin said, guiding their group farther into the room. "Let's circulate so we don't look like country bumpkins."

But as soon as they stepped out from beneath the cover of the balcony, Edgin looked up, and his mouth dropped open.

"Found the orchestra," he said, pointing to the ceiling.

"Oh my Gods," Forge said, and Kira laughed in delight.

To be fair, Alyanna had warned them that Torlinn planned different attractions and set pieces for each of his parties, and even she wouldn't know everything he had in store for the evening, since he kept things a secret from all but a select number of servants who helped him set up.

Therefore, the first surprise of the evening was that Torlinn had hired what looked like a twenty-person orchestra, and they were playing on the ceiling. Not just on the ceiling, but upside down on the ceiling. Flautists, lute players, singers, even the conductor were all playing their parts as if nothing out of the ordinary was happening, as if they performed this way all the time.

And if that weren't enough, situated in the middle of the orchestra was one of the largest pipe organs Edgin had ever seen. A dwarven man with bright copper hair and a long, braided beard sat at the instrument, happily playing along with the rest of the orchestra.

"Well, Alyanna said each party has a different theme," Edgin said. "Guess tonight the theme is 'How Weird Can a Wizard Get?'"

"This is the best party ever," Kira declared as she stared up at the orchestra. The organ player somehow caught sight of her and waved. Kira waved back.

"Impressive, isn't it?" A gnomish woman with short, curly brown hair stopped beside them. She was wearing a half mask of purple silk embroidered with blue butterflies. "I asked Torly—sorry, Torlinn— what spell he was using to keep them all up there like that, instruments and everything, and do you know what he told me?" The woman was a bit tipsy, her eyes a little too bright. "He said it was powered with the suspension of disbelief!" She chortled loudly and sailed away, waving an empty glass at a nearby server.

"More likely some kind of reverse gravity spell," Edgin mused when she was gone. The three of them wove through the crowd, pausing to get drinks from another servant bearing a loaded tray. The red wine was sweet, not at all what Edgin cared for.

"Maybe with an added dose of magical boots," Forge said, pointing to a far corner of the room, where one of the lute players was calmly walking up the wall to switch out with one of the other members of the orchestra.

"Oh, now that's interesting," Edgin said, tracking the other lute player's progress down the wall to the floor of the ballroom. "Forge, if those boots *are* magical, do you think you can acquire us a pair? You never know when they might come in handy."

"I'd be delighted," Forge said, grabbing a second glass of wine from a passing tray as he made his way across the ballroom floor to head off the lute player and offer him the drink.

"So, that's one pair of magical boots all but acquired," Edgin said, offering Kira his arm. "Should we explore?"

Kira's eyes sparkled behind her mask, but then she tilted her head curiously. "Where do you think Torlinn is?"

That was a good question. There were several dragonborn in the crowd, but no one that matched Alyanna's description of Torlinn or had the presence that Edgin associated with the wizard in his mind. No one who threw parties like this would ever fade into the background. When they spotted Torlinn, they'd know it.

"Let's try in there," Edgin said, pointing directly across the expansive ballroom to yet another set of double doors, which were thrown open and from which the sound of raucous laughter echoed.

Kira nodded but gave the dance floor a long look as they crossed the ballroom. Edgin nudged her. "Save your dad a turn for later? Before your dance card fills up?"

Her eyes lit up. "You got it."

CHAPTER 24

They passed through the doors, leaving the crowded ballroom and the music behind, only to find an even wilder scene.

The back wall of this room was dominated by a huge bar carved out of oak, with designs of trees and flowers worked into its length. Lined up along the bar were what looked like cocktails of every color, flavor, and strangeness. Some of them leaked smoke. Others had flames dancing around the stems. There were gold and silver chalices next to cups that Edgin swore were made out of feathers. That wasn't logical and couldn't possibly be sanitary, but Edgin was intrigued.

The bartender, a tall, dark-haired man with a thin goatee, wearing an open vest and costumed as a centaur—or maybe he was an actual centaur, Edgin amended as they got closer—stood behind the bar, which luckily had plenty of space behind it. He waved a hand at the cocktails as people crowded close to examine them.

"Drink up, friends, if you dare!" he shouted ominously but with a wicked grin on his face. "The specials tonight are Tyr's Juice of Justice, Dragon's Morning Breath, and Torlinn's new favorite cocktail, Volo's Folly. Come and try a sample!"

Edgin approached the bar, watching to see what everyone else was trying. The Juice of Justice seemed the popular choice, with several people picking up the orange drink and taking a sip. Seconds after they did, their arm muscles swelled, tripling in size. The crowd shrieked with laughter at the illusion, and the drinkers flexed their imaginary muscles and clinked glasses until the effect faded.

Farther down the bar, people were doing shots of Volo's Folly, which made their skin literally sparkle, as if they were drenched in glitter. The effect was blinding. Edgin had to shield his eyes as he passed through the crowd.

He found an open space near the corner of the bar, and there was Holga, loading up a tray of drinks. She turned and saw him but kept her expression neutral and bored, like a servant who'd seen a thousand of these parties. "Interested in trying the Dragon's Morning Breath, sir?" she inquired politely, showing off her tray of fluted glasses.

"Don't mind if I do," Edgin said, reaching for a drink.

"I wouldn't," Holga muttered in a low voice. "Tastes like Dragon's Morning Piss."

"Good to know." Edgin removed his mask, tipped the glass up to his lips and then poured it over his shoulder into a potted plant. "Tasty stuff!"

Kira came up behind Holga and gave her a quick hug where no one could see. "Hi, Holga," she whispered.

"Hey, bug," Holga said. "Go ask the bartender for two Fizzy Cherry Delights." She glanced at Edgin. "They're actually pretty good, and they won't muddle your head."

Kira slipped away while Edgin pretended to look at the drink selection on her tray. "This place is weird, even by rich people standards and wizard standards," he commented.

"Tell me about it," Holga said with a sigh. "From what Simon and I could get from the servants, the parties last all night and sometimes into the next day. Basically, until everyone collapses. Half the staff wants to quit because of the long hours and constant parties, but the pay is just good enough to keep everyone here, except . . ."

"Except?" Edgin prompted, pretending to take another drink while tossing it back into the plant.

"Everyone's on edge," Holga said grimly. "Like they're afraid, but they're not sure of what. Makes me twitchy."

"Focus on the plan," Edgin said as Kira returned with two tall glasses full of shockingly pink fizzy liquid swimming with cherries, their long stems twisted into curlicues. "When's Torlinn planning to do his little demonstration with the Staff of Aorth?"

"Alyanna says not until midnight," Holga said, with another sigh.

Edgin sympathized. They had a long night ahead. "All right, Kira and I are going to explore more of the guest areas."

"Keep an eye out for Simon," Holga said. "He's jumpier than usual too. Might need a pep talk."

They separated, with Edgin and Kira fading back into the crowd. Kira removed her mask so she could take a sip of her own drink.

"Holga was right, it's actually really good," Edgin said, clinking Kira's glass with his own. "Where next?"

Kira pointed to a door on the opposite end of the room. "I think there's some kind of lecture going on in there," she said. "There's a bunch of people sitting around and a woman standing at the front talking."

"Let's check it out," Edgin said.

They finished their Fizzy Cherry Delights first and donned their masks again, then made their way across the room, passing through the door Kira had indicated into a grand library. Bookshelves lined every wall, crammed with books on every subject imaginable. A balcony ran the length of the second story, just like in the ballroom, with more books up there along with the occasional portrait of a dragonborn. Torlinn's ancestors, perhaps.

Rows of chairs had been set up on the ground floor of the library, and here people lounged with their drinks and listened to the speaker at the front of the room, a halfling woman holding a large red leather tome with gold writing on the spine. Edgin was too far away to make out the title.

"This excerpt from the seminal works of Vrestus Honore of Neverwinter is the pride of Torlinn's collection," the woman was saying as Edgin and Kira slipped into a couple of seats near the back of the room. "I'll be reading three verses from the poem 'Winter Enervation to Spring Innovation.' I ask for silence as we contemplate the gravity of Honore's words."

It was difficult to contemplate the gravity of anything when people were shrieking with laughter from the bar in the next room, but the audience obediently fell quiet for a whole thirty seconds while the woman launched into her poem, and then they went back to talking amongst themselves.

The winter snow coats the world
Cold flakes like the dandruff of Silvanus
The spring buds burrowed and furled
Beneath the soil they shivereth.

Life sleeps, snores, and waits
Crushed in an icy hand
Hungry to rise and enervate
Its dreams, and flow across the land.

The woman had promised only three verses, but after a few minutes with no end in sight, Edgin leaned over to Kira. "I'm not a great judge of poetry, but does this strike you as being a bit . . . nonsensical?"

Kira nodded. "I don't think the poet knows what the word 'enervation' means."

A willowy elven woman sitting in front of them turned in her seat. She was wearing an eye mask of white lace to go with her pale pink gown and silver hair. Edgin thought she was going to shush them, but she rolled her eyes in commiseration. "It's always like this," she whispered. "Every party it seems Torlinn has a new favorite poet or novelist that he simply *must* share with his intimate friends. I never listen, I just sit here to rest my feet from all the dancing." She winked at Kira and turned back around in her seat.

"I think we've seen enough here," Edgin said. "Back to the ballroom?"

"I'm getting hungry," Kira agreed, "and we still haven't seen Torlinn yet."

True. Where was the wizard hiding?

They rose from their seats and made their way along the back wall to the door. As they reached it, the hairs on the back of Edgin's neck prickled. That sensation of being watched struck him again, stronger than it had when he'd stepped into the house. He turned, scanning the crowd, but no one was looking their way. The guests were either talking amongst themselves or, Gods help them, actually listening to the poetry.

He was about to turn away when his gaze rested on a familiar face in the crowd. Edgin's mouth went dry as he recognized the Lady Sofina sitting near the front of the room, politely listening to the poetry, though her dark eyes had a slightly glazed look, as if she were trying to stay awake. She wore a black cloak and hood. She wasn't looking at him now, but Edgin couldn't rule out that she might have been watching him before and he just didn't know it. He hoped his mask concealed his identity.

"We've got company," he said to Kira, quickly leading her out of the room.

"Who?" Kira asked, glancing over her shoulder.

"Don't look," Edgin said, pulling her through the bar and back into the ballroom. "It's Lady Sofina. We knew she was going to be here, but I hoped in a party this size we might be able to go the night without running into her."

"Did she see us?" Kira asked anxiously.

"I don't think so, and we're both wearing masks, so she shouldn't recognize us even if she did see us." Edgin glanced back at the library doors to be sure, but no one appeared. "I think we're good for now." He glanced down at Kira. "Snack table?"

"Definitely snack table," Kira said.

At least, Edgin had been picturing a snack table, but he should have known better. It was more like a buffet of every possible sweet or savory food you could imagine all in one place, in a riot of color and smell that was like a punch to the senses. Just like everything else at this party.

"Wow," Kira said as they joined the line moving along the table. "Lobster tails, apple pie, vegetable skewers, clams in cream sauce,

roast beef, roast chicken, roast pears—and that's just in this section!"
She picked up a plate and took a big scoop of mashed potatoes, but
she froze with it hovering above her plate.

"What?" Edgin asked, alarmed. "Is there a fly in the food? I knew
this place was too good to be true."

Kira shook her head and pointed down the table with the potato
scoop. "Is that . . . Torlinn?" she whispered.

Edgin looked. "I think you might be right."

Of course they'd end up finding the eccentric dragonborn wizard
and host of the biggest party on the Sword Coast standing in line at
the buffet table amassing a plate of sauteed shrimp and chatting
with the guests in front of and behind him like it was no big deal.

He was wearing long, flowy robes in deep purple that sat well
against his golden scales and curved horns. He had a diamond nose
ring fastened to his snout and wore a necklace that winked with glittering opals. As Edgin watched, someone whispered something in
his ear, and he laughed.

"He seems . . . normal?" Kira said, uncertain.

"Yeah," Edgin agreed. He wasn't sure what he'd been expecting.
Something more ostentatious, definitely, with the theme of the party.
Torlinn wasn't even wearing a mask.

Or maybe he'd been expecting someone more dangerous, considering what Holga had said about the mood of the servants. What
was *really* going on in this house? Was Torlinn a terrible employer or
not? Was he a sinister villain spiriting people away in the night? Or
just an eccentric wizard who loved to throw elaborate parties?

A good way to find out might be to talk to the dragonborn himself. Edgin weighed the risk. Normally, he wouldn't go near the person whose estate he intended to rob, but in this case, it might be
worth it to know the kind of person they were dealing with, to separate the rumors and wild speculation from the truth. It also wouldn't
matter that Torlinn didn't know them, since Alyanna had said the
dragonborn regularly issued invitations to people he'd heard about
but never met, from nobility to commoners, and never took the trouble to keep close track of his own guest list. He left that job to his
servants.

The only problem was Torlinn seemed always to be surrounded

by people who wanted the wizard's attention. There was no way to get close to him without being rude.

"I think we should arrange an introduction," Edgin said, nudging Kira. "Weren't you and Forge working on some attention and distraction scenarios a few days ago?"

Kira's eyes lit up with a gleeful fire. "The Walking Disaster," she said, in a tone of relish. "That's our newest one. Should I do it right now?"

"No time like the present."

Kira turned back to the buffet table, quickly stacking her plate with some of the messiest food within reach: mashed potatoes and brown gravy, blackberries in honey, and some lemon custard that was starting to go runny. Then she stepped out of line, threw her shoulders back, lifted her chin at a haughty angle, and started walking across the room. When she was within sight of Torlinn, she took a step to the right and rammed her shoulder into the nearest passing party guest, a tall human man who was weaving drunkenly through the crowd, his egg-white skin beaded with sweat.

"Oh no!" Kira shrieked. Her plate went flying into the air as she "tripped" and sprawled on the ground a few feet away from Torlinn. Her food crashed down after her, shattering her plate and leaving a rainbow of stains smeared across the marble floor.

The entire back half of the ballroom paused what they were doing to look for the source of the commotion.

Kira sat up slowly. Behind her mask, her eyes were bright with tears.

"I'm so . . . s-sorry," she said. "I wasn't watching where I was going and then . . ." She ducked her head, as if it was all just too much to bear.

Edgin was so proud he thought he might burst.

"Now, now," Torlinn said in a deep, soothing voice, putting down his plate of shrimp and gliding over to kneel beside Kira like a gallant rescuer from a storybook. "No need to be upset, young one. There's no harm done here." He gestured to two servants standing nearby, one of whom was Alyanna. "Can you get this cleaned up please while I see to my guest?"

They hastened to obey while Torlinn offered his clawed hand to

Kira to help her stand. "Are you all right, my dear?" he asked. "That was a nasty tumble you took."

"I'm f-fine," Kira said, "just so embarrassed. I didn't mean to make such a mess!"

With everyone's attention still fixed on the mini drama playing out, Edgin was able to sneak up behind the dragonborn. He wasn't sure what he was hoping to learn. Maybe a quick pickpocket to see what he was carrying around with him? No, not worth the risk if he was caught and thrown out of the party. But maybe he could see if the wizard had any weapons or magical objects or—

Just then, Torlinn pivoted, and Edgin swallowed a gasp.

Tucked into the crook of Torlinn's arm, blending in so well with his robes that Edgin hadn't noticed it until that moment, was a slender staff. The wood was engraved with strange arcane symbols, interrupted by a long, thin crack down the middle of the shaft. Simon would probably know what the symbols meant, but Edgin had no clue. The grooves seemed to catch the light, creating a twinkling effect like starlight, but not the garish display in the bar where people were drinking magical cocktails. This was deeper, richer, and mesmerizing to watch.

Embedded in the top and bottom of the staff were two gems cut into rough ovals no larger than Edgin's thumb. The one at the top, near Torlinn's shoulder, was a diamond that sparkled in the lights. The one at the base was a perfectly cut emerald.

The Staff of Aorth. It had to be. It matched every description Edgin had ever read about the artifact. And Torlinn was just carrying it around the party like a prop. According to Alyanna, he would put it away later, after the midnight demonstration, but somehow Edgin had a hard time believing that. If *he* were a wizard who owned a powerful magical artifact, he'd never let it out of his sight.

"Now then, all cleaned up and everything's fine," Torlinn was saying, snapping Edgin back to reality. The wizard bowed over Kira's hand as the servants whisked away the bits of broken plate and food. Alyanna caught Edgin's eye and gave him a significant look. She knew he'd seen the staff. Edgin gave her a minute nod and then turned back to Kira and Torlinn.

"There you are, Ellie," he said, as if he hadn't just been standing a few feet away. "Is everything all right?"

"Oh yes, Father," Kira said brightly, gesturing to the dragonborn. "Torlinn, this is Frederick, my father. Father, this is Torlinn, our host. He's been ever so kind to me."

"My thanks to you, Torlinn—and great party, by the way," Edgin said, holding out his hand. Torlinn clasped it briefly, and a strange tremor went through Edgin's body. His heartbeat sped up, and he felt that same prickle of uneasiness he had earlier, like someone was watching him. But then Torlinn released his hand, and the sensation faded.

"It's my pleasure," the dragonborn said. "Your daughter is delightful. Now, if you'll both excuse me, I must greet some guests who've arrived fashionably late."

He glided away before Edgin could reply, leaving him and Kira alone by the buffet table. The curious onlookers had mostly dispersed, but Edgin still lowered his voice when he spoke.

"He was weird, wasn't he? Tell me that wasn't just me?"

Kira shook her head. "It wasn't just you," she said. Her eyes were troubled. "He was . . . it felt like he was using magic the whole time we were talking, even though I never saw him cast a spell the way Simon does. And he stared at my pendant a lot."

Edgin bit back a curse. "He probably has ways to detect any magic items people might be carrying. We should have thought of that before we drew attention to ourselves."

Sloppy. He should have known better.

Kira clasped her pendant protectively. "Do you think he'll ask us to leave?" she whispered.

Edgin watched Torlinn move through the crowd, stopping by a pair of dragonborn and the Lady Sofina, who walked up right when Torlinn did. Edgin tensed, wondering if she was about to blow their cover and warn Torlinn about them. But she never even glanced their way. She seemed to be speaking mostly to the other dragonborn, and after a moment of what looked like polite conversation, the group broke up, and Torlinn wandered away.

Edgin released a sigh of relief. "I don't think so," he said, "and it looks like Torlinn has better things to do playing party host than worry about us."

They still had at least another two hours before midnight. "Kira," Edgin said, glancing across the ballroom. "I think it's time you and I had that dance. Blend into the crowd for a while."

"Good idea," Kira said excitedly.

Edgin led her out to the dance floor just as the orchestra struck up a lively tune, similar to what Edgin and Zia used to dance to in the village square during festival season. The organ player addressed the crowd from above, proclaiming, "Torlinn's favorite dance, the Light-Footed Maiden! Come and join the fun!"

The crowd who took up the challenge divided into four different groups, each forming a circle with their hands clasped. Edgin led Kira to the circle farthest from where Torlinn had gone, and the people made space for them.

When Kira told them she was new to the dance, a smiling couple happily showed them the steps, and soon enough, he and Kira were dancing in the circle, spinning, clapping, and stomping their feet in time with the music. Kira's eyes were bright with laughter, and she shrieked happily when Edgin lifted her and spun her around at the dance's conclusion.

If nothing else came of this night, at least Kira seemed to be having the time of her life. And, despite his worries, Edgin had to admit that he was too. The heist, the masquerade, the strange party theme and even stranger host—this was a night he wouldn't soon forget, and he was happy that he got to share it with his daughter.

They danced three more dances in their circle before Edgin had to beg off to rest and get some water. He also wanted to find Forge and Simon. Holga circulated the ballroom often, serving drinks, and Alyanna popped up here and there, running errands for Torlinn, but Edgin hadn't seen either of the others, and he hadn't forgotten what Holga had said about Simon being nervous.

Like magic, Holga appeared with two glasses of water on her tray right as they were leaving the dance floor.

"You read my mind," Edgin said, reaching for a glass.

Holga batted his hand away. "I got it for Kira," she said, handing her the water. Only once Kira had taken off her mask and had a big drink did Holga hand Edgin his own glass. "You can have some too, I guess."

"That's what I love about you, Holga," Edgin said, removing the cat mask and taking a long swig. "Your kind and caring nature."

Holga snorted. "And my axe skills."

"And your axe skills."

"Did you see me dancing, Holga?" Kira asked, tugging on Holga's pant leg.

"You were beautiful, bug," Holga said, smiling down at her. "Drink your water. You're all flushed." If she hadn't been posing as a servant, Edgin thought Holga would have ruffled Kira's hair.

There they were again, those subtle gestures that showed how Holga was always thinking about Kira, always watching out for her, whether it was making sure she had enough water or defending her to the death with her axe.

"I'm going to freshen up," Kira declared, pointing to an area marked for guests just off the main ballroom. "I'll be right back."

Holga chuckled as Kira swept grandly across the ballroom, her skirt swishing around her. "What a lady. Growing up too fast." Her voice caught, and she cleared her throat hastily.

"Tell me about it," Edgin said. "Every day she gets a little bit taller and gets a few more opinions." He laughed, but it died quickly, replaced by an ache in his chest. He turned to Holga. "Listen, I never apologized for what I said to you in the boat after the hag fight. I was way out of line."

Holga looked briefly taken aback. "Wasn't sure you remembered."

Edgin sighed. "Yeah, well, I ought to remember when I behave like a jackass." He put a hand on Holga's arm. "I'm really sorry. I thought I was going to lose Kira, I was terrified, and I took that all out on you. Which is especially terrible considering you've always been there, protecting Kira from danger." He looked around the strange ballroom and the glittering throngs of people. "This is a weird life to raise a child in, and even though I wouldn't have chosen this for Kira in the beginning, I've always felt better knowing you and the others are there looking out for her, being a parent to her."

Holga cleared her throat again, and her eyes looked suspiciously bright under the driftglobe lights. "She's a good kid," Holga said. She dug her elbow into Edgin's ribs affectionately. "You're all right too sometimes, Ed."

"Thanks," Edgin said, rubbing his side. He decided not to mention that she'd probably bruised a rib with her elbow.

CHAPTER 25

Holga was called away to help with an emergency in the kitchen—something about a stove fire, or maybe a gnome on fire. Edgin had trouble understanding the babbling halfling who came to fetch her, but apparently, her muscles were needed for something.

When Kira returned a few minutes later, she pointed out another door off the ballroom that they hadn't checked out yet, but he remembered it from studying the layout of the house.

"Alyanna said that's the theater room." Kira looked up at him hopefully. "Can we go see what they're performing?"

"Might as well," Edgin said, although going by Torlinn's taste in poetry and party themes, this was bound to be another exercise in strangeness. "Maybe we'll find Forge and Simon."

They were in luck. Edgin spotted both of their companions as soon as they entered the darkened room. It wasn't your typical arrangement for a theater. Instead of rows of seats, there were silk-covered couches and divans spread all throughout the room. People lounged on these alone or in groups, eating, drinking, and watching the tableau playing out onstage. Simon appeared to be delivering a platter of snacks to Forge as he sprawled on a couch near the back of the theater.

"Look at that!" Kira said, pointing to the stage.

Edgin used the word "stage" loosely when describing what he was looking at. Platforms arranged at various heights dominated the front of the room. Some were decorated to look like clouds, others like clusters of floating trees or rocks, and still others as flying mounts like griffons or pegasi.

Actors in masks and body paint performed acrobatic feats from platform to platform or acted out battle scenes using the airborne mounts. If there was an overarching story there, Edgin couldn't see it, but it looked like they'd come in right in the middle of the play.

Most interesting, to Edgin's mind, was that a few of the performers seemed to actually be *flying* from platform to platform. They weren't suspended from any wires that he could see, unless they were hidden very well.

"Kira," Edgin said, jerking his head in the direction of backstage. "I think it's time for Operation Invisible Hand."

"Really?" Kira grinned. "Let's do it!" She put her mask back on and cupped her invisibility pendant in one hand. "What am I looking for?"

"See how those acrobats are flying there?" Edgin pointed. "I'm willing to bet they're using some kind of potion for that. They don't look like they're wearing any jewelry, and they're barefooted. If they have flying potions backstage, I want one."

Kira nodded. "I'm ready." She glanced around to make sure no one was watching them, then activated the pendant and vanished from sight.

"Be careful," Edgin said to the empty air.

He took a deep breath and released it. Kira would be fine, he told himself. The performers backstage would be too distracted by the show to catch her. This would be easy pickings. Still, he couldn't help worrying. He would always worry. He was her dad.

He made his way back to where Forge was sitting. The con man was still selecting snacks from the tray Simon held out, his jester's mask sitting beside him on the couch. Edgin decided it was safe to leave his own mask off in the dark theater, so he tucked it into his vest.

"You say the bacon-wrapped scallops are to die for?" Forge was asking as Edgin plopped down next to him.

"For the hundredth time, yes," Simon whispered, rolling his eyes. He glanced at Edgin. "There you are. We were wondering where you'd gone off to. Where's Kira?"

"Backstage to get us some flying potions, I hope," Edgin said, taking a scallop and popping it into his mouth. Rich, buttery, delicious. He could get used to eating like this.

"Good thought," Forge said. "On that note." He lifted the cuff of his pants to reveal a pair of black leather boots with stylish silver buckles fashioned to look like spiders. "I haven't tested them yet, but they worked well for the lute player. Who is currently sleeping off a terrible drinking binge in one of the anterooms," he added. "Drank so much wine, he lost consciousness, poor thing."

"Happens to the best of us," Edgin said. He leaned over to peruse Simon's tray for other treasures. "How's it going with you, Simon?"

"Alyanna's happy," Simon said, adjusting the collar of his shirt as if it were choking him. "She thinks this is her last night and that she'll never have to work a day in her life again."

"She has the right idea," Edgin said, taking a fig tart. "That is the plan, after all. But I was asking about you. What's got you so jumpy, Simon? You're as nervous as . . . what's that expression about the cat and the rocking chairs?"

"As nervous as a cat in a rocking chair," Forge supplied.

"Exactly," Edgin said.

"That's not the expression." Simon scowled at them both.

"Well, I've never liked rocking chairs, so if I were a cat sitting in one, I'd be nervous," Edgin said, shrugging. He pointed to the spot next to him. "Sit down."

"I can't," Simon said peevishly. "I'm supposed to be serving everyone scallops and tarts."

"No one's paying any attention to you." Edgin took the tray out of Simon's hands and put it on his lap, then he pulled the half-elf down beside him. "The plan's going well," he said under his breath. "Everyone's in place, and Kira and I even met Torlinn. He's just carrying around the Staff of Aorth, if you can believe it. I was close enough to touch it earlier."

"Are you serious?" Forge turned his attention from the stage, where two acrobats painted and costumed to look like lions had been performing a complex midair acrobatic maneuver that had somehow gotten their tails tangled. "You're sure it was the staff?"

"Yes, and I'll tell you what, I think it's the genuine article," Edgin said. He nudged Simon. "You see? Everything's going our way."

"But what if I—what if we can't deliver?" Simon asked. "Everyone's gotten their hopes up, and I'm supposed to be a hero, remember?" He tore the bacon off a scallop he'd grabbed from the tray in frustration. "That's what my family expects, but this is bigger than anything I've ever done before. This wizard—I didn't realize how powerful he was until I walked in this place." He looked at Edgin for support. "There's magic everywhere. Torlinn must have been collecting it for decades. I thought it was impressive that he'd beaten a beholder just a few years ago, but that seems like nothing now compared to what I've seen in this place." He stared at his lap. "There's no way my magic could ever compete with his."

"All right, well, now you're starting to freak *me* out," Edgin said. "Simon, we *need* your magic tonight. If you think you're not up for this, or if we're in over our heads—"

"Whoa, whoa, whoa," Forge said, cutting him off. "Let's not start losing focus right now. We are absolutely not in over our heads, and Simon *is* up to this challenge." He turned to the half-elf. "If you truly want to be a hero—and, let me stress, that is *not* required in this case, because no one here is a hero, and Edgin is allergic to heroics anyway—"

"They give me hives," Edgin interjected.

"—then this is the perfect opportunity," Forge continued. "You have a famous ancestor, a legend in magic and lore who probably farted rainbows and rescued kittens from red dragons. Do you know what you absolutely have in common with that man?"

Simon shook his head. "I've never saved a kitten from anything."

"But there's still time for you to start," Forge said, poking Simon in the chest with his index finger. "That's what I'm talking about. This Elminster fellow was just an untested youth like you once. He had to start somewhere, and so do you. This"—he waved his hand at the theater and the manor house at large—"is your chance to begin making a name for yourself. To push yourself and test your limits, just like your ancestor once had to." He looked at Edgin. "We're all pushing our limits, but that's how we find greatness, how we seize bigger lives than the ones we've got now. We don't have to be content with mediocrity."

Edgin wasn't sure he'd ever seen Forge so passionate in one of his speeches. The theater must have been rubbing off on him.

Or maybe he was talking about the things he wanted for himself too, in his own life. Edgin couldn't help thinking back to their conversation in the cave, when the hag was taunting each of them about their weaknesses. She'd mentioned envy in regard to Forge, and Edgin had no trouble seeing that. Forge was more ambitious than all of them put together. He envied the wealth and power that others had, and beneath his genial good humor, he had his own desires and the will to make them happen.

And with good reason, Edgin thought. Life was hard and short, and they had to try to seize what they wanted. No one was going to hand it to them. Edgin had tried the noble life, hoping he'd be taken care of in his turn. That hadn't happened, and he'd lost everything.

He put a hand on Simon's shoulder, feeling the tension in the young man's muscles. "Forge is right," he said. "It's time to show us what you've got, Simon. We need you to commit to this. We're counting on you. Are you with us?"

Simon swallowed, his throat bobbing nervously. "I'll try," he said. "I'm not going to back out, if that's what you're afraid of."

"Good to hear," Forge said, patting Simon on the back. "Now stop tearing up that food and eat some of it." He gestured imperiously to a passing servant and snatched a shot glass off the man's tray. "Here, have a shot of Volo's Folly. I hear it's our host's favorite."

Edgin winced. "Um, maybe you shouldn't—"

But he was too late. Simon tossed back the shot, and his body began to sparkle, just like the people at the bar.

"What did you give me?" Simon demanded, looking down at his

twinkling self. "And that flavor." He licked his lips, then puckered them, going cross-eyed as he fanned the air in front of his mouth. "It's . . . spicy. No, sour. With hints of . . . oh Gods, is that cinnamon and hot peppers? And *mint*? This is the worst thing I've ever had in my mouth, and I accidentally ate grave dirt once."

"Yes, you are looking a little green beneath the shine," Forge said. "Eventually, we'll talk about the grave dirt too, because I have to hear that story, but are you feeling any calmer?"

"I suppose," Simon said as the glittering effect slowly faded. "I'm too distracted by the awful taste to be nervous anymore."

"Mission accomplished then—*oof!*" Edgin said, just as an invisible weight that was roughly the size and shape of his daughter landed on his lap and knocked the breath out of his lungs. "Help, I've been ambushed," he gasped, collapsing back on the sofa.

Simon stood up as Kira giggled and became visible, holding up two small vials filled with blue liquid that shimmered like the ocean on a sunny day. "Got the potions!" she said.

Edgin quickly took them from her and slipped them into the innermost pocket of his vest. "Excellent work," he said, giving her a quick hug before he rolled her off his lap and into the space Simon had vacated. "Did you have any trouble?"

Kira shook her head. "It was easy. Everyone was distracted by the two lions that got tangled up during their act. I heard someone say they had to end the performance early, so Torlinn's going to move up his demonstration of the staff. It's happening in ten minutes."

"Well, that's our cue to get back to the ballroom, then," Edgin said, climbing off the sofa and pulling Kira up after him. He put his cat mask back on, and Forge became the jester again. "Everyone ready?"

They all nodded, and Edgin was pleased to see Simon looked steadier than he had when they'd first started talking.

Everything was going to be fine. They had it all under control.

CHAPTER 26

The ballroom was packed by the time Edgin and the others arrived. Word must have spread that Torlinn's demonstration was imminent. There was a small cleared space in the center of the room, directly beneath the pipe organ, where Torlinn stood holding court with what looked to be some VIP guests, including Lady Sofina. Edgin checked to make sure his mask was in place when he saw her, but she wasn't paying any attention to the crowd. Her gaze was firmly fixed on Torlinn and the Staff of Aorth, which Torlinn held with the emerald pointing toward the floor and the diamond pointing toward the ceiling.

Edgin found them a spot near the back wall by one of the windows, where Kira could stand on the narrow window ledge to see over the heads of the crowd while using Edgin's and Forge's shoulders to help her keep her balance.

"Friends, honored guests, welcome to my home," Torlinn said, his voice magically amplified to carry over the crowd noise. "I'm so happy all of you could be here with me tonight for the first masquerade of the season. I hope you've been relaxing and making yourselves at home." He raised the staff, and a collective hush of anticipation fell over the crowd. "I thought we might have a bit of entertainment to liven things up even more. What say you, friends?"

The crowd whistled and cheered enthusiastically. Torlinn beamed.

"Look at the diamond," Forge whispered to Edgin and Kira.

Edgin watched as Torlinn twirled the staff theatrically, and the diamond began to pulse with a faint glow that gradually got stronger and brighter. The orchestra played some subtle music that thrummed in time with the flashing light. Edgin found himself clenching his fists. He was edgy, and he wasn't sure why.

Maybe it was the artifact itself that was making him uncomfortable. He swore he could feel the power of the thing even from across the room. It hummed, creating a charge in the air that made his back teeth ache. Edgin felt like they stood on an open plain, listening to the thunder of an approaching storm, waiting for it to break and relieve the tension that continued to build.

"Now," Torlinn said, "as a token of my gratitude to all of you for attending my little party, behold! The power of Aorth!"

Every light in the ballroom went out at the same time, plunging the room into darkness.

Just enough moonlight filtered in through the nearby window to allow Edgin to see his companions. He instinctively grabbed Kira's hand, and Forge maneuvered himself in front of her protectively.

"Well, now, this is dramatic," Forge said, his voice deceptively calm.

Fortunately, the darkness didn't last long. The light from the diamond in Torlinn's staff flashed again. Sparks flew from the gem, spiraling toward the ceiling like shooting stars, until the whole orchestra looked like it was bathed in starlight.

Gasps, oohs, and aahs echoed from the crowd, and the music became a soft, dreamlike melody, almost like a lullaby. Then, the light changed, the false starlight becoming a rainbow of colors that grew and expanded as the music picked up tempo. Now there were floating spheres of color drifting along the ceiling, glowing in reds, greens, blues, purples, and yellows, illuminating the faces of the watching crowd as they applauded the performance.

Edgin glanced at the spheres, but mostly he watched Torlinn

and the staff. All throughout the show, it was only the diamond that seemed to glow and pulse and power the spectacle. The emerald at the bottom of the staff remained dark and dormant the whole time. It struck Edgin as strange, but then, he wasn't an expert in magic. Maybe the gem had no power at all and was merely decorative.

As he watched, Torlinn twirled the staff again, and the music swelled, as if the show was approaching its climax. The floating spheres exploded one by one, showering the room in colorful sparks, all of it done in time to the music. Edgin reached out a hand to the falling light and felt the warmth of magic touch his fingers before fading away. His skin tingled strangely, but that too was fleeting, and he thought he might have imagined it.

Simon was right, though. There was more magic in this place than Edgin was comfortable with.

The crowd broke into wild applause and raised their glasses in salute as the music and colors faded, and the ballroom driftglobes came to life again, flooding the room with its normal illumination.

Edgin blinked against the sudden brightness. Across the ballroom, Torlinn bowed and left before the applause died down. According to Alyanna, Torlinn would return the Staff of Aorth to its place in his treasure room, then rejoin the guests afterward for some dancing. She said he was usually gone only a few minutes.

She was right. Less than ten minutes later, Torlinn returned and headed right for the dance floor. The Staff of Aorth was nowhere to be seen.

"That's our cue," Edgin said. "Simon and Holga will be waiting. Time to get what we came for."

According to their drawings of the mansion, there was a short servant's hall on the other side of the door Torlinn had left through that ran the length of the first floor, ending at a back stair that led to the second-floor landing. The rooms up there were off-limits to guests. That was where Simon and Holga would be waiting to meet them.

Edgin led the way casually across the ballroom, stopping for another drink while Forge and Kira grabbed a pair of cream puffs from a passing tray. They mingled, pretending to wave to people they knew, admired the upside-down orchestra again, and finally reached the door Torlinn had used. Alyanna had gotten them a copy of the key for it weeks ago, which Edgin had stashed in his vest.

Edgin handed Forge the key and swept the ballroom with another casual glance, just to make sure no one was watching. He looked for Lady Sofina too, but thankfully she was nowhere in sight.

Forge tried the key in the door. "It works," he said, sounding relieved.

"You didn't trust Alyanna to keep her end of the deal?" Edgin asked. Truth be told, Edgin hadn't entirely trusted her either, but so far, she'd come through with everything she'd promised.

"Don't get me wrong," Forge said. "She seems lovely, and ambitious too, which makes her a woman after my own heart, but she's an unknown. I trust *my* people." He looked at Edgin and Kira as he spoke.

They went through the door, closing and locking it behind them. The hallway beyond was musty, dimly lit by a couple of smaller driftglobes. The loudness of the party was muffled here, and Edgin was surprised by how soothing the sudden quiet was after all the noise and excitement.

He was back in his element, sneaking around and searching for their target. This was the real party.

"Kira," he said, "time for you to disappear. Just in case we meet someone up here, we need you hidden."

Kira nodded and activated her pendant, vanishing from sight. She squeezed Edgin's hand briefly to let him know she was still close by.

The stairs were at the end of the hall, exactly where the drawings had indicated. To the left, a few feet away, was the door to the kitchen and food prep stations. They could hear the clattering of pots and pans and casual cursing from multiple voices. Preparing all that food probably took a small army. Edgin hurried up the stairs, Forge on his heels, before someone could step outside for a break and see them.

The stairs creaked under their weight, but Edgin wasn't too worried. No one in the kitchen would hear them over all that banging and yelling. He hoped that Holga had managed to put the stove fire out. Or the gnome fire, whichever it was.

At the top of the stairs, there was another door, which Alyanna had promised to make sure was unlocked for them. Forge listened at the door, his ear pressed to the wood. This was the tricky part. They were headed into a part of the house where guests definitely weren't allowed to be, and, technically, neither were any but the most senior servants. Alyanna wasn't a senior servant, so if they ran into anyone up here, depending on who it was and how they had to deal with them, it could blow the whole operation.

"Hear anything?" Edgin whispered.

Forge shook his head. He stepped back and eased the door open, standing behind it. "Kira, if you please?"

Kira didn't respond, but Edgin felt a stirring of the air as she passed by him and out into the upstairs hallway. A few seconds later, she pinched his arm. Edgin tried not to jump.

"Kira," he warned. "We're on the job now. Be serious."

A soft giggle. "Sorry. The hallway's clear," she said. "Simon and Holga are waiting, and Holga's wearing her elk mask!"

"Excellent." Cautiously, Edgin stepped out into the hall. His feet sank into plush carpet. More driftglobes hovered in polished brass fixtures along the walls. The air smelled of fresh flowers from vases at either end of the hall.

Simon and Holga were indeed waiting at the far end of the hall, in front of a pair of doors. Holga turned, removing her mask when she saw Edgin, and her shoulders loosened in relief.

"Took you long enough," she whispered.

"We didn't want to make it seem like we were bailing on the party early," Edgin said. He took off his cat mask so he could see better. Forge did the same, and Kira became visible again. "Everyone ready? Where's Alyanna?"

"I'm here." Alyanna hurried down the hall toward them, brandishing one of the butler's keys in her hand. "This'll get us in."

"And no one's going to notice it's gone, right?" Edgin asked.

"Nope. Grimes took the tainted cocktail I gave him and is now sleeping it off next to a lute player," Alyanna said, grinning. "We're in the clear. Let's do this."

There were excited nods all around, and Alyanna slid the key into the lock. There was a soft click, and as the door swung open with nary a sound or disturbance, some of the tension in Edgin's body eased.

And then he got a glimpse of the room beyond the doors, and it was all he could do not to dance around like a boy on holiday.

The room was full of treasures. No fewer than three large chests were situated at the far end of the room. Weapons and art covered the walls. Not the kind of art that you saw in sitting rooms and salons—this art was old and valuable. The kind that would fetch an astounding price on the black market.

In the center of the room, two life-sized statues held pride of place. The one on the left was a depiction of the goddess Selûne, dressed in robes, with a sheer veil over her face that was probably meant to represent the moonlight shining down on her. Edgin had seen such depictions before. The other statue was the god Lathander, arms spread, with his face tilted to the sky, eyes closed in a rapturous expression. In between them, there was a gold display stand, and upon that was the Staff of Aorth, situated vertically with the emerald facing up.

Edgin walked over to examine the staff more closely. Simon came to join him, but he didn't immediately reach for the artifact. "We should wait until we have everything else and are ready to leave before we take it," Simon said. "I don't sense any traps or other magic on the stand, but it's . . ." He hesitated, holding his hand up, palm out toward the staff. He closed his eyes.

"While he's doing the wavy hand magic thing, the rest of you get to work," Edgin said, directing Holga, Kira, Alyanna, and Forge to the chests and art. "Remember the rules: platinum before any other coins, grab the paintings that are easiest to move and conceal, and leave no trace if you can help it."

Immediately, Forge and Alyanna set about picking the locks on the chests while Holga called for Kira to help her remove a painting of a desolate mountain landscape from the wall. A tarrasque roared from the top of the mountain peak, head thrown back in a terrible howl of rage and power. It was by far the creepiest painting, and it would fetch the highest price.

His crew was truly the best.

Edgin turned back to Simon, who still had his eyes closed, hand out toward the staff, as if he were meditating.

"Come on, Simon," he muttered under his breath, trying not to distract the sorcerer. "I want to know this thing's secrets."

Just then, Simon's eyes flew open, and, almost as if he were in a trance, he turned to the statue of Lathander, reaching out his hand to clasp the God's outstretched palm. There was a soft click, and Edgin whirled as he heard the shift and scrape of wood on wood.

A panel on the back wall next to a massive fireplace was shifting aside to reveal a secret passage.

Edgin's mouth dropped open.

"We got a jackpot over here," he said, snapping his fingers to get the others' attention. He went over to Simon and grabbed the half-elf by both cheeks. "Simon the sorcerer, I could kiss you."

"Please don't." Simon pulled away.

The others gathered around the mouth of the dark passage. "Well done," Forge congratulated Simon. "How did you find it?"

"Don't get too excited," Simon said, and that's when Edgin noticed the sorcerer's shoulders were slumped, his expression unhappy. "I cast a spell to make sure there was no additional magic guarding the staff while it was on its stand," Simon explained. "I didn't find any kind of alarm system or anything like that, but there are two magical tethers attached to the statues. One of them runs to the secret door, which conceals it, and when I investigated, I found a hidden button to activate it."

"Where does the other tether go?" Kira asked.

"That's the bad news," Simon said. "It connects to the staff, creating another magical effect." He reached for the staff, and his hand passed right through it as if there wasn't anything there.

Edgin's gut clenched. "It's an illusion," he said. "Torlinn doesn't keep the staff here at all, he just pretends to."

Of course. In a house with so much magic, they should have known it was too easy to get into this room and reach the staff. Even with Alyanna's help and inside knowledge, Torlinn would have been prepared in case one of his servants betrayed him. This room, for all its treasures, was probably just a decoy. Torlinn's most valuable possessions, including the staff, were likely hidden elsewhere.

"So where *does* he keep the staff?" Holga looked at the illusion and then at the dark passage. "Think it's at the end of this?"

"Only one way to find out," Forge said, putting into words what they were all thinking.

Edgin glanced at the loot they'd already gathered in one corner of the room. On its own, it was a sizable haul, and with the flying potions and the wall-climbing boots they'd acquired, they were one swan dive out the second-story window from getting away from this gig free and clear—but without the main thing they'd come for.

And that dark passage sat waiting, the worst, best temptation.

He met Forge's gaze across the room. No great stretch of the imagination to guess what he was thinking. Edgin voiced it for everyone else.

"This room has all kinds of goodies," he said, "but I think Torlinn's hiding the staff and who knows what other treasures in a more secure location, and we might have stumbled right onto it, thanks to Simon."

They all looked back at that passage.

"We need to see what's down there," Kira said in a hushed voice.

Edgin held up a hand. "It's possible we're wrong about this," he said, "and whatever's down there could be dangerous. We need to put it to a vote. All those in favor of taking what we found here and clearing out, raise your hand."

Edgin waited a beat, but no one raised their hand.

"All those in favor of trying our luck in the secret passage?"

Everyone's hand went up. Forge grinned.

"I think that settles it." Edgin pointed to the passage. "Forge and I are in front, with Simon and Kira right behind us, then Alyanna, with Holga watching our backs. We need to move quickly, quietly, and not waste time. Everyone got that?"

There was a soft chorus of "yes," and Simon cast a spell to summon his three globes of dancing lights, which he set to follow just behind Edgin and Forge so they could see where they were going. Holga fiddled with the secret panel and managed to slide it back into place manually, leaving a tiny crack so they could open it again.

They stepped into the passage.

CHAPTER 27

J ust beyond the hidden door, there was a set of stairs leading
down. Cautiously, Edgin led the way, with Forge right behind
him. He listened as they descended, wondering if he would be
able to hear sounds of the party through the walls. They must be
near the servant's areas at the back of the house. But there was nothing. Only silence. Either the walls were very thick or there was some
kind of magic dampening the sound.

At the bottom of the stairs, a passage led off straight ahead—
roughly north, by Edgin's reckoning, assuming he hadn't gotten his
directions confused. The floor and walls here were dirt and some
worked stone. It reminded Edgin vaguely of the hag's lair, minus the
killer plant life.

"Looks like we're beneath the house now," he said. "I wonder
how far this goes."

Fortunately, the passage was wide enough for two to walk abreast,
and the ceiling was high enough that Edgin could stand to his full
height. The tunnel sloped gradually but noticeably down as they
walked. Someone had taken a lot of time and care to excavate this
underground hidey-hole, or whatever it was. Edgin's heartbeat

quickened in trepidation and excitement. What had they stumbled into here?

After several minutes, the passage gradually leveled out, but Edgin thought they had to be deep underground at this point, and it was even money whether they were under Torlinn's mansion any longer.

A light appeared ahead of them at the end of the passage. Edgin slowed the group, holding a finger to his lips for quiet. Forge gestured to himself and then pointed down the passage, silently asking if he should scout ahead. Edgin nodded and halted the group while Forge went on.

Holga came up, holding her axe in her hands. "Not liking this," she said gruffly, but she lowered her voice so only Edgin would hear.

"Me either, if I'm honest," Edgin said. Only a few minutes ago, this had seemed like a great adventure, but now . . . "Is it just me, or does this place seem less like a hidden treasure hold and more like a forgotten dungeon?"

Holga sighed, which Edgin took for agreement. "Don't like that we brought Kira," she said.

Edgin's chest tightened, but he tried to push aside his doubts. "It'll be fine. We'll see what Forge finds up ahead, and then we'll backtrack and get out of here if we need to." He glanced at Holga. "But you'll be watching over her, just in case?"

"Always," Holga said, her eyes glittering with a fierce light as she gripped her axe.

They waited. Edgin could see Forge's silhouette at the end of the passage. He wasn't moving into the room beyond. Edgin stopped himself from calling out to him, just in case there was someone—or something—in the room waiting.

Finally, after what seemed like an age, Forge came slowly back down the passage to them. He had a strange look on his face.

"What?" Edgin demanded. "Gnolls? Hags? Stirges?" Come to think of it, they really should stop going into underground spaces. "What are we looking at here?"

Forge opened his mouth, closed it again. Shook his head. "You really need to see for yourselves," he said, motioning everyone to follow him.

Fantastic, Edgin thought as they trooped down the tunnel to the source of the light. At least it wasn't anything dangerous, or Forge would have been making an effort to be quiet.

They reached the end of the tunnel, which spilled out into a large underground cavern lit by more magical driftglobes.

Edgin stopped, staring at the scene in front of him.

The cavern was done up to resemble the ballroom in Torlinn's mansion, like a strange, underground mirror image. But instead of marble tile, there were dark flagstones. The window treatments were exactly the same as in the mansion, only there were no windows.

And on the ceiling, just like in the ballroom, there was a full orchestra, with a large pipe organ in the center.

No one was manning the instruments. They simply hung there upside down in eerie silence, waiting for someone to come along and play them.

"This is too weird," Simon whispered. Holga nodded.

"Alyanna," Edgin said, "any idea what's going on here?"

The woman shook her head. "Not a clue. I didn't know anything about this place."

Kira stepped closer to Edgin. "Should we go inside?" she asked. She pointed across the ballroom. "There's another door there, just like in the other ballroom upstairs."

"Which led to the bar," Edgin said, nodding as he remembered the layout. "I suppose it wouldn't hurt to check it out, see if there's a mirror of every room in the mansion."

"Maybe a mirror of the treasure room as well," Forge said thoughtfully.

Edgin patted Forge on the arm. "Always optimistic. I like that." The pat became a gentle shove. "You go first and make sure it's safe."

"Somehow I knew you were going to say that," Forge grumbled. "Fine."

He walked onto the dance floor, heading for the opposite side of the room. After about ten feet, the stone beneath his left foot dipped, and there was a loud *click* that echoed in the chamber.

Forge froze. "Oh dear," he managed to say before a loud rumble filled the chamber, and suddenly, one of the violins suspended from the ceiling let out a discordant note, the bow ripping along the strings by itself, the sound ringing painfully in Edgin's ears. The air shimmered around the instrument, and then the violin vanished, replaced by a large boulder dangling precariously above Forge's head.

"It's an illusion!" Simon shouted. "Forge, look out!"

Forge dove out of the way just as the boulder came crashing down, slamming into the floor right where he'd been standing. He rolled, jumped to his feet, and sprinted the rest of the way back to where they were standing in the tunnel.

"All right, that was a bit close," he said, hands braced on his knees as he took great gulps of air while Kira patted him on the back.

"Good reflexes," Holga said. She stared up at the ceiling and the remaining instruments. "Those all fake?" she asked, gesturing to the orchestra.

"I think so," Simon said, squinting up at the ceiling. "It's some kind of trap, obviously, triggered when you step on certain stones crossing the room."

"I think we've seen enough here," Edgin said. "New plan. We have plenty of loot waiting for us upstairs. I say we head back up, then split up. Half of the group will take the loot we already have and get it out of here. That way we make certain we get something for our trouble here tonight." He'd also make sure Kira was in that group to get her to safety. "The rest of us will come back down and explore a little further to try to find the staff. Agreed?"

Everyone nodded. For once, even Forge didn't have an argument to make about the plan.

"Wait, where's Alyanna?" Kira asked, looking around. "She was just here."

Edgin did a fast head count and cursed under his breath. "We're short one crew member," he said, glancing at Forge. "And I think I know where she's gone."

Together they turned and made their way quickly back up the passage toward the secret door. They caught the half-elf right as she reached the secret panel.

"Hold up!" Edgin called, making Alyanna jump and turn to face them guiltily. "You bailed out of the team meeting back there. Going somewhere?"

She crossed her arms. "I was just scouting ahead to make sure the way was clear. You're welcome."

Forge loomed next to her with no trace of his usual affable smile. "You mean you weren't planning to sneak back up here ahead of us and grab all the loot you could carry, perhaps sealing us in for good measure?"

"Of course not!" Alyanna took a step back, almost bumping into Holga, who'd circled behind her and was reaching for the panel, at the same time serving as an imposing wall of muscle and axe.

"Uh-huh," Edgin said. "Well, no harm done, since we're all together again and safe. Let's just get out of here, and we'll go our separate ways as soon as possible."

And good riddance.

He glanced at Holga. "How you doing with that door?"

Holga stood there, grunting, trying to slide the hidden door open. Her face reddened with exertion.

"Everything all right?" Edgin pressed, trying not to let his voice betray any anxiousness.

"The door closed," Holga said, grunting harder as she put all her strength into trying to wrench the panel open. Forge went to help her, and together they pulled as hard as they could, but it was no use. Panting, Holga leaned back against the tunnel wall. "I left it open," she insisted. "Someone shut it, or it closed by itself."

"We're trapped," Alyanna said bleakly. "Aren't we?"

They all looked at Edgin. By the light of Simon's orbs, their faces were pale and tense.

"We can't be sealed in," Edgin said, trying to sound reasonable as he made his way to the panel. "There's got to be a lock here to pick or a mechanism we can disable. Simon, bring your light thingies closer."

Edgin crouched by the door, his heart pounding as he ran his fingers along the edges, searching for something—a knob, a latch, a hinge—anything that he could manipulate to force the door open.

There was nothing. The panel was sealed tight, and no amount of prodding or prying made it move. Edgin didn't realize he was sweating and swearing until Holga put her hand on his shoulder and gently tugged him to his feet.

"It's no use, Ed," she said quietly.

"What do you mean it's no use?" Edgin snapped, pulling away

from her. "If I don't keep looking, it means we're *trapped* here! It means we can't get out, so we're either going to die down here in the dark or hope that Torlinn finds us and turns us in to the authorities in Longsaddle or Neverwinter or wherever he wants us to rot in prison." Edgin ran his hands through his hair, tugging on the strands. "It means this is all my fault. I dragged my family down here and trapped them!"

He was breathing hard. The walls of the tunnel seemed to be closing in. All the anger, fear, and helplessness he'd felt over the past nine years suddenly boiled up inside of Edgin all at once. He turned and punched the tunnel wall.

Pain exploded in his knuckles, shocking him out of his rage. "OW!" he cried, slumping against the wall. "That was . . . OW!"

"Dad!" Kira ran over to him and threw her arms around his waist. "It's all right, Dad," she said shakily. "It's going to be all right."

Edgin didn't know whether he wanted to laugh or cry as he stood there while his daughter comforted him. He should be the one comforting her, *protecting* her. But he'd failed at that too, just like he'd failed at everything else. Failure as a Harper. Failure as a father.

The others stood there, huddled in an uncertain group. Finally, Holga sighed and came over to him. She sat down near the tunnel wall and pulled him and Kira down next to her. The others automatically followed suit, until they were sitting in a loose circle, the lights hovering just above their heads. The only sound in the tunnel was the rasp of their breathing.

"We voted," Holga said after a moment.

Edgin looked up at her in confusion. "What?"

She shrugged. "We voted to come down here. You didn't drag us anywhere."

"Yes, but—"

"No, she's right," Simon said glumly. "I'm regretting it, but . . . it's not your fault, Edgin. We chose this."

"We are all capable of making our own decisions," Forge pointed out. "Misguided though they sometimes turn out to be."

"And at least we're together," Kira said, her voice muffled as she buried her face in Edgin's shoulder, hugging him tightly. "That's all I care about."

Edgin stroked her hair, his heart breaking. "You deserve better than this," he said.

She laughed, but there was a little bit of a sob in it. "You always say that," she said. "When will you believe I have everything I want here? It's like you said. We're a family."

Edgin stilled. He *had* said that, hadn't he? He flushed, glancing at the others, but they hadn't corrected him. And in that moment, he realized, as strange as it was, he really had come to think of all of them—well, except Alyanna—as family. A strange, dysfunctional, often dishonest family, but a family nonetheless.

Why had he waited so long to admit that to himself? Maybe it was because he was afraid if he admitted what was important to him, it would all be taken away from him, just like last time with Zia. But now that they were trapped down here, and there was a good chance they were going to either die or be caught, Edgin found he didn't want to deny it to himself anymore. Out of the tragedy of his past, he'd made a life for himself that made him happy, and he'd surrounded himself with people he cared about. They *were* his family.

And he wasn't going to fail them now. He wasn't just going to sit here feeling sorry for himself. He was the leader, the planner, the plotter. He just had to plot their way out of this mess.

Alyanna sighed, leaning back against the tunnel wall. "It's not like I can complain either," she said. "I wanted to get out of here so bad, and you all were my ticket. Guess if I'm going to die down here, this isn't a bad bunch to do it with."

"Yeah, we haven't forgotten about the part where you were about to betray us and leave us for dead," Simon reminded her.

"We're not going to die," Holga said, sounding exasperated. "We just have to get out."

"Sounds great," Alyanna said, "but how—"

"Holga's right," Edgin said, sitting up. His knuckles were still bruised and aching—punching walls was truly counterproductive—but he ignored the pain. "There has to be a way out of here. We just need to explore the rest of this weird mirror house, or death dungeon, whatever you want to call it." He turned to Alyanna. "You're sure Torlinn never mentioned having a death trap dungeon at any of the employee meetings?"

"I'm pretty sure I would have remembered," Alyanna said dryly. Then she paled. "But what if . . . what if the servants who left . . . the rumors about party guests going missing . . . you don't think they ended up down here somehow, do you?"

They all looked at one another, the unspoken thought being, *And they were never heard from again.*

"All right, let's not get ahead of ourselves," Edgin said. "We don't know anything yet. For now, we focus on getting out of here, and since I'm theorizing that the only way out is *through,* then we go through."

And that meant confronting the ballroom and its potentially deadly falling rocks. It also meant dragging Alyanna with them and hoping she didn't choose the wrong moment to betray them. Well, no time like the present.

Edgin led the group back down the passage to the underground ballroom. They clustered in the doorway while Edgin and Forge crouched to examine the flagstone floor. The depression in the stone where Forge had activated the trap was still visible, and of course the giant boulder lay nearby, an ominous warning.

Edgin's thoughts raced. This place was a mirror of the ballroom above. The Staff of Aorth had two gems, one at each end, and the artifact itself had a dual nature, according to Forge. Something about that tickled his senses, telling him it was connected, but how? What was the purpose? And why was Torlinn seemingly using a powerful artifact for party tricks and light shows?

Had the people that disappeared somehow figured out what was going on in this place?

Edgin shook his head. The "why" didn't matter right now. They could figure that part out later. Right now, they were in the middle of a puzzle they had to solve if they wanted to move forward.

"If this room is supposed to be a mirror of the one in the manor," Edgin said, "why isn't there any music? Seems like an important detail to leave out."

"Aside from the fact there's no one to listen to it," Forge pointed out, "there aren't any musicians."

"No, there was music," Simon said. "The violin—or the illusion of it—made a sound right before the boulder fell."

"That wasn't music," Kira said, shuddering. "That was horrible."

"Right," Edgin said, pointing to her. "Ear-bleedingly horrible, but maybe that was because Forge stepped on the trap." He clenched his fist in sudden realization. "It wasn't music, because Forge wasn't dancing! We need music and dancers to beat the trap!"

Holga looked at him with a cocked eyebrow. "Seems overly complicated."

"But it does make a certain kind of sense, if you know Torlinn," Alyanna said thoughtfully. "He loves convoluted and elaborate displays, especially of magic." She rolled her eyes. "He cackles gleefully for weeks while he's planning his party themes."

"He really is the worst dragonborn ever," Edgin agreed. "All right, so if my theory is correct, then all we have to do is dance our way across the floor to the door on the opposite side. No problem!"

The others stared at him.

"If you're wrong, we'll look real stupid for a few seconds, and then we'll be crushed by rocks," Holga said.

"Succinctly put, as always," Forge said, with a tip of an imaginary cap to Holga. "Let me point out an alternate suggestion. We do have the flying potions Kira so kindly acquired for us, and I have the climbing boots that I could use to walk along the walls. With those tools at our disposal, we could avoid the floor altogether."

"True," Edgin said, "but we don't know what's waiting for us on the other side of this. There could be more traps, and we might need those potions later on." He looked down at Forge's boots. "Could you use those to walk along the walls to the other side of the ballroom, then throw them across to us, and we could all get around the trap that way?"

Forge shrugged. "Possibly, but it took me a while wearing the boots for the magic to activate. I'm not sure how long it would take for everyone to use them. It might be hours."

Edgin didn't think they had that kind of time. "Do you think you could carry someone else and still use them?"

"I could probably carry Kira," Forge said, "but I don't think I could manage any of the rest of you. The magic holds my weight, but it doesn't feel like it's meant for more than one person."

"Good enough," Edgin said. "Take Kira across. The rest of us will try our luck on the dance floor." He pointed to Simon. "You and Alyanna pair up. Holga and I will go first. Everyone ready?"

They nodded. Edgin turned to Holga, who had her arms crossed, a scowl on her face. "What?" he said. "Don't worry, I'm an excellent dancer."

"No," she said flatly.

Edgin waved an impatient hand. "We'll just do the dance that Kira and I did earlier. There's nothing to it, just some clapping and spinning and prancing around."

"I'd rather be crushed by the boulder."

Edgin put a hand dramatically over his heart. "You wound me, fair one. Will you not favor me with your company for just one dance so that I may die a happy man?"

"Or I could kill you right now." Holga brandished her axe.

"I want to see you dance, Holga!" Kira said, smiling at her encouragingly. "You'll be great!"

Edgin watched with amusement as Holga's resolve cracked and shattered into a million pieces under the weight of Kira's smile. She heaved an exasperated sigh.

"Fine," she said, teeth gritted. "Let's get it over with."

They moved quickly. Forge activated the boots, scooped up Kira, and walked along the cavern walls to the other side of the ballroom without any trouble. While they stood in the opposite doorway, Edgin took Holga's hands. He knew that if he so much as cracked a joke she would throw him in the path of a falling boulder, so he kept his face expressionless and started into the dance he and Kira had done earlier, gliding out onto the stone floor, trying his best to pretend there wasn't a gruesome death hovering above their heads. He had a flying potion palmed in his right hand, just in case.

As they spun in a circle, music suddenly filled the room. Edgin instinctively flinched, but it wasn't the discordant note that had preceded the boulder falling. It was the same music that had played during his and Kira's dance number. He risked a glance above them and saw that the illusory instruments were all playing at once, an almost perfect mirror for the ballroom in the mansion.

Holga was stiff as a board in his arms, her face set in a formidable frown. Edgin squeezed her hand. "Lighten up," he said. "It's working, and you're dancing just fine."

"I know I am," Holga snapped. "I'm a terrific dancer."

"Oh, well . . ." Edgin was confused. "Then why—"

"Because I haven't danced with anyone since Marlamin," Holga said, her face reddening. "It's just . . . not the same with someone else."

"I see," Edgin said quietly. "Sorry, I didn't think."

"It's okay," Holga muttered. "It's in the past anyway."

But that didn't mean it didn't still hurt. Edgin knew what that was like. He started to say something else, but suddenly he noticed they were dancing to the edge of the ballroom and off the stone floor.

Safe and sound.

"You did it!" Kira clapped her hands and ran to them, throwing her arms around them both. Edgin hugged her back, and Holga ruffled her hair affectionately.

"See? Easy," Edgin said, motioning to Simon and Alyanna. "You two are next."

The music was still playing. Simon and Alyanna danced across the room in a kind of awkward waltz, their steps faltering as they kept glancing up at the illusionary orchestra.

"Don't look up, just keep dancing," Edgin said, gesturing at them to hurry. "You're almost there. Come on!"

But something was wrong. The music abruptly turned to a shrieking mess of squealing notes, and the floor beneath Simon and Alyanna dipped, just like it had for Forge. The flautist section of the orchestra shimmered above their heads, and an ominous rumble echoed through the chamber.

"Move it!" Holga yelled, but Simon and Alyanna didn't need to be told. Holding hands, they ran the rest of the way across the ballroom as fast as they could, activating two other trapped floor stones as they went. Boulders rained down around them, but Simon and Alyanna dove off the dance floor and rolled to the safety of the doorway just as the last boulder crashed down a few feet away.

Dust rose in thick clouds throughout the room, making everyone cough. Edgin knelt next to Simon and Alyanna, checking them over for injuries. "You two intact?"

"I think so," Simon said, wiping a trickle of sweat from his temple. "That was close."

"I don't understand why it didn't work," Alyanna complained, sitting up and dusting herself off. "We danced, didn't we?"

"Awkwardly, but yes," Edgin said. "I could give you a few pointers if you—" He broke off as the pair glared at him.

"From what I could see, the only thing that was different was the type of dance," Forge said. "You did a waltz while Edgin and Holga did—what was that, anyway?"

"The Light-Footed Maiden," Kira supplied. "Didn't they say it was Torlinn's favorite dance or something?"

"Torlinn's favorite," Edgin murmured, as realization dawned. "Of course! It had to be a specific type of dance! Nice work remembering that, Kira."

Simon stood up. "I hate this party," he grumbled. "No more parties after this. Let it be known, I'm never having fun again."

Edgin glanced at the ruined dance floor, now choked with boulders. "You just need to find the right kind of party," he said. "Once we get out of here, we'll do just that, but for now, we need to move on."

And confront whatever other deadly traps awaited them.

CHAPTER 28

Beyond the ballroom, there was a short tunnel that ended in a closed door. They waited while Forge listened, then checked the door and the lock for any signs of a trap. Finally, he shook his head and motioned the others back while he tried the latch. There was a soft creak.

"It's unlocked," Forge said. "Everyone brace yourselves."

He didn't need to warn them. After the boulder ballroom, everyone was on edge. Edgin kept Kira close beside him as Forge pulled the door open.

The room beyond was familiar in the same way the ballroom had been. It was the bar Edgin and Kira had visited, positioned just off the ballroom, exactly as it had been in the mansion. He wondered if the entire layout was the same. No, it couldn't be. There'd been only one exit from the boulder ballroom, whereas in the mansion there had been several. That meant this was at least a smaller version of the mansion above. Edgin was glad. He had no desire to trek through dozens and dozens of trapped rooms trying to find an exit.

Instead of a polished wood bar, there was a long stone slab covered in drinks of all kinds, just as the bar had been upstairs. To their right was another closed door, which, if the pattern continued, would lead into a mirror of the library. Forge and Simon went to examine that door, but after a few minutes, they came back to the bar, frowning.

"It's magically locked," Simon said. "I tried to dispel it, but it's too strong for my magic." He looked away, jaw tight.

"Don't worry about it," Edgin said. "I didn't expect you to be able to open it. This is just another puzzle room we need to figure out."

"What's the puzzle this time then?" Alyanna asked. She paced in front of the bar, examining each of the cocktails. "Are we supposed to drink one of these?"

"And what happens if we drink the wrong one?" Forge crossed his arms, looking doubtfully at all the choices.

"Upstairs, people would have funny things happen to them when they drank," Kira said, "like the people who sparkled or got fake muscles."

"So down here, if we drink the wrong drink, at best we'll be poisoned," Edgin said. "At worst . . ." He let the thought trail off.

"Wonderful," Holga said. She squared her shoulders. "I'm not choosing, but it ought to be me that drinks."

"Why you?" Edgin said sharply, at the same time Forge was nodding in agreement with her.

Holga tapped her chest. "I'm the strongest. Biggest muscles. I can take it."

"That is not how poison works," Edgin said, rubbing his temples in frustration. "All right, everyone, think. Which drink is it? There's got to be a clue here somewhere."

Simon looked thoughtfully at Kira. "The Light-Footed Maiden—you said that was Torlinn's favorite dance. Did you happen to hear if he had a favorite drink too?"

Kira's eyes lit up. "He did! It was . . ." Her brow furrowed as she tried to recall.

"Volo's Folly," Holga said, wrinkling her nose. "I served dozens of them. They smelled funny, like mint and hot sauce."

"It's a terrible drink," Simon agreed.

"Perfect!" Edgin said. "Find me a Volo's Folly!"

They combed the bar, carefully sniffing each of the drinks until finally Holga found one in a shot glass near the end of the bar. She lifted it to her nose and sniffed again just to make sure. She gagged. "Yep, this is it."

"Great," Edgin said. "Now we'll draw lots to see who—"

Holga tossed back the shot.

"Drinks," Edgin said, throwing up his hands. He swore sometimes Holga was worse than Kira in the *listening to instructions* department.

They all stood around Holga, tense, waiting for something to happen.

"She's not turning green in the face or choking," Alyanna said. "That's got to be a good sign, right?"

"But nothing else is happening," Forge said. "What are we missing?"

"Maybe she should try the door," Simon suggested.

"Couldn't hurt," Holga said, letting out a minty belch. She walked over to the door, hesitated, then grasped the latch and pulled.

The door swung open.

The group let out a collective cheer. Edgin punched the air while Kira ran to give Holga a huge hug.

They'd done it, and no one had suffered a scratch. Maybe they were getting the hang of this dungeon.

Inside the underground library, dusty wooden bookshelves were arranged along the walls, filled with hundreds, if not thousands of books. There was even an upper balcony with a wrought iron railing, just like there had been above in the mansion. Instead of chairs set out for a lecture, there were several statues in various poses throughout the room. There was a door on the north wall, which was predictably locked with strong magic. As before, they weren't getting out of here until they figured out the puzzle.

"Each of these rooms just gets creepier," Forge said as he examined the closest statue. It depicted a cleric on her knees clutching a holy symbol of Tymora. Stone tears streamed down her face, her arms raised as if in supplication to her goddess.

"Nobody touches anything until we figure out what we're looking for," Edgin warned them as they spread out through the room. "And watch your step. We don't want to trigger more falling rocks."

Holga glanced up at the ceiling, and Edgin followed her gaze, but there was no orchestra or any other objects dangling above their heads, just smooth stone interspersed with some stalactites. Actual stalactites, as far as he could tell—no ropers this time around.

"What was going on in the library in the mansion?" Simon asked. "Were there certain books on display?"

"Worse," Edgin said, wincing. "There was a poetry reading in progress." He brightened. "But the woman giving the lecture did make a point of saying it was one of Torlinn's favorites."

"So Torlinn was giving clues about each of these rooms, like he knew *someone* was going to end up down here," Simon mused. "Do you think he found out about us and our plan?"

"I think it's bigger than that," Edgin said grimly. "I think all this is connected to the staff and to the other people that have gone missing, like Alyanna was saying."

"Well, if we survive this, I'm not sticking around to ask him about it," Forge said, turning away from the statue. "I just want to get the staff and get out of here. What book was the poem from?"

Edgin pursed his lips. His mind was a blank. He looked to Kira for help. "You remember it, don't you? Couple of verses that went on and on and made you want to stab yourself in the eye."

"Um." Kira shook her head, looking anxious. "I wasn't really paying attention."

"Neither was I." Edgin held up his hands defensively when the others glared at him. "How were we supposed to know there'd be a test later in a murder dungeon? I don't know about you, but that's not the kind of thing that happens at the parties I attend!"

"Great," Alyanna said, sweeping her hand in front of her to encompass the thousands of books. "We just need to choose one at random and hope it's right."

There was a collective groan. Forge pointed to the shelves. "All right, spread out. We can at least look for a poetry section, and maybe the title will jog Edgin and Kira's memory."

They spent the next fifteen minutes searching the ground floor while Forge used his boots to scour the upper level, but they found no poetry section. In fact, there didn't seem to be any rhyme or reason to the arrangement of the books. They weren't shelved alphabetically, or by subject, or by author, or even by color.

"This is ridiculous," Edgin said. "Where did he get all these books anyway? Are they even real?" He reached for one as he spoke.

"Don't!" Simon grabbed his wrist. "If we grab the wrong one, it'll probably trigger the trap!"

"Of course we're going to trigger the trap!" Edgin snapped. "Look at this place. What are the odds that we'll pull a book at random and it'll be the right one? Let's just pick one and get it over with."

"Works for me," Holga said. "We triggered the boulder trap and escaped. How bad could this be?"

They all stared at her incredulously.

"What?" She shrugged.

"Way to tempt fate, Holga," Alyanna said, sighing. "All right, I'll grab one. Everybody ready?"

Forge drew his dagger while Holga lifted her axe. Edgin made sure Kira was close by and that Simon was ready to cast . . . something. "Let's do it," he said.

Alyanna nodded, reached for the nearest shelf, and pulled out a book with a red leather cover. "*The Haberdasher's Harrowing Day*," she read from the spine. "Sounds riveting. Now what do I do with this?"

"Try the door," Edgin suggested. His gaze swept the room again. It was eerily quiet. Too quiet. He'd expected something terrible to happen as soon as Alyanna grabbed the book, which honestly would have been preferable to this tension.

Alyanna walked over to the door, still holding the book in her hands. She tried the latch, but the door didn't budge.

"We're still locked in," Forge said. "Oh Gods, you don't think we have to try every book, do you?"

Holga groaned, and Kira made a face. "I don't want to be stuck in here forever," she said.

"We won't be," Edgin assured her. "Holga, maybe it's time we tried to force the door, or—" He stopped. Listening. "Did you hear that?"

"Hear what?" Holga cocked her head. Her eyes narrowed. "Wait, I hear it now. It sounds like . . ."

"Like thunder or . . . someone pounding on something far away," Simon said.

The sound was growing louder. A distant *boom boom boom boom.* It couldn't be thunder. They were too far underground to hear anything like that.

Forge frowned. "It almost sounds like—"

"Footsteps," Edgin said, "coming closer . . . running . . ." He spun to face the back wall. *Boom. Boom. Boom. Boom.* "Heads up, everybody!"

BOOM.

A section of bookshelves exploded, throwing paper and splintered wood in every direction. Edgin grabbed Kira and ducked behind the nearest statue for cover. He peeked out and saw that the back of the library had a false wall. Another dark tunnel gaped from behind the destroyed bookshelves, and there, emerging from the shadows, was a huge, multi-legged lizard creature. It easily filled the space at the back of the library, its bluish-gray body covered in jagged spikes. Wide, fanged jaws opened, dripping viscous drool as the monster sniffed the air and growled, but before Edgin could study it further, he heard Simon shout.

"Don't look directly at it!" he cried. "It's a basilisk! If you catch its gaze, it'll turn you to stone!"

CHAPTER 29

Edgin tore his eyes away from the creature, tipping his head back to look up at the statue he crouched behind. It was the cleric of Tymora. With a jolt, Edgin realized that he *recognized* her. He hadn't at first because when he'd seen her earlier, she was wearing a mask. It was the elven woman they'd spoken to during the poetry reading upstairs. The one who hadn't paid attention to the poem either. Now she was somehow down here, on her knees, staring at the sky and praying to her goddess.

Except she wasn't really staring at the sky. She was staring into the face of the basilisk that had turned her to stone.

They were in trouble.

The creature charged, butting aside the wrecked bookshelves. Holga raised her axe and came at it from the side, sinking the axe blade deep into its hide. The creature howled and spun toward her, but Holga kept her eyes on the ground.

Big and powerful, but it could also be hurt. "All right, everyone, let's do this," Edgin yelled. "Holga needs backup. Attack it from anywhere but the front, and don't look it in the eyes!"

The others moved at his command. Simon and Alyanna grabbed

another of the fallen bookshelves and braced it awkwardly on its side to create a barrier while Simon started casting a spell. Forge ran behind Edgin, grabbing Kira and using his boots to run up the wall with her to the balcony. *Good.* She'd be relatively safe up there as long as she didn't meet the creature's gaze.

Edgin took his reinforced lute off his back. He'd brought it along to the party just in case, but he hadn't touched it all night. Grabbing it by the neck, he charged and swung it as hard as he could at the basilisk, connecting with its plated body.

It was like hitting stone with a stick. The monster didn't even flinch.

Edgin scrambled back as the basilisk swung its head toward him, catching him in the chest and knocking him flat to the ground. He rolled to get out from under the creature's legs before he could be crushed, and for just a split second, he looked up and caught the basilisk's gaze.

A strange, heavy sensation crawled over Edgin's limbs. His fingers felt stiff, his tongue suddenly thick in his mouth. The sounds of the battle became distant and muddled. It felt like everything was slowing down, though his heart was still hammering wildly in his chest.

No, no, this couldn't be happening. He wasn't going to let it. The others needed him.

With a ragged shout, Edgin forced his sluggish limbs to move, pulling himself to his feet and backing away from the basilisk. With every step, he shrugged off more of the magic that had been trying to take hold of him and turn him into a statue.

That had been close.

Thwarted, the basilisk turned around and lunged at Holga, grabbing her axe blade like it was a toothpick and shaking her like a rag doll. Holga held on stubbornly, keeping her eyes closed as she engaged in a tug-of-war with the creature.

"Simon!" Edgin cried, swinging his lute again, this time aiming for one of the creature's many legs. "Magic, please! Ideally sometime today!"

"He's working on it!" Alyanna hollered back. "Stop distracting him!"

A dagger sailed past Edgin's shoulder and buried itself in the creature's backside. Edgin glanced behind and above him to see Forge and Kira standing at the balcony railing. Forge had thrown the dagger, and now he and Kira were working to push one of the heavier statues toward the edge of the balcony. They were going to try to drop it on the basilisk. Edgin hastily got out of the way.

But in the meantime, the basilisk won the tug-of-war. Edgin watched, heart in his throat, as it casually tossed Holga across the room. Her axe went flying in the opposite direction, and her body slammed into the bookshelves. She collapsed, curling in on herself in the corner.

"Holga!"

It was Kira screaming.

Edgin dropped to his belly as the creature swung around, barely missing him with its spiked tail. He rolled clear just as Forge and Kira tipped the statue over the rail. It hit the basilisk in the head, shattering against its spikes in an explosion of jagged stone shards. The creature lost its balance under the blow and collapsed onto its stomach, looking momentarily stunned.

"Simon!" Edgin hollered. "Magic!" He listened for the sound of arcane gibberish, something to indicate Simon was attempting a spell, but he heard nothing.

Cursing in frustration, Edgin leaped to his feet and ran to where Holga was lying prone on the floor. She groaned when he touched her shoulder. "Are you all right?" he demanded.

"M-f-fine," Holga said, slurring the word alarmingly. "Getting a second wind. Any second now."

"'Course you are," Edgin said, hurriedly rummaging in his vest pocket. The basilisk was slowly getting back to its feet, shaking its head and sending stone shards flying. "Never doubted it. We're going to fix you up, turn you into a super basilisk killer. How's that sound?"

"If you s-say so." Holga looked at Edgin blearily as he pressed two potion vials into her hands. "What're these?"

"Drink the red one first, then the blue one," Edgin said. "Side effects may include headache and dizziness, followed by impressive battle advantages." He got to his feet and stood in front of Holga as the creature growled loudly and swung its head back and forth, as if trying to decide whether to go for Edgin and Holga on one side of the library, or Alyanna and Simon on the other.

Edgin made the choice for it. He downed the other blue potion in his pocket, then took up his lute, belting out the opening lines to a song with his head high and his eyes closed.

> There once was a lizard
> with a terrible face
> Sharp of form but short of grace
> Turned all to stone
> But throw us a bone
> We just want it to give us some space!

The ground shook. Edgin wasn't looking directly at the basilisk, but he was pretty sure the creature was charging in his general direction. He felt the hot, sour gust of the creature's breath on his face right before he jumped straight into the air and took flight, opening his eyes as he soared up to the second level of the library, the power of the flying potion holding him aloft.

The basilisk slipped, its clawed feet skittering across the stone as it jumped, snapping at Edgin with its jaws, but it couldn't reach him. The creature let out a roar of rage and frustration.

"Not listening and not looking at you," Edgin said airily, and continued to sing his improvised basilisk ballad and pluck at his lute strings.

He glanced down to see Holga back on her feet, the healing potion having taken care of her head wound. She stalked across the room while the basilisk was distracted, snatched up her axe, and, with a murderous cry, she downed the second flying potion and launched herself into the air like a flying storm of muscled death.

"Go Holga!" Kira shouted. "Get it!"

The whites of Holga's eyes were very large, her jaw clenched with rage as she bore down on the basilisk. At the last second, she veered up sharply, flipping in midair and hovering above the nest of spikes on the creature's back. She brought her axe down, cleaving into the thing's neck. The axe blade cut deep, and the basilisk let out a howl of pain as its blood ran freely onto the library floor. Holga yanked out her axe and struck again before the creature could recover, and with a third chop, the basilisk's head came off its body and rolled across the floor in a red, soppy mess.

"Oh, that's going to need more than a bandage," Edgin said, but the joke wasn't as gratifying as he'd hoped because he started gagging at the stench of basilisk blood that filled the chamber.

He floated slowly to the floor, careful to avoid the spreading blood, while Holga cleaned her axe on the thing's hide. Forge and Kira came down from the balcony, and Edgin made his way over to where Alyanna and Simon were still behind one of the tipped-over bookshelves.

"You two all right back here?" Edgin asked, looking at Simon, who was sweating profusely, his hands clasped together like he was trying to keep them from trembling.

"We're fine," Alyanna said. She had her hand on Simon's shoulder. "Just a little shaken up."

Simon pulled away from her. "I couldn't even get one spell off! Not even one!" He kicked at the ruined bookshelf, scattering books everywhere. "I tried, though!" He looked at Edgin beseechingly. "I really tried! This is why I'll never be a great sorcerer. Hells, I'll never be a sorcerer at all if I can't get my magic to work when I need it. You'll all throw me out of the group, and I'll deserve it because I can't come through for you. It's hopeless!"

Edgin considered Simon as his rant wound down and he plopped on his backside on the floor. Edgin glanced at Kira, and then came over and sat down beside Simon.

"Look, we don't have a lot of time for pep talks here, so I'll make this short and sweet," he said. "Yes, we could have used your magic in that fight, but Holga had it handled. She came through when we needed her, and I think—I hope—the times when we really need your magic, you'll come through too."

"But how can you know that," Simon asked, "when everything I do is so hit and miss?"

Edgin shrugged. "I know I'm at least going to give you a chance, because you came through for Kira when she needed you in the hag's cave, and you didn't even know her then." He patted Simon's shoulder. "Maybe you're not as hopeless as you think."

Simon blinked. "So, you're not throwing me out of the group?"

"Well," Edgin said, "let's see if we survive this death dungeon first, and then I'll decide. Sound good?"

Kira swatted him on the arm. "Dad!" she scolded. "We're not throwing him out."

Edgin let out a dramatic sigh. "Looks like our leader has spoken. Chin up, Simon, we're getting out of here."

"Do I sense a plan in that confident tone of voice?" Forge asked hopefully as he held out a hand to pull Simon to his feet.

"Something resembling a plan is forming," Edgin confirmed.

"Door's open now," Holga called out from across the room. She'd finished cleaning her axe and was standing over by the library exit with her hand on the latch.

"Hold that thought," Edgin said, and pointed to the gaping hole in the wall where the basilisk had smashed through the bookshelves. "I want to see what's back there. Maybe we can get behind the scenes of this weird play and take a shortcut out of here."

"So far, I like this plan," Forge said.

Simon summoned his lights again and sent them drifting over to the newly exposed tunnel. It curved away into the distance and ended in what looked like a T-shaped intersection. Edgin and Forge again took point, and they set off down the tunnel. At the intersection, Edgin chose to go right, hoping they weren't being led into a maze, but when he glanced to the left, he saw the tunnel dead-ended in a pile of collapsed stone blocking the passage.

"Looks like the caves here aren't as sturdy as they look," Alyanna said. "I wonder how long it took Torlinn to have this all dug out."

"And how long it took to transport a basilisk down here to be part of a trap," Simon said. "Can you imagine? I hope there are no more where that came from."

They continued down the tunnel until, up ahead, Edgin saw light. It looked like more driftglobes, but there were sounds as well—soft snorts, growls, and occasionally some high-pitched yips, like dogs barking. The tunnel curved, and Edgin stopped to peek around the wall to see what lay ahead of them.

"Oh boy," he said.

"What?" Forge demanded. "*Is* it another basilisk?"

"Nope, not a basilisk," Edgin said, "but if you're in the market for any other monsters, Torlinn's got quite the menagerie in here."

The rest of the group came slowly around the corner, where the tunnel emptied out into another large chamber. Two rows of cages were separated by a central pathway. Some of the cages were empty, including one that had its door hanging open. Edgin suspected that up until a few minutes ago, that might have been the basilisk's home.

The rest of the cages were very occupied.

To their right, a pair of giant spiders rested in the center of a thick white web that filled the cage they were in. Their long, hairy legs made Edgin shudder, and their glossy black eyes fixed on the group as they shuffled cautiously down the path between the cages.

Opposite the spiders was a group of four wolves, two black and two gray, but they were bigger than any wolves Edgin had ever seen in the forests around Targos. Their teeth were large and sharp as their lips pulled back in a chorus of snarls. Bones littered the floor of their cage. Edgin didn't have to look too closely to know they weren't animal bones.

"Dire wolves," Holga said.

"Are you sure?" Alyanna asked.

Holga nodded. "My tribe used to hunt them. Nasty beasts."

The wolves continued to growl as the group walked past, their eyes glowing yellow in the light of the driftglobes. Kira pressed her body against Edgin's leg. He put his arm around her shoulders.

"It's all right," he said. "Just don't get near the bars, and we'll be fine."

There were some kobolds snoring in the next cage, and in the one across from it there was a huge two-headed snake coiled up in the corner. Edgin was so distracted watching the heads—which were easily the size of his thighs—bob and bump against each other, tongues flicking the air, that he didn't immediately register that Kira was tugging on his arm.

"Dad," she whispered.

"It's all right," he repeated, thinking she wanted comfort. "The snake's too big to get through the bars. Seriously, look at the size of that thing."

"No, Dad, *look*," Kira said, tugging harder. "Over there."

Edgin turned and saw a hunched figure leaning against the back wall of the last cage, wrapped in a filthy brown robe, head bent as if they were asleep. A hood covered their face, obscuring any clues to their identity. As the group drew closer, the figure shifted and raised their head.

Edgin sucked in a breath. Kira dug her fingernails into his arm until it hurt, and the rest of the group just stood frozen.

"T-Torlinn?" Alyanna whispered.

CHAPTER 30

The dragonborn, who bore a striking resemblance to Torlinn—well, if Torlinn had suddenly decided not to eat, sleep, or bathe for several months—raised a shaky, scaled claw and pulled back his hood, squinting at them in the light. "How do you know my name?" he asked. His voice was little more than a croak, as if he hadn't used it in a very long time.

"We . . . er . . . I mean." Edgin cleared his throat and tried to process what was going on here. "You . . . *you* . . . are Torlinn?" he asked. "Torlinn, the wizard who owns the mansion up top and the murder dungeon down here?"

Torlinn blinked at him. "I . . . yes, I once owned the estate aboveground." His expression turned dark with hate, so quickly it took Edgin's breath away. "It was Sharrestren who built the dungeon and imprisoned me here."

"I'm sorry, who is Sharrestren?" Forge asked, stepping forward. "Hello," he said, waving when the dragonborn tilted his head to look at him. "Sorry, we're probably being rude, it's just we've found ourselves trapped and are trying to find a way out."

"Plus, we just fought a basilisk, so we're all very tired, and this was a twist we did not see coming," Edgin added.

Torlinn looked them up and down, taking in the blood and dirt stains, their torn clothing and exhausted faces. "You've come farther than any of the others," he said. "They all perished in the first few rooms, or so I was told."

"Yes, but let's not get ahead of ourselves," Edgin said. He had a list of questions swirling in his mind, but he forced himself to focus. "Who is this person that trapped you down here and is impersonating you up there?" He pointed to the ceiling.

"Sharrestren," Torlinn said, making the name into a curse. "My rival. The eye tyrant I battled decades ago who usurped my life, my power, and everything I'd built." He spat the words, his frail body trembling with suppressed anger.

"The eye tyrant?" Simon said in a choked voice. "Oh Gods, you don't mean—"

"The beholder," Edgin said. Cold dread crept over his skin. He raked both hands through his hair as the full impact of how badly he'd screwed up swept over him. "You lost the duel," he said, putting the pieces together. "You lost the duel, and the beholder used his magic to take your place."

"Correct," Torlinn said. "He wears a magical opal around his neck that allows him to shape-change into a semblance of myself."

Edgin didn't care about the logistics. He was too busy trying not to freak out. "You're telling us that all this time, we've been robbing a mansion controlled by an insanely powerful monster who throws extravagant parties, enjoys sauteed shrimp, and built a secret death dungeon in his basement."

"Breathe," Holga advised, patting him on the back, but Edgin ignored her. Kira had been right next to the beholder at the buffet table. Edgin had *sent* her to go meet him. He'd had no idea what they were dealing with. They'd been in way over their heads this whole time, idiots stumbling around in the dark.

"Wait a minute, why should we believe you?" Alyanna cut in, stepping forward to grasp the cage bars. "This could just be one more trick in this weird dungeon. Torlinn—Sharrestren, whatever—has servants around all the time. Surely, one of us would have noticed something before now. He can't have kept this charade up for that long without slipping. No one's that good."

"You're right," Torlinn said. Using the wall to brace himself, he climbed to his feet and hobbled closer to the bars. Instinctively, the group took a collective step back. "Those around Sharrestren, be they servant or guest, who got too close to the truth were cast down here to the 'mirror house,' as he likes to call it, where they were quickly killed, their essences added to his power."

"That sounds ominous," Forge said, shifting agitatedly from foot to foot. "What exactly does that entail?"

"The Staff of Aorth," Edgin said. "That's what you're talking about, isn't it? This place—the mansion and the dungeon—are tied to the artifact somehow, aren't they? It has to do with the two gems, the dual nature of the staff."

"Clever of you to have noticed," Torlinn said, fixing Edgin with a piercing gaze. "Are you sure you're all just common thieves? I wouldn't have expected a group like you to have made it this far." His gaze fell on Kira, and his eyes widened. "And you brought a *child* down here with you?"

"All right, shut up a minute," Edgin snapped. He wasn't going to put up with a lecture on parenting from a wizard who'd let himself get replaced by a beholder. "Tell me how it works—the Staff of Aorth, I mean. What does it really do?"

Torlinn coughed, a wheezing sound that didn't seem at all healthy. Simon untied his waterskin from his belt and held it between the bars.

"Careful," Holga warned. She was never quick to trust anyone. "Could still be a trick."

"He can't do anything," Simon said. He pointed at the drift-globes hanging around Torlinn's cage. They glowed a deep crimson color, different from the soft light of the other driftglobes they'd seen. "There's an anti-magic field surrounding the cage. I didn't notice it until I got close enough and my light spell went out."

"That, a very complicated lock, and the power of the Staff of Aorth have managed to keep me trapped here quite effectively for . . . you know, I've lost count of the number of years now." Torlinn took Simon's waterskin with a grateful nod. He drank deeply, his eyes sliding closed in pleasure. "The staff," he continued, when he'd finished drinking, "has a dual nature, as you surmised, embodied by the two gems set at either end. The diamond feeds on positive emotions, especially as they relate to pleasure and excitement."

"The party guests," Alyanna said. "*That's* why he throws these elaborate, messy, ridiculous affairs every few weeks?"

"All that unbound energy swirling through the mansion works to feed the staff," Torlinn said. "You see, when I first found the artifact, it was drained of power and nearly broken. There were cracks running all through it. In fact, it was so damaged that I had nearly given up the notion of repairing it, but when Sharrestren discovered I had the staff, he had . . . other ideas."

"So that's why you had the duel in the first place," Edgin guessed. "It was over the Staff of Aorth. And ever since Sharrestren won, he's been working to repair the artifact." Edgin remembered the dormant emerald on the other end of the staff. "If the diamond feeds on positive emotions and grows more powerful that way, I suppose the emerald feeds on the bad stuff?"

Torlinn's expression darkened once again. "Fear, pain, death—he stores the staff down here when he's not using it at his parties in order to feed off the emotions of his victims before they perish. And he uses it to feed off me, of course."

Silence fell as they all absorbed the implications of that. Kira gasped, horrified.

"It's been feeding off of you for *years?*" she whispered. "That's terrible!"

Torlinn actually smiled faintly. "It is, little one. Believe me."

"But if Sharrestren wants people to die down here, why does he go to the trouble of giving his guests clues to the dungeon's secrets upstairs?" Simon asked. "It doesn't make sense."

"Sharrestren is twisted and evil, but he knows what he's doing." Torlinn sighed. "No one ever collects all the clues, so the dungeon always claims its victims in the end. But giving people hope for their own survival, only to have that hope ripped away in fear and terror, is like sweet meat for the emerald in the Staff of Aorth. And his work has paid off. The power Sharrestren has collected over the years has been gradually repairing the staff, though it's a very slow process."

"Not that slow," Edgin said. "I saw the staff upstairs in the ballroom. There was still a sizable crack running down the shaft, but other than that, it looked like the thing was in great shape."

Torlinn closed his eyes. His scaled throat bobbed as he swallowed. "Then soon, the staff will be fully repaired, and Sharrestren will be able to unleash the artifact's power on Faerûn at large. That will not be a good day for anyone."

"Not to mention he's going to unleash every one of his eyeballs on us when he finds out we came to steal the staff and wrecked part of his murder dungeon," Forge said bleakly.

He was right. And worse, Edgin had been the one to lead them all here. This was his fault.

He looked around at the tense, fearful faces of his friends, his daughter. He'd worked so hard over the past few years to give Kira a better life. He'd gathered a group of people around him to work with, and somehow, against all odds, they'd become like a family to him. Now all of that was in danger because of him.

No, not again. He wasn't losing another person he cared about. Not while he was still breathing and charming and capable of making a plan to get out of it.

"I'm sorry about this," Edgin said, looking around at everyone. "I'm the leader of the group, and I should have done better by all of you on this heist. If I had, we wouldn't be in this mess." He stood up straight, squaring his shoulders. "But I swear, we're going to get out of this dungeon, we're going to get our loot, and one day, when we're old and gray, we'll be telling stories about this heist and sitting around the fire talking about that time we robbed and outsmarted a beholder." He glanced at Simon. "It'll be the stuff of legends. That's a promise."

His words were met with silence from the others. Even Torlinn didn't have anything to say. He'd lapsed into another coughing fit and was leaning against the bars of the cage. Edgin felt some of the wind go out of his sails. What if his friends didn't believe him? What if they no longer trusted him?

But then Kira stepped forward and wrapped her arms around his waist, hugging him tight. "It's not your fault," she said. "No matter what, we're in this together."

A lump rose in Edgin's throat. He swallowed and felt a heavy hand on his shoulder. He turned around to see Holga looking at him with a fond expression.

"We're with you," she said. "Let's get out of here."

"Yes, as novel as this murder dungeon is, I've had quite enough," Forge agreed.

"Sounds good to me," Simon said.

"Yes, if I make it out of here alive, it's safe to say I'm officially giving my notice," Alyanna said. "I don't work for beholders."

"Yeah, I don't blame you there." Edgin's chest swelled with unexpected emotion. His friends were standing by him, and he was going to make sure they all came out of this in one piece.

He shook himself. Enough with the feelings. They needed a plan, and he was the planner. Finding Torlinn had given them some crucial answers, and maybe even the breakthrough they'd been looking for.

He squeezed Kira one last time and gently pulled away to approach Torlinn. The dragonborn had recovered somewhat and was drinking from Simon's waterskin again.

"Torlinn," Edgin said, "if we were to get you out of that cage, could you show us the way to get out of the dungeon?"

Torlinn gave a wan smile. "I appreciate the offer, but the lock on that cage is too complex. I've examined it thoroughly, and I've made no progress over the years trying to open it." He held out his hands for emphasis. Several of his claws were chipped or broken, evidence that he'd used them to try to pick the lock numerous times.

"No offense, but those are hardly the tools you need for work like this," Edgin said, examining the lock on the cage door. It was definitely one of the more elaborate locks he'd ever seen, but he thought between him and Forge, they could crack it. "Think about it. We get you out of here, you lead us safely through the dungeon, and we all escape this place in one piece."

"If you think you're going to just sneak out of here without Sharrestren noticing, you're sadly mistaken," Torlinn said, a laugh rattling his chest. "He knows everything that goes on down here. You can bet he knows you're here. He expects you to die here, but if for some reason you do not, he'll never let you leave the estate grounds."

"We appreciate the vote of confidence, sunshine." Edgin tried not to let his sudden anxiety show. "Come on, there has to be a way," he insisted.

"Once you get beyond the anti-magic field, can't you use your magic to help us?" Simon pressed. "You're supposed to be a powerful wizard!"

"My magic was no match for Sharrestren's in our duel, remember?" Torlinn said dryly. "And that was years ago. In order to even have a chance against him, I'd need to acquire the Staff of Aorth. It's the only way we'd be evenly matched."

Edgin caught the sudden gleam in Torlinn's eyes when he mentioned the staff. *Of course.* That's what Torlinn was angling for. The wizard wasn't feeling nearly as hopeless as he tried to appear. He knew they were a party of thieves who'd gotten farther into the beholder's murder dungeon than anyone else. He was hoping they could get the staff for him.

"*If* you had the staff," Edgin said, "you'd use it to help us escape?"

"To be perfectly blunt, I'd use it to make that Gods-thrice-damned beholder pay for everything he's put me through," Torlinn said, his voice dripping with venom. "But yes, in the process of doing that, I would also help you and your group escape the estate."

"Works for me," Holga said, and Simon nodded.

"Better than dying here," Alyanna said.

"Edgin, could I have a word?" Forge asked, motioning to him to step away from the cell.

Edgin followed him down the row of cages until they were standing near the giant spiders. Edgin kept a watch on them out of the corner of his eye. "What is it?" he asked in a low voice.

"You realize if we make this deal with Torlinn, we're giving up the Staff of Aorth," Forge said. "My contact who wants to buy it will be none too pleased, and we'll be out a large portion of the loot we'd counted on for this job."

"I know," Edgin said, scratching at the beginnings of beard stubble on his chin as he considered their dilemma. "But even the best thieves can't spend coin when they're dead. We may have to cut our losses on this one. Or," he said, a thought occurring to him, "some of us could stick around just long enough for Torlinn to get his revenge on this beholder, then, in the aftermath, maybe we grab and dash with the staff while he's still recovering."

"Interesting thought," Forge said. "I like it, as long as we avoid being part of the collateral damage when those two face off."

"Once we're out of here, we'll put a plan together to make sure that doesn't happen," Edgin assured him.

They shook on it, and as they turned to go back to the group, one of the giant spiders jumped, landing on a strand of web right next to the bars of its cage, inches from Edgin and Forge. They leaped back out of reach, automatically clutching each other to stay on their feet.

The spider stared at them through the bars, its eight eyes large and unblinking, showing them their tense reflections in the black depths.

From down the row of cages, Holga snickered. "It's all right," she said, "the big, mean spider can't get you."

Edgin shuddered and turned away. They returned to the group, and Edgin addressed Torlinn. "You have a deal," he said.

Torlinn inclined his head, but he eyed the lock on his cage doubtfully. "We'll see soon enough if what you propose will work."

"Forge, time to show off," Edgin said. "The rest of you keep a lookout and watch those cages to make sure nothing gets loose."

Edgin knelt next to Forge so they could both examine the lock. Forge whistled as he fiddled with the mechanism. "I've started seeing these in Neverwinter in recent years on the estates of city officials and higher nobility. This is going to be interesting." He cracked his knuckles and smiled cheerfully at Torlinn. "Not to worry. We'll have you out in no time."

Twenty minutes later, Forge snapped his fifth lockpick and sat back with a curse, wiping the sweat from his forehead.

Torlinn sat serenely on the ground near the door, his tattered robes wrapped around himself, eyes half closed, as if he were contemplating a nap.

"It was a very good effort," the dragonborn said. "But I did tell you I'd tried for years with that lock. It's not something that can be easily picked, I'm afraid. Please don't be upset," he said, when Edgin slapped his palm against the floor in frustration.

"You seem really calm about all this," Kira observed. She was sitting near Edgin and Forge, watching the process and watching Torlinn at the same time.

He turned a benign gaze on her. "I've had years of sitting in this hovel to rage and snarl and howl at the unfairness of the Gods," he said. "I'm done with that now. I've accepted my fate, whatever comes."

Edgin didn't quite buy that Torlinn was as calm as he seemed, especially since his eyes fired up with hate whenever he spoke of the beholder. But he was doing an admirable job of hiding it now.

And Edgin wasn't ready to give up yet.

"Forge, let me get in there," he said.

Forge gestured to the lock with a frustrated wave of his hand. "Be my guest," he said.

They didn't have that many sets of lockpicks left. Edgin took the instruments in his hands and examined the lock. He took a deep, steadying breath and closed his eyes as he slid the lockpicks in.

"Edgin, this isn't the time to be showy," Forge said in irritation.

"Shh," Holga said. "Let him work."

Edgin shut out all their voices, falling into a trance as his fingers moved the lockpicks, listening for the telltale clicks that would let him know that he was succeeding. It was a technique he'd learned with the Harpers, this way of cutting himself off from everything else and just focusing on the immediate moment and what he had to do. He'd never wanted to have to use those techniques again, but if it got them out of here, he was all for it.

That's it. Move it a fraction to the left, just a whisper. Now bring the other pick and just . . . gently . . . gently . . . shift the . . . there!

Still absorbed by his task, Edgin didn't notice that Kira was shaking him.

"I did it!" Edgin opened his eyes as the cage door swung open. His gaze fixed on Kira's wide eyes. "What is it, sweetheart?"

"Incoming!" Holga put her body in front of Edgin and Kira, so Edgin had to look around her to see down the row of cages.

The spider cage door was open.

The spiders were coming out.

"What the Hells?" Edgin scrambled to his feet, shoving his lockpicks back into his vest.

"It appears some of the cages are linked," Forge said. "Opening this door opened that door."

"Let's get out of here!" Alyanna shouted. She held her hands out to Torlinn, who was getting slowly to his feet.

The dragonborn passed through the cage door and stepped out of range of the anti-magic aura. He took a deep breath, drew himself up to his full height, and turned toward the advancing spiders. He raised a trembling claw and pointed at the creatures, chanting the words to a spell in what sounded like Draconic, though Edgin wasn't familiar with the language.

A sphere of fire grew from Torlinn's hand, glowing brighter and brighter, expanding until Edgin had to look away from the blazing light. Torlinn released the fireball with a shoving motion, launching it down the row of cages and into the path of the advancing spiders. In the other cages, the dire wolves yelped in fear, and the kobolds were awake and screaming.

"Run!" Edgin scooped up Kira, and they fled in the opposite direction, the heat of the explosion scorching their backs. Edgin grabbed Torlinn by the arm and tugged him along with them. He'd just been standing there, staring at the fire and the dying spiders, the orange light of the flames gleaming in his eyes.

CHAPTER 31

Torlinn knew where the Staff of Aorth was kept.

As Edgin had suspected, when Sharrestren wasn't showing it off for his guests upstairs, he kept it down here in the murder dungeon. But when Edgin asked how it was guarded, Torlinn had hedged, preferring to have the group see for themselves.

Edgin did not like that at all, but he had no choice but to follow the dragonborn.

Torlinn led them along a series of smaller tunnels—the "backstage" area of the dungeon, he called it—picking his way over broken piles of stone, using Simon's dancing lights to guide their way. Now that Torlinn was out of his cage, he seemed much more energetic—driven, almost, to get them to the staff as quickly as possible.

"I have to say, you know your way around this dungeon remarkably well for a prisoner," Forge said, and it was a credit to Forge's personality that he made it sound like a compliment rather than a suspicion.

Torlinn glanced over his shoulder. "Sharrestren kept me well informed during the building process," he said bitterly. "He showed me the layout, the mirroring of certain rooms upstairs. It was a very exciting time for him. He even had the gall to ask for my opinion on which monsters to populate the dungeon with, all while wearing my form like a second skin."

The passage, to Edgin's surprise, started to slope gradually upward, and he felt a flare of hope within his chest. Going up meant they were closer to being out. Around a bend, the tunnel widened into a midsized chamber, with a high ceiling that seemed lower because of the thick nest of stalactites hanging overhead.

In the center of the chamber, there was a large slab of what looked like obsidian, its flat surface gleaming in the light of the driftglobes scattered throughout the room. It reminded Edgin of nothing so much as an altar, and he suppressed a shiver.

Resting on its surface was a familiar object.

Edgin caught his breath and unconsciously took a step forward, but Simon stopped him with a hand on his shoulder.

"This room feels wrong," Simon said. "Something's . . . there's a lot of contained power here."

"Your friend is perceptive," Torlinn said, eyeing Simon. "Do you wield powerful magic yourself?" he asked.

"Sometimes," Simon said, looking away.

"You won't be able to tell, but we're at the heart of the dungeon here," Torlinn explained. "The central hub that all the other rooms feed into."

"'Feed,'" Holga said gruffly. "You mean the fear?"

Torlinn nodded grimly. "All the terror, the screams of the dying, the hatred that comes from my heart—it all gets channeled here into repairing the staff."

Edgin could see now that the emerald in the staff was glowing faintly, pulsing with a sickly glow, while the diamond lay dormant. The crack running along the center of the staff was still visible, the damage equidistant from each gem.

Funny how he'd been so anxious to get his hands on the staff before, but now that it was within reach, knowing how it obtained its power, he was reluctant to go anywhere near it or have any of the group touching it.

"All right, I take it we can't just grab the staff off that altar," Edgin said. "So what's the trick? What's the test? How do we get it?"

Torlinn's face was grim. "Only someone capable of wielding magic can claim the staff. Even then, you must be able to withstand the artifact's power. It will naturally try to draw on all your emotions, positive and negative, pulling the life energy out of you if you aren't strong enough to resist."

"That sounds more like a curse than a test to me," Edgin said. "I don't want a curse of doom laid on my crew."

"It's not a curse," Torlinn assured them, "but yes, it will be very . . . unpleasant. And I wouldn't ask any of you to take the staff. *I* will be the one to wield it."

"Wait," Simon said as the wizard stepped toward the altar. "I should take it first, just to make sure Sharrestren didn't put any traps on it. He'd be most worried about *you* taking the staff, right? So he might have specifically protected it from you."

Torlinn cocked his head. "That is true," he allowed. "You're quite brave to offer yourself in my place."

"Simon, you don't have to do this," Edgin said as the half-elf stepped toward the altar, but Simon was already closing his eyes, reaching his hand out to hover over the staff. Edgin found himself holding his breath. Kira squeezed his arm in a death grip.

"If I don't do it," Simon said, "none of us are getting out of here."

His fingers brushed the staff lightly, and then he picked it up in one smooth motion. The whole group flinched, waiting for an explosion or an alarm or something else to happen, but nothing did.

No, that wasn't true. Edgin looked at Simon's face. His eyes were open, but his face was a tight mask of pain. Sweat beaded his forehead, and his chest expanded suddenly, as if he were drawing a breath to scream.

"All right, drop it!" Edgin moved toward Simon, but Torlinn caught his arm, holding him back with surprising strength.

"It's too late," Torlinn said. "He'll claim the staff, or the staff will claim him. There's nothing you can do."

Helpless, Edgin could only watch as Simon's eyes rolled back in his head, showing the whites. It looked like he was fighting a battle inside his own head. Torlinn was right. None of his friends could help him.

Simon slid to his knees. The group tensed as the gems in the staff flashed a brilliant green and white—and then the light faded, and, just like that, it was over. Simon opened his eyes and looked around, a dazed expression on his sweat-soaked face.

"Simon?" Forge asked, stepping forward. "Are you all right?"

Slowly, Simon got to his feet. He shook his head. "This thing is . . . bad." His voice was strained. He stared at the staff in wonder and disgust. "I can feel everything you described," he said, looking at Torlinn. "All the pain and fear mixing in with the pleasure and positive emotions—it's like this terrible stew of things you shouldn't feel all at once. I just want to throw it across the room. But there are no special protections on it. You can touch it . . . if you really want to."

Torlinn came up beside him and gently took the artifact. For a moment, he seemed to wage the same inner battle that Simon had, though it was over quicker. "It's the damage to the staff," Torlinn said when he could speak again. "If the artifact were whole, you wouldn't be able to feel its power so strongly. But yes," he said, patting Simon lightly on the shoulder. "I regret the day this came into my possession and made me a target of that abominable creature."

"We should go," Edgin said. "There was no alarm, but I'm assuming Sharrestren still knows somehow when someone is touching his toys?"

Torlinn nodded. "He'll be alerted, yes. We must move quickly." He pointed to an adjoining tunnel. "That way leads to the back exit from the dungeon. It comes out in a secret passage just off the ballroom, but it's well hidden. None but Sharrestren and I know of its existence."

Edgin cocked his head as they moved quickly down the tunnel. "That's why the drawings of the mansion looked so strange," he said. "The shape of the ballroom was off, but I couldn't figure out why. It's because of the exit to the dungeon being there."

"I had originally intended it as a way to escape the ballroom during a party," Torlinn said. He held the staff gently, almost reverently, in his hands. "I don't like large gatherings, you see. They're very tiring. I prefer to be alone with my books and my cats."

"Well, then you're definitely not going to like what's been going on upstairs these last few years," Edgin said. He didn't mention the fact that he hadn't seen a single cat anywhere in the mansion. Did beholders eat cats? Best not to bring that up either.

Up and up they went along the tunnel, and there were more rooms with traps and magical barriers along the way, but Torlinn disabled all of them with just a touch of the staff. The artifact seemed to function as a sort of master key to the dungeon itself.

Finally, their journey ended, somewhat anticlimactically, at a nondescript door in a wall. It was magically sealed, but again the staff served as the key, and they stepped out into a small sitting room with a few bookshelves along one wall and a pair of leather chairs with a side table between them. The room had none of the gaudy extravagance of the other parts of the mansion, and Edgin surmised that Sharrestren probably just hadn't bothered to change the décor of this hidden room when he'd taken over the mansion.

Torlinn looked around the room as if seeing it for the first time, his eyes glassy, mouth slightly open. In a daze, he wandered over to one of the leather chairs and picked up a small book with a green cover. One of the early pages was dog-eared.

"Just like I left it," he said softly, "so many years ago." He glanced up at Edgin, tears shining in his eyes. "I always wondered how the book ended," he said. "Sharrestren wouldn't even leave me my books during my imprisonment."

They all stood silently, at a loss for what to say. It hit Edgin suddenly just how many years of his life Torlinn had lost, imprisoned in a hole in the ground without ever seeing the sun. He couldn't imagine such a thing. There were no windows in this room, and it wouldn't have mattered anyway, because the sun wouldn't be up for a few more hours, but Edgin wondered if Torlinn was looking forward to seeing it again.

"Time to go," the dragonborn said, setting the book carefully back down on the chair. He turned and pointed to a panel in the wall. "That's the hidden door to the ballroom. I have an old friend to confront." There was a dangerous gleam in his eyes now.

"Hang on," Edgin said, stepping in front of the dragonborn. "We can't just go spilling out into the ballroom shouting, '*Surprise,* we survived your death dungeon and we're here for some sweet, sweet revenge.' We need a plan, and you promised an escape for me and my group so we're not caught in the crossfire of your tiff with the beholder."

Behind him, Forge coughed. "And we need to collect our loot," he said.

"That too," Edgin amended.

Torlinn looked them all over, a veil of calm settling over him. For some reason Edgin couldn't explain, that made him feel more uneasy instead of less. "I appreciate all that you've done on my behalf," the dragonborn said, and if nothing else, his words sounded genuine. "But I've waited too long for my revenge." He sounded sad as he spoke. "It's eaten me up inside, and there's nothing left of me but that." He looked at Edgin. "If you try to stand in my way, I'll kill all of you. Be smart. Take the child and your friends and run. You don't want to linger here for what's about to happen."

Edgin watched, slack-jawed, as Torlinn strode to the wall, made a gesture at the panel, and slid it aside effortlessly. Music, laughter, and the smells of food spilled into the room as the ballroom was revealed, the party in full swing as if they'd never left it.

"Is this actually happening?" Alyanna said as Torlinn walked out into the room, the group following.

Edgin and Forge exchanged a glance. Edgin knew what he was thinking. Their window of opportunity to get the staff was shrinking fast. But if they weren't careful, they would lose the chance to get the rest of their loot too, and this would have all been for nothing.

"Forge, you, Simon, and Alyanna go upstairs to get the loot we collected from the treasure room," Edgin said. "Holga, you and Kira head outside, go get the wagon, and bring it around to the pickup point."

"What are you going to do?" Holga asked, grabbing Kira's hand before the girl could protest.

Reason with Torlinn? Try to get him not to start a magical battle in the middle of a ballroom full of innocent people? Grab the staff and run? All those options flitted through Edgin's mind as he trailed behind Torlinn across the ballroom.

"I'll figure something out," he said, making a shooing motion at Holga. "Go!"

By now, some of the party guests had spotted the real Torlinn in their midst and were pointing and murmuring. Edgin quickened his pace to catch up to the wizard, but as it turned out, like in many critical moments in his life before now, he was just a breath too late.

"Torlinn," or, rather, Sharrestren in the form of Torlinn, stepped into the middle of the ballroom. The two mirrored dragonborn faced off amid the confused crowd. The upside-down orchestra ceased playing, the musicians craning their necks to look down on the proceedings from above.

"Well, well," Sharrestren said, his voice smooth and cold. "You escaped your cage, little rat."

"Shit," Edgin said.

CHAPTER 32

"I've come to take back my household, Sharrestren," Torlinn said, brandishing the Staff of Aorth. "This party's lasted long enough."

Edgin winced. Not a great opening line, especially considering Torlinn had been in a cage for the last several years. He'd had plenty of time to come up with a killer piece of banter for this confrontation.

Edgin decided it was time to go. Much as he hated to admit it, he had to give up on the staff and whatever he'd been about to say to Torlinn to convince him not to make this battle so very public. Whispers of unease were moving through the crowd, and a few people were working their way subtly toward the exit.

Edgin had turned to join them when a hand wrapped around his arm, bony fingers holding him in place.

He turned and there was Lady Sofina, staring at him with her dark eyes. "How did I know you'd be involved in this somehow?" she asked.

Oh Gods. He'd forgotten he'd taken off his cat mask, so of course she'd recognized him at once. Here were a set of chickens he did not need coming home to roost right now.

He tugged her with him toward the front doors. "You were absolutely right," he said in a rush. "We came here to rob the place, steal the legendary Staff of Aorth, and get away with enough loot to retire on comfortably, but things hit a snag when we got trapped in the death dungeon in the basement and found out about the beholder, and I'd be happy to explain every last detail of the story outside in the yard where it's safe."

Lady Sofina's face had gone several shades whiter. "Beholder?" she said incredulously, tightening her grip until it was painful. "What are you talking about?"

The two Torlinns were slowly circling each other, and most of the crowd, though confused, were hanging around to watch the drama play out. They had no idea what was about to happen.

"Look, can we just talk about this outside?" Edgin was practically dragging her toward the door. He looked across the room and noticed that Holga and Kira were still inside. They'd gotten stuck in the small crowd bottlenecked at the exit. People were just standing around whispering, speculating about what was going on. Edgin's heart lodged in his throat. He needed to do something. Now.

"Fire!" he shouted. "Fire in the kitchens. Gnome on fire! Everyone, please clear out, quickly!"

Lady Sofina looked at him as if he'd suddenly polymorphed into a monkey. "What are you doing?" she asked.

"What does it look like I'm doing? I'm trying to start a panic! The biggest panic on the Sword Coast if that's what it takes to move this crowd," Edgin snapped. "Fire! Did anyone hear me about the REALLY BIG FIRE in the kitchens?"

"Enough!" Sharrestren's voice boomed unnaturally loud through the ballroom, drowning out Edgin's shouts. Everyone in the room froze like startled deer. Lady Sofina's hand slid off his arm as she turned to look at the two dragonborn.

"No one is going anywhere." Sharrestren lifted his arms, and pale green light erupted from his hands. It struck the ceiling and began to spread outward and down the walls.

"Oh no," Lady Sofina murmured, evidently recognizing the spell. "He's sealing us in."

At the same time, the real Torlinn raised the Staff of Aorth and fired a beam of radiant light from the diamond. It struck Sharrestren in the chest, driving him back several steps and leaving a large black singe mark on his robes. Otherwise, it looked like it had done no damage.

"That's it?" Edgin shouted in frustration. "That's all the legendary Staff of Aorth is good for?" He turned his attention to Holga at the door. "Get Kira out of here!"

Holga was already shoving her way through the crowd, knocking people aside to get to the foyer and the front doors, which started to close on their own as the green light reached them. Setting Kira on her feet, Holga grabbed the closest door with one hand, holding it open with all her strength. She grabbed Kira with the other and shoved her through the small gap just as the green light came down on their heads. There was a sharp crack, like lightning splitting the air.

The door slammed shut, the green light touched the floor, and there was now a glowing barrier covering every window and door out of the place.

They were trapped.

But Kira was safe. Edgin repeated that to himself. Or, at least, she was outside the mansion, which was safer than here.

The ballroom had turned into a stampede as the crowd surged toward the doors and windows, pounding against the barrier. Lady Sofina had disappeared into the chaos, no longer interested in Edgin. Above his head, the orchestra members abandoned their instruments and scurried down the walls like ants in formal wear. A few of the guests came forward to cluster in a group around the false Torlinn, ignoring the scorch mark on his chest, waving their hands for attention, their faces flushed with anger.

"This practical joke has gone far enough, Torlinn," bellowed a dwarf whose graying mustache quivered with indignation. "Release us at once!"

"I'm never coming back to one of these vulgar events again!" screeched a human woman whose eyes were glassy from too much drink. She swayed on her feet in front of Sharrestren, shaking his arm like a child.

Sharrestren looked at the people clustered around him with a wicked light dancing in his eyes. In fact, something was suddenly very strange about his eyes. Edgin cursed as Holga made it through the crowd back to his side.

"Find cover!" He grabbed Holga's arm, and together they sprinted across the ballroom, back toward the secret room, whose panel was still open. They'd just made it to the doorway when the screaming began.

Edgin turned in time to see Sharrestren . . . twisting. Or, at least, that's what it looked like. The false dragonborn had one hand on the opal necklace he wore, and as he murmured some arcane phrases, his body began to bend and swell at the same time, clothes ripping and falling off of him in tatters as his scaled flesh darkened to a bluish black, his limbs drawing inward toward his body at the same time his head seemed to shrink. It was a horrifying transformation to watch.

But the worst of it was yet to come.

A huge central eye with an iris the color of dried blood slowly opened in Sharrestren's newly bulbous form. A gaping mouth split its bottom half, lipless and full of blackened teeth, curving in a ghastly parody of a smile.

Then, as if that weren't terrible enough, with a soft popping sound, ten smaller stalks sprouted from all over the beholder's rotund surface, each one cracking open a singular eye, each iris a different color, all of them looking in different directions, the stalks waving like tentacles.

"Holga, can you shut us in here?" Edgin shouted to her.

Holga glared at him. "What do you think I've been doing?" Only then did Edgin notice she was feeling along the wall for the mechanism to close the panel back up and seal them in the secret room, but like the secret door upstairs, it refused to budge. "I hate these things! Why don't they make normal doors!"

Edgin looked back at the ballroom. It was bedlam now, nothing but screams and shouts as people trampled one another to get away from the newly revealed beholder—except the dwarf and the woman who'd been shouting at Sharrestren, who were both frozen in terror on the spot, staring up at the monster.

The beholder had risen several feet in the air to hover above the ballroom, grinning with that tooth-filled maw at all the panic its appearance had caused. It turned a single eyestalk toward the dwarf, and a beam of energy burst from a yellow eye, spearing him like a fish.

The dwarf's body disintegrated in a swirl of dust and necrotic energy.

Edgin gasped. He'd heard tales of the powers of a beholder's eyestalks, but he'd never seen anything like this up close before. With the basilisk, you could avoid the power of its gaze by not looking at it. This was different. He'd never seen anything that had the power to just look at you and make you die.

"We have to get that barrier down," he said to Holga, "or this is going to be a bloodbath."

"We need Simon for that," Holga said.

They exchanged a look, then took off across the ballroom toward the door to the servant's area. They had to shove aside people running blindly for cover or trying to get to one of the other rooms to hide. Several of the doors off the ballroom were closed, and it looked like people had barricaded themselves on the other side. Guests stood at the doors, banging on them and shouting to be let in, but they received no answer. It was everyone for themselves.

In the middle of the ballroom, Torlinn and Sharrestren had engaged in a full-on magical battle, with Torlinn using the staff and Sharrestren his eyestalks. In their blind panic, party guests ran into the path of the eyestalks while trying to get away and were struck down. Some of them were killed instantly; others fell to their knees, screaming in terror as they tried to crawl away from the beholder. And still others fell into a kind of trance, staring up at the beholder with serene smiles on their faces.

Edgin reached the servant's door just as Simon, Alyanna, and Forge were forcing their way through it from the other side. The door slammed at their backs, and it sounded like heavy furniture was being pushed against it on the other side.

"We heard screams," Forge said, "then the green light appeared and blocked the exits, so we came back down and . . ." His voice trailed off as he surveyed the chaos and the duel between Torlinn and Sharrestren. "Oh," he said faintly.

"Yeah, so we're trapped in the mansion," Edgin said, ticking the disasters off on his fingers as fast as he could. "Kira's outside getting the wagon, but we have no way to get to her, so she's all alone. Torlinn and that beholder are probably going to kill each other and everyone in the house, and they don't seem to care. Also, we're probably not getting the staff," he added, although that part was surely obvious to everyone by now.

They moved together, taking cover behind the buffet table, but it was crowded. Other guests had had the same idea, and they didn't look too keen on sharing. Holga glowered at them and they backed off.

"We just need to cut our losses and get out," Forge said. "We don't want any part of this fight."

"How do we get through the barrier then?" Edgin asked, turning to Simon. "Can you bring it down?"

"That?" Simon pointed to the net of green energy covering the walls and shook his head. "It's not a normal spell," he said. "I'm guessing this is like the hag's cave, only on a bigger scale. She'd made the island her lair, and she could control things on it like the vines."

"You're saying Sharrestren can manipulate this house the same way," Edgin said, "control who gets in and out?"

"I think so," Simon said. "To get the barrier to come down, Sharrestren has to either die or decide to take it down himself."

"Lovely," Alyanna said, rolling her eyes. "We just have to ask really nicely, then."

Edgin glanced toward the dance floor as Torlinn's magic shattered some large potted plants arranged by the window, sending shards of pottery flying like tiny missiles everywhere. He ducked as several pieces flew over his head, embedding themselves in the wall. It was only a matter of time before the fight migrated in this direction and everyone took an eye beam to the face. They needed to do something to tip the scales in their favor before that happened.

"We need a new plan," he said slowly, reluctant to even speak the idea aloud. "We have to get on team Torlinn and make sure he wins the duel this time."

There was a brief silence.

"You serious?" Holga asked. She was looking at the beholder doubtfully. Edgin didn't blame her. Hovering at least ten feet in the air, the eye tyrant was well out of reach of her axe unless she threw it at the thing.

"I'm extremely serious, and I'm really feeling good about this plan," Edgin said, trying to sound reassuring. "I think we can do this."

"I think Edgin's also suggesting we don't have any other choice," Forge said, "and I'm inclined to agree. What should our roles be in this?"

They were going to absolutely hate this part, Edgin thought, but he plowed on. "I think our best bet is distraction," he said. "Get Sharrestren to waste some of his powers on us to give Torlinn an advantage with the Staff of Aorth."

"It's not just the eyestalks," Simon put in. He'd been watching the spell duel closely as they spoke, studying the combatants. "Beholders have this thing they can do where they render an area dead to magic, just like with Torlinn's cage. They make it so wizards can't cast spells in a certain area, and magic items like the staff won't work either. Look." He pointed to Torlinn, who was running as fast as he could to reposition himself near the south windows before he fired another beam of energy from his staff. "Torlinn has to get out of the anti-magic field before he can attack, so he has to keep moving. I think Sharrestren will wear him down that way before he can get anywhere with his attacks."

"You're right," Edgin said. He could already tell Torlinn was fatigued. The dragonborn's chest heaved with each breath, and his hands trembled on the staff. "All right, everyone, we have a mission. Operation: distract the beholder and don't get in front of the eyestalks."

They all stared at him. Edgin shrugged. "I'll come up with a better title later. Let's go!"

Taking a deep breath, Edgin sprang up and ran out onto the dance floor, grabbing a shard of broken pottery as he went. "Hey, Sharrestren! Beady-eyes! Over here! How about you play with us too!"

He threw the pottery shard at the beholder. It bounced harmlessly off its tough skin, but Edgin was undeterred. He picked up shard after shard, throwing them at the beholder until Sharrestren swiveled one of his eyestalks to face him.

He was taunting a beholder. He was taunting a beholder with pottery shards. Edgin vowed he would seriously reexamine his life choices if he survived this night.

"Watch out!" Holga cried.

There was a flash in the smaller eye as it narrowed on Edgin, then a beam of energy speared in his direction. Alyanna shoved Edgin out of the way, the beam narrowly missing him.

But Alyanna didn't manage to dodge.

The beam clipped her in the shoulder, the force of it spinning her around. She swayed on her feet like a rag doll about to tip over. Edgin's heart lodged in his throat.

No.

Alyanna dropped to the floor, her body going rigid, eyes open and staring straight ahead. To Edgin's relief, her body didn't turn to dust, so she hadn't been hit by the disintegration ray, but she wasn't moving either. Was she breathing?

The beholder swung away from them, focusing its attention on Forge and Holga. Forge had thrown his dagger, and Holga was shouting at Sharrestren to come down to face her.

Edgin ran to Alyanna's side, reaching her just as Simon did. Her body was stiff and unmoving, but her chest rose and fell steadily. Her eyes focused on them, and Edgin could see her lips trying to move, jaw muscles clenching and unclenching, but she couldn't speak other than to make an incoherent groaning noise.

"It's some kind of paralysis," Simon said. He squeezed Alyanna's stiff hand. "I think you'll be okay," he said. "You just have to wait until it wears off." He looked at Edgin. "We have to get her somewhere safe. She can't defend herself like this."

And she'd saved Edgin's neck. If not for Alyanna, he'd be the one lying there paralyzed.

Simon scooped Alyanna awkwardly into his arms, and together he and Edgin ran across the ballroom to the door to the bar. It was closed, of course, but Edgin kicked it with all his strength. It splintered and swung open on creaking hinges. Luckily, there hadn't been any furniture barricading it.

Inside the room, a bunch of people were hiding behind the bar or huddling in groups pressed against the walls. Spilled cocktails and broken glass lay everywhere. The room reeked of alcohol and blood. Some of the guests were tending to the wounded.

"Little help over here!" he called out.

A half-orc man with a curling beard turned, and his eyes widened when he saw Alyanna's condition. He handed some strips of cloth he'd torn from his shirt to an elf crouching beside him and indicated that he should finish bandaging a dwarf with a bleeding arm. He made his way through the crowd to Edgin and Simon.

"She's paralyzed," he confirmed after he'd done a quick examination. Around his neck, he wore the holy symbol of Helm. "It'll wear off soon enough." He and another guest took Alyanna gently from Simon's arms. "I can make sure she's comfortable in the meantime."

Edgin nodded his thanks, and he and Simon hurried back to the ballroom to rejoin the battle. People who hadn't managed to find cover or hiding places were still clustered in groups along the walls, screaming and running whenever the fighting came near them.

Suddenly, another of the beholder's eye rays struck Holga, lifting her off her feet and hurling her into the air. Edgin gave an incoherent shout of fury, but there was nothing he could do. He could only watch helplessly as Holga twisted and managed to land on her feet, keeping a grip on her axe. She stumbled, though, as if the fall had hurt her leg. Her face was creased with pain, but at least she wasn't dead.

If nothing else, Torlinn was using the distractions well. Every time Sharrestren attacked Edgin's friends, the wizard was able to get a spell off or a shot from the Staff of Aorth. These, more than anything else, were taking a toll on the beholder, leaving scorch marks and gaping wounds on his body.

But it wouldn't be enough. Edgin could see that his friends were tiring, and Torlinn wasn't strong enough to keep up his attacks forever. Someone was going to die if they didn't do something fast.

"Simon," Edgin said, putting his hands on the half-elf's shoulders, "new plan. We have to kill the beholder. What can you do to make that happen?"

Simon stared at him incredulously. "Um, nothing? I told you my magic is no match for theirs! What do you expect me to do?"

"Use your head!" Edgin poked him hard in the forehead with his finger. "You may not have the power, but you have more knowledge about magic than all of us. Think! What would be strong enough to kill the beholder?"

Simon bit his lip. "At this point, the Staff of Aorth, but only if you could release its power all at once somehow," he said finally. "That's all I can think of."

"All right, good thinking," Edgin said. He scrunched his forehead. "Why isn't Torlinn doing that then?"

"Probably he's too weak," Simon said. "He's been imprisoned too long. To release all of an artifact's power at once like that would either take an extremely powerful wizard or . . ." He sucked in a breath, his eyes widening.

"What?" Edgin demanded. "What is it?"

"It's . . . no, we can't possibly do that," Simon said, shaking his head. "Forget I said anything."

"Are you serious?" Edgin shook him. "We don't have time for well-thought-out plans, Simon, we're at the desperate gamble stage. What. Can. We. Do?"

"We can destroy the staff!" Simon choked out.

Edgin released his grip on the sorcerer in surprise. "Destroy it? I didn't think that was something you could do with an artifact?"

"You can't, not easily," Simon explained. "But the Staff of Aorth is still damaged. I think that means that with enough physical force we could shatter it. Except . . . we don't want to be anywhere in the vicinity of the explosion it'll create."

"But we have to make sure Sharrestren is," Edgin said. He could see why Simon thought it wasn't a plan worth mentioning. The timing it would require meant it was almost impossible to pull off.

"All right, I'll do it," Edgin said.

"Just like that?" Simon spluttered.

"Just like that," Edgin said, with a smile of bravado that, judging by Simon's expression, was not very convincing. "We need to gather up the others. I want everyone for this. You still have any spells that can get rid of magic?"

"Yes," Simon said, confused. "But I told you I can't dispel the barrier."

"We're going to do something different," Edgin said. "I can't even believe I'm saying this, but it's time for a hero moment, Simon, and you're going to help me."

CHAPTER 33

This was a terrible plan. The worst one Edgin had ever come up with, and yet, here he was, crouched in a corner of the ballroom, holding a barrel-sized potted plant in his arms—the only intact decoration left in the ballroom, by his calculation—ready to stake his life on this terrible plan.

"Why did we need the potted plant again?" Forge asked him as he crouched next to Edgin behind a ruined set of upholstered chairs.

"It's my stand-in," Edgin said, as if that made things obvious. "I named him George. George, meet Forge."

Forge looked at him intently. "You're not losing it on me, are you?"

Edgin laughed, and there was just a touch of hysteria to it. "Of course not. We're about to try to murder a beholder by unleashing magic so powerful that it might blow up this entire house and everyone in it. I'm feeling *excellent* about all of this."

"Well, if it helps at all, there's no one else I'd rather have in charge of guiding us to glory or certain doom," Forge said. He glanced across the ballroom to where Holga was limping her way into position with Simon. "Looks like we're ready." He held out his hand to Edgin. "Nice conning with you, Ed."

Edgin shook his hand, the gesture made only a tad awkward with George in his arms. "You too, Forge Fitzwilliam."

Just then, Torlinn shouted the words to a spell, sounding frustrated and exhausted. Edgin looked over just in time to see a fireball spiral from the wizard's hand up toward the beholder. Sharrestren floated straight down, dodging the spell, and the fireball engulfed one of the crystal chandeliers above the buffet table. The flames quickly spread to the drapes hanging by the windows.

"Well, now it's a party," Forge said. Fresh screams echoed from the guests as smoke filled the ballroom.

Holga signaled them frantically from across the room. She was in position, and Sharrestren, in dodging the fireball, had drifted down nearer to the floor than he'd ever been. It was exactly the move they'd been waiting for.

"Go!" Edgin shouted.

All the players came onto the board at once, like a well-coordinated dance. Edgin had always sensed he had a good crew, that they worked in a harmony that would be envied by other thieving groups up and down the Sword Coast. Maybe it was because they were family too, and they were driven by more than just the motive to steal for themselves. They wanted to protect one another.

Or maybe Edgin was about to die, and this was just his life flashing before his eyes, a reexamination of all the choices that had brought him to this point. Either way, there was no turning back now.

The first move was Holga's. She left Simon standing near the ballroom's double doors and charged across the room toward Sharrestren. The beholder ignored her, focused entirely on retaliating against Torlinn for the fireball. Because of that, Holga, dropping her axe as she ran, was able to get right up to the beholder, but instead of attacking, she launched herself into the air with a fierce battle cry, landing on the beholder's body. She wrapped both arms and legs around its bulbous form, grabbing two eyestalks to use as handholds.

And squeezed.

Sharrestren let out an incoherent shriek, spinning and bobbing in the air, trying to dislodge the large woman clinging to him like a stirge.

Torlinn's face lit up with a wild grin, and he again brought the staff to bear, aiming it at both Holga and Sharrestren.

Edgin's belly tightened with fury. A part of him had hoped that Torlinn wouldn't try to attack, knowing that he'd hurt Holga in the process. But he was too far gone in his desire for revenge. Edgin recognized that mad light in his eyes. He'd felt the same way after Zia was killed.

But Edgin had also counted on Torlinn being too distracted to notice Forge coming up behind him. In a comically similar move to the one Holga had just made, Forge tackled Torlinn from behind, driving them both to the floor. In the tangle of arms and legs, Torlinn lost his grip on the staff, and it went rolling across the ballroom floor.

"What are you doing?" Torlinn screamed in rage, clawing at Forge's face. "I had him!"

"Get ready, Simon!" Edgin shouted. He ran to the staff and wrapped his cloak around his hand before scooping it up. It was a risky move, but he was out of options. Now he had a potted plant and an ancient artifact.

Perfect.

He ran to the center of the dance floor, setting the potted plant down and driving the Staff of Aorth into the pot like a stake stuck in the ground.

Directly above him loomed the massive pipe organ, the centerpiece of the orchestra that Sharrestren had been so proud of. Around it, one by one, the other instruments were catching on fire, creating a disturbing tableau on the ceiling.

"Now, Simon!"

Across the room, Simon began to cast a spell. His hands trembled, his eyes fixed on the pipe organ.

"No!" Torlinn wrenched himself free of Forge and muttered a spell. A thunderous wave of energy hit the con man and tossed him across the room. The back of his head hit the buffet table and he collapsed, unmoving, on the floor.

Not good. "Simon, hurry!" Edgin shouted. He wanted to run to help Forge, and he wanted to get as far away from the staff as possible, but he couldn't leave it. He couldn't risk Sharrestren or Torlinn getting it again.

Luckily, Sharrestren was still distracted trying to get rid of Holga. Eye beams flashed, lighting up the ballroom in eerie glows, but Holga managed to dodge them, wrenching the eyestalks with her bare hands to throw off Sharrestren's aim.

But Torlinn was getting to his feet. Edgin grabbed the staff, prepared to run, but Torlinn turned to face Simon, evidently divining what he was trying to do.

"Stop!" he cried, thrusting a hand at Simon, claws dripping blood from a wound Edgin couldn't see. "I've waited too long! I won't let you take it from me!"

Fire bloomed at his fingertips, pointing at Simon.

And Edgin saw something he'd never seen in the young half-elf's face before. Simon stared at the fire growing in Torlinn's hand, and a wave of calm seemed to wash over him. His hands stopped trembling. He lowered them, turning his attention from the pipe organ to Torlinn. He chanted some arcane phrases that Edgin recognized.

A counterspell.

Torlinn's face, which had been alight with wild triumph, crumpled as the fire in his hand guttered and died. At the same instant, Simon looked up at the pipe organ and calmly chanted another spell, looking more confident in that moment than Edgin had ever seen him. It was as if, when his life was on the line, his back to the wall, Simon finally stopped being afraid.

Above him, the pipe organ groaned loud and ominous as Simon stripped away the magic holding it to the ceiling. Across the room, Sharrestren flung Holga off and spun to face Edgin.

"Die!" Sharrestren shouted at him. He was already firing an eye beam at Edgin as he screamed.

Edgin had that moment again, the moment of his life flashing before his eyes. Whatever that ray was, it was going to kill him. He knew it. He'd heard the stories of the eye tyrant rays that could kill with a touch, and he'd seen the dwarf disintegrated before his eyes.

This was it, then. He hadn't gotten to say goodbye to Kira. His heart lurched in his chest, and his eyes burned, but somewhere inside him, he felt a sense of peace.

Holga. Holga would take care of her, would protect Kira no matter what, because she loved her. He'd always known that. And the rest of them would be there too. They were all a family of misfits. They would look out for one another, and he would do this one last thing to protect them.

Then the world was filled with light as a shudder rocked the ballroom.

"Edgin, move!" Simon was screaming at him.

But the beam . . .

Edgin turned just in time to see Torlinn in front of him, crumpling to the ground. He'd been running toward Edgin, and the beam had struck him in the back. He lay in a heap on the floor.

Sharrestren was coming at him—no, coming for the staff—and the pipe organ shuddered again as, freed from its magic, it fell.

Edgin dove out of the way, leaving the staff standing upright in the potted plant just as the pipe organ came down on top of it *and* Sharrestren.

A thunderous crash shook the house and knocked Edgin off his feet. He crawled to the wall, dragging the remains of a sofa down on top of his head just as a tremendous explosion rocked the ballroom, deafening him. He covered his face with his hands and curled into a ball.

Heat washed over him in a wave, hotter than flame, blistering in its intensity. Magic crackled in the air, lifting the hairs on his arms, invading his nostrils with the scent of lightning and burning flesh. His eyes watered, and he coughed on the smoke that was invading every part of the room. His heart thundered in his chest. Never in his life had he felt such an outpouring of magic as when the Staff of Aorth was destroyed.

And then, just like that, it was over. Silence reigned except for the loud ringing in Edgin's ears. Slowly, he uncurled his body and thrust the remains of the sofa—which was now blackened and on fire—off of him. He got to his feet, knees wobbling. The driftglobes in the room had all gone out. The only light now came from the moonlight at the windows and the fire licking along the ceiling and walls.

There was a pipe organ–sized crater in the center of the ballroom, but little else remained of the instrument. Ash drifted in clouds in the air. *That* seemed to be all that was left of Torlinn, Sharrestren, and the Staff of Aorth. They'd all been consumed by the magical explosion.

Edgin called out through the haze and smoke for his friends.

Holga emerged from behind a pile of rubble with Simon at her side. Edgin's head swam with relief. "We're here," Holga said. "Forge?"

He'd been unconscious by the buffet table. Edgin ran over there, boots crunching on bits of the crystal chandelier, which had come down and shattered on the floor.

Forge was lying where he'd fallen, but someone else had reached him before Edgin. Lady Sofina was bending over his chest, listening for a heartbeat.

"Is he dead?" Edgin asked tightly, kneeling next to her.

Lady Sofina looked up at him in surprise. "You're alive?" she said, blinking at him. "I thought for sure you'd been caught in that blast."

"Is he dead?" Edgin repeated sharply.

"No," she said. She reached into a pocket of her dress and pulled out a potion, unstoppering it with her thumb. "I can't believe I'm using this on him, after our history." She sighed and poured the potion down his throat.

Forge's eyes popped open and he sucked in a breath, coughing weakly on the smoke. "Am I dead?" He groaned and clutched his head. "Or hungover?"

"He'll be fine." Lady Sofina got to her feet with Edgin's help. She looked exhausted, and she was bleeding from a deep cut on her cheek. "I believe I've had enough revelry for one evening. I'm leaving."

"Who are you?" Edgin asked, a suspicion he couldn't ignore gripping him suddenly. "Are you really just a party guest here?"

"I'm as much a party guest as you are," she said with a daggerlike smile. "Let's just say I represent a group in Neverwinter who wanted Torlinn's magical activities investigated."

Ah. That could mean she was a Harper, or a member of the Lords'

Alliance, or even the Zhentarim. There were any number of organizations that kept an eye on threats to Faerûn.

"I thought that you and your crew were involved somehow," she went on, "though obviously not in the way I expected." She cocked her head as she looked at Edgin. "Who are *you*, if I might ask?"

Did she know him? Edgin wondered if she'd asked around about him. It wouldn't be terribly difficult to find people who remembered him from his days as a Harper.

It didn't matter. Edgin shook his head, giving her that charming smile he'd perfected. "We're just common thieves, ma'am," he said. "We were in the wrong place at the wrong time."

She raised an eyebrow. "Just common thieves," she repeated skeptically. "Well, if that's the case, you'd better leave soon if you want to avoid more than just my own questions. My backup will be arriving shortly, you see."

"That's our cue, then," Edgin said, giving her a bow. "Oh, and you might tell your people that there's a fairly extensive complex beneath this estate. It's full of monsters and murderous traps. Just, you know, if they want to check it out."

Lady Sofina's eyes sparkled with interest. "I will. My thanks, Edgin. Perhaps we can work together again in the future."

Edgin nodded politely, though he sincerely hoped they never met again. He helped Forge to his feet, slinging an arm around the con man's shoulders. "Holga, Simon, can you get Alyanna and meet us out front?" he said. "I need to find Kira."

"And the loot," Forge mumbled.

"We'll take care of it," Holga said. She and Simon turned away, but Edgin called out to the half-elf, who turned back to look at him. There were dark circles of exhaustion and pain under his eyes.

"Way to come through, Simon," Edgin said. "Thanks."

CHAPTER 34

The barrier was down. It had fallen with Sharrestren's death. Edgin, Forge, and the other survivors who were well enough to walk burst through the doors to find a crowd of people waiting outside. The guests who'd managed to escape the mansion before Sharrestren transformed were confused and frightened, but Edgin didn't spare them a thought. He was only looking for one person.

He found her standing at the very front of the crowd. She was clutching her domino mask in her hands, which now sported a jagged crack down the white side of the mask.

Edgin's gut clenched. That's how close he'd come to losing her. Never again, he told himself. He'd promised Kira she could be a part of his work, but not like this. He wasn't involving her in any more heists that involved wizards and powerful magic. It was too dangerous.

When Kira saw him, she ran and leaped into Edgin's arms. He caught her with a grunt and hugged her tight.

"Dad, I can't breathe!"

"Tough," Edgin said, stroking her hair with a shaking hand. He set her down and pulled back so he could get a look at her. "I was so worried, Kira," he said, his voice trembling.

"Me too." Kira's eyes were huge in her dirt-smudged face. "We all kept pounding on the barrier, but we couldn't get through, and then there was that huge explosion!"

"That was us," Edgin said. "What happened to your mask?" He touched the crack with one finger.

"When Holga pushed me outside, the barrier caught the edge of it and cracked it," Kira said. She waved a hand, as if that didn't matter. "But where are Holga and the others? What happened to Sharrestren and Torlinn?"

"Holga and our crew are fine," Forge assured her. "I don't suppose you managed to bring the wagon around?"

Kira nodded, grinning. "It's around back by the servant's entrance, just where you wanted it when we were planning everything."

Edgin swept her up in his arms again, spinning her around. "You are the best daughter ever!"

The wagon was indeed waiting at the servant's entrance, and Holga, Simon, and Alyanna were already there, loading up all the loot they could carry from the treasure room upstairs. Edgin was surprised any of it was intact, but apparently Sharrestren had some extra protection magic on the room, so they were able to collect a sizable amount of coin and paintings that would sell for a handsome price.

It wasn't the same as acquiring the staff, but at that moment, Edgin didn't care. He had his crew, his family. They were safe, and they were getting away. He felt a surge of relief and exhilaration as they all piled into the wagon and took off for home.

THEY GATHERED AT Edgin's house to split up the treasure. Alyanna wasn't sure of her welcome at first, but Edgin insisted they were square after what she'd done protecting him from the beholder. Edgin broke out some wine and a cask of ale, and they used the last of their healing potions to treat Holga's leg and some other wounds she'd taken while she was attacking Sharrestren with her bare hands.

"Not many people can claim to have wrestled a beholder," Forge said, saluting Holga with his wineglass.

Holga just shrugged and shifted Kira so she was more comfortable on her lap. She'd fallen asleep there almost as soon as Holga had sat down by the fire. They were all exhausted, but there was a nervous energy humming in the room, a recognition that they'd all survived something harrowing together, and they were irrevocably bonded by the experience.

"To Holga and Simon," Edgin said, raising his glass. "Beholder slayers!"

"To all of us, and to new beginnings," Simon said, clinking his glass against Alyanna's. She seemed none the worse for wear after the beholder's paralysis had ended. She was just tired and dirty like the rest of them, and reeking of smoke. Edgin was going to take the longest bath in the world at some point tonight.

The party broke up soon after. Alyanna wanted to be far away from the area before sunrise to start her new life. Edgin was surprised that, in addition to her share of the loot, Forge gave her his climbing boots.

"In case you ever decide to pursue thievery as full-time work," he said. "I've plenty of other tricks to use."

Edgin had no doubt of that.

After Alyanna left, with Simon escorting her to the edge of town, Holga took Kira to her bed, laying the domino mask on her bedside table, a souvenir of the heist. Then Edgin, Forge, and Holga stepped outside for a bit of fresh air.

Edgin looked up at the sky. It was a cloudless night, and the darkness was thick with stars, the air cool and crisp on his face. He sighed in contentment.

"You know, this is almost the perfect night," he said, and he meant it. He had the family he'd made for himself around him, a profitable heist behind him, and the future looked bright. The only thing missing, the thing that would have made everything perfect, was if Zia had been there to share it with him.

Some of his thoughts must have shown on his face, because Holga swatted him on the shoulder. "No one gets a perfect night," she said. Her voice was a low rumble in the darkness. "But you've got us, and we've got you."

Edgin looked up at her. "Always?" he asked.

She smiled faintly. "Always. So be grateful for what you have." Then she turned and went back inside the cottage, leaving Edgin and Forge alone.

"I suppose she's right," Edgin said, speaking half to himself. "No one gets the perfect night or the perfect life, do they?"

"Oh, I don't know," Forge said thoughtfully, taking a sip of wine. "Tonight, you faced down a beholder and a powerful wizard and came out on top. I think you're capable of great things, Ed, greater than you realize." He shrugged. "And who knows, maybe it's possible to steal the perfect life. We are a crew of thieves, after all."

Edgin chuckled. He wasn't sure he shared Forge's optimism, but at that moment, it didn't matter. He didn't have the perfect life, but what he had was precious, and for now, it was enough.

EPILOGUE

Kira's eyes had drifted closed sometime during the denoue-
ment of Edgin's story, and she was snoring softly in her bed.
Edgin rose slowly from his chair and pulled the blankets
up around her chin. He straightened and looked down at his daughter for a moment. She resembled Zia more and more every day, and
Edgin felt a pang of loneliness pierce his heart. Zia would have loved
telling her bedtime stories too.

He checked the fire in the small hearth before he left, which had
burned down to nothing but embers softly glowing in the darkness.
Partially closing the door behind him, he went into the kitchen for a
glass of water before bed.

There was no sign of Holga, though Edgin had been sure she'd
been out here listening to at least part of the story. She must have
gone to bed sometime near the ending too.

She'd kept her promise all this time. They had each other's backs,
and they were always there for each other.

He stood looking out the kitchen window into the darkness. For
some reason, his thoughts kept returning to the ending of the story,
the memory of the conversation with Forge outside the cottage.

Maybe it's possible to steal the perfect life.

He'd laughed off the words at the time, but now he wondered. After all he'd seen and done, Edgin was willing to admit that his crew was capable of an awful lot. And Forge had been hinting lately about a job that he thought Edgin would be particularly interested in, but he hadn't offered more than those cryptic words.

Time would tell, but for now, Edgin drank his water and listened to the sounds of the night around him, to Holga snoring in the next room, to Kira shifting and sighing in her sleep. For now, he vowed he'd just be grateful for what he had, and he would try not to want anything more.

Well, maybe just a little bit more. He was still a thief, after all.

ACKNOWLEDGMENTS

I have surrounded myself with so many geeks, gamers, and all-around cool people over the years who have made my life richer and more exciting for their presence. To Elizabeth Schaefer and the team at Random House Worlds, you are editors after my own geek-girl heart, and I loved every minute of working on this book and talking D&D with you. Thanks for making this project such a blast. To the folks at Wizards of the Coast, past and present, I love watching you do what you do and am grateful I've gotten a chance to go along for the ride at different times over the years. To my agent, Sara Megibow, I know these two things to be true: I couldn't do this without you, and I would fly across the country anytime to play Terraforming Mars with you. Game on. To my own home gaming group, and especially to my husband and my brother, whether we're playing board games, roleplaying games, MMORPGs, and everything in between, it's been a heck of a ride. Let's still be busting out new games when we're in our nineties. I'll put the coffee on and keep the dice ready. And finally, to my dad, who is not a gamer but who started me on the path by putting books into my hands whenever I wanted them. You really have no one to blame but yourself. I love you.

READ ON FOR AN EXCERPT FROM

THE
DRUID'S
CALL

BY E. K. JOHNSTON

In her parents' defense, they did try. They didn't do a very good job, and they definitely gave up the moment things got difficult, but they did try.

And that is how the tiefling Doric survived babyhood.

CHAPTER 1

The sharp twang of a bowstring had a way of attracting attention. Arrows could be quiet if they were fletched properly, and a well-trained ranger could move through a pile of dry leaves without making a noise. But some things were just unavoidable. If you were going to take a shot, you had to be sure your aim was true, because you might not get another chance.

Doric's arrow went wide, and the herd of deer that she and her fellows had been diligently tracking split up in a panic and melted into the trees.

"That was better!" said a chipper voice beside her. Torrieth could always be counted on for encouragement, even when Doric wasn't in the mood for it. It was the foundation of their relationship and had been since the first time the slender, dark-haired elf had laid eyes on her.

Doric crashed through the brush to retrieve her arrow. She didn't even try to be quiet, and her tail thrashed at the low-growing shrubs in the underbrush. She looked up and saw a snowy owl perched above her. Even the owl looked judgmental. She stuck her tongue out at it, but it didn't react.

"We can't eat what we don't shoot," Doric pointed out, returning to her friend's side.

"There are plenty of deer," Torrieth told her. "Maybe the others will have better luck."

Doric wanted to tell her that it wasn't luck. It was skill, and it was a skill that she couldn't seem to master no matter how long she practiced. She knew the other hunting parties were positioned so that after she screwed up, they'd be able to take advantage of the panicking deer. Her incompetence was part of the plan, an example of how she was able to contribute. She hated that.

"You know," Torrieth continued, "no one expects you to be out here. You don't have to hunt with us. You don't even eat that much."

She did, sometimes, eat what the hunters brought home. Perhaps if she were a more able hunter, she would feel differently, but she wasn't, and so she ate things the elves couldn't when no one was watching and held herself to minimal portions from the communal hearth. She didn't want to remind the elves that she was different too frequently, but even more than that, she didn't want to be a burden.

There were deer aplenty. In fact, there were probably too many deer. The farmers and woodcutters along the forest edge killed the wolves that preyed on their livestock, thinning them out until there weren't enough to keep the deer population in check. Then the deer ate everything that was green and below shoulder height, leaving little for the other forest animals. So the elves ate the deer in order to restore the balance. It was a work in progress, but it was progress all the same.

The Neverwinter Wood was a strange place where seasonal norms didn't precisely apply. Something was always flowering or fruiting or mating, and that meant that food was rarely hard to come by. But that food always tasted like guilt to Doric, and if her demon-given stomach could handle fallen tree bark and the occasional piece of limestone, she'd let it. The wood elves had taken care of her ever since she'd first come to the forest, which was a rare blessing from the reclusive forest-dwellers. She was nothing like them, but she owed them a lot. The least she could do was make it easy for them.

"I want to help," Doric said.

"I know," Torrieth said. "Maybe you just need more practice."

It was kind of her—Torrieth was usually kind—but Doric had already decided that this would be her last hunt if she was unsuccessful. She'd try something else. Like berry picking. It had to be hard to screw up berry picking.

"Whatever you're thinking, I reject it utterly," Torrieth said. "And I will kill you if you leave me out here in the forest alone with all the boys."

Doric laughed in spite of herself. Torrieth wasn't the only girl in their age-group with ranger talents, but she'd dragged Doric into training with her anyway. Lately it seemed like a few of the boys were inventing reasons to spend time with Torrieth, and she wasn't particularly interested in most of them. Doric definitely understood wanting to avoid attracting attention.

"Fine, I'll keep practicing," Doric said. "But maybe I should talk to Liavaris about another apprenticeship or something, just in case."

Torrieth only rolled her eyes, and the two girls headed back down the game trail towards the elven encampment. It was a sunny day in the Neverwinter Wood, which was not uncommon, and the air was warm. Outside the forest it was early spring, cold days broken up by warming breezes. Here, under the dappled green light of the trees, the sun wasn't particularly hot, but it could get humid quickly. The elven hunters had gone out at first light to avoid the worst of it.

Now that they weren't focused on the deer, Torrieth's gaze wandered to and fro through the trees. Doric watched her, wondering if she could learn to see the forest the way her friend did. She wanted to love the strong, tall trees and the grappling shrubs that tried to grow up from the forest floor, but she didn't feel it the way Torrieth seemed to. No matter how hard she tried to forget, the forest held dark memories for her, so she could never be entirely comfortable here. She could tell if animals were healthy or if plants were hale, but her experience was hard won. And yet Torrieth breathed the forest in, always knowing exactly where she was and remembering every leaf and twig she saw.

"Berries." Torrieth pointed away from the game trail. She knew Doric hated to come home empty-handed. "Did you bring a bag?"

Doric had already pulled a foraging bag out of her satchel. The girls went into the brush, and a few steps later, they were surrounded by fat red partridgeberries, dark as blood. It took them only a few minutes to fill the bag, stripping three-quarters of the berries from every plant, leaving some for the birds. They were nearly back to the trail when one of the other hunting parties caught up with them.

"Torrieth, look!" Deverel was almost staggering under the weight of the young deer he carried across his shoulders. He'd been part of their training group, and this was his first successful hunt. He was clearly thrilled. "It was awesome. The deer came crashing through where we were set up, and my shot was perfect."

Doric could see he was telling the truth. There was almost no blood, and from her angle, the deer looked unmarked. Deverel was right to be proud of himself, and he was genuine enough that it wasn't obnoxious. He'd practiced his aim day and night for months now. Torrieth congratulated him, and Deverel's copper skin flushed a few shades pinker.

"Doric, Torrieth," said Deverel's mentor, a seasoned ranger named Fenjor. "I'm glad we found you. I've got to get this one back to camp, but there's something strange going on southwest of here, by the river. It's too quiet, and the water doesn't feel right. We didn't have time to check it out before the deer came. Could you make sure nothing is amiss?"

"Of course," Doric said. She handed over the berries a bit reluctantly. She was going to be empty-handed after all. But there was no way she'd say no to a request from one of the elders.

"Oh, these are perfect," Deverel said, looking into the bag. "Your berries and my deer wrapped up and roasted together all afternoon—it's going to be delicious. I'm going to tell everyone."

Fenjor rolled his eyes, but his smile was indulgent. Torrieth covered her smirk by checking her quiver. Of all the clan members, Deverel was the one she liked best after Doric, though as far as Doric knew, neither of them had talked to the other about it.

"Ready to go?" Torrieth asked.

"Always," Doric replied.

They plunged back into the forest in the direction that Fenjor and Deverel had come from. It was an easy walk through the underbrush. The way down to the river was always easier than the way home. For most of its course through the Neverwinter Wood, the river was slow and meandering, its banks gentle. Near the camp, the river was narrow and quick, with steep, rocky banks that were easy enough to scramble down but a challenge to climb. Doric would never complain. At least she wouldn't have to do it carrying a deer.

"Deverel seems nice," Doric said after a few moments walking in silence.

"Oh, he's absolutely gone on me," Torrieth said. "We could have collected a basket full of slugs, and he'd still be all excited at the idea that we worked together to get dinner. It's kind of cute."

Doric snorted. She'd been with the elves since she was a child, but sometimes the things they did still perplexed her.

"You laugh, but someday someone's going to look at those pretty red curls and fall head over heels for you," Torrieth said.

Most of the wood elves had brown hair, though a few, like Torrieth, had darker shades. Doric's hair color was the least of her concerns when it came to her head. Her horns gave her away as a tiefling instantly, and just as quickly many equated her with the destructive tendencies of demons. Doric had spent almost every waking moment since the elves had taken her in doing her best to make sure that they had no reason to think poorly of her.

"You're making that face again," Torrieth said. "I'm not sure how many times I can reject your thoughts in one day."

Torrieth's complete refusal to be put off by Doric's horns, tail, and general insecurity was one of her best qualities. She'd been adamant about her friendship since the girls had first met, when Doric had spent her first season with the elves. Doric had been mystified as to why Torrieth had taken to her so quickly. Torrieth eventually confessed that at first it had been sheer stubbornness: her uncle had been one of the few who'd wanted Doric to leave. The more time they had spent together, though, the truer Torrieth's affections had become. In the near decade since, Torrieth had never wavered, even when some of the others expressed distaste for Doric.

They continued down to the river, which was flowing cheerily over the rocky bed. The water was clear and cold, no matter how warm the forest got. It wasn't immediately obvious why Fenjor had said the water didn't feel right, but he was much more experienced than they were.

"Let's go downstream," Doric said. "Upstream must be fine, because the water's still clear."

They kept going, and Doric began to sense that something was wrong. Dark memories of the forest, the unpredictable flooding preceded by too-quiet animals and birds, pulled at the back of her mind. She didn't want to think about it, not even to do what Fenjor had asked.

"Being out here is giving me the creeps," Doric said.

"Do you think we should go back up?" Torrieth asked.

Doric considered it. "No. We'll just take a quick look and then decide what to do from there."

The girls moved as quietly as they could, which for Torrieth was totally silent. Doric felt like a mammoth by comparison, even though none of the animals around them seemed to notice her. They followed the riverbank around several bends, and just when Doric was mentally kicking herself for coming up empty on even a simple scouting run, they came upon what they were looking for.

A huge pile of logs stood on the far side of the river. The branches had been stripped away, and all of the detritus had been swept into a giant pit that was still smoking. All around the pile were tree stumps, short and hacked off, and the brush had been thoroughly trampled. A few of the logs had been stretched across the river. The water flowed over them, but it was clear that when they were ready to transport the timber, there would be a dam.

"What is happening?" Torrieth asked, but Doric knew the signs.

"Humans," she hissed. "These trees are probably worth a lot of money."

"We're still in the middle of the woods," Torrieth pointed out. "Why are they cutting down trees here? How are they going to get all the logs out of the forest?"

Doric remembered the rush of water, the endless drag and pull.

"If they finish the dam, the water will build up behind it,"

Doric said. "It'll flood the area we're standing on, but when they break the dam apart, all that water will go downstream really fast."

"Pushing the logs all the way to the city," Torrieth finished.

They stared at the wood and water, envisioning the surge and all that it would sweep away.

"I don't like this," Torrieth said. "There have always been humans in the Neverwinter Wood, but not like this. The wood-cutters we know wouldn't cause this kind of damage. And it's more than just the trees: this will throw off hunting patterns— and not only ours."

Doric didn't like it when humans did anything, but this in particular dug under her skin. Like with hunting deer, the elves respected that some trees had to be cut. When wood was dead or someone needed a house or to stay warm outside the forest, they felled only the amount they needed. But this was on a devastatingly larger scale. And it seemed like it was just the beginning.

"We should go back," Doric said. "We have to tell the others right away."

"They'll have a better idea of what to do," Torrieth agreed with a wise nod.

From across the cleared area came an angry roar. Doric and Torrieth froze immediately, recognizing the sound. Elves and bears usually avoided one another in the forest, but if Torrieth was right and the logging had disrupted the bear's hunting, it might be hungry enough to try its luck on other territory and prey. Doric grabbed Torrieth's shoulder and they both dropped to the ground.

The bear crashed into view. Thankfully, it was both upwind and on the other side of the river. The bear shambled around the logging stand, sniffing at piles of wood and traces of human habitation. It made its way to the water and splashed its front paws in the shallows.

"There should be fish," Torrieth breathed so quietly in Doric's ear that she almost thought she'd imagined it. "It's probably more interested in food."

While Torrieth deduced the reason for the bear's appetite, Doric could imagine its rage. It should be well fed and happy. This was the Neverwinter Wood; this was a bear's paradise. Yet now its territory had been spoiled. It would have to stay and starve or leave and fight for a new home.

"Very slowly," Torrieth said. "While it's in the water. Follow me."

Torrieth slid through the brush, and Doric followed, choosing every step with utmost care. In spite of her very best attempt to stay quiet, she broke a stick underfoot, and the dry crack might as well have been a thunderclap. Both girls froze, and the bear looked right at them.

"Make yourself big!" said Torrieth, no longer needing to be quiet. "Don't run. Stand your ground!"

She swiftly turned towards the bear and planted her feet shoulder width apart with her arms outstretched. Doric meant to match her friend's movements but caught her foot on a tangle of roots. Her ankle buckled, and Doric went down with it. Down like a prey animal.

"Doric!" Torrieth strained to keep her voice calm. The bear needed only seconds to cross the river, and it stalked up to Doric with its ears laid back. A low growl rumbled in its throat. It snapped its jaws threateningly.

In a panic, Doric stood up to her full height and faced the bear down. It was just over her wingspan's length away, salivating and desperate.

"Stop!" she said, one hand held up imperiously, her legs trembling.

The bear stopped. It stood up and tilted its head, sniffing the air inquisitively. They stared at each other. In that moment, the massive creature seemed to soften, its face all but pleading.

"We're going to help," Doric said firmly. "We can't help if you eat us."

The bear huffed, an almost petulant sound. Its sad eyes were sunken into its head from weight loss. Its fur had become dull and patchy. Doric remembered being so hungry she thought her stomach would chew right through her spine.

"Stay back." Doric set her jaw.

She felt her blood boil—not at the bear, but for it. The bear wouldn't be baring its teeth at them if its home hadn't been ruined. It wasn't wrong to be angry.

The tranquility between tiefling and bear suddenly snapped. Fury once again filled the bear's eyes. It dropped to its front paws with a heavy thud and roared at the top of its lungs.

"Doric, back away." Torrieth's voice tore from a whisper to a cry. "Keep your arms up and back away!"

The bear snapped its attention past Doric and effortlessly bolted towards Torrieth. With a terrifying snarl, it swiped a dense paw at the elf. She was nimble, but not nimble enough to escape the bear's claws. The razor-sharp tips caught her skin and dragged five weeping red lines across her bicep.

"STAY BACK!" Doric shouted from deep in her gut, fingers curled like talons. She stamped the ground and closed the gap to be closer to the starving bear than any self-preservation instinct would normally have allowed.

Suddenly, the bear hushed. It stopped, already in motion for the final blow, and nearly stumbled straight into Torrieth. It ducked its head low, and for a second that seemed entirely like fantasy, it looked afraid. The bear backed up a few steps before turning and running back into the woods from which it came.

"How—" Torrieth panted, clamping her hand down on her wounds. "How did you do that?"

"I . . . don't know," Doric said. She didn't want to talk about it. It was new and different, and Doric had spent a lot of time trying not to be new or different. "Let's get out of here. We need someone to take care of your arm right away." She tore a length of fabric from her sleeve and wrapped it tightly around Torrieth's bicep. She could still feel that famished, angry roar in her ears.

The girls didn't talk as they made their way back home. Doric stared at her feet as they walked, allowing her vision to lose focus. Torrieth was hurt, and all because of her. Long before they reached the treetop village, they smelled roasting meat and heard the clan celebrating Deverel's first hunt. It was familiar, an almost-home. And somehow, she'd have to tell the people who had taken pity on her what they'd seen on the river-bank, what she sensed might be coming, and that she'd gotten her only close friend hurt.

CHAPTER 2

There were enough elves spread across the realms that making generalized comments about their living habits was next to pointless. The clan that had welcomed Doric had lived in and with the Neverwinter Wood for generations and didn't need to move around much to follow seasonal rhythms. High up in the trees, the wood elves built intricate treehouses, platforms connected by sturdy walkways, and broad verandas where many could gather. Dwellings had roofs of woven grass and reeds with waterproof hides beneath to keep out the rain. They didn't have fires inside, though some of the elders had braziers that could be filled with bright embers on nights when there was a chill. There were large huts for extended families, small huts for one or two people who wanted privacy, and everything in between.

Doric's hut was one of the newer ones. Torrieth had helped her build it two years ago when she moved out of Liavaris's home. The elder had kept Doric as close as family but respected the tiefling's wish for a place of her own. Now Liavaris's apprentice, one of her grandnieces, slept in the spot where Doric used to, because the old elf didn't want to be alone.

"Then why don't you move in with us?" Liavaris's youngest niece, Sarasri, had asked. "We have plenty of room."

Liavaris had watched as three elf babies wrestled on the floor, getting under the feet of the adults who were working, while fourteen other children careened in and out of the enclosure.

"I said I didn't want to be alone," the old elf said. "Not that I wanted to be surrounded by complete mayhem. I get enough of that at council meetings."

And so everyone ended up more or less where they wanted to be. The grandniece certainly had no complaints about her new, significantly quieter, living arrangements.

Doric's bungalow was built on a sturdy branch that was usually downwind of the main gathering area. Torrieth had chosen the spot, guessing (correctly) that if Doric were left to her own devices, she'd live in the farthest corner she could wedge herself into. Instead, she was just outside the main circle, with a tiny firepit of her own and a straight line of sight to the central hearth. It was an acceptable compromise for everyone.

The central fire was already roaring when the girls returned to camp. A large portion of Deverel's deer was on a spit, slowly turning above the crackling flames. Deverel had been true to his word: Doric could see the dark red juice of the berries he'd stuffed it with dripping into the fire as they roasted and burst out of their skins. The rest of the deer was being portioned off for drying or smoking, with the hide and bones set aside for later use. The mood was celebratory, and Deverel himself was seated next to the elders while his parents beamed at him from across the fire.

When he saw them, Deverel nearly bounced out of his seat in his enthusiasm to wave them over. Torrieth blushed and pulled her cloak over her arm. Doric would rather cut out her own liver than step on Deverel's moment. Their report could wait until someone asked them about it, as much as it was gnawing at Doric's mind. Torrieth was smiling despite the gashes in her arm. Doric had always found it difficult to stay stoic when Torrieth grinned at her, so by the time they made it to the fire, both of them looked convincingly like they were excited to be there.

"And, as I was telling you"—Deverel was clearly winding up the story of his hunt—"the deer came straight at me. Doric must have spooked it exactly right. I couldn't have done it without her."

Doric felt her smile freeze. The worst part was that Deverel was being completely serious. He actually thought she had missed her shot on purpose, to give him the chance. Torrieth had made her first successful hunt weeks ago, and since then she and Doric had landed enough small game that no one openly derided Doric's participation, but everyone knew she wasn't actually very good. And yet here was Deverel, the star of the hour, going on like she was an integral part of his success.

Fenjor looked at her sympathetically, and the other elders reacted with varying degrees of amusement. Only Liavaris kept a straight face. Doric had never been able to tell what her guardian was thinking, and today was no different. She had a few guesses, though. Most of them revolved around Doric being a constant frustration. She wanted to shrink to nothing, to disappear, but Torrieth had a hold on her arm, and she couldn't leave without making a fuss.

"That's why we hunt in groups," Fenjor said, finally breaking the moment. "We celebrate individuals, but we remember that everyone contributed."

Deverel's smile grew even wider.

The cooks announced that the meat was ready and began slicing portions off the roast. Everyone's plate was filled with portions more generous than usual to celebrate. There were fennel and fiddleheads to go along with it, as well as more berries and toasted wildgrains. The taste was rich and green and only a little bit gamey. The deer must have been in good shape.

Plates were passed around, and Doric took a seat close to the fire. It could get crowded on feast nights, with everyone coming together to eat, and since she wasn't affected by the fire as much as the others, Doric had no problem taking the closest place. Torrieth joined her, her face already turning a bit red from the heat. Tonight, Doric would eat from the main meal. There was plenty to go around, and Torrieth would make a face if she ate only a little bit and then snuck away. It was so easy to be Torrieth's shadow. Everyone liked her, and for some reason, she'd decided she liked Doric. If only Doric's aim with a bow could improve, her life would be all but perfect. She wouldn't be important, but she'd be useful, and the clan would never have any reason to ask her to leave.

Wood elves weren't overly trusting of strangers, and yet for some reason they allowed Doric to stay, though she had never fit all the way in. Their skin was a pretty copper with a greenish cast in the dappled forest light, while Doric was pale as a porcelain dinner plate. No one had her hair color either. But those two things were the least of her differences. A tiefling was one of nature's inexplicable hiccups—a demon child born to otherwise human parents—and Doric counted herself as such. Liavaris had clearly taken her in out of pity. It was Doric's responsibility to earn the right to stay, and that meant winning the approval of the elders.

The clan was overseen by ten of them. The position wasn't necessarily tied to age, though that was part of it. More, it was experience and willingness to put up with one another. Fenjor and Liavaris were the two that Doric was the most comfortable around, but tonight even they were exchanging looks over her head. She was going to practice firing arrows tomorrow until her fingers cramped, she decided. She was going to get a deer.

"Did you two find anything troubling down by the river-bank?" Fenjor asked, shifting closer to Doric and Torrieth. He spoke loudly enough that others close by could hear.

"What's this?" asked Marlion. He might have been Torri-eth's uncle, but he didn't share his niece's affection for Doric.

"There was something in the woods, and I asked the girls to look, that's all," Fenjor said. He was sitting with his legs out in front of him, the picture of relaxation, but Doric knew he was on edge: he was digging his fingers into the wood of the seat beneath him. "I had to see Deverel back to camp, so I asked Doric and Torrieth to investigate for me."

"Out with it, then," said Marlion. He was clearly talking to Torrieth.

"Doric talked to a bear!" Torrieth was apparently done holding it in. Her cloak shifted off of her hurt arm while the words erupted out of her.

Every eye snapped to Doric, and she wanted to sink into the ground.

"I didn't *talk* to it exactly," Doric said. "It was more like . . ." But she struggled to find the words to describe her moment of connection with the bear.

"I think it would be best if you started at the beginning," Fenjor said gently.

"It didn't take us very long to follow Fenjor's directions," Torrieth said, wrestling her tone under control. "We found a logging stand. At least a hundred trees had been cut, mostly oak and ash. They were stacked neatly, so someone's clearly coming back for them."

"Humans?" Marlion pressed. When Torrieth nodded, he sat back and glowered. "They'll never clear enough trees to get a wagon in here, and dragging the logs behind a horse would take forever. What are they up to?"

"Doric thinks they're going to use the river," Torrieth said.

Any eye that had left Doric turned back to her, and Doric fought off the urge to flinch. Torrieth squeezed her knee encouragingly.

"I think they're building a dam," Doric said. "It's not done yet, but once it is, they can leave it for a few days to fill with water and then use the flood to push the logs downriver to the city."

"And the bear?" Fenjor asked.

Doric relayed the story as calmly as she could, trying to make everything seem relatively normal given the circumstances. Considerable murmurs rose up from the listeners as Doric spoke, and concerned looks were exchanged. Marlion in particular looked sour and upset.

"So because you managed to frighten off a ravenous bear, you think it is passable that my niece was wounded?" he snapped.

"It's superficial, honestly." Torrieth folded her arms with a frown, and she did her best to swallow a wince as she agitated her injury. "The bear would have done a lot worse if Doric hadn't been able to deter it."

"I'm sorry, Torrieth. I—" Doric started, but her friend only squeezed her hand reassuringly.

"We can talk about Doric and this bear more later," Fenjor said, clearly directing his statement to Marlion. "Both made it back safe enough."

"In the meantime, the woods can survive a bit of flooding," Marlion said unhappily. "Fenjor, have your hunters shift their routes over the next few days to avoid any upset to the animals in the area. Make sure to leave game behind. We'll send a few more experienced scouts to keep an eye on the situation, and once the humans are clear, we can go back to normal."

"That's it?" Doric surprised everyone, including herself, by speaking up.

"What else would you suggest?" The question came from Liavaris, so it was kindly asked.

"I—I don't know," Doric stumbled. The bear loomed in her mind, frustrated and furious. She couldn't stop her tail from twitching even though she was sitting down. "I just thought, well, I thought that humans don't usually come this far into the woods, and they never cut down trees here, and maybe we should find out why?"

A few of the elders were nodding and mumbling in agreement, but Marlion held up a hand for silence.

"No," he said. "We will leave them alone and they will leave us alone. It's better for everyone that way. And safer, too. They'll be gone soon enough, and then everything will right itself. A few days training near camp will be good for our younger hunters."

Doric knew she was turning red, but she couldn't do anything about it. She swallowed hard and nodded.

"Of course," she said. "I apologize for interrupting."

The subject changed with blessed quickness, and Doric shoveled down the rest of her dinner without tasting it. There was music starting up—it was a celebration, after all—but Doric didn't feel like dancing. She watched as Deverel, blushing to the roots of his hair, held out a hand to Torrieth, and the two of them joined the growing number of revelers. With no one to pay attention to her, Doric was finally able to make her escape. She picked up a few embers before she stood, closing her fingers around the bright coals with no fear of burning. She would eat them later.

Her hut was small, but it was hers, and it was welcome. She threw open the door, letting the late-evening sun cast its light into her domain. Inside there was only a bedroll, a small chest, and a place to hang her bow. She unclipped her quiver from her belt and put it away, and then returned to the opening to sit and check her arrows' fletching.

She worked quickly and efficiently, stopping every now and then to watch the dancing. She had joined them in the past, and the elves always took her hands and spun her about in their circles. Torrieth said she was good at it, light on her feet and aware of where her arms and legs were in relation to everyone else. Firelight brought out the gold in her hair and turned her horns to dark twists on her head. Her tail would flash around her, spinning her more. Sometimes, if there were visiting elves from other clans, they would stare, unused to tieflings but well versed in the dark and demonic stories about them. Her clan might not uniformly welcome her, but they did know that tieflings weren't inherently evil, and they didn't care about the old stories anymore. Doric worked very hard to make sure that it stayed that way, even when her own mind would take time out of its day to make her feel despicable. If no one cared, then no one would spend too much time thinking about whether a tiefling really belonged with the clan.

The sun set behind the trees, casting long, fingerlike shadows that darkened and spread into one another until the fires were the only source of light. Doric watched the silhouettes of the dancers as they whirled, their laughter rising into the night with the sparks from the flames. Liavaris and Fenjor were still sitting close to each other, heads bent so that they could talk quietly. It made Doric nervous. She was sure it was her they were talking about, but she couldn't imagine any good reason why.

Doric looked up at the stars. Most people saw the sky with some regularity, but Doric's childhood had been such that she remembered exactly when she saw stars for the first time. She'd been about six years old, and they had filled her with wonder. They still did, more than ten years later. It was a permanence that was lacking in most parts of her life, and Doric always felt calmer when she could look up.

She was fed and she was housed. She could come and go as

she pleased. She was slowly learning how to be a part of the clan, not as a child who needed support and guidance, but as an adult who could pull her own weight. She remembered the time before the stars and shuddered.

What she had here was enough.

THE WINDOW, OF COURSE, WAS HER PARENTS' UNDOING.

It wasn't a particularly happy childhood, but she had no other points of reference. As far as she knew, her parents told their fellow villagers that their baby had died during the delivery and then kept said baby in an attic loft packed with straw to muffle the baby's cries. She thought it was normal for parents to lock the bolt on the outside and pull away the ladder that allowed access to the trapdoor. If there was a way to feed a child other than sending up bladders of goat milk and, later, slightly stale bread in a basket on a rope, she wasn't aware of it. All she knew was the straw floor and the wood ceiling, and the tiny window in the wall through which she could look down on the outside and see a pocket of the world.

When she grew tall enough, she would rest her chin on the windowsill and watch the seasons pass. There was a tree in her little slice of the universe, and she watched it bud, leaf, change color, and die every year. It always came back, which was comforting for reasons she couldn't understand. Her parents made sure she could walk, and she learned to speak by listening to them. She didn't think they knew how well she could hear what they talked about downstairs. It wasn't particularly interesting. The weather, some animals that she had no visual reference for, and names of people whom she had never met. She wasn't sure how long it was before she was tall enough to reach the windowsill, but she knew she'd watched the tree die and resurrect three times when the conversations changed.

Her parents whispered. There was no one living close to them, but still they spoke in the hushed tones of those who feared nothing more than being overheard. Her pointed ears were keen, but not that keen. She didn't know what they were talking about. When her father walked past her window with his scythe or shears, he was in a hurry, steps short and determined. When her mother walked past with her water pail or garden shovel, her belly was distended, and her steps were more of a waddle.

Finally, there came a day when her mother was no longer quiet. She screamed and cried, and when she wasn't doing that, she gasped out directions to the girl's father. The girl could tell she was in pain, and she wanted nothing more than to go to her mother, to hold her hand and tell her that it would be okay, but the bolt was still fastened. After what felt like an eternity, a new cry split the air. It was thinner, more vulnerable, and she finally understood that there was a new baby in the house.

She ran her hands through her hair, finger-combing it as much as she could and picking out bits of hay. She made sure the nubs on her head didn't have any snarls of hair wrapped around them. Sometimes her curls had minds of their own. She split the straw that made up her bed into two piles. She kept most of it for herself, but she put the softest blanket she had over the smaller pile, tucking away the bits that poked out. There hadn't been anyone to take care of her when she first came to the loft, but the new baby would always have someone to watch over it.

The crying had stopped. She could hear her parents laughing. They weren't whispering anymore. Her mother sang a sweet song, soft and low, to the baby in her arms. The girl wished she had the memories of that part of her babyhood. The lonely nights in the attic might be easier to tolerate if she had some recollection of being held. She would hold the baby when her parents sent it up here. She would help it remember.

The hours went by, and the baby never appeared through the trapdoor. She waited patiently, but soon the hours turned to days, and then to weeks. She could hear the baby crying, hear her mother feeding it. She could hear her father speaking in a strange voice that made her mother laugh and the baby coo. And still she was alone.

Eventually, she gave up. She couldn't figure out why her parents kept the new baby downstairs instead of sending it up to her in the attic. She had been ready. She went back to the windowsill. She was tall enough now that she had to hunch over to avoid hitting the roof with her horns, but she could still see clearly into the little bit of the world that was her own.

She lost track of time once the tree grew its leaves that year. It got hot, and she watched the ground bake. It must have been fairly close to the time of year when the tree changed color that it happened, or at least that was what she decided a few years later when she'd finally figured out how human babies worked.

The child that toddled beneath her window that hot, humid day had red curls just like her. The child was unsteady on her feet, but when she fell over, there was no tail clumsily trailing behind her. There was no sign of any horns on her head, not even the smallest nubs, which the girl remembered having as long as she'd had memories. When the child shook her head, the girl saw that her ears were round.

The baby didn't look like she did, and their parents let her go outside.

She felt something shift in her chest. It wasn't anger, not quite. It was determination. If her sister got to go outside, then she was going to go outside, too. If it was safe for a baby, it must be safe for her. She had never run anywhere before, but she was pretty sure she could do it. She'd get out there, and maybe find out what grass felt like before it was dried.

The first thing she had to do was figure out how to get out of the attic.

ABOUT THE AUTHOR

JALEIGH JOHNSON lives and writes in the wilds of the Midwest. Her middle grade debut novel, *The Mark of the Dragonfly*, is a *New York Times* bestseller and was chosen for the ABA Kids' Indie Next List. Her other books include *The Secrets of Solace*, *The Quest to the Uncharted Lands*, and *The Door to the Lost*. She has also written fiction for Dungeons & Dragons: Forgotten Realms and Marvel. Johnson is an avid gamer and lifelong geek.

jaleighjohnson.com